DANCES OF DECEPTION

A LEGENDS OF TIVARA STORY

JC KANG

This is a work of fiction. Names, places, characters, and events are either fictitious or used fictitiously. Any resemblance to actual events, locations, organizations, or persons, alive or dead, is entirely coincidental and unintended.

Cover Art by Binh Hai
Cover Layout and Maps by Laura Kang.
Second Edition: March 2021

Dedicated to Yuki, Kristina, and Nina, the joys of my life. Thank you for putting up with my writing.

TIVARALAN
IKSUVI
LIETUVI
TELERI
ROTUVI
KANIN WILDS
CATHAY
DRAGON LANDS
KANIN
ANKIRA
MADURA
AYURI CONFEDERATION
LEVASTYAN EMPIRE
AKSUMI TRIBAL LANDS

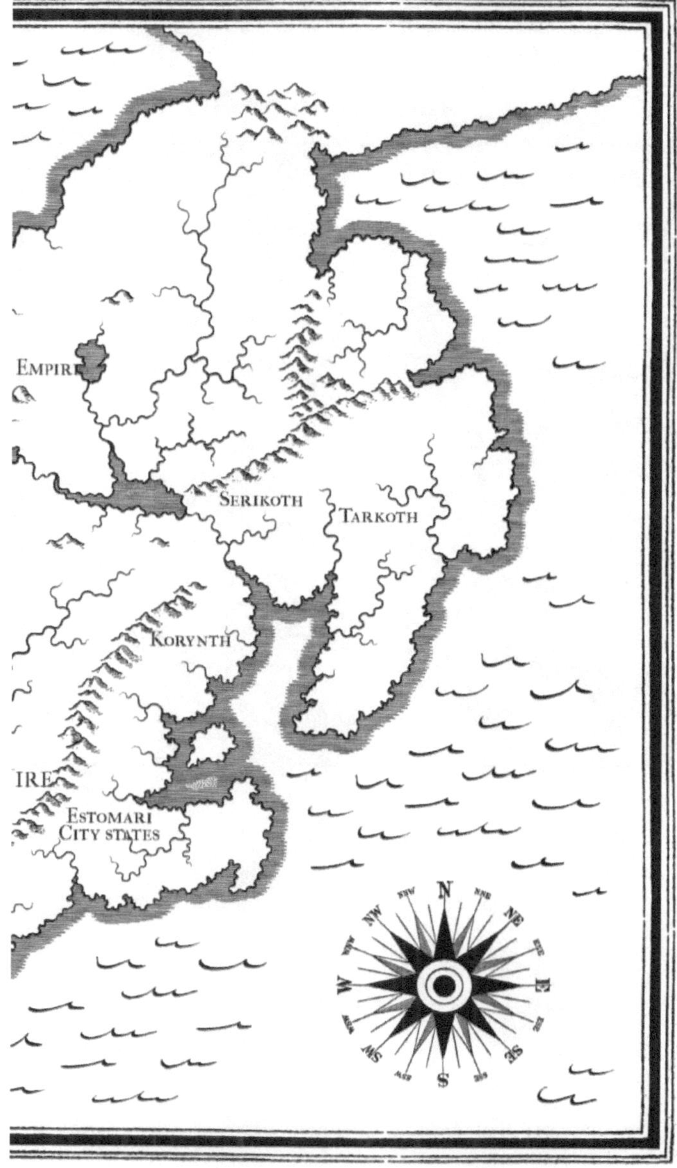

EMPIRE
SERIKOTH
TARKOTH
KORYNTH
IRE
ESTOMARI
CITY STATES

Map of the Nothori Northwest and Kanin Wilds

Who's Who in Dances of Deception

Kaiya's Retainers:

Chen Xin	Captain of Kaiya's imperial guard detail
Han Meiling	Kaiya's handmaiden and decoy
Li Wei	Imperial guard
Ma Jun	Imperial guard
Xu Zhan	Imperial guard
Zhao Yue	Imperial guard
Zheng Jiawei	General of the imperial guard

Black Lotus *Black Fist*

Cheng	Newest member of the Iksuvius cell
Shun	Black Fist
Old Tong	Eldest member of the Iksuvius cell
Yan Jie	Kaiya's half-elf bodyguard
Zheng Tian	Head of the Iksuvius cell
Zu	Black Fist

Cathayi Embassy Staff in Iksuvius

Wu Liming	Ambassador
Zhu	Trade officer

Teleri

Geros Bovyan	First Consul
Marius di Bovyan	General
Thieros Bovyanthas	Ambassador
Feiying	Black Lotus defector, head of the Nightblades

Dignitaries in Iksuvius

Arvydas	King of Lietuvi
Ausra	Queen of Iksuvi
Evydas	King of Iksuvi
Gunvydas	King of Rotuvi
Manuwaya	Ambassador from Kanin

Pyramid Quest

Cyrus Estazadeh	Akolyte from Selastya
Brehane	Aksumi Mystic
Sameer Vikram	Paladin knight
Fleet	madaeri guide

Eldaeri Nations

Aelward Corivar	Prince of Tarkoth
Ciro	Marine
Thielas Starsong	Elf ranger
Alaena Vardamcar	Princess of Serikoth
Keril	Ranger
Markel	Ranger
Rami	Ranger

Maki Tribe

Hati	Chief's son
Kona	Young warrior
Kosa	Young warrior
Lahi	Village beauty, Yuha's sister
Lana	Yuha's sister, shaman
Nadi	Yuha's daughter
Noki	Refugee
Nuwa	Chief
Yuha	Shaman
Waka	Yuha's son

Prologue:
Childhood Scars

Sweat rolled off Zheng Tian's forehead and stung his eyes as he fumbled with the tiny key.

"H-H-Hurry up, Tian!" Kai-Long hissed.

Tian's hands trembled even more than his companion's voice. The loose robes and pants usually afforded ample mobility, but now seemed as restricting as a silkworm's cocoon.

He shot a panicked glance out the circular window, where his friend stood on lookout. Beyond, two men wearing dark blue robes hurried down the garden path.

Kai-Long's shoulders quivered. "Come on! We're dead if they catch us!"

"Shut up! I can't focus." Tian took a deep breath and eyed the rectangular golden lock. It taunted him as it dangled between the double doors of the eldarwood armoire. Everyone knew Dwarves forged the sharpest blades and strongest armor, but who knew they could also make such intricate locks?

And in truth, it hadn't been that difficult to unlock the first time he opened the armor cabinet. Now his fingers had minds of their own. He again tried to ease the spindly key into the hole, praying to all his ancestors. If they would please, please just let him open this lock, he'd place incense at their altars every day, both morning and—

Behind him, the training hall doors crashed open. Tian's heart leaped into his throat, and he stumbled backward, his legs tangling in the mess of armor pieces strewn at his feet. He tumbled onto his behind. Face hot from panic and embarrassment, he looked up.

The two imperial guards approached, marching in unison across the worn wooden floors. Etched into their burnished breastplates, a five-clawed dragon—the symbol of the ruling *Tianzi*—glowered down at him. Already racing, ten-year-old Tian's heart now hammered like a drum at a New Year's Lion Dance. His stomach twisted in knots.

"What are you doing, Young Lord Zheng?" Though lanky with a boyish face, the newly minted imperial guard Chen Xin still radiated intimidation.

Cowering, Tian whipped the key behind his back. "I-I... nothing... "

Chen Xin leaned down and clamped Tian's concealed wrist in an eagle's grip. The guard dragged him to his feet, revealing the key in the same motion. He looked from Tian's hand to the lock. "Silly boy. This is the wrong key."

How had that happened? Tian shrugged with a sheepish smile. "Oh, what do you know... "

Chen Xin's jaw tightened. His comrade's shoulders shook as he tried to swallow a laugh.

Behind the guards at the door to the master's study, thirteen-year-old Peng Kai-Long scowled at him. He held up the correct key and mouthed, *Get them out of here.*

The guards followed Tian's gaze back towards Kai-Long. The boy stood there gaping, key out for everyone to see. The older guard gestured him to come, and Kai-

Long's head sank as he moped over. Chen Xin swiped the key away.

"What are you doing in the swordmaster's armoire? Trying on his armor?" Chen Xin scowled as he looked at the mess on the floor, and then began fiddling with the lock.

Oh, no. Tian tried to open his mouth to say *something*, but his tongue refused to move. He had been clenching his teeth. What had seemed like a harmless joke three hours ago might now have serious consequences. If the guard opened that chest, even Father wouldn't be able to save him from banishment, or even death.

His mind raced for a good answer until he caught sight of the hanging scroll with the character for *calm*. The magic imbued in its tranquil script rippled over him, slowing his heart and cooling the heat in his head. "No, no, the master. He ordered us to oil his armor. We were just putting it back. We can take care of—"

The lock yielded in Chen Xin's hands with a whispering *click*.

Oh, no.

The armoire doors swung open, revealing an eight-year-old girl standing as motionless as a statue. She wore the same cotton robes as Tian and Kai-Long, suitable for martial training. Her typically porcelain complexion blanched into an ashen pallor. Her fists squeezed so tightly her knuckles whitened, and her brown eyes, too large for her head, stared straight forward, unblinking.

"*Dian-xia!*" both imperial guards boomed in unison, using the formal address for an imperial princess. They sank to their right knees, right fists to the floor.

The princess steadied herself on the armoire wall and took a tentative step out, limbs stiff as the corpses that the bronze-skinned Southerners embalmed. After having spent a few hours in the equivalent of a coffin, all of her delicate grace seemed lost. Chen Xin rose and hurried over to support her, while the other guard fixed his glinting glare on the two boys.

Tian and Kai-Long both dropped to their knees and placed their foreheads to the ground, hands splayed in front of them.

"Forgive us, *Dian-xia*!" Tian's own voice sounded wrong to him, almost a squeak.

"Us? It's not my fault, it was *your* idea!" Kai-Long peered over, expression almost mirthful.

"Liar," Tian muttered under his breath. It *had* been Kai-Long's idea, but there was no use protesting. He was the *Tianzi*'s favorite nephew and would escape blame.

The princess' catatonic expression remained unchanged for a few seconds before her eyes welled up with tears.

"I'm sorry, Kaiya. It was just a stupid prank." Tian sobbed as Chen Xin grabbed him by the collar and hauled him to his feet. Was he crying because he faced certain, and possibly severe, punishment? Or because he'd hurt his best friend—and if he admitted it, his love? He'd spent almost half his life with her, learning archery, swordsmanship, literature, and the other educational foundations of the noble houses.

Stumbling to keep up as Chen Xin dragged him along, Tian craned his neck to catch one last glimpse of the girl who'd promised to marry him. Kaiya was now weeping inconsolably, while her cousin Kai-Long comforted her with reassuring pats on the head.

He didn't want this to be his last image of the princess. Would she only remember him as the one who locked her in an armoire? Servants scurried past him, obscuring his view of her. Attention forward, Tian shuddered as Chen Xin prodded him through the grounds of Sun-Moon Palace for his inevitable audience with the *Tianzi* himself. The other guard ran ahead.

All Tian could do was count, like he always did: His paces. His breaths. The number of flowering fruit trees.

Tian climbed the one hundred and sixty-eight white stone steps to the entrance of the Hall of Supreme Harmony. The final step, the knee-high spirit-tripping threshold, took the last of his strength. Inside the cavernous room, eighty-eight gold-lacquered columns vaulted upwards to support a tile ceiling mosaic of circling dragons.

Inebriated by the cloying incense hanging in the air, Tian stumbled down an aisle between ninety-two seated ministers in blue robes. His footsteps clicked on the white marble floors, faltering as he came to a bloodwood dais carved with countless auspicious symbols of bats and lotuses.

Two thrones loomed above him. One was chiseled from a gigantic chunk of jade to resemble a coiled dragon; the other was gold, worked to resemble a resting phoenix. Seated on the larger jade throne was a man of middling years, dressed in yellow robes with blue-and-red dragon heads on the breast and sleeves.

The *Tianzi*.

Tian gulped. Despite spending much of his time at the palace, he'd never seen Kaiya's father, the man who would pass sentence on him.

His gaze strayed to the Broken Sword, borne by the commander of the imperial guard, who stood behind the *Tianzi*. Maybe they'd use it to behead him or run him through; or maybe order him to cut his own throat.

Tian threw himself to his knees, nearly knocking himself unconscious as his forehead hit the ground. He knew his history well: three centuries before, the first *Tianzi* had executed five generations of an entire family over a child's mischief.

"Raise your head, boy."

Despite Tian's fear, the man's tone of command compelled him to rise into a kneel. He stared downward, keeping his eyes averted from the *Tianzi*.

"You convinced the princess to hide from her guards, and then locked her in an armoire for three phase-hours of the Iridescent Moon. What have you to say in your defense?"

Tian's words stuck in his throat. He opened and closed his mouth, but only a squeak came out.

"*Huang-Shang*," a new voice from behind said, using the formal address for the *Tianzi*. "May I speak?"

"You may."

"Young Lord Zheng, face me." The same voice now came from the opposite side of the room.

What? Tian shifted his position and looked in the direction of the voice. He found only pitying stares. No one acknowledged him. He turned again, back in the direction from which the voice had initially originated.

A minister with one knee down, fist to the floor, gazed back at him with dark eyes that seemed to be looking into his mind. "You were counting the number of guards on your way in, weren't you? It's okay, answer freely."

Tian nodded. He *had* counted them. Counting was a compulsive habit with little use.

"How many?"

"Thirty-six," Tian said.

"On your way to the Hall of Supreme Harmony, did anything seem out of the ordinary?"

These questions had nothing to do with the princess. Why was he asking? "There was an enormous palanquin. With wheels. Borne by large horses instead of porters."

"And?"

"The door was dark green. With a nine-pointed star of silver."

The minister's lips twitched. "As you entered the hall, who was standing where you are now?"

"A barbarian from the East."

"Where in the East?" The minister was smiling now.

Where? How was he supposed to know? Just as he was about to shake his head, he remembered his heraldry lessons. Tian swept his gaze towards the area he thought the man's voice had come from the second time.

A teenage boy with a slim build and sharp features looked back at him. The boy had an olive skin tone and a long brown mane, so different from everyone else's darker complexions and black hair. And although he wore silken court robes, the *wen* emblem on his chest was the same foreign-looking star he had seen on the palanquin.

He was an Eldaeri human, part of a tribe that had mingled with elves thousands of years before. The circlet indicated nobility, and the crest belonged to the Kingdom of Tarkoth. "He is a prince of Tarkoth."

"Crown Prince Elrayn, to be exact." The *Tianzi* nodded a fraction. "Impressive."

"*Huang-Shang*," the minister said. "With your permission, allow me to decide his sentence and administer the punishment."

Fear had partially given way to curiosity, and Tian now spoke with no thought to his predicament. "Will I see the princess? Before my punishment?"

The minister shook his head. "No. Where I am taking you, you might never see her again."

CHAPTER 1:
Value of a
Dragonfly's Life

Zheng Tian knew many ways to kill the smuggler, but none to ease his own conscience.

A column of sun streamed in from the dusty warehouse's skylight, reflecting off his target's seventeen glittering rings. All it would take was a signal to assassinate him and his two bejeweled henchmen.

Hold the dragonfly with care, eight-year-old Princess Kaiya's voice chimed in his head, quoting an old Cathayi proverb. *For even their fleeting lives have value.*

What was the value of a *man's* life?

Now twenty-one, Tian banished memories of the gentle girl to the recesses of his mind.

Time to focus on the most distasteful of his duties. Just eleven feet away, the olive-skinned Estomari merchant walked from crate to crate, checking items off a cargo manifest and barking orders.

The twenty-four wooden crates contained legitimate trade goods, for sure. However, Marcus Larruso also trafficked in the local girls, sending them to the South, where their fair complexions and blonde hair would fetch a handsome price. Perhaps he deserved death.

Tian's goals weren't particularly noble, either. As much as he wanted to, he wasn't here to rescue impoverished girls from a short and miserable life of exploitation, far away from home.

Larruso reached the last of the two crates, while one of the heavily-armed bodyguards stepped onto the spot where he would die.

The power of life and death, in Tian's hands. Perhaps that burden was a form of punishment, one which widened the gulf between his carefree youth and the ruthless spy he had become.

He flashed the hand signal from his vantage point.

Six *Black Fist* brothers fell upon the three unsuspecting smugglers in clinical silence.

Old Tong, the most experienced of them, darted from between the last two crates. He covered Larruso's mouth and slashed his throat with a black-lacquered knife.

At the same time, Pockmarked Zu dropped from the rafters. He stomped through the largest man's knee and applied an unremitting chokehold. His victim's frantic clawing only hastened his demise.

The most recent arrival to their embassy in Iksuvius, Cheng, burst out of the shadows and hacked at the third henchman's neck with his curved sword. Blood sprayed, and the man let out a choked screech before falling dead.

"Clear." Six voices echoed the word in quick succession. Lives, so easily snuffed out.

Pockmarked Zu eased the body to the hard-packed dirt floor. "Brilliant plan, worthy of the Architect."

"And executed with the precision of the Surgeon and the Beauty." Young Cheng's eyes crinkled as he opened one of the many crates.

Tian snorted. His plan had not been much more than picking a hiding place, and choosing the right timing against overmatched thugs.

"Now, which one of you is the Beauty?" Old Tong looked from Young Cheng to Pockmarked Zu before shaking his head. He was old enough to have known the three legendary masters, all struck down in their youth a generation ago. Under clan orders, he never spoke their names, though he animatedly recounted their exploits when given a chance. "Neither, you're both too ugly."

Like the rest of his comrades, Tian held the deceased masters in awe. Nonetheless, he silenced the men with a scowl. "Cheng. Use a more effective technique. He made a sound. Others could have heard."

The boy hung his head. "But you timed it so the rest of them—"

"It's all right. Just learn from your mistakes." Tian swept his gaze around the warehouse. "Now. Where's our primary target?"

Old Tong motioned him over. "Here."

Larruso lay dead, his curly brown hair matted in a pool of blood. The Pirate Queen's agent in the frigid Northwest, Larruso was a known associate of Tian's former friend and current fugitive, Peng Kai-Long.

Tian sighed. Three more murdered, bringing the total he'd arranged to thirty-two, on top of sixty-seven he'd killed with his own hands. All necessary to protect the homeland. He gestured towards Young Cheng. "What's in this shipment?"

"Just fine glassware." The boy shrugged.

"And wool," Pockmarked Zu added, looking up from another crate.

Tian tapped his chin. They'd tracked Larruso for weeks after receiving word of increased weapons orders.

With a Cathayi trade ship coming into port later today, it would be the perfect opportunity to smuggle his cache. "No weapons?"

Old Tong looked up from a table and waved a blood-smeared sheet of paper. "Here is a diagram for repeating crossbows."

Tian nodded. Without access to firepowder for muskets, Peng would need Cathay's other great invention. Or innovation rather, since the Repeater design had originally come from the Eldaeri people of the Northeast.

"Here are the parts," Shun said from the far corner. "Uncrated."

Uncrated. So they weren't being shipped home to Cathay, to arm the dwindling insurgency. At least not yet.

Tian took the diagram from Old Tong and scanned it. He then traced the cocking mechanism with his finger. "This is an Eldaeri crossbow. Not one of ours." Just like the ones he'd seen two years ago when the Eldaeri attended the wedding of Second Prince Kai-Wu.

"You're right." Shun tossed over the trigger component.

Tian swept it out of the air. "Dockworkers will arrive later. Shun, impersonate a merchant. Make sure the crates get loaded. The rest of you. Dispose of the bodies. The locals won't miss this criminal. Then regroup in my office."

"As you command," his men responded in unison.

Three knocks rapped on the skylight, the prearranged signal from their lookout that someone was coming in.

The Black Fists melted back into shadows, dragging the bodies with them. The door opened, revealing a young man with a repeating crossbow.

He took a tentative step in. "Master Larruso?" A thick local accent weighed down his Arkothi.

Tian raised a fist, ordering his men to stand down. No point killing a hapless servant who had the bad luck of walking in at the wrong time. He stepped out into the light. "Master Larruso is indisposed."

The man looked at him, his eyes intermittently glancing to the space behind him. "Who are you?"

"Feng. Trade officer. From the Cathayi embassy." Tian motioned to the crates behind him. "I am here to make sure everything is in order. This shipment is going out tonight."

The man licked his lips. "By yourself? That's not like him."

"Oh, yes. Lord Larruso had another matter to attend to. He told me to make arrangements." Tian covered the bloodstain on the cargo manifest as he held it up. "Wait here. If you want. Or I can pass your message to him."

The man presented the crossbow. "I can't read. I just wanted to make sure I assembled this correctly."

Tian flipped it over in his hands. Cathay had improved upon the inefficient magazine and unwieldy cocking mechanism a century ago. To think the most advanced weapon in the North was almost obsolete back home.

He looked back at the man and held the weapon as if it were a venomous snake. "I'm only a clerk. I don't know weapons. But I will leave this... *thing*... on his table. How about I write a note for you?"

The man nodded enthusiastically. "Just let him know the workers are confused and need directions."

"I will do that." Tian flashed him a warm smile as he walked the man to the door. As the fellow walked out, Tian flashed a signal to Tong. *Follow.*

Old Tong zipped through, and Tian closed the door and let out a long sigh.

"Why'd you let him go?" Young Cheng emerged, shaking his head.

Tian held the boy's gaze. "Shun, was he an immediate threat?"

"No, the crossbow was uncocked," Shun said.

Tian nodded. "Zu, was he close to Larruso?"

"No, Larruso's lieutenants are all literate and wear their wealth," Pockmarked Zu said. "He was just a local peasant, looking for work."

Cheng cocked his head. "But shouldn't we tie up loose ends? He didn't matter."

"What did you make of his bracelet?"

"Crudely weaved, with faded colors," Cheng said. "Fraying in spots."

Tian nodded. "Very good. What does that tell you?"

Cheng's forehead furrowed.

"The poorest cannot afford rings. When they exchange wedding vows, the use bracelets. Unlike Larruso, he would be missed."

The young *Black Fist* shrugged. "What is one life worth?"

"A dragonfly. Now, clean up here. Then meet back in my office."

With a last glance, Tian slipped out the door and into the bright afternoon sunlight. He blinked a few times to let his eyes adjust, and then set off for the embassy, just on the other side of Iksuvius' western marketplace.

Guilt pricked at him, even more so than the marketplace's scent of oily foods, fresh vegetables, and salted fish. Had they needlessly killed those men? He'd lost his innocence many times over since his banishment from the capital. What would his ten-year-old self think of who he had become? Princess Kaiya would be disappointed.

Her *again*. He'd last seen her from afar on the battlements of Wailian Castle, eight hundred seventy-eight days ago. She'd rarely visited his thoughts in the last four thousand and twelve days; maybe only on the several occasions when he'd had to kill an enemy of the state. Otherwise, there was no use wondering about someone he'd never see again. Or who'd undoubtedly forgotten about him. His chest squeezed. There were more pressing matters.

Tian started to pick his way through the crowded market. After two years, he'd grown accustomed to being surrounded by the large, light-skinned, fair-haired Nothori folk. Even so, their sweat stank of raw onions and goat's milk. He weaved through them with careless grace, loath to brush up against their hairy bodies.

Along the way, he cut the purse of a brothel owner, and later slid a copper Iksuvi *kroon* into the pocket of a destitute boy. When asked by his spies about this peculiar habit, he always shrugged it off as an exercise to keep his skills sharp. And if a child happened to notice his handiwork—or even tried to pick *his* pockets—he or she might be recruited as another set of eyes and ears for Tian's information network.

A network whose information he'd misinterpreted. The weapons weren't meant to arm the insurgency back home. A pit formed in the bottom of a stomach. He'd ordered an unnecessary murder.

What had he missed? Tian stood before the spongewood board that took up the entire northern wall of his second-floor office. The setting sun peeked in from the windows, splashing the middle of the room with gentle light. It left the walls cloaked in shadows, concealing his Black Lotus brothers.

A cool breeze wafted in, bringing with it a breath of salt water off of Cold Harbor. It dislodged the crossbow diagram from one of the strings crisscrossing the room, and sent it fluttering. Tian plucked the page out of the air as it drifted by, without looking at it or creating a whisper of sound.

He snaked through the organized tangle of zigzagging lines like a contortionist, and tacked the diagram to a new spot on the southern wall board. Satisfied, he stepped back and pondered. The carelessly scribbled notes, objects, and twine connections formed a chaotic net of interrelations between events, people, and evidence.

The embassy staff referred to his office as the *Cobweb*. If the embassy as a whole presented the face of his homeland's commerce with its northern neighbors, this room was the brain. Here, twelve Black Lotus Fists gathered information on potential enemies who otherwise masqueraded as trading partners.

The systematized mess of data mirrored the rest of the room, from the cluttered wooden desk to the random positioning of the chairs, bookshelves, and even the richly-colored wool rugs on the dark wood floors. In the middle of it stood Tian, his mind the calm eye in the storm of facts and figures, bringing logical order to the chaos.

He pointed out a single strand of curly red hair, which Old Tong had retrieved from the crossbow workshop, dangling on one of the threads.

"There," he said, keeping his voice just loud enough to carry over the din of the late afternoon bustle in the western marketplace. "Only Northerners have red hair. This strand is coarse. It probably belongs to an Eldaeri. There was a huge order for Eldaeri crossbows. Not from the rebel Peng. Maybe the Eldaeri are planning to disrupt treaty negotiations."

Gliding untouched through the web of strings, he traced that particular thread back towards the northern wall board, to a note labeled *Northwest Conference*.

"An assassination attempt?" queried a voice from the dark corner of the room.

Tian tapped his chin. He'd been wrong about Larruso. He spoke slowly, making sure not to trip over the words. "Maybe. It would be their best chance. The Teleri Empire's First Consul will be here. With less protection. If the Eldaeri kill him, they can split the Northwestern alliance. And we would benefit. Stay on the lookout for the Eldaeri. If they are here, we will make contact. To help them."

"Understood," answered a chorus of voices from the shadows.

He waved his hand, dismissing them. The sounds of their breaths disappeared, indicating they had melted away.

Tian smiled to himself. His spies might now consider him the second coming of the Architect, but when he had first been posted here, as a young man who couldn't speak in complete sentences, they probably thought it was because of his family connections. As if any aristocrat would choose to work in these barbaric lands. He returned to the tendril of hair, rubbing it between his fingers.

An unfamiliar young man appeared at the door, guided by the Mistress of Chambers.

"I have just arrived on the *Wild Orchid*," he said, "and have been instructed to bring you to the docks."

"Me?" Tian snorted. The cargo that would fatten Cathay's coffers mattered little to him. "You're looking for Trade Minister Zhang."

"I was explicitly ordered to summon you." The messenger reached into his robes and drew forth a thin jade plaque. Carved in the likeness of a five-clawed dragon, it symbolized the *Tianzi*, ruler of Cathay.

As protocol demanded, Tian sank to his right knee, head bowed, right fist to the floor. It was strange to see a plaque here. "Please. Take me to the ship."

The two descended through the main residence, a three-story mansion of wood and immaculate white stone with sloping eaves of blue tile, which stood at the center of the embassy compound. Situated on a low hill and encircled by a twelve-foot-high stone wall, the spacious grounds overlooked the only deep-water harbor in the Northwest of the continent.

With the arrival of a cargo ship, the embassy buzzed with activity. On his way through the courtyard to the main gates, Tian weaved around trade officers, guards, and porters, who all hurried between the two-story trade office building, the stables, the barracks, and a warehouse.

Monks' chants and the cloying smell of burning incense emanated from the East Light Temple in the southeast corner of the compound. Dedicated to

Cathay's patron god Yang-Di, the wooden temple rose to the height of six men and boasted sharply pitched, yellow-tiled eaves. Sailors from the *Wild Orchid* already streamed in to thank the Lord of the Sun for the ship's safe arrival after a week at sea.

Tian paused at the wrought iron gates and looked back to see the messenger still near the residence, stutter-stepping through the crowd. There was no need to wait; they both knew where to go. He continued out of the embassy and maintained a brisk pace through the bustling streets. Near the docks at the far end of the marketplace, now shrouded in the long shadows of late afternoon, a crowd of locals gathered to witness the arrival of a Cathayi trading ship.

They jostled each other to catch a glimpse of the black-haired, honey-toned Cathayi people. Many gawked at the giant ship, and fought to get first pick of the gadgets and wares imported from all over the continent. In this, they would be disappointed. With lords and kings visiting for the quinquennial Northwest Conference, this particular shipment contained luxury items far beyond commoners' means.

When Tian reached the head of the quay, a stocky Cathayi sailor nodded and waved him past the cordon. As Tian waited for the less dexterous messenger to catch up, he studied the dark planks of eldarwood that made up the *Wild Orchid's* hull.

It was eldarwood that made the otherwise small, mountainous nation of Cathay so rich. The straight-trunked evergreen was the only tree thriving on the west coast which could be made into ocean-going ships, and it grew in abundance in Cathay. Cathay's navy and trading fleet dominated the western seas, making it the envy of its neighbors.

The messenger arrived a moment later, interrupting his musings. Tian followed him up the gangplank to the main deck, where the bright light of the setting sun caused him to squint. Here, their roles reversed—the messenger's sea legs allowed him to jaunt across the deck towards the aft cabin, while Tian lurched after him.

The man stopped at the door, placed the imperial plaque in Tian's hands, and then gestured for him to enter.

The door closed behind him, plunging him into darkness. He instinctively reached into a secret pocket in his vest, withdrawing a twelve-pointed, razor-sharp throwing star. A year spent blindfolded prevented Tian from panicking. His other senses kicked in.

Incense had recently been snuffed out. A man breathed at the far end of the cabin, near a closed porthole.

"Young Lord Zheng, thank you for coming." The man's sonorous voice carried a certain tone of command bred into Cathayi royalty. It belonged to Crown Prince Kai-Guo, the first son of the *Tianzi*, whose voice Tian had heard only once, a decade ago.

Tian sunk to his right knee, right fist to the floor, head bowed. Yet suspicions tugged at his mind: why would the Crown Prince be here? Unannounced? In the dark? Why the secrecy? There had been no imperial guards on the ship. "Your servant obeys," he answered, nonetheless.

"You are being recalled to Cathay, to inherit your father's place on the *Tai-Ming* Council."

Tian's mind swam at the implications. Something had happened to his father and his brothers. Dead? Branded traitors? He took a deep breath to settle his grief.

The scent of incense had faded, and a different smell, a more flowery fragrance, percolated in. The Crown Prince's breathing changed in depth.

Tian whipped the throwing star toward the voice. Metal clanged, the tone of the reverberation suggesting a small knife had deflected his weapon. He bounced up onto his feet and into a half-hearted defensive stance. There was no real threat.

"Hey! That was dangerous." Gone was the prince's deep, commanding tone, replaced by a familiar high-pitched, girlish voice, with a hint of laughter wrapped around the complaint.

Tian snorted. "My aim isn't so bad. It would've missed you."

The imposter giggled. "I still would've deflected it, had your aim been any better."

Light flooded the room as the half-elf Yan Jie opened her hand to reveal a magical Aksumi light bauble. Half the households on the continent owned one, but the sprite-like girl might have a dozen hidden in her black linen dress. Unarmed to the untrained eye, she was a walking arsenal.

She bounded across the cabin to envelop him in a warm hug. He fought off her affectionate embrace and stepped back. Making a mental note to check his pockets for any stolen items, he took a good look at his best friend.

Short and lithe, she hadn't changed in eight hundred and ninety-two days, her father's ageless elf blood giving her the appearance of a tween. It also accounted for her particularly large brown eyes and slightly pointed ears. Her pulled-back dark hair framed sharp features.

She flashed an impish grin. "How'd you know it was me imitating the Crown Prince?"

"Your *Mockingbird's Guise* technique couldn't deceive my *Seeing Ears*. Or maybe that was the most outrageous command. About me inheriting. I *do* hope my family is well?"

"Yes, of course, your father was never better. Your eldest brother Zheng Ming, in fact... " She shook her head. "But I forget why I'm *really* here. I've come by imperial command."

He smirked. "What mischief have you been wreaking? On the imperial court?"

"Oh! It's been so exciting, you'd never believe it. I was assigned to protect Princess Kaiya—"

"You're right. I wouldn't believe it." The shock of hearing the princess' name stirred not so much memories, which had faded with time, as a sense of nostalgia for innocence lost a decade ago.

"It's true! And she's nothing like your childhood memories. She's not fun or playful. She's very serious, very proper, very guarded."

"*Really?*" Serious, proper, and guarded would never describe the girl he'd grown up with. She'd been adorable then, and stories said she'd grown into a once-in-three-generations beauty. How could she have changed so much? "Now I really don't believe you."

"Have I *ever* lied to you?" Jie cast him a wounded look, which he dismissed.

"Maybe stretched the truth. A little... "

Her mouth spread into a toothy smile. "Well, if I told you everything that happened, you'd think I was a golden-tongued storyteller inspired by the old tales from the War of Ancient Gods. Like how she vanquished a dragon and enchanted the entire Ayuri Paladin Council of Elders."

"So, if you were the princess' prized bodyguard. Why are you here? Telling me tall tales. Instead of enjoying more adventures?" Tian raised a suspicious eyebrow.

"Oh right. It's a long story, but basically, I was sent ahead *by imperial command* to deliver a message to Ambassador Wu—"

Tian rolled his eyes. "So why all the secrecy? Why have me come here? So urgently?"

"Oh, I was just having fun with you." She grinned and winked at him.

"Impersonating royalty. It's a capital offense."

Her lip twitched as she fought off another grin. "I risked my life, hoping you wouldn't report me."

"I don't understand. Why do you have an imperial command? Just to deliver a message? Why didn't the court just send it? With the diplomatic packet?"

"You never did let me get to that." Or rather, she'd kept changing the subject. "I'm also supposed to learn about the operations here and arrange security. The princess is coming in a month."

CHAPTER 2:
The Games We Play

If there was one thing Jie knew better than spying, interrogation, and dirty fighting, it was the psychology of Zheng Tian.

His eyes widened and lips parted for a split second. Then his face blanked as only a Black Fist's could. If he thought the empty expression she'd taught him could hide his thoughts, or make him look objective...

Objective indeed! There she was again, lingering on his lips. He probably knew exactly how many days had passed since they'd last seen each other, though more out of habit than for any affection he might have for her.

Jie arranged her own expression into playful nonchalance, while Tian's face reverted to his sometimes endearing, always infuriating *Older Brother* look.

His voice droned in trained disinterest. "Why is she—"

She held up a hand to silence him. "You're on a need-to-know basis, and—"

"I don't need to know," he said, finishing their oft-repeated exchange.

"Actually, you do." Heavens, it was fun to mess with his head. It had been too long. "Just not this second. It's been a long journey, and I would really like to put my feet on solid ground. More details when I settle in, I promise."

Before he could press the matter, she dropped a few boxes of her personal effects in his hands and ushered him out of the cabin and onto the deck. After disembarking from the ship, he placed her things on a wooden cart, atop carefully crated and stacked trade wares. They then joined the two dozen sailors and porters heading back to the embassy compound.

Their group drew so many stares from the locals, they might have been a circus troupe, with a pointy-eared half-breed as star of the freak show. She'd need to cover her ears to move anonymously through the city.

No sooner had she set foot in the marketplace than the foreign culture began its assault on her senses. The drab colorlessness of Iksuvius only emphasized the confounding diversity of foul smells. The spoiling crustaceans had chosen long-dead fish as dancing partners, with rotting onions and garlic as an audience. Did the gamey odor come from the squalid goats tethered to a vendor's dilapidated wooden stall, or from the unwashed vendor himself? She'd seen splattered human brains and disemboweled entrails without flinching, yet now had to fight down rising bile.

"You get used to it." Tian's crooked smile made her stomach flutter in a completely different way.

He always knew what she was thinking. Heavens, she was becoming just as sappy as Princess Kaiya around a certain flamboyant lord. Her lips curved into a grin of their own accord. "When?"

"Winter. When it cools down."

"It's already chilly enough, and it's still summer!" Jie tightened her shawl around her shoulders. It wasn't just her. Beggars in tattered woolen clothes huddled together by weathered storefronts to soak up the last rays of afternoon sun, while shopkeepers and merchants donned flannel and wool jackets.

"Oh, it gets worse. In the dead of winter the cold will freeze you to the marrow. Unfortunately it will do the same to the homeless and destitute. "

They continued down the packed dirt road. Although her training emphasized detached observation, the abject poverty was appalling. Cathay had been stable for almost three centuries, and wealthy her entire lifetime. Sure, there were still many poor people, but it didn't begin to compare to here. So many beggars in one place! A toothless girl in rags crouched near a squat wooden building, gumming down a crust of moldy bread.

"Abandoned child." Tian must be reading her thoughts again, or at least following her eyes. "Taxes are so high. Parents can't afford to raise more than a few children. Many girls are sold into brothels. Or simply kicked out onto the street."

Abandoned! Jie shuddered. She might have shared the same fate as these discarded girls had her father not left her as a bawling babe at the front gates of the Black Lotus Temple. Master Yan had raised her as his own, though he had lost the only hint of her identity. The letter pinned to her swaddling blanket spoke of a human mother who died giving birth and a father too busy to be burdened. Jie would always carry that resentment towards her father—and the aloof elves in general.

She sucked on her lower lip. There were no elves to be found here. They were too prim and prissy for a stinking backwater like this. Up ahead, a group of ruffians extorted protection money from a protesting baker. Yet the greasy-looking man and his half-dozen thugs wore the light blue and yellow uniforms of Iksuvi soldiers. Longswords hung at their sides.

"Tax collector," Tian whispered. "Iksuvi pays a king's ransom in tribute. To the Teleri Empire. They call it an alliance. It places a heavy burden on the citizenry. Still, the Iksuvi commoners are generous. That baker will give leftovers to the beggars."

The shopkeeper bobbed his head and proffered a purse.

The tax collector swiped it away, though his grin transformed into a scowl as he looked inside. He started to say something, when one of his henchmen leaned over and whispered in his ear. Both men turned and looked directly at Jie. Nothing good would come of this.

A lurid smile appeared on the tax collector's face, and he gestured for his men to follow him as he approached. "Who is in charge here?" He spoke in Arkothi, the common language of the North, though it was heavily laced with a Nothori accent.

A young trade official strode forward and offered a few papers with a curt nod. "You will find that all documentation is in order," he said in his own accented Arkothi.

The tax collector waved the papers away while his attention edged towards Jie. "I am sure they are. But I have heard *vicious* rumors that you Cathayi are smuggling in contraband. Certainly you will not mind if we take a quick look to dispel this hearsay?"

Tian leaned over and whispered, "This is a common occurrence. We have to bribe them. Otherwise, they'll keep us here for hours. Young Zhu has a few silver coins ready. For these contingencies."

Just as Tian said, Zhu reached into his wide sleeves and produced a dozen Cathayi coins, strung together through square holes in their centers. "I am sure this more than covers any import duties."

The tax collector shook his head, his expression wounded even as he took the coins. "No, no, I am not that kind of man. I take my responsibilities very seriously." On a hand signal, the Iksuvi soldiers began to move among the carts, while he himself sauntered over to Jie.

And not to give a warm welcome, no doubt. She cast her gaze downwards, assuming the role of a servant, even as she mentally prepared for confrontation. Tian sidled closer to her.

"Do you have papers, girl?" The man lifted her chin, his hand reeking of a musk which did little to cover his pungent sweat. His pigeon-like eyes leered at her. It would be easy to dislocate every joint from his elbow to finger tips in two seconds. Still, she feigned nervousness, trembling at his scrutiny.

Tian's hand closed around hers, the electricity of his touch breaking her concentration. Angry at herself for the lapse, she refocused on the situation.

"My wife," Tian said. "Just arrived from Cathay."

A lie to counter a lie. Still, her heart fluttered.

"She looks too young to be married." The man turned her head to the side, jolting Jie out of her fantasy. "I need to see documentation for all females. We do not want those of an... unsavory profession... coming to our noble kingdom."

Noble, indeed. If anyone was unsavory—

"I've never heard of such rules," Tian said.

"New guidelines. She will have to come with us." The tax collector shrugged and drew Jie closer.

The games adults played. Jie made a show of turning her head. She'd play along until an opportune moment to escape presented itself, then find her way to the Cathayi embassy.

Tian stepped forward. "I will accompany her."

"I am afraid that is out of the question." The tax collector's tone was apologetic. His grin was anything but. "You are in our country and will follow our laws. Now step back before I have all of your cargo impounded."

Tian's grip loosened, while his weight shifted. He was readying himself to fight! Over such a trivial matter, no less.

She clasped his hand tighter, leaving her index finger free to tap on his palm in a clan code. *Don't. Only seven. I have this. Not here. Non-lethal.*

He relaxed and turned to her, eyebrow raised. "Are you sure?" he asked in their native tongue.

"It should be easy to slip away from these oafs."

A male with a deep voice boomed from behind her, in perfect Arkothi: "That is no way to treat a married woman."

Everyone turned to the half-dozen Teleri soldiers in impeccable black tunics emblazoned with a nine-pointed golden sun on their chests. Onlookers gave them a wide berth as they approached in precise formation. The ruling race of the Teleri Empire, the Bovyans stood half a head above even the tall Nothori folk. With the exception of their even taller leader, whose dark locks fell to his shoulders, they all sported close-cropped hair.

Jie gritted her teeth. Her own experiences with Bovyans—a two-year mission in the Teleri heartland, as well as several run-ins with the Bovyan spies in Vyara City, and Bovyan charlatan Akolytes in Selastyas—had been less than cordial.

The tax collector stiffened, his hand slipping from Jie's chin. He looked around for his men, but they conspicuously kept their distance. He licked his lips. "As if a Bovyan knew the first thing about marriage. This is an Iksuvi state matter, and none of your business."

The young Teleri leader, a general by the sun insignia on his collar, stepped closer to the cowering man. His chiseled features might have belonged to the Arkothi Sun God Solaris, from whom the Bovyans descended. "It *is* our business. The Teleri care deeply about how our allies treat our trading partners. Now, run along and harass your own citizens. I would hate to see an incident mar our nations' relations on the eve of the Northwest Summit."

The tax collector scowled as he backed out of the general's shadow. Turning on his heel, he snapped his fingers at his men. Heads down and shoulders slumped, the lot of them slunk towards another shop.

What a surprise; a noble Bovyan. Jie dipped into a curtsey. With Tian still clasping her hand, they might have been about to start a Northern-style dance. "My deepest gratitude for your intervention on my behalf."

The general dipped into a sweeping genuflection reminiscent of the old Arkothi Empire. When he straightened, he was grinning. "It's me, Marius di Bovyan. I am only returning the favor from two years ago. You can always find me at the Teleri Embassy in the city center."

Jie maintained a smile, even though she had no idea what he was talking about. Perhaps all half-elves looked alike, because obnoxious sailors, a Paladin Master, a fraudulent fortune teller, fake Akolytes, and now a Bovyan general all claimed to have met her. Sometimes in places she'd never visited.

One of the Teleri cleared his throat. "General, we are late."

"Of course." General Marius winked. At his command, the column marched out of the marketplace with the same precision they had entered.

"Well. That was interesting." Tian released Jie's hand, scuttling any hope that he'd maintain the act.

She nodded. "Yes; he was more the image of the Bovyan Knights of old, and not like the Teleri brutes and rapists they have become. And I have no idea what favor he is referring to."

The caravan proceeded without further incident, and arrived at the embassy.

Jie stared wide-eyed at the amount of white stone that had gone into its construction. It gave the grounds the feel of a northern-style fortress, even if the sloping blue roof tiles hinted at a Cathayi architectural influence.

Tian led her to the main residence, through the vaulting foyer and up the broad wooden steps to the second floor. Her room had a window facing west towards the harbor. The red sun hovered just above the water, bathing the room in a fiery glow.

"So. Why is the princess coming here?" Tian's tone was impatient.

Let him squirm a little. Jie placed a few boxes by the foot of the bed.

"Especially during the Northwest Conference," he added.

It was more fun to keep Tian in suspense. Jie walked across the room and leaned her elbows against the window sill, looking out onto the city. The side streets, which a drunkard must have laid out, provided many bottlenecks, ambush points, and escape routes.

Tian shuffled behind her. He was close to his bursting point.

She turned around to face him and spoke with detached nonchalance. "The princess is to be betrothed to the Teleri First Consul." It was a clan interrogation trick: glibly throwing out nonsense to gauge a reaction.

The twitch of his lips, flashing before he buried it under years of training, betrayed his disappointment. Yet, he didn't miss a beat. "Bovyans don't marry. They *breed*. Prolifically. To sustain the Teleri war machine."

Jie forced a laugh. "Zheng Tian, you have become gullible since we last met. Has the cold frozen your brain?"

Again, his mask dropped briefly, the brow above his high-bridged nose relaxing.

So he still had feelings for the princess after all these years. Now it was her turn to hide disappointment behind an inscrutable expression.

"Why is she *really* coming?" He locked eyes on her. Beautiful, intelligent eyes. Her heart skipped a beat.

Where to start? She could write a novel. Jie withdrew a lacquered box from her things. "Here, an imperial edict. I was instructed by the *Tianzi*'s own order to deliver this into the hands of Ambassador Wu."

Frowning, Tian bowed to the edict as protocol demanded. He then extended his hand towards the door. "Come. Let me introduce you to the ambassador."

Ambassador Wu Liming's office was on the other end of the mansion, on the second floor, a spacious anteroom to his personal quarters. Two large windows looked east out onto the Alto River. Hanging scrolls with brush-and-ink style paintings and calligraphy adorned the walls.

The ambassador sat behind a meticulously clean sablewood desk, between the windows and facing the doors. Stocky and middle-aged, he wore a blue silk robe. His long hair, drawn back into a pony tail, was as white as his short mustache and thin beard.

Jie had visited the Foreign Ministry archives in Cathay before her departure, and had already learned about him. He'd been assigned to establish the embassy in Iksuvi twenty years ago—ostensibly to bolster trade, but more importantly to keep an eye on this crossroads between the Nothori Kingdoms and their Teleri masters.

Tian guided Jie across the plush Ayuri carpet covering the hardwood floors, and cleared his throat. "Godfather," he said, "the *Wild Orchid* carried some unwanted cargo." He coughed as Jie jabbed him in the back with her finger. "This is Yan Jie. My sister from the temple."

Jie bowed, putting her right fist in her left hand.

A broad smile crossed Ambassador Wu's face as he rubbed his knees and eased himself out of the chair. He spoke with a warm, fatherly voice. "Welcome to Iksuvius, my dear. Unwanted cargo? Little Tian! Such a beautiful girl, it looks more like a surprise gift!"

Jie fought back a smile. "Thank you, Ambassador Wu. I—"

He shook his head. "I insist you call me *Godfather*. Since Tian is your Temple-Brother, and he calls me Godfather, we are virtually related."

Jie nodded. "Thank you, Godfather. However, I am no ordinary stowaway here to see the sights. I have come by order of the *Tianzi,* to personally deliver this message into your hands."

Opening the lacquer case and withdrawing a scroll, she approached the desk and dropped to a knee. Head bowed, she extended both arms to offer the imperial edict.

The ambassador received it with both hands, bowing. He unfurled the scroll, revealing the large, dark red mark of the *Tianzi*'s imperial seal. His pupils swept across the text before he passed it to Tian.

Of course, she'd already read it. Princess Kaiya would meet with First Consul Geros Bovyan of the Teleri Empire and negotiate the rebel Peng Kai-Long's extradition. Ambassador Wu would be tasked with making all arrangements. And she'd be responsible for security.

The ambassador leaned back and sighed. "The timing is bad. The First Consul is here to bask in glory. He won't acquiesce to the demand, let alone to a woman."

Jie shook her head. This was the Dragon Charmer he was talking about. "Princess Kaiya is no ordinary woman. She vanquished the Last Dragon with only her voice."

"Very well." The ambassador didn't sound convinced. "We will prepare for the princess' arrival in a month. Little Jie, you have had a long journey and need some rest before you begin your duties here. Settle in, avail yourself of the bath house. If you need anything, please don't hesitate to let me know."

"Thank you, Godfather. I will be taking my leave, then." Jie held a bow as she backed out of the room, with Tian not far behind.

Walking back through the halls towards Tian's office, she hid her smile. Her first duty had been accomplished: delivering the edict. Now came the interesting part: reminding Tian how amazing she was.

Tian patted her on the head. "My little sister. All grown up. Protecting princesses."

Curse her elvish blood: at thirty-two, she was eleven years older than Tian, yet still looked like an adolescent. She forced a coy smile. "My big brother, still hasn't grown up, still in love with princesses."

Where he'd normally have a quick retort, his silence and pursed lips spoke louder than words. She quickly changed the subject. "Remember how we used to play blind Cathayi chess, without a board?"

"Of course," he answered, almost before she finished asking. "Do you want to play again?"

"I want you to teach me Arkothi chess."

He nodded. "The pieces are fairly similar. The game reflects our cultures' differing mindsets. The Arkothi play between the lines. Controlling space. We play around the space. Controlling lines."

She laughed. "Seems simple enough. Let's start. I learn best by immersion."

"Very well. I will be white. Since your soul is obviously black. Queen's pawn forward two."

How appropriate a move. For the princess' pawn.

CHAPTER 3:
Plant Expectations, Reap Disappointment

Standing on a balcony of the Cathayi embassy's main residence, Tian gazed out across Cold Harbor. A warm, early autumn sun settled over the shallow waters, its yellow shimmer in the waves dancing among the fishing boats. In the distance, a larger, three-mast, phoenix-headed ship approached, flying the sky-blue flag of Cathay. His pulse quickened.

The oars slid through the waters, rhythmically following the hollow drum beat and accompanying shouts that echoed over the bay. It would take at least another half-hour for it to navigate the deeper sections of the inlet. Smaller boats zigzagged by, coming and going from the dozens of shallow landings. Only one dock could accommodate the deep-drafted vessels, which the Cathayi and the Eldaeri nations alone could build.

At last! For the past several days, Tian had stolen a few minutes from his duties to come here and scan the horizon for the ship. Now it was here, his unexpected reunion with Princess Kaiya close at hand. An unlikely chance to relive, if only for a moment, childhood memories and an innocence cut short by his training at the Black Lotus Temple.

Jie's voice from the balcony door interrupted his nostalgia. "Knight takes pawn. Check."

"A daring move," Tian said, turning towards his best friend. "You're exposing your knight to danger. Though it takes pressure off your queen."

"That's the knight's duty, right?" Jie emerged from the shadows. A pink ribbon held her dark brown hair in a bun. She wore a simple linen gown, pink with black floral borders, looking very much the servant.

"You're beginning to think like a Northerner. Your move is strategically questionable, though. Cathayi chess and Arkothi chess share one goal. Protect your king. Capture your enemy's. Every other piece is expendable."

Jie remained silent, and Tian surreptitiously studied her empty expression. The message in her move was obvious. She was still goading him over his *childhood* relationship with the princess. For someone who was a decade older than him, Jie still looked and sometimes acted like a girl just into the awkward years before womanhood.

"So, what news have we gathered?" he asked.

"The Teleri First Consul has crossed over the Alto River and just passed through the marketplace by the eastern gate. His retinue includes three thousand heavy infantry, armed with spears and longswords, and two hundred heavy cavalry with sabers and spears."

Tian tapped his chin. So many soldiers. The First Consul didn't need that much protection in an allied nation. It was quite an investment, feeding and lodging so many men. "They can't all be staying at the Teleri Embassy. I'll send Old Tong to learn where the rest will be quartered. In the meantime, let's join the princess' welcoming party."

"Like that?" She laughed and pointed at his head, proffering a jade comb that appeared in her hands. "Your hair's a tangled mess! You haven't been sleeping well lately, have you?"

He took the comb, drawing it through his hair from crown to shoulder, noting a passing rise in the right corner of Jie's lip. She offered him a pink ribbon, which he ignored, and instead withdrew a black tie from his dark-blue silk robes. His palms sweated. A reunion, four thousand and fifty-one days in the making, was close at hand.

She ushered him inside and through his office, tugging the wrinkles out of his robes. His white silk vest was embroidered with four-clawed, blue-and-gold dragons, a symbol of his family's standing as *Tai-Ming* lords. His heart pattered. Soon. He gathered up his curved *dao* sword as he passed the door, and both went down to the courtyard to join the princess' welcoming escort.

Twenty embassy guards dressed in dark blue cotton tunics and black leather breastplates assembled there, joining four horses and a stable boy. Each soldier was armed with a broadsword and a spear with red horse hairs near its head. A single sky-blue banner emblazoned with a five-clawed golden dragon, held by the lead soldier, fluttered in the light breeze.

Jie fell in behind twelve runners who carried an elaborately carved palanquin on their shoulders. Another pair of men pulled a cart with two mounted drummers on either side of a three-foot round drum. A hundred musketmen watched from the top of the white stone walls.

Ambassador Wu arrived, wearing his own formal robes and a black square hat. He mounted a horse, and Tian and two ministers bowed and followed suit. Wu's voice, still strong despite his advancing age, carried through the courtyard. "To the docks. Our princess will be disembarking soon."

Turning to Tian, he whispered, "Little Tian, we are entrusted with one of the *Tianzi*'s most treasured jewels. What movements are we seeing thus far?"

Keeping his voice low so that only Ambassador Wu could hear him, Tian said, "The kings of Lietuvi and Rotuvi arrived several days ago. They have small contingents of a few hundred each. They are staying in their own embassy compounds in the city center. The Teleri First Consul just arrived within the hour. With three thousand foot soldiers and two hundred cavalry. I have sent men to investigate."

Wu nodded, then signaled the party to depart with a wave of his hand. They left in exacting formation, led by the four mounted officials. The palanquin went next, followed by the foot soldiers. The drummers took up the rear, setting a slow, thunderous beat as the gates swung open.

As the procession made its way down the hill and through the market, citizens cleared the road and pointed and stared. The deliberate pace extended what would normally be a five-minute walk into a fifteen-minute parade. Other Cathayi residents of Iksuvius joined in, faces solemn. Tian's heart beat twice as fast as the drum. It wouldn't be long now.

By the time they arrived at the head of the dock, the sun cast a red glow from low on the horizon. Coming to a stop, the foot soldiers moved to secure the quay and prevent any of the gathering crowd from approaching.

The drummers slowed the beat to half-time. Tian joined the officials, dismounting from his horse and walking to the landing. The palanquin bearers followed close behind, with Jie in tow. Dockworkers bustled about, tying down moorings and extending a ramp to the second deck of the ship.

At a distance, the *Golden Phoenix* was impressive. Up close, it inspired awe. The Dragoncarved figurehead resembled a regal phoenix surging forward in flight, making the ship seem in motion even when stationary. It towered above them, dwarfing all of the other nearby vessels and casting shadows across the docks. As the *Tianzi*'s flagship, it was the fastest ship in the fleet.

Tian slowed his breath to calm his excitement. The drummers on deck sped up to double-time, and those on shore responded to match the pace. Members of the imperial guard, in their sky-blue silk tunics and immaculately polished steel breastplates, appeared on the deck. They lined up eight in a row on either side of the ramp.

General Zheng Jiawei, Tian's cousin and commander of the imperial guard, stepped to the head. Dropping to one knee, fist to the ground, he announced, "Princess Wang Kaiya from the Empire of Cathay."

The drummers on shore and on deck ceased simultaneously. With a jangle of armor, the other imperial guards sank to their right knee, heads bowed, right fists touching the ground. All the Cathayi on the dock and shore followed suit, a wave of color rippling down the procession.

Tian stole a glance up. A single figure stepped onto the ramp and billowed down at a deliberate pace. Here she was.

His stomach leapt into his throat. He quickly lowered his head. The soft rustling of her heavy linen gown approached. A single red brocade slipper covering a delicate foot came to a stop just in front of him.

"Rise." Just one single word. It was resonant and melodious, so unlike the voice from his childhood. Tian looked up, avoiding direct eye contact as protocol demanded.

He suppressed a gasp. Even in the waning light, it was clear the stories were true: the gangly child he knew a lifetime ago had blossomed into an unparalleled beauty. Her waist-length hair, braided into a single queue, hung over her shoulder. Large, doe-like eyes accentuated her high-bridged nose, the perfect curve of her lips, and her pearly complexion.

Ambassador Wu labored to his feet, maintaining a bow, and spoke: "Welcome to Iksuvius, *Dian-xia*. I am Wu Liming, the *Tianzi*'s representative in the Northwest. I yield that honor to you." He motioned to the officials as he introduced them, and as she nodded to recognize each one, they bowed deeply in response. "Lastly, this is Zheng Tian, Chief of Information."

The princess tilted her head at a slight angle, revealing the elegant line of her neck. Looking up at him through her lashes, she smiled with a radiance that brightened the afternoon shadows.

She spoke in a gentle, yet clear and mellifluous voice, which a nightingale would envy. "It has been many years since we last met, Young Lord Zheng. You have grown into a fine gentleman. I trust you have been doing well."

Tian's voice caught in his throat. "I am, um, honored. That you... remember me. *Dian-xia*." Somewhere behind him, Jie was undoubtedly laughing at his expense.

She tilted her head. "I do not forget my friends."

Warmth rose to his face, and he cast his gaze at her feet. Hopefully the late sun would prevent her from seeing him blush.

Luckily, Ambassador Wu relieved his awkward moment. "We should get back to the compound before the sun sets. Perhaps you can reacquaint yourselves over the princess' week-long stay." He motioned the palanquin bearers over.

A handmaiden shuffled forward, knelt, and opened the palanquin door. Nearby, Jie's lips quivered in a half-laugh.

"I shall ride a horse." The princess waved the handmaiden away. "It is not often that I leave Cathay, and I will see this foreign city."

The officials looked at one another in confusion. For a member of the Imperial Family to ride exposed in a foreign country was unheard of. Jie stared at the sky.

Someone had to say something. Tian cleared his throat. "*Dian-xia*. That is not wise. We must ensure your safety. The locals have never seen one of your stature. Our enemies' agents may be among the crowds."

"Nevertheless, I will ride." The last three words trilled like a song.

Her voice washed over Tian like a wave. All his misgivings now seemed inane, and he found himself compelled to obey. Around him, the ambassador, all of the officials, and even the imperial guards nodded. Jie sucked her lower lip, perhaps too concerned with protocols to entertain the princess' completely reasonable command. Nonetheless, she kept silent.

As an embassy soldier went for a horse, General Zheng sidled up to Tian. "It was like this on the *entire* journey. She insisted on doing *everything* her way. Kicking the captain out of his quarters on the poop deck so she could move in. Constantly getting in the way of sailors on deck. She is so headstrong, and nobody can defy her."

"It sounds like she gave you quite a headache," Tian whispered back.

"Now your headache, too, Cousin." General Zheng swallowed a laugh, motioning to one of the imperial guards to accompany the horse. "Zhao Yue, come!"

With his triangular face, Zhao Yue looked familiar. Of course; he'd been at Wailian Castle two years ago. Now he knelt, and the princess used his knee as a footstool to mount the horse. The Nothori on the shore pointed and laughed at this humiliation, too ignorant to know that any of the Cathay would consider it an honor.

Tian took the reins to guide the horse, but the princess pulled them away. The procession, now joined by a hundred of the imperial guards and three handmaidens at the rear, began their return to the compound. Though it was almost dusk, the Nothori commoners clogged the streets, jostling to catch a glimpse of the Cathayi princess. Excited shouts and chatter erupted as she passed.

Tian scanned the crowds for potential threats. Why had he ever conceded into letting her ride high on a horse, exposed to danger? This was such a bad idea.

Maybe he had little to worry about. The imperial guards radiated an aura of awe. Commoners, and even Iksuvi soldiers, shrank back as the procession passed. When they reached the compound, the gates opened.

Once inside, a stable boy took the reins of the princess' horse and guided the mount towards the mansion. She looked back and flashed Tian a demure smile as she rode off.

Tian's mouth gaped. Was the pounding in his ears the echo of the drum, or his own heart?

"Queen takes knight," Jie muttered under her breath.

He turned to glare at her, and caught sight of a large Cathayi youth watching from between two buildings across the street. As their gazes connected, the boy darted back into the dark shadows of the alley.

It was not someone he recognized, and he knew almost every one of his countrymen living in the city. And his size... it was reminiscent of the boys who'd assassinated Old Lord Peng two years ago.

CHAPTER 4:
Heart of a Princess

Kaiya suppressed a laugh. Zheng Tian, with his mouth agape, oblivious to onlookers, stirred nostalgic feelings of their carefree childhood. Despite what Jie had said about him being a deadly swordsman and incomparable spy, he seemed just as innocent as he was ten years ago. She rubbed the river pebble he'd given her back then as a token of his affection. After all that had happened in the past two and a half years, it was nice to remember the idealistic girl she'd once been.

His bewildered expression vanished as quickly as it had appeared.

She would have traded an armful of jade bangles to see that look again, to remember a life before court intrigue, putting down rebellions, and singing to dragons. Before being manipulated by both Avarax and Cousin Kai-Long. If only she could be that idealistic girl again, the one who didn't question the motives of anyone who was kind to her.

Heavens, there was that ugly bitterness invading her thoughts again.

She gazed at Tian. If anyone could restore her faith in humanity, and reassure her of her worth, it would be him.

The moment passed, and Kaiya composed her countenance to one of regal aloofness. She slid off the horse near the steps of the main residence.

Solid ground. Open space. Fighting to keep her legs from unsightly wobbling, she looked up at the building. It was quaint, almost reminiscent of a Cathayi noble's villa with its steeply-pitched tiled eaves.

The ambassador bowed low. "We attempted to recreate the architecture from back home, but I am afraid all the stone gives it a cold appearance."

The steward, bowed on one knee at the entrance, echoed the ambassador's apologetic tone. "We have reserved the entire south wing of the second floor for your use. I am so sorry we cannot do better."

The kneeling Mistress of Chambers was equally contrite. "We have tried to train the servants in proper court etiquette, but I am afraid it will never meet the standard you are used to."

As if to emphasize the point, a porter bearing one of her ornately-carved rosewood boxes nearly ran into her. He sank to his knees, forehead touching the ground, almost dropping the box in his haste. Other servants followed suit, bowing abjectly.

She fought off the impulse to reassure the porter, since such displays would only embarrass him more.

Everyone was making such a big deal out of trivial matters. No, it was enough just to escape the stifling cabin that had been her home for a week at sea, to be out of the narrow confines of the ship.

"We have prepared a bath for you." Bowing, the Mistress of Chambers invited Kaiya inside with an open hand. "I will take you there while the servants bring your train to your suite."

A bath! It would have been her first order of business as well, had she set the itinerary herself. A chance to wash out a week of travel. Sea salt seemed to clog every pore. Worse was the awful stench of the filthy harbor and marketplace, which clung to her like a grimy second skin. She hid her enthusiasm as she followed the Mistress of Chambers through the foyer to a side door.

A short walk across a raised, covered walkway through an enclosed garden brought them to the embassy's wooden bathhouse. Kaiya's nose crinkled at the fresh varnish that made the wood gleam. Along with the manicured shrubs and combed white gravel, it was a clear sign the staff had prepared for an imperial visit.

Her most faithful imperial guards, Chen Xin and Ma Jun, kept watch outside the door, while several others blocked the two access points to the courtyard and patrolled the perimeter.

A kneeling maid slid the door open, bowing low as Kaiya entered. Although the enormous soaking tub inside could tightly hold a dozen men at once—and probably did on busy evenings—the entire building had been cleared. Her handmaidens swarmed around to assist her. Waving them off, she sat on a stool outside the bathtub and scrubbed the salt out of her skin and hair until she glowed pink. She then stepped into the tub and sank into the steaming waters.

They warmed her to the core, chasing away the cold sea breezes that had lodged in her bones. To think it was already so chilly in early autumn! Why was *she* the one sent to this frigid wasteland to negotiate Cousin Kai-Long's extradition?

Beyond the bathhouse walls, the imperial guards shared her complaint in low whispers. They should have known her keen ears would hear them.

"I could have sworn it was summer when we left Cathay," Chen Xin grumbled.

"And it will still be summer when we get back," Ma Jun said cheerfully.

"Well, I can see my breath."

"At least we will be able to see it coming before we have to smell it."

Kaiya choked back a giggle. No one bantered with her like that, except for maybe the Last Dragon when he'd taken on the form of Hardeep to dupe her

"My breath doesn't smell bad," Chen Xin said.

"Compared to this city, no. It *is* cold, but at least you're not posted here like the embassy staff. We get to go home soon enough." Ma Jun could always see the bright side of things.

"Yes, but who knows where they will send us next? The last trip almost got us killed."

"You got to see a real dragon... the last one in all of Tivaralan."

"We were almost his dinner. And I suppose getting diced up by the Maduran Scorpions is your idea of adventure?" Chen Xin was no longer complaining as much as bragging.

"Well, as the classics say, *Travel is worth more than a thousand books in cultivating wisdom.*"

"If you survive... "

Kaiya smiled. Oh, to have a deep camaraderie like those two enjoyed. Like the one she and Tian once shared. Playing the Dragon Scale Lute almost three years ago had changed everything, burdened her with unwanted responsibilities in the imperial court. Vanquishing Avarax with a song had elevated her to legend. Nobody could relate to that, and now her closest confidante was an impertinent half-elf whose idea of opening a heart was more literal than figurative.

With a sigh, Kaiya sprawled out in the tub, sinking beneath the water. Her hair floated on the surface, filtering light from the baubles on the ceiling. In the three hundred years of the Wang Dynasty, the Founder's consort—who had reigned as Dowager Regent for eight decades—was the only woman who had played a more important role in the Cathayi court. She must have felt so isolated.

Kaiya emerged to catch a breath, brushing hair and water out of her face while affording herself a moment to daydream about the dashing *Tai-Ming* heir who'd been courting her. She'd rejected a dozen suitors before him, but his quick wit and charm made her entire body tingle. A delightful fluttering erupted in her stomach.

Maybe after marriage, people would forget about the Dragon Charmer, and life would regain a semblance of normalcy. Maybe it wouldn't feel so... *lonely*.

Quickly banishing these thoughts, Kaiya mused over her reunion with Zheng Tian. Despite the assurances that he had become a magnificent swordsman, he seemed just as adorably awkward as ever. His puppy-dog reaction to her smile! Just like when they were children. Apparently, the right facial expression or gesture could still evoke his response. A laugh escaped her, but she covered her mouth. If the guards heard her outburst...

A handmaiden opened the doors and shuffled in, head bowed and eyes averted. She presented a towel with both hands. "*Dian-xia*. The Iridescent Moon waxes to half. The reception is at the second gibbous."

Sighing, Kaiya reluctantly left the waters' warm embrace. She stepped out of the tub and into the open towel, again fighting off a handmaiden and wrapping herself. Perhaps other Cathayi nobles expected servants to do all the work of washing and dressing them. After a particularly insolent retainer had admonished her, Kaiya took more responsibility for herself.

Barefooted, she glided across the room and to a private changing area. While handmaidens fussed at drying her hair, she donned a simple white silk robe and draped a heavy fur shawl over her shoulders. She slid her feet into fur-lined sandals. Kneeling maids opened the sliding doors.

Kaiya stepped out and tasted the brisk night air with a deep breath. The Iridescent Moon Iridescent Moonfloated a little more south from its usual position, waxing halfway towards its first gibbous. There was only an hour and a half until the reception for the senior embassy staff and prominent Cathayi families living in Iksuvius.

Her nose wrinkled at her imperial guards' odor. To think she must have smelled just as bad just half an hour before. She shuddered. "Ma Jun, Chen Xin, be sure to bathe before the banquet."

Both guards dropped to their right knee, heads bowed. "As the princess commands," they both bellowed.

Satisfied, Kaiya nodded and strolled down the walkway, handmaidens in tow. The other half-dozen imperial guards fell in behind her, keeping a respectful distance.

A shallow breathing hid in the muffled sounds of the city, buried among the quiet footsteps and swishing robes of her maids and guards.

Kaiya paused mid-stride and raised a hand, signaling all to stop. The guards behind her placed their hands on their *dao* and deployed into defensive positions around her.

"Jie," Kaiya said.

The Insolent Retainer melted out of the shadows and dropped to her right knee, right fist to the ground. "*Dian-xia*. As always, I am amazed that you can hear me."

Kaiya covered her laugh with a hand. The half-elf's straightforward nature and witty quips were always endearing. No one else dared speak freely to her. "Maybe I just guessed you would be lurking the halls. Either way, I am pleased to see you again."

"Me, too." Jie rose to her feet at Kaiya's hand gesture and followed her down the walk and through the side door into the embassy. The guards again fell in behind.

"So," Kaiya said. "You have already been here a month. What are your impressions?"

"The people are big and standoffish," Jie said. "The level of poverty crushes their collective soul. It is amazing that the nation has not collapsed under the weight of civil disorder."

Kaiya sighed. "It does not sound like a very hospitable place. The sooner we are done negotiating with the Nothori Kings and their dreadful Teleri masters, the sooner we can leave this land. You have made security arrangements?"

"Yes, *Dian-xia*," Jie said as they arrived at the foyer's grand staircase. "Taking your itinerary into account, I have selected the safest routes and ensured that my clan's Fists will be watching for potential threats. Zheng Tian has been helpful in organizing them."

"Tian." Kaiya tasted the name and decided it was the flavor of nostalgia. "What do you think of him?"

The usually quick-witted half-elf was unusually slow to respond. Within those three seconds of silence, the average Black Fist could probably plan the invasion of a small country. When Jie finally answered, her tone carried forced objectivity. "He has an exceptional grasp of the situation here. He sees connections between seemingly unrelated pieces of information. You will find his insight and advice invaluable."

"Yes." Kaiya covered her laugh with her fingers, deciding to test her theory. "But what do you think about *him*? You have not seen Tian for three years. I have not seen him for ten. But he has hardly changed at all. Still awkward, despite his good looks."

Even if Jie did not betray an emotion in her expression, she was again uncharacteristically quiet for a few seconds. "There's a lot going on in his head, all the time."

A hint of defensiveness floated in the answer. Could Jie actually have affections for a boy? *That* boy? How could such a pretty and talented girl fall for someone so... *Tian*? Kaiya rubbed his pebble.

No, Tian was a man. Not the gullible ten-year-old, despite initial impressions. Surely, he'd still always be the reliable ear to keep her secrets and a solid shoulder to lean against.

Jie's ears twitched. Outside, bird calls rang out. Fake bird calls.

CHAPTER 5:
Things That Go Bump In The Night

From Tian's vantage point on his office balcony, the marketplace in the near distance appeared an oasis of light in a desert of dull grey, lit by Aksumi glass baubles brought by the citizens socializing there. The nearly-full White Moon blanketed the city in dim light, while the larger Blue Moon Guanyin's Eye was almost closed.

Muted sounds of laughter diffused from the market and filled the otherwise empty city streets. Farther out, individual lights from fishing boats bobbed in the harbor, like fireflies dancing in Cathay's gardens at midsummer.

He and seven-year-old Princess Kaiya had once caught fireflies in one of the many courtyards of Sun-Moon Palace. It seemed like a lifetime ago; a time of innocence, before the realities of duty and responsibility took over.

Tian looked up and south to find the Iridescent Moon in its usual place, swirling in translucent pinks and purples like an opaque soap bubble. It waxed towards its first gibbous. Just an hour remained until the reception. With so little time, he returned to the office to ponder his convoluted web of information.

Just as he was about to pin a note about the strange boy, the annoying squawks of peacocks erupted in the courtyard below. The fake caw, a Black Lotus code indicating an intruder, repeated twice from different parts of the compound. Old Tong and Shun.

The little hairs on the back of his neck stood on end. An intruder, just when the princess arrived, couldn't be a coincidence. Sheathed sword in hand, he slipped out onto the balcony. A quick search along the perimeter revealed nothing. Perhaps it was related to the young man in the alley a couple hours earlier.

At a spot near the middle of the western wall, two drunken Nothori ruffians argued, loud enough to scare ghosts away. At the top of the wall, half a dozen Cathay musketmen pointed and laughed.

The lack of discipline! Especially with the princess visiting. Tian clenched his jaw as he raked his gaze back and forth over the grounds. Maids and servants hurried about, preparing for the reception. Beyond his line of sight, a caller announced the names of prominent Cathayi families at the main gate.

Young Cheng's bird call shrieked from the north, then Pockmarked Zu's answered from the east. At least three intruders. Any could be a threat to the princess. Tian's hands clenched. He started to leap down into the courtyard, but paused with a leg over the railing. Something didn't add up.

Ducking back into his office, he closed the door and locked it behind him. He shuttered the Aksumi light-bauble lamp. The room blinked into dim darkness, with only the feeble blue rays of Guanyin's Eye filtering in through the window. Tian sank into a crouch in the darkest shadow of the southwest corner.

Settling his gaze without focus on the middle of the room, his field of vision encompassed the entire space. His right hand rested on the wooden floors, while another pressed against the wall to feel for the vibrations of someone's approach. His hearing reached out beyond the floors and walls and ceilings.

The sounds above and below suggested nothing out of the ordinary, beyond preparations for the princess' reception. On this level, a large group climbed the central stairs and then passed through the east corridor, heading south. It was likely the princess and her retinue heading to her spacious quarters, oblivious to potential danger.

Outside where the Nothori ruffians had been arguing, the ruckus increased. Embassy guards yelled at them to quiet down and leave. Yet hidden in the commotion was a faint new sound just outside his balcony, the unmistakable scraping of the cat-claws the Black Fists used to scale walls. Tian's heart squeezed. His own men wouldn't come up the walls like that, not without announcing themselves.

Feet landed on the balcony with almost inaudible sound, followed by the indistinct clicks of the door lock being picked. None of his men would do that. Every nerve stood on edge as Tian gripped his sword.

A blink of light and shadows under the threshold of his hallway door broke his concentration. Just outside, Princess Kaiya's unmistakable voice spoke in muffled whispers. What was she doing here? Right when a possible attacker was nearby, no less.

Both doors simultaneously opened.

At the balcony, the intruder stood taller and broader than any of Tian's spies. Dressed all in black and wearing a hooded mask, the man remained at the half-open door, surveying.

In the same second, the princess glided into the room, light from the hall flooding in.

Tian vaulted through gaps in the twine, simultaneously flicking three throwing stars behind him.

The stars arced between the strings and whistled through the space of the closing balcony door. Behind him, a youth's muffled shriek pierced the night. Tian hit the ground shoulder first, rolled, and sprang again through more openings in the twine. On his descent, he tackled the princess, shoving her back into the hall. He twisted to soften her fall, so that she landed on top of him.

Six *dao* rasped from scabbards as the imperial guards closed on him. He ignored them, instead signaling in clan code to Jie who slunk behind the princess' group. *Intruder, balcony.*

Jie responded even before he'd finished. She charged into the office and swam through the web of twine with effortless dexterity. And then she was out of his line of sight. The balcony door crashed open, followed by a loud thud. Then silence.

Tian's stomach clenched as he craned his neck to see through the Cobweb. Had Jie taken care of the intruder? Or had he—

Hands pressed against his chest. He looked up. A beautiful woman lay on top of him. Wearing only a silk inner gown. His arms were wrapped protectively around her. Her warmth and fragrance and softness smothered him. His armor of martial and mental training failed.

She was trying to push herself off of him. Five, now six, of the realm's deadliest swordsmen pointed the sharpest swords in the world at him.

"Unhand the princess," snarled one, the belligerent, flat-knuckled guard from the Wailian battle.

"Let go of me!" the princess panted, her face flushed, regal bearing lost in her panic. She took a deep breath. When she spoke again, it was with the imperial tone of command. "Zheng Tian, release me."

The confident voice woke Tian from his own state of shock. Heat rose to his face. He'd just touched a member of the Imperial Family. Ended in a compromising position, no less. Such a trespass, even to protect her, might invite a death sentence.

He let go.

With a sharp push on his chest, the princess extricated herself. Her luxurious locks cascaded over her face as she staggered to her feet and stumbled back. She tightened her gown around herself and brushed the errant hair away, revealing a flushed face and glinting eyes. In that moment, she seemed less like the elegant princess and more like the child he remembered.

An imperial guard charged, *dao* raised.

Tian sprang to his feet with a windmill kick, just before the sword came down. He sidestepped the follow-up thrust, caught the guard's wrist, and twisted. As the man's grip loosened, Tian plucked the blade free. In the same motion, he wrapped up the guard's elbow into a lock and started to slash his throat. He stopped the technique. Heavens, his automatic reactions almost killed one of Princess Kaiya's personal guards.

The other guards closed in around him, naked blades held in defensive positions. He was skilled enough with the sword to confront one of the vaunted imperial guards in a fair fight; but had very little chance against five, regardless of what underhanded tactics he might use.

Even now, the magical aura of intimidation from their breastplates sent his heart racing.

"Stop," the princess said, her voice shaking. She stared, her gape one of shock and horror.

He dropped the sword and released his hostage.

CHAPTER 6:
Plots Unraveled

Jie had finished binding the intruder on the balcony when she heard the sounds of warriors assuming fighting stances in the hallway.

Imperial guards, always late. She twisted through the Cobweb, coming back to the hall.

Her jaw slackened. Five of the princess' personal imperial guards—whom she had come to appreciate, despite any jokes she made at their expense—surrounded Tian with naked blades. Face red, Xu Zhan was climbing to his feet. Princess Kaiya stood near the wall, gown clutched tightly around her, tears glistening in her eyes.

It had happened so fast, the others must not have known about the infiltrator. Jie dropped to her knee, head bowed. "*Dian-xia*, Zheng Tian was protecting you. An intruder is bound, out on the balcony." She glanced up to see the princess' cold stare, tears gone. Had she imagined them?

All attention turned to the princess. After two seconds, she motioned the guards with a wave of her hand. "Zheng Tian, the prisoner is yours. In the future, do not dare touch me without my permission."

There was the princess Jie knew. Afraid to show vulnerability, hiding embarrassment behind regal carriage.

"Understood, *Dian-xia*." Tian sank to both knees and pressed his forehead to the ground. He held himself in this most contrite bow.

The princess lifted her chin and straightened her back, not deigning to afford Tian another glance.

It was time to diffuse the awkwardness. "*Dian-xia*," Jie said, "allow me to go ahead of you and check your rooms. There might be more than one intruder. Please wait here."

The princess cast a sidelong glance in Tian's direction. "I shall not wait here. I am well protected with you and my guards." Despite her defiance, her voice carried a hint of embarrassment and her hand trembled.

"Forgive my insolence, *Dian-xia*," Jie said without a hint of sincerity, "but if there is someone in your rooms, I want to apprehend them. If they hear you coming, they will try to escape. Unfortunately, Chen Xin and Ma Jun could not sneak up on a deaf man. If anyone, send Li Wei several paces behind me." She flashed a grin at the imperial guards.

The princess nodded. "As you suggest, Jie. The rest of us will take the north hall, which should give you plenty of time." With a flourishing sweep of her robe, she turned and glided up the corridor, guards and handmaidens scurrying to keep up.

Only after the princess had disappeared around the corner of the hall did Tian lift his head. He wore an expressionless look, save for his rigidly set jaw and twitching neck muscles.

When had he ever had such a reaction before? Was he angry or humiliated? She grinned. "You did the right thing. At first, that is."

Without ever making eye contact or acknowledging her comment, Tian slipped into his office and closed the door.

Attitude from him, too. Jie snorted and turned back towards the princess' suites in the south hall. She drifted lightly along the hardwood floors, motioning for Li Wei to wait at the corner.

Another imperial guard, Zhao Yue, stood at the door to the suite. She signaled for him to stay put as she approached. The crack beneath the door was dark. She placed a hand and an ear to it. Even if her father had abandoned her, at least he had left her with superior hearing.

Inside, there were almost inaudible sounds of activity. Whoever was in there was good. Black Fist-good. Jie looked first at Zhao Yue and then back towards Li Wei at the junction of the west and south halls, and then made simple hand gestures. *I am going in. You,* she pointed to Zhao Yue, *follow. You,* she nodded at Li Wei, *go down and to the other side.* A three-year-old would understand. An imperial guard was another matter.

She withdrew four magical light baubles from a pocket concealed in her dress sleeves. A quick push on the door opened it a crack. Grasping a knife, she tossed the beads through and burst in.

All had been in order when Jie had checked the suite an hour earlier. Now, several ornate lacquer and brocade boxes were open, revealing extravagant gowns, musical instruments and jewelry.

A large fair-haired youth, his face darkened by pitch, rose to his feet near one of the boxes. He screened his eyes with one hand and reached for a shortsword with the other. Beyond him, at the double doors leading out onto the grand balcony, a young Cathayi male squinted at her.

With her left hand, Jie reached into the fold of her dress and flung a throwing spike at the man near the balcony doors. In the same motion she surged towards the youth by the box.

He swung his sword with such precision, his vision must've already adjusted to the sudden light.

She whipped out another knife from her sleeve with her left hand, leaving her left flank exposed to bait him. As he lunged with a thrust towards the opening, she twisted out of his line of attack and slashed through the tendons in his wrist.

Even before the sword slipped from his limp fingers, Jie passed under his arm and severed his knee ligaments with a backhand slash. She finished the motion with a shoulder butt to his floating ribs. Despite being more than twice as large, he tumbled to the ground with a grunt.

Zhao Yue and Li Wei charged in. Both of them. Jie kicked the sword out of the youth's reach before turning her attention towards the young man near the balcony doors.

Her spike had lodged on the right side of his chest, likely puncturing a lung. It had him keeled over on all fours, gasping for breath. As Jie approached, he lobbed a knife at her. Thrown with little force, it was easy to sidestep. The blade clattered harmlessly along the floor behind her.

In two steps, she kicked his hand out from under him. Cocking her foot back, she drove her heel into his temple. He collapsed in a heap with a muffled groan.

Not wasting a beat, Jie edged over to the door into the sleeping chambers and peeked around the corner. Empty.

However, one of the eastern windows overlooking the bathhouse courtyard stood open. After a quick glance into the dressing room, she went to the window and screeched out a birdcall that would notify her Black Lotus brothers of potential danger.

Jie returned to the antechamber, where the imperial guards kept a watchful eye over the intruders. "I will take the princess to the east-wing guest room until we clean up this mess. Get one of the embassy guards to bring these prisoners down to the storerooms, and tell them to bring the doctor. This one needs help if we want him to survive long enough for interrogation."

She slipped out of the room and up the east hall, where she found the princess and her entourage.

The princess' posture was straight and her pace deliberate, her regal bearing suggesting that she'd put the awkward incident with Tian behind her. However, her jawline quivered and her eyes locked forward, unfocussed. Hiding her embarrassment, no doubt.

Jie dropped to her knee. "*Dian-xia*, we are dealing with a security issue in your quarters. I will report to you when the entire picture is clear. Until we resolve things, please use these guest quarters, next to the ambassador's suite." She motioned with an open hand towards a door.

The princess simply nodded, and Jie went to listen at the door.

Satisfied that it was empty, she opened it and took a quick look in. Her night vision—another legacy of elven parentage—penetrated the darkness, casting the bed and table in hues of green. Nothing seemed amiss.

Meiling, the princess' handmaiden and decoy, glared at her. "The princess will require appropriate attire for the reception tonight."

Jie motioned for Meiling to follow her as she turned back towards the princess' suite. It had transformed into a beehive of maids and guards in the short time she was gone, with the Mistress of Chambers directing cleanup efforts. Embassy guards carried out the prisoners.

Jie smirked as Meiling blanched. "Which robe did the princess intend to wear tonight?"

"The plain white silk, hanging in her changing room." Meiling waved an open hand towards the sleeping chambers and the dressing room that lay beyond.

Jie slunk in and examined the robe under the bright illumination of a light bauble. She sniffed and ran her hands over the luxuriant fabric, which felt almost like mist made solid. Undraping it, she handed it to Meiling. "This is safe. Wait while I check her cosmetics."

Face powders of crushed pearl, rouges of *danhua* flowers, jade combs and make-up brushes of phoenix feathers lay neatly arranged on a rosewood table with ornately carved borders. Jie caught herself looking at her reflection in the large silver mirror, imagining herself made-up, wearing a silken gown. What would Tian think of that? The last time he'd seen her like that, he'd been a boy of ten, newly inducted into the clan.

The reflection of Meiling, lips pursed in amusement, brought her back to the present. How silly, to think of such vanity. She returned to the make-up, again smelling and taking the minutest of tastes.

"This lip rouge might have been tainted." Jie held up a small mother-of-pearl case before stashing it in her sleeve. "The others are safe. You may take these to the princess so that she might prepare."

She dismissed the handmaiden with a jerk of her head and returned to the antechamber to examine the boxes. Suspicious powdery residue clung to the three finest court gowns. Those she placed in a box, which she had embassy guards take to her own quarters.

After an exchange of fake bird calls to confirm the compound was secure, Jie descended into the network of tunnels and rooms beneath the grounds.

Originating from the warehouse, the network had started as cold storage, hewn into the subterranean rock. It had been further excavated over twenty years to include several rooms and two escape routes into the city sewers.

She found Tian in a musty room filled with wooden crates. Two of the intruders, now bound and blindfolded, sat motionless in deceptively flimsy-looking bloodwood chairs.

Unlike other young Cathayi males, the tall, brawny youths sported the close-cropped hair favored by mercenaries and Teleri soldiers. Balcony Boy's knee and ankle wounds had since been bound, using strips of cloth torn from his loose-fitting black pants. Those pants were part of an ensemble that resembled the utility suits the Black Fists wore on night missions.

Blond Boy was similarly dressed and coifed, his face now washed to reveal the fair skin of a Nothori. The last, also Cathayi, lay on a blanket, hands bound in front of him. His breathing was labored and blood flecked his lips. With wounds like that, he wouldn't last the night.

Tian would not look at her, and instead made himself busy rummaging through the prisoners' effects: climbing cat-claws, a kit of lockpicks, Aksumi light beads, straight shortswords, small flasks, various small throwing weapons, hemp twine, and other tools.

In almost every respect, they appeared like Black Fists. However, the Cathayi youths did not resemble any of the recruits who had passed through the Black Lotus Temple in the last three decades Jie had been there.

After an up-close examination, it was clear *what* they were: Nightblades, whom she'd tracked and researched for two years in the Sundered Empire.

If only Tian would acknowledge her so they could confer. He was still keeping to himself, sulking from his encounter with the princess.

"Knight takes queen, and looks stupid doing it," she said.

Tian looked up from the tools, scowling.

She flashed her most innocent smile, and his expression softened.

Not wanting the prisoners to overhear, Jie used the clan's silent body signals. *Teleri Nightblades. Bovyans trained by Black Lotus traitor. I was tracking. You fought one in Jiangkou.*

Tian pointed at the two who looked like their Cathay countrymen. *These not Bovyan. Are Cathayi.*

Jie waved her hands back and forth. *Bovyans always look like mother. See, huge for Cathayi.*

After another look at the two, Tian shrugged. *But small for a Bovyan.*

Jie nodded. *Small ones do other military specialties. Spies. Logistics.*

"You should've told me. Earlier," Tian said.

Jie shrugged. *Not many Nightblades at all. All in East.*

At least three here. Tian pointed at the two bound boys, and the dying one.

"I will find out more," Jie replied. *You prepare for reception.*

A sheepish grin appeared on Tian's face. "That will be awkward. I am sorry. About earlier."

She waved him off with a smile, though saying in her most lethal voice, "You had better be."

The tone was for the benefit of the prisoners, to whom she turned her full attention once Tian disappeared from the room.

Balcony Boy sat, seemingly unfazed by his predicament, his breathing calm and shoulders relaxed.

Jie had many ways to unsettle a man.

She reached into the sleeve of her dress and withdrew a single-edged knife with a sharp rasp. Slowly, she ran the blunt side across the top of the boy's lip, pausing for a brief second of pressure in the divot under his nose.

His knuckles whitened around the chair's delicately curved armrests, and he let out a sharp breath of air. Despite his initial calm, he was not trained as thoroughly as a Black Lotus Fist *Black Fist*.

She leaned over and whispered in his ear, "You *will* talk. Save yourself the misery."

He laughed, but it was half-hearted, forced. When he spoke, his voice straddled the divide between puberty and adulthood. "Do what you will, bitch. I won't talk."

"You were trained by a Black Fist spy. I can tell." Jie took out a small flask and uncorked it. A sweet fragrance diffused through the small room. She held it under his nose. "So tell me, what is this?"

He bit his lip.

"I suspect you know quite a bit about contact toxins, since you put a powder in the princess' cosmetics. And staged toxins, since I found some deer horn velvet in her dresses. So you know that if I took the first powder and mixed it with *yinghua* flowers instead of the deer horn, it would make a male-specific toxin instead of a female-specific one. Like what is in this bottle."

He cast his gaze downward. He knew.

Dabbing a small amount of the fluid onto her lips, she slid behind his back. She then lightly pressed her chest against his back and brushed her lips across his neck. Feminine wiles would probably be enough to bend a hot-blooded teen boy to her will. The euphoric intoxication he would feel from the toxin would make him soft clay in her hands.

Now why would the Teleri want the princess in such a state?

CHAPTER 7:
Princesses Unraveled

First the humiliation of being manhandled into a compromising position; then enemy spies rummaging through her clothes and jewelry. Throughout it all, Kaiya had maintained her composure, had tried to seem aloof even if her heart had raced. Now, with her handmaidens and imperial guards waiting outside the guest room, the privacy afforded her a chance to unravel.

The worst part was seeing the awkward, gentle boy from her fondest memories transform into a brutal killing machine. Letting out a long sigh, she threw herself down in a chair in front of the writing desk that now served as a make-up table. In the mirror, her straight carriage slumped back and her placid expression contorted into distress. Tears welled in her eyes. Her hands trembled freely, matching the rhythm of her fluttering heart.

She shook hair into her face, as if it would hide her shame.

It was her fault.

After years of having no real friends, here was a rare chance to reconnect with her one-time confidante. Perhaps even share secrets like they had as children. She should've waited until morning to call upon his cobweb sanctuary instead of visiting unannounced.

Tian had been trying to protect her from what he perceived to be a clear and present danger. She *knew*. Even so, Tian holding her down on top of him was too reminiscent of Rumiya seizing her face.

With the need to always project the image of control, it was hard to feel so powerless. The memory of dark confinement rushed back, threatening to unravel her at a time when Cathay needed her resolve. She was holding her breath. Her chest tightened.

No, she wouldn't go there. She wasn't that helpless girl anymore. She'd secured a mutual protection pact with the Paladins. Transformed a dragon with her voice. She was in control of her own destiny.

She closed her eyes and took several deep breaths.

Her heartbeat slowed. Kaiya opened her eyes and looked in the mirror to find the lines of weakness gone from her face. The Dragon Charmer had replaced the scared little girl. Tilting her neck at just the right angle, she tested a demure smile, a mischievous rise of an eyebrow, an innocent blink, a flirtatious pout—all tools that could be just as useful as the magic of her voice.

One more deep breath, and she rose to her feet. She slipped on an outer robe with long hanging sleeves.

As she brushed her hair, a light rap on the door was followed by her handmaiden Han Meiling's voice. "*Dian-xia*, the Iridescent Moon has waxed well towards its third gibbous. Your guests have been waiting almost half an hour."

How had the time slipped away from her? She must seem like a spoiled brat to everyone around her. Her heart quickened a beat, but she fought back the rising flustered feeling with another deep breath.

"Enter," she commanded.

The door swung open, revealing her handmaidens in silken floral gowns, kneeling. Her most trusted imperial guards stood behind them, now immaculate in their dark-blue robes and burnished breastplates. The five-clawed dragons etched into the steel seemed to wink at her with their gleaming eyes.

Confidence building, she smiled. They might be late, but at least they wouldn't dishonor Father with their appearance!

Ambassador Wu stepped forward from behind the imperial guards and bowed. "*Dian-xia*, please follow me to the banquet."

With a nod, she glided out of the room and fell in behind the ambassador, following him down the grand stairway and into the central hall.

If the rest of the embassy compound felt like an imitation of Cathay, the enormous banquet room was nothing but. Modeled on ancient Arkothi-style architecture, it took up the northern end of the building, vaulting two stories with an overlooking mezzanine. A dozen windows on the northern wall, made by Estomari glassmakers in Iksuvius, reached nearly to the ceiling and looked out onto a meditative rock garden. Color brush-paintings and black-and-white calligraphy by some of Cathay's most famous masters graced its walls.

Prominent Cathayi families and senior embassy officials alike had arrived well in advance. They formed a rectangle on the dark hardwoods, each person kneeling on a cushion of light blue silk with gold-colored embroidery. As she entered, all bowed, bringing their foreheads to the ground, open hands on the floor in front of them. If only they knew she'd been a quivering mess of nerves just half an hour ago.

There—Tian sat in the far corner of the rectangle. Although all avoided direct eye contact with her as etiquette demanded, he was doing a particularly good job at it.

Maybe it was for the better.

She glided to her place at the head of the rectangle, then settled to her knees onto a cushion.

She nodded her head. "Please sit comfortably."

All bowed again. The male guests switched into a cross-legged position, while the women shifted their weight to relieve pressure on their knees. General Zheng of the imperial guard took a seat on her left. Ambassador Wu, on her right, motioned for the servants to bring the food.

They placed a low, small table in front of each person. Chopsticks rested at exacting angles on every table, accompanied by a bowl of rice, a plate of boiled Nothori clams, a small saucer of soy sauce-braised pork belly, a low-rimmed bowl of stir-fried Nothori greens, a small plate of fried Nothori squash, and a lacquer bowl of turnip soup.

Several porcelain flasks of rice wine were passed around, to be poured into small white cups. Thinking back to that humiliating brush with wine and a drunken traipse through Huajing with Avarax, Kaiya waved it off.

"Unfortunately, many of our leafy vegetables are past harvest in this cold climate," the ambassador said. "However, we import some of our spices and seasoning and use local produce to imitate cuisine from home. It is quite delicious if not authentic. Please, try some."

Kaiya had been clenching her jaws. She must have quite a dreadful expression. With a shy smile, she took her chopsticks in hand and extended them towards the only dish she recognized: the braised pork. Hand cupped beneath, she lifted it.

The entire room had fallen quiet. Everyone was trying to hide the fact that they were watching her. When she slid it into her mouth and nodded graciously, the collective sigh of relief was silent but obvious.

How ironic. Her recent flare-up of food allergies was a state secret, to prevent tarnishing the image of Perfect Princess. As hard as it was to maintain that façade, her countrymen tried even harder to accommodate her.

Pretending to ignore their stares, Kaiya raised her rice bowl and scooped out a small clump with her chopsticks. She took a few small bites, and the weight of attention gradually fell away. Thank the Heavens for the reprieve from the guests' scrutiny. She tentatively picked at the unfamiliar dishes.

The evening wore on, with the slow trickle of individuals coming to introduce themselves with deep bows soon building up to a torrent of bobbing heads. It became the perfect excuse for ignoring the food. Even if socializing was tiring and not particularly enjoyable, at least she excelled at it. Her neck would certainly be sore in the morning from all of the nodding. After the ritual exchange of pleasantries, she committed each person's name to memory.

Tomorrow's welcoming reception at the Teleri Embassy would be more of the same, albeit with a bewildering plethora of foreign names and faces. Among those would be First Consul Geros Bovyan of the Teleri Empire, and she'd be relying on Tian to guide her.

Tian. She'd have to apologize to him in private, and then share her biggest secret: the imminent announcement of her betrothal. He'd want to know.

She looked towards his corner, only to find that his seat was empty.

CHAPTER 8:
A Losing Game

Summoned by Jie, Tian was grateful to escape the reception and focus on something other than the slow and tortuous death of his childhood memories. From the shadows of the hall, he shot a last glance back at the princess. How could she be so picky? She wouldn't so much as look at the clams, an expensive delicacy and the main course of the meal.

The girl he remembered was open-minded and adventurous. He was just now coming to grips with the notion that that girl was gone, transformed by years of extravagance in the Cathayi imperial court.

How different from the austere life and demanding training he'd endured. Hopefully, she would return home soon, before the memories of his youth were completely poisoned, leaving him only with the realities of the present.

"King's rook forward three," Jie said even before he set foot in his office. "Check."

"Interesting move. You've played an unorthodox game so far."

Jie shrugged, her expression blank.

Tian absently ran a hand over one of the Cobweb lines. "Did our prisoners have anything to say?"

"If he's to be believed, one said that their goal was to catalog this office, to see what you knew."

"You don't believe him."

Jie smirked. "I have no doubt he was telling the truth. But I couldn't get them to say why they'd placed a staged intoxicant in the princess' lip rouge and gowns."

Tian nodded, pondering. "They breached our security. How?"

"They're recent arrivals, hired by the Zhou family as bodyguards." She traced relative locations in the air. "After escorting them here, they told the gate guards they would wait in the barracks to meet some friends. That is when one tried to access the Cobweb and the others snuck into the princess' chambers. Hired hands and some other Teleri soldiers made a concerted effort to create distractions outside the walls."

Tian scrunched his nose. Such poor planning, and even worse execution. "Where are the prisoners now?"

Jie pointed down. "Still in the warehouse tunnels. I was waiting to see what you wanted to do with them."

"Find out more about the Nightblades. Who trains them. How many there are here. This might be our best chance. I trust that you can do that? Given a little more time?"

Jie brushed a lock of hair behind her ear and looked up through her lashes. "Unfortunately, with my limited tools, teenage boys are a difficult lock to pick."

That seductive look! It made perfect use of her exotic elf-influenced features.

Heavens, Jie was quite beautiful. How had he missed it all these years? Maybe calling her *Little Sister* so many times had consigned her to the *inappropriate* category in his mind. Or perhaps idealized memories of a child princess had blinded him to the young woman right in front of him.

Jie wasn't just cute. She was beautiful. Such a novel concept.

She looked up, one eyebrow raised. He had paused for more than a beat, and she was waiting on his answer.

"Um, good." What was the question again? Tian quickly changed the subject. "Now. What about the Teleri? Their troop movements?"

Jie produced a map of the city from the fold of her dress. It depicted Iksuvius' location between the west bank of the Alto River on the east and Cold Harbor to the west, with city walls surrounding the Old City on the north, east, and south sides.

She pointed to the center of the city, close to the Teleri compound. "Their cavalry are stabled here." She then indicated a spot near the Cathayi embassy. "Here, off of the western market, are five hundred soldiers; and near the northern and eastern gates are three hundred soldiers each. Another three hundred at the southwest and northwest gates. The rest are staying on Teleri embassy grounds."

"That's not protection for the First Consul. That's an army. Three thousand additional Teleri soldiers. That triples the number of Bovyans in Iksuvius."

Jie sucked on her lower lip. "A simple show of force? The Northwest Conference is when they demonstrate that they are the real masters of the region, to show they are the inheritors of the Arkothi Empire."

Tian glanced up at his nest of notes, then back at the map. "Look at their positions. They control all of the main gates into the capital. Except the southern gate."

Jie's eyes widened. "The summit is a distraction. They're staging an invasion. The capital is their prize. "

"Four thousand Bovyans. Against twenty thousand Iksuvi soldiers and city guards." Tian shook his head.

Was it possible? Bovyans weren't just the most physically imposing men in the world, but also the best trained. From six months of age, when a Bovyan was weaned from the breast, he'd be raised by men in a warrior culture.

Jie made a show of counting on her fingers, though she'd likely run several scenarios through her head already. "Almost an even match, but it would leave the First Consul exposed. And with the Nothori nations already paying an exorbitant tribute, what would the Teleri have to gain from an invasion?"

Tian tapped his chin. Of course. If anything besides brutal training and constant warfare kept the Bovyans' population in check, it was the Orc God Tivar's curse on their ancestor. Because of it, their race had no females, and women of other races would miscarry a second Bovyan pregnancy. They procreated through the institutionalized gang rape of every last flowering girl in their vast territory. Tian's face scrunched up. "Breeding stock."

Jie fidgeted. No doubt she'd seen it played out during her deep reconnaissance into the heart of the Teleri Empire. How could it not be unsettling, especially with the Teleri Empire's inhumane process? After giving birth, a new mother would never even hold her own baby. He'd be taken away, so that the empire was the only mother he'd ever know. Meanwhile, the young woman would serve as a wet nurse for a different lot of boys before being sent back to her life. To marry, give birth to more girls. To continue the inhumane cycle.

"Ignore the motives," Tian said. "For now. Can four thousand Teleri soldiers take the city? I don't think so."

"There's another piece of the puzzle. We believe there is a Keeper from the Shrine of Geros," Jie said, referring to the Bovyans' most sacred temple in their capital of Tilésité. It housed some of their progenitor's personal effects—most importantly, his final testament, which laid down his vision for establishing peace and stability. The Keepers were trained to read and interpret its arcane language, and provide guidance as to how the Testament should be applied to the modern Teleri state.

Tian sucked in his breath. "Keepers don't leave the Shrine. Let alone Tilésité."

"There's something much bigger going on than just the Northwest Conference," Jie said. "We have proof they tried to poison the princess. Even if it seems more like a prank than a threat, the Teleri are up to no good. We should call off her meeting with the First Consul and send her home sooner."

Tian shook his head. "Cathay would appear weak. It's a drastic decision. We need to find out more. Tomorrow's reception at the Teleri embassy. It's the perfect opportunity. Every dignitary will be there. The princess gives us a reason to be there, too. I've never been inside."

Jie glared at him. "Be careful how you use the princess. She's not just a chess piece to set out as bait."

Chess piece? Tian grinned. Jie's unusual strategy had given him the upper hand, but maybe he was missing something. "Speaking of which. Queen takes rook."

"King's knight to king's three. Check."

Tian sighed. He could sacrifice his knight now to save his queen, but it would only prolong the inevitable. "It's just as I feared. My queen is hopelessly lost."

"Your move."

CHAPTER 9:
Rogues' Gallery

With spears in their left hands, the black-clad soldiers thudded their right fists against their chests as First Consul Geros Bovyan XLIII passed. The sound of their salute and his own heavy boots echoed down the bare stone halls of the Teleri embassy, the rhythm reminding him of cocking Eldaeri repeating crossbows.

A titan among giants, he absently nodded down to his fellow Bovyans, thinking more about the impending meeting with his spymaster.

The embassy steward shuffled toward him, his impeccable dress coat rustling with his incessant bowing. A balding Nothori man of middle years, he barely came up to Geros' chin. "Your Excellency, you have a visitor in the audience hall."

Already. Geros harrumphed. The local sycophants were so pathetic. Without slowing his pace, he waved a hand. "Yes, yes. The Nothori kings undoubtedly heard of my arrival and are coming a day early to kiss my feet. However, I gave you specific instructions that I was not to be disturbed by outsiders tonight."

The man's head bobbed, and he licked his lips. "Your Excellency, it is not the kings. This one... I could not keep him out. He just... appeared."

Geros paused mid-stride. "Appeared?"

"Yes, Your Excellency. He was in the audience hall, demanding to see you. He is... is... sitting on your throne."

On his throne! Someone would die tonight. Geros suppressed an angry snarl, looking back to see if his shadow was still following him. He lengthened his gait towards the audience hall, motioning for the guards stationed along the walls to follow. "My men did not remove him?"

"They are trying... "

Geros slammed the double doors open and stalked into the spacious audience chamber. It was almost as he remembered it from five years before: stone, cold, and bare, save for the banners of the Teleri Empire and each of its army divisions hanging from the walls and columns.

One difference was the sight of his soldiers littering the floor, all alive but nursing wounds with low groans. The other difference was on the throne directly in front of him.

Slouching back with legs splayed sat the King of the Altivorcs himself. Bedecked in a sharp dress uniform and sporting a thin silver crown, he lazily twirled a magic wand around a finger. A half-dozen stocky, turquoise-skinned altivorc guards in chain tunics flanked him with arms crossed, though their broadswords remained sheathed.

With a shout, one of Geros' guards surged forward, lowering a spear.

Geros' vision flashed with lines of yellow as the Eye of Solaris in his skull processed the guard's vector of attack. It would hit the Altivorc King's chest.

The wand stopped spinning and settled in the King's hand. Pointing it at the guard, he grunted a grotesque-sounding syllable that the human mouth probably couldn't imitate. A blast of blue energy burst out from the wand and slammed into the guard.

Knees buckling, his man crumpled to the floor in a heap. The spear clattered away.

Two more guards roared out challenges and stepped forward with weapons lowered.

Geros raised an open hand. "Enough!"

Both soldiers snapped to attention, while the King grinned and resumed the twirling of his wand.

"You." Geros regarded the King of the Orcs through narrowed eyes, evaluating. No one was sure how old he was, and some suggested that he was not even the same individual over the centuries. He had first appeared in history almost a millennium ago, as his people were losing control of Tivaralan during the War of Ancient Gods. Unlike other altivorcs, whom humans would consider short and quite unattractive, the King combined the handsomeness of an elf with the frame of a Bovyan.

"Thank you for answering my summons so promptly." The King grinned, revealing his fangs.

Heat surged into Geros' head, but he held his tongue. Only this pompous boor could lift the curse the first Geros—the mortal son of the Sun God Solaris, and progenitor of the Bovyan race—had submitted to. In return for strength, he had sacrificed his descendants' life force to sustain the Altivorc King. Until the King relinquished this benefit, all Bovyans would expire just past their thirty-third birthday.

A date in Geros' near future. He clenched his jaw.

The King stood and stepped down off the dais, laughing. "Geros, Geros, forgive my bad joke. We're all friends here." He sheathed his wand and sat down on the edge of the dais, patting a spot for Geros to join him.

"Of course." Geros didn't bother to disguise the disdain in his voice as he walked over and sat. "To what do I owe the pleasure of your company? I am sure you have more important matters to attend to."

"Nothing is more important than giving an old friend advice. Especially on the eve of, shall we say, his crowning moment."

Crowning... How did the King know so much? Geros scowled, the underlying messages in that one statement not lost on him. "And what advice is that?"

"Bovyans have a propensity to underestimate what you humans would call the fairer sex. My counsel is this: do not take the princess of Cathay lightly. Your allies in the South did and fared the worst for it. So did Avarax." The King produced a grey metal collar and tossed it at Geros' feet. "Put this around her neck, if you have a chance."

Geros laughed. "I was not elected First Consul by my peers in the Directori for my charm. Nor have I defeated all of my enemies by looking down on them. Your advice is duly noted. But rest assured, I have taken measures to ensure the girl's capacities will be impaired."

"Your Excellency." A small Bovyan soldier in dress uniform stepped forward, pounding his fist against his chest. Fair-skinned with short-cut blond hair, he was clearly of Nothori stock. "I am your chief of spies in Iksuvius. Might I discuss the matter of Princess Kaiya in private?"

"No need," Geros said. "We are all friends here. Speak."

The spymaster's gaze darted from the First Consul to the King and back again. "I am afraid the outcome of our attempt to influence the princess with an intoxicant is uncertain."

"Uncertain?" Geros frowned, and the spymaster shrunk under his glare.

"Our insertion into the Cathayi embassy was countered. The lone survivor reports that the intoxicants were delivered into the princess' effects, but that they might be discovered by their Black Fists."

The Altivorc King chuckled. "Black Fists? What ever happened to the Black Fist traitor we recruited for you, what—twenty, thirty years ago? The Surgeon? It sounds like he'd do a better job of planning than this fool."

The spymaster snorted. "With due respect to Master Feiying, he is not Bovyan."

The King burst out laughing again. "Neither were the ones who *countered your insertion*. I like the sound of that, by the way. Quite wholesome."

Geros snapped his fingers.

A shadow by the throne coalesced into a slim humanoid shape, dressed all in black. In the light, the short, wiry man was revealed to be Cathayi, with a honey-toned skin coloration that emphasized the sharp cheekbones and sunken eye sockets in his gaunt face.

The spymaster's eyes widened, and he hit his chest with his right hand. "Master Feiying."

Feiying's expression seemed frozen in a perpetual frown. "I may not be Bovyan, but as the King of Orcs says, I would not have been so foolish as to send my Nightblades in a place protected by Black Fists. You may have the physical assets, but not the right mentality."

"Which is exactly why I brought Feiying with me from Tilésité." Geros frowned at the spymaster while jerking his head towards Feiying. "Debrief the master—and the rest of us—while you are here."

The spymaster bowed his head in acquiescence. "A dozen Black Fist spies operate out of the Cathayi embassy. They mostly function as information-gatherers. However, since a half-elf girl joined their ranks a month ago—"

"A half-elf Black Fist?" The King sat up straight, his aloof demeanor jolting into one of keen interest. He and Feiying exchanged glances.

The spymaster continued, ignoring the King. "—their duties have shifted towards security. We assumed that was in preparation for their princess' arrival. After our failed attempt to penetrate their security, only two of our Nightblades remain. "

"Then it was truly foolish to attempt an infiltration," Feiying said. "It would be difficult to get in and out of a place protected by a Black Fist cell without being noticed, unless you had superior numbers and skill."

The Altivorc King rose to his feet and turned towards Geros. "It looks like you have your hands full with your plots, so I won't bother you any more with idle chatter. One of my sons will coordinate with you regarding our deal." He looked again towards Feiying.

Geros stood. He hid his relief at the King's imminent departure behind a broad smile. "Have no doubts, the Teleri always honor our arrangements. If you provide the support you promised in our Northeast Campaign, the pyramid in Lietuvi will be yours to administer."

"Farewell." The King of the Altivorcs grinned again. He barked a series of harsh syllables, and his guards fell in behind him. Geros watched as the King led his entourage out of the hall, their clopping steps the only sound.

Once the orcs had disappeared, Geros turned to the steward. "Summon the healer to attend to these injured men."

The steward bowed and hustled out of the room, leaving Geros alone with his soldiers. He threw himself down onto the throne and motioned the spymaster and Feiying over. "I want you to combine your great minds and come up with a plan that will give us an upper hand when negotiating with Cathay. I don't want the princess harmed in the process."

After all, he was looking forward to seeing if the Dragon Charmer was really as beautiful as the rumors said. He picked up the collar and turned it over in his hands. The metal resembled the Teleri imperial crest pinned to his chest, which blocked magic.

CHAPTER 10:
Battle of Wills

Tian's heart felt like a chunk of ice as he weaved new lines into his web early the next morning. The names of each person working in the Cathayi embassy—all of whom he knew, liked, and trusted as much as a *Black Fist* could—dangled from those threads. The list even included the ambassador, his spies, and Jie. None escaped his scrutiny as suspects in abetting the attack the night before. The only person whose innocence he was absolutely certain of was himself.

The task had taken much longer than expected, but after the better part of a morning of subtle questioning, he was now relieved to have torn down over half the names. Nothing he could think of even remotely implicated any of the other half, with the exception of Jie.

Jie. She was unaccounted for in the minutes before the attack. The very thought of her betraying the princess was ludicrous. Nonetheless, evidence exonerated a suspect, not personal feelings.

And just what were those personal feelings? Tian was not even sure anymore. Adopted Sister. Best Friend. Unexpected Beauty. He laughed at this last and newest revelation. How stupid he'd been all these years. As he stood amid the zigzagging lines, his mind was more tangled than his convoluted web of information.

Fresh air would help restore clarity. He huffed out onto his balcony, accidently dislodging several of his threads in the process. He didn't bother to tack them back up.

Tian settled down with his back to the door, looking out onto the harbor. No sooner had he eased into a comfortable position than a crisp sound cut through his troubled thoughts. What was it?

A torrential resonance of the *guzheng*, a Cathayi zither, drowned out the late morning din of the western marketplace. Not only that, there were no other sounds. Not because the *guzheng* was *that* loud. Rather, it seemed that even the birds had stopped chirping to listen.

Tian rose to his feet and looked past the compound walls. Hundreds of people gathered outside, held spellbound by the mystical quality of the music.

Curious, he leaped down from the balcony and followed the song to the southern side of the main residence. To a spot below the princess' suite. The placid melody seemed to tangibly billow out of her window, wrapping tendrils of sound around him and settling his scattered thoughts.

The princess' renowned music! It had vanquished a dragon, and now, like the ocean's lullaby, it calmed him. Worries forgotten, he stood entranced for several minutes before returning to his task of rooting out the traitor. His efforts took the rest of the day, and ended with more names removed from his list.

As dusk approached and the Iridescent Moon waxed to its fifth crescent, Tian put aside his work. He descended into the courtyard to join the official procession to the Teleri Embassy. Like Ambassador Wu and the other officials assembled there, he wore a dark-blue silk robe, with his pony tail hanging from beneath a square black hat.

Sixty-four of the imperial guard stood at attention. The dragons etched on their sparkling breastplates glowered, inspiring as much fear as the *dao* swords that hung at the guards' sides. Drummers and palanquin bearers all wore shiny blue coats with high collars embroidered in gold. A porter carried a *guzheng* in a silk brocade bag.

The princess was conspicuously absent. Her music had continued through the day, but no one had seen her. If it were up to him, he wouldn't have to look at her again. Minutes passed, though all hid their impatience with irreproachable decorum. Maybe his wish was coming true.

When she finally emerged from the residence with her handmaidens, all in the courtyard bowed in unison. The sound of ruffling clothes and clinking armor stuttered through the ranks.

"Rise." Her voice could have shamed a nightingale.

Tian stood and gasped. The entire embassy staff gasped as well. Even the ambassador stood with his mouth agape. While the princess may have been stunning after a long journey the day before, her appearance now, after an afternoon of preparation, was nothing short of divine.

She wore a sleeveless, strapless pure white silk inner dress, with an undecorated bust that just barely gave a hint of the soft curves beneath. From her waist down, the white silk was embroidered with a bright blue dragon-and-plum-blossom pattern. An open-face outer robe of translucent sky blue, bordered by a thicker dark-blue silk with gold embroidery, trailed behind her lightly on the courtyard stones. Its long sleeves hung to her ankles. A broad, dark-blue silk sash encircled her slim waist, accentuating the curve of her hips.

Her lustrous black hair, which had been straight and tied back the day before, now appeared in full-bodied tresses, fragrant and curled into a slight wave by *shouwu* berry juice and adorned with simple platinum jewels. It fell nearly to her waist and just partially obscured her delicate neck and collarbones. Her pearly complexion was now slightly tinged with light rouge from *danhua* petals.

Tian blew out a breath. In ancient times, wars would be fought over this beauty.

Behind her stood three of her handmaidens dressed in dark-blue gowns, holding the train of the outer robe so that it would not touch the ground. Although all would be considered beauties in Cathayi, they didn't warrant a second glance in the company of their princess.

Yet Tian did linger on one. Jie, in disguise, would use this opportunity to enter the Teleri Embassy. He'd never seen her in such elegant dress or exquisite make-up. Though she'd always seemed like a girl not quite to the edge of womanhood, tonight she had transformed into a delicate blossom, rivaling the princess herself. If she felt awkward primped up as such, she hid it well.

The princess interrupted his moment of admiration. "My horse," she commanded.

The order was audacious, even from her. For such an official function, dressed as she was, it was absurd to consider.

The officials and guards looked among themselves, but none dared speak. Tian dropped to one knee, rehearsing his lines in his head. "*Dian-xia*, it is unwise. Even your father, the *Tianzi,* would ride in a palanquin."

Her large eyes glinted as sharp as a knife. "I am not my father. I *will* ride a horse." Her voice took on a musical quality and tugged at his mind.

Expecting the tone of suggestion, Tian braced himself. His resolve weakened, yet her voice didn't wash over him as it had the night before. He glanced around for support, but even Ambassador Wu just shuffled on his feet. "Please *Dian-xia*. We must protect the image of Cathay."

"What better show of confidence is there than a procession with a member of the imperial family at the head, in full view?" She raised a perfect eyebrow.

"It is not just image." Tian kept his tone less than deferential. "Consider your safety as well."

She waved a hand at the procession. "Will the foreigners dare attack when we are protected by the imperial guard?"

The ambassador stepped forward and bowed. "Please, *Dian-xia*, I humbly recommend following Zheng Tian's advice. He has been monitoring troop movements, and he thinks it is best for your own protection."

"If we were truly in danger, would it not be better to be on a horse so that we can escape quickly?"

Ambassador Wu fell silent, head bowed.

So stubborn! In this, Princess Kaiya had not grown up. Tian clenched his jaw. "If we do not set off now, we will be late. An imperial princess, of all people, should understand protocol. Being late, riding in the open, allowing the common foreigners to behold the daughter of the Dragon Throne. It would be unacceptable."

Her eyes flashed.

Though he withered under her glare, he stood resolute. In this battle of wills, for her own good, he would not give in. And Heavens, he'd probably just uttered the longest sentence of his life.

Behind the princess, Jie flashed a grin unbecoming a handmaiden, while the rest of the procession shifted nervously.

The seconds dragged by before Imperial Guard Captain Chen Xin stepped forward and dropped to his knee. "Please, *Dian-xia*. We must trust the judgment of the embassy staff, who know this area. After we return to Cathay, we will see to it that this uncultured cur be reassigned to the most uninhabitable, forsaken excuse for a country with which we have relations."

"Which would be here," the princess said with a sigh. She afforded Tian one last contemptuous glare, which he returned with detached nonchalance, before ducking into the ornate palanquin.

He'd prevailed. For now. No doubt there'd be more struggles to come. The tomboyish streak and unrelenting stubbornness from their childhood was still there, even if it were wrapped in a pretty package.

The gates swung open and the procession embarked on the half-hour march down a tree-lined boulevard to the Teleri embassy in the city center. Along the way, crowds gathered, marveling at the Cathayi, whose colorful regalia still stood out in the light of the full White Moon, Renyue.

Tian broke formation on his horse and fell back to be closer to Jie, who walked with as much grace as the other handmaidens behind the palanquin.

Little Sister beautiful, he signaled.

Her cheeks flushed slightly, all the way to the tips of her pointed ears. He chuckled.

Beautiful like your princess? she gestured back.

What kind of question was that? He just smiled and spurred his horse back towards the front of the formation. Though not before seeing Jie sucking on the right side of her lower lip.

Arriving at the Teleri embassy, the procession passed through the heavy steel gates, set into twenty-foot walls of grey-speckled stone. The compound looked more like a fortress than an embassy, with battlements and crenellations manned by hundreds of stoic Bovyans.

Tian tapped his chin. Getting in or out, without permission, would not be easy.

The front wall stretched hundreds of feet, with guard towers at regular intervals. Flanking the vaulting metal-and-glass reception hall stood an equally impressive official residence that easily dwarfed its Cathay counterpart. Several stone barracks were on the left.

The procession came to a stop in front of the reception hall. The bearers lowered the palanquin and a handmaiden dropped to one knee as she opened it. Ambassador Wu extended his hand to meet the princess', and she glided out with his help.

Was her hand trembling? Did her face seem somewhat paler? Was that sweat on her brow? Perhaps their earlier confrontation was still on her mind. If so, all of those signs of nervousness instantly disappeared when she met Tian's eyes.

She faced forward, and Tian hurried to take his place on her right side. With the ambassador on her left, she glided up the dozen stairs. How elegantly she moved; the embodiment of grace. Her handmaidens followed, stiff in comparison.

Four enormous Teleri guards with close-cut dark hair and bronze skin flanked the top of the landing. Their formal black overcoats had gold-embroidered cuffs over high-collared black shirts, accentuating their strong, chiseled features. They stood unmoving as statues, longswords held at their chests in salute. Tian's fists clenched as he passed between the hedgerow of blades. These were the people who tried to intoxicate the princess, and now she was walking into their stronghold.

Two equally imposing men greeted them near the doors. The Teleri ambassador to Iksuvi on the right had long blond hair and a short beard that covered his sharp jawline. Fair skin and blue eyes marked him as local Nothori, except for the telltale Bovyan height and muscular frame. He bowed in grand Arkothi fashion. "Ambassador Wu, welcome."

Hands at his side, Ambassador Wu returned the bow. "Thank you," he said in perfect Arkothi. "Allow me to present Princess Kaiya Wang, daughter of the *Tianzi* of the Heaven-Mandated Empire of Cathay."

"Delighted to meet you," the princess said in Arkothi with a lilting Cathayi accent. She afforded the Teleri ambassador the slightest of nods as he took her hand to kiss it. Her fingers looked so small and delicate compared to his. No telling how many other hands his lips had touched already. Still, she didn't appear taken aback by the barbaric custom of the North.

The uncouth greeting didn't begin to rate with the boorish leer of the man on the left. Towering a head and a half above Tian, he undressed her with sharp eyes, one the color of anodized steel, the other brown—The Eye of Solaris. Streaks of grey in his tied-back hair suggested he was not far from his inevitable expiration day. A scar over his right cheek marred what was otherwise a perfectly smooth olive complexion.

The Teleri ambassador gestured towards the larger man. "I present Geros Bovyan XLIII, First Consul of the Teleri Imperial Directori, King of the Arkothi Three Lakes Province, and Prince of the Western Plains."

Tian assessed the famed Geros Bovyan, elected by his peers as head of the Teleri Directori two years ago. Supposedly, he was born to a virgin, begotten by the Arkothi Sun God, Solaris. His military, political, and economic acumen had expanded the empire to its historic pinnacle. A giant among men. No doubt, Princess Kaiya was overmatched. She'd likely make a fool out of Cathay tonight.

The First Consul bowed ever so slightly, sending the medals on his left breast jingling. One curious pin stood out. Circular, with irregular squiggly lines etched into it, its dull grey surface absorbed all light.

The Pin of Geros. Both it, and the Eye of Solaris were heirlooms to the Bovyan people.

As he snapped out of his bow, Geros drew up to his full height, towering above her. "Enchanted to meet you, Kaiya. We are pleased at Cathay's participation tonight. You will enjoy yourself." With an unwavering stare, he took her hand in his and pressed his lips to it.

Tian stiffened. The First Consul hadn't even bothered to address the princess by her title. Beads of sweat gathered on Ambassador Wu's brow. Behind them, Jie shuffled while the other handmaidens quivered. If the princess panicked now, like the rest of them...

Yet she stood steadfast beneath the First Consul's hulking frame and overbearing stare. Her gaze remained on his, impassive, and she barely nodded in acknowledgement. "Many thanks for your gracious invitation. We look forward towards fraternal relations and eternal peace between our countries."

Tian bit his lip. She was goading him! An ill-advised game of indiscreet messages, meant to let the First Consul know that Cathay saw the Teleri as equals. He'd earned a reputation for quick wit, and his retort would slap her down, taking Cathay's honor with her.

The First Consul's mouth open and closed, while tight lines in his brow faded and the arrogant smirk melted. His eyes, only seconds ago sharp and penetrating, now softened as the princess held him with her gaze.

Seconds passed as other dignitaries queued behind them. Finally, she smiled coyly, and spoke in a playful tone with the same lilting voice. "My hand please, First Consul... "

With a gape, he released her hand and bowed to the waist in a show of deference. A diplomatic faux-pas. The most powerful man alive, outwitted by a delicate blossom.

Tian hid his smile while their entourage passed the humbled First Consul. He'd misjudged her. As introductions continued behind them, all who witnessed the encounter would think that in the game of statesmanship, the Cathayi had won the first engagement.

All because of Princess Kaiya. No longer the naïve eight-year-old of his memories, nor the willful diva from the last two days, she was the *Tianzi's* envoy. A well-honed weapon of diplomacy.

Tian looked out into the banquet hall beyond. If he were the one planning a Teleri invasion of the Northwest, this is where he'd start: a gathering of prominent leaders.

107

Tian looked out into the banquet hall beyond. If he were the one planning a Teleri invasion of the Northwest, this is where he'd start: a gathering of prominent leaders.

CHAPTER 11:
Change of Fortune

The buzzing of a hundred conversations quieted to a sudden hush as Kaiya stepped into the grand reception hall, with her retinue in tow. A thousand eyes met hers, though all of them combined were not as disconcerting as Geros' brown one.

The Eye of Solaris. According to everything she'd read, a new First Consul would gouge his own eye out and replace it with the glass orb, which contained a spark of the Arkothi sun god's divinity.

Suppressing a shudder and shaking the thought out of her head, she held the gathered dignitaries with a gaze for a brief second, before tilting her head a fraction down and to the right and offering a shy smile.

Whispered murmurs erupted, all echoing the same sentiment: never before had they seen such beauty. Whether it was the power of theatrics or the gullibility of males, a glance had captured the room more effectively than a thousand musketmen could with their guns.

Her head spun at the dizzying swash of national colors: an explosion of blues, scarlets, yellows, blacks, and golds. Yet the vibrant mélange of livery paled in comparison to the majesty of the prism-shaped hall itself. Spaced at regular intervals, arching metal columns framed the building. They vaulted some forty feet towards a central spine, with stained glass forming the walls.

The glass panels might have been a history lesson if not for the propaganda. The first few depicted stories from the Arkothi Empire, which had collapsed after the Hellstorm three hundred years before. The next showed their Sun God Solaris impregnating the mother of the first Bovyan, Geros I. The rest celebrated the Bovyan Knights of old, then the soldiers of the modern day Teleri Empire.

Kaiya suppressed a snort. While not known for their appreciation of fine art, the Bovyan rulers of Teleri sent a clear message in the awe-inspiring architecture: they were inheritors of the ancient Arkothi Empire.

Yet there was something more, something deeper than just the view. She closed her eyes and listened. A subtle resonance hummed with an uncanny familiarity. Where had she heard it before?

Perhaps the Temple of Heaven back home. Or Shakti's Hill in Palimur, where she'd confronted Avarax.

She opened her eyes to meet a familiar face. Light-brown in complexion, with flowing black hair and a short, pointed beard, Sameer Vikram approached with a fluid grace. It'd been nearly half a year since they'd parted ways at the Temple of Shakti.

"Sir Sameer," she said, switching to the Ayuri language. After months of not speaking it, her accent lilted in her ears. "I did not expect to see you here."

"Nor I. What an unexpected pleasure." Sameer pressed his hands together and bowed his head. A white cotton *kurta* shirt and matching surcoat hung to his knees. The gold embroidery on the collar and hems, along with his curved *naga* sword, all marked him as an Ayuri Paladin. A weariness clung to him, one that hadn't been there just months before.

"I cannot thank you enough for your support when we faced Avarax," she said.

"Support?" Sameer laughed. "I was merely a bystander. You were the only one who did not wither under the dragon's stare. To be honest, I have never been so frightened in my life."

"Your presence gave me courage." Kaiya pressed her hands together. "But how is it that you are in Iksuvius? I did not hear of you taking a Cathayi ship. I would have ensured the most comfortable berth at no cost to you."

He chuckled. "Your Highness, you assume that Cathayi ships are the only way to travel from my homeland to here. But to answer your question, I am en route to the ancient pyramid in the Kanin Wilds, by command of the Paladin Council. It will be the fifth I have visited. Perhaps Jie or your, uh, male friend, told you about our journey to Levastya?"

Male friend. Kaiya's belly fluttered. Neither said male friend nor the Insolent Retainer had mentioned anything about a side trip. Tian shuffled beside her.

She turned to glare at Jie, who was apparently admiring the architecture.

With an eye on the others who jostled toward her, Kaiya turned back to Sameer and talk of pyramids. There were several different architectural styles, one for every region of the continent, dating back to ancient times. Her ancestors, slaves to the altivorcs, likely worshipped the Orc Gods at the pyramid in Cathay. "If your duties find you in Cathay, I would be delighted to take you to our pyramid. However, in Iksuvius, I can only offer you a room in our embassy compound."

Sameer waved a hand. "I appreciate the gesture, but I am staying with my father, who is the Ambassador from the Ayuri Confederation to the Nothori lands. Allow me to introduce you." He beckoned over a dignified-looking gentleman with a darker skin tone. Streaks of white punctuated his long black hair, which was pinned up in an intricate braid. Unlike the white *kurta* of the *Bahaduur*, the older man's clothes shone with a copper hue.

The ambassador approached with a broad smile of white teeth. He placed his hands together and bowed his head. "Princess Kaiya, it's a pleasure to meet again."

Kaiya pressed her hands together and bowed her head. "Ambassador Vikram. The honor is mine."

"You know each other?" Sameer cocked his head.

The older man laughed from his belly. "I attended the wedding of her brother, Prince Kai-Wu. Her cousin, Lord Peng, introduced us, and a fabulous Blind Musician."

Kaiya's chest tightened. One was a traitor, her reason for coming to this frigid land; the other, Avarax in disguise. Both had made a fool of her. Never again. She took a deep breath to calm her nerves. "I hope you found Sun-Moon Palace hospitable."

He pressed his hands together again. "First rate. Please do me the honor of paying a visit to our embassy during your stay in Iksuvius."

She turned towards Ambassador Wu, who'd been deflecting well-wishers. "Please see if there is time on my schedule." Hopefully not, if Ambassador Vikram intended to reminisce about traitors and dragons.

Ambassador Wu bowed at her command and stepped forward to take over her conversation with the Ayuri. On her other side, Tian talked animatedly with Sameer, the first hint of warmth she had seen in him since their reunion.

She looked around the hall, her gaze pausing at the group of a dozen stout altivorcs who stood away from the conversations and crowds. Their coarse black tunics and large broadswords did little to enhance their blunt noses, huge foreheads, and blocky faces. The altivorc prince they protected, however, would put a human to shame with his good looks.

Kaiya shuddered. Her previous encounter with these ferocious humanoids involved a Maduran prince who'd tried to kidnap her. She turned towards Jie and whispered, "Find out who they work for."

Jie nodded and slunk in their general direction. Despite her worry, Kaiya suppressed a giggle at the thought of Jie trying to be discreet while dressed in a gown designed to draw attention.

Indeed, it did. Before Jie had even taken a dozen steps, a gigantic Teleri general intercepted her with a friendly smile on his face. He leaned down and whispered in her ear. Kaiya barely picked out his words from the background noise. "Where is your husband tonight?"

Husband? That had to be a mistake. Had Tian and Jie eloped without anyone knowing?

Jie looked down and to the side, covering her mouth with her hand. It was a cute gesture, though with better execution, it might overwhelm a man's willpower. Kaiya had practiced it enough.

A uniquely accented male voice from behind interrupted her thoughts. "Princess of Cathay. Well met."

She turned to see a rough and wrinkled face with a ruddy complexion. Greying black hair hung freely from his shoulders, decorated with brightly colored bird feathers. His flaxen coat had tassels of braided horsehair along its borders and was covered in the front with a rectangular plate of interlocking shells painted in red and blue.

A Kanin plainsman, famous for their magnificent horses and equally amazing equestrian skills. He placed his worn right hand over his heart and swept it out in an arc. He spoke in Arkothi with a heavily nasal accent. "The stories of your beauty do you no justice."

She imitated his salute. "Well met, sir. I'm afraid you have me at a loss."

"Yes, there are far fewer tales of my beauty." He chortled with an endearing sincerity.

She leaned in with a conspiratorial grin. "The secret is to shower the storytellers with gold and jade. Before long, everyone in Tivara will know your name. How many of my platinum hairpins must I part with to learn yours?"

"My name is hardly worth a strand of your lustrous hair. So I will settle for a kiss." His eyes sparkled mischievously as he patted his cheek.

She turned her head and covered her lips with a hand in mock modesty. "I am afraid these lips have never touched a man before, and as much as I would like for you to be the recipient of my first friendly kiss, my future husband would not be pleased." She plucked a strand of her hair and proffered it. "Since you say your name is not worth a single hair, then I expect to hear your entire family tree for this."

"I would have preferred the kiss." He pouted, not at all looking his age.

Tian came to her side and ruined their banter. "He is Ambassador Manuwaya from the Kingdom of Tomiwa. He is renowned for the role he played in the unification of their tribes a generation ago."

"I can see why. He has quite a way with words."

Manuwaya grinned. "In those days, words alone were not enough to unite the plains. I was better at negotiating with a spear than my mouth."

Kaiya bowed her head. "I apologize for being presumptuous."

His laugh was infectious. "That was then. Now I am just an old man trying to impress a pretty face with tall tales of past martial prowess. And you cost me a kiss, Mister Zheng. You will have to let me win our next game of mahjong."

Kaiya pressed a hand to her chest. "Mahjong? I did not realize our national pastime had found its way so far north."

"Oh no, Mister Zheng taught me, and we occasionally play over your country's delicious rice wine. I presume he is trying to get me drunk while we discuss trade."

She looked towards Tian, eyebrow raised.

"Military supplies," Tian said. "Our guns to arm their palace guard, their corn wafers to feed our soldiers when they travel."

Manuwaya waved him off. "Of course, we are interested in cultural exchange as well. Please ask your father to send a trade mission to Tomiwa, hopefully with you at the head. Our king is a connoisseur of fine teas and teacups, most of which he acquires from the Ayuri Confederation. However, the Cathayi teas are the most famous, and very hard to obtain. He owns one single Cathayi teacup, which he treasures above all others for its exquisiteness. I know now after meeting you, my dear, that your country, besides teacups, produces other unique beauties as well."

Kaiya turned her head to the side and smiled. "For our teas and cups, we would certainly hope to acquire some of your peerless horses. They are renowned throughout the world—strong, intelligent and courageous, much like their masters, the Kanin people."

"They are headstrong, brash, and difficult to break," he responded, his tone proud.

"The people? Or the horses?" She flashed a hint of a smile.

Ambassador Manuwaya burst into a loud guffaw. Turning to Tian, he said, "Mister Zheng, I have been completely disarmed! Our king's son is a debonair and spirited warrior, who is indeed hard to control. But perhaps your princess could tame him!"

Spirited, to be sure. Prince Tani had visited Cathay the past New Year, and made a proposal of a different nature. She looked to Tian to gracefully extricate her from the sudden shift in topic.

His face remained devoid of expression, making Kaiya wonder if an Aksumi biomancer had switched out her childhood friend with a zombie.

"Greetings, distinguished guests." First Consul Geros' commanding voice boomed over all conversations. The room quieted and all eyes turned to where he stood on the dais. "Take your seats. We have prepared several courses of Nothori and Arkothi delicacies for you to enjoy."

More strange foods. Her poor skin might erupt with ugly red blotches by the end of the night. Kaiya's stomach twisted in dread anticipation as dozens of male servants circulated through the crowds and ushered guests to assigned seats. There must've been over forty tables, each surrounded by ten heavy wooden chairs with armrests and black upholstery.

From the livery, dress, and military symbols, it seemed that the kings of Northwest countries—

participants in the Northwest Summit—sat at the front center table. Other guests sat at distances commensurate with their importance. It appeared that everyone who was anyone in Iksuvius was there. Teleri generals, influential Iksuvi families, government officials, and ambassadors. As representative of a sovereign state, no doubt she'd sit somewhere in the middle.

A servant placed a hand on her elbow—so rude! No one else was getting grabbed—and guided her toward the front. After several steps, she looked over her shoulder.

Other servants guided Tian, Jie, Ambassador Wu, and her handmaidens toward the back. The ambassador protested. He moved to follow her, only to be blocked by a Bovyan soldier.

Her own usher kept an insistent tug on her elbow, pulling her along until he came to a halt. Kaiya turned to see where they had stopped, only to find a wall of elite guards in the livery of their respective nations. Standing in stoic attention around their rulers, they parted to make space for her to pass. Her eyes widened.

She stood directly across from First Consul Geros himself.

To his left, seventeen-year-old King Arvydas of Lietuvi rose to his feet. He wore a dark-blue jacket over a scarlet, high-collared shirt. Like most Nothori nobles, he was tall and well-built. Sandy blond hair, coifed flat with oil, framed his heavy features. Wisps of light-colored hair shadowed his upper lip and jaw line. Despite his youth, he exuded an air of confidence, perhaps bordering on foolhardiness. "What a pleasant surprise that such a jewel will adorn our table."

"There must be some mistake," Kaiya said. To sit here would suggest Cathay was joining the Northwest alliance—and becoming a vassal state to the Teleri.

"None at all," the Teleri Ambassador Thieros said. "The First Consul wished to give the Cathayi princess all due respect and place her here, with her noble peers."

Or rather, make it look like she was submitting. Kaiya waved off the suggestion with a sweep of her hand. "That is not necessary. Cathay is a mere observer to this gathering and would not deign to aspire to more significance." Gripping her toes to the ground and borrowing the pulsating energy of the chamber, she sang, "Please allow me to join my countrymen."

Ten syllables of command, necessary to maintain the formal wording of diplomacy. Far more than she'd ever tried. Her vitality guttered. She thrust a hand out to the chair to keep from collapsing.

Still, the dignitaries all nodded.

The magic had worked! Now to return to the safety of—

"Nonsense," Geros said. "Take it as my atonement for being such a boor at the gates. Now, I insist you be seated."

Kaiya kept herself from gaping. The First Consul had somehow resisted her power.

The usher pulled out the empty chair, right next to King Gunvydas of Rotuvi, who harbored Cousin Peng. With hair and long beard greying, he bore lines of care drawn by a lifetime of failed dreams. His light-blue coat seemed as dreary as his demeanor.

Had they intentionally chosen this seat for her? Two years before, Rotuvi's soldiers had pinned down General Lu at Wailian Castle, necessitating her use of the Dragon

Scale Lute to subjugate Lord Tong's rebellion. Now, King Gunvydas protected Cousin Kai-Long.

The First Consul, at eye level with her despite being seated, again motioned for her to sit. Behind her, soldiers moved closer.

There was no other choice, besides embarrassing herself and Cathay by making a scene. Kaiya settled on the edge of the chair, next to Queen Ausra and King Evydas of the host nation, Iksuvi. Both were young, fair-skinned and blond; both tall and attractive by Nothori standards. The queen wore a white satin dress that spilled loosely down to her ankles. Its plain neckline plunged low, revealing a lilac-colored topaz necklace that matched her violet irises.

King Evydas' light blue eyes glinted, his face held tight in uncontained anger as he exchanged glares with King Arvydas. Ambassador Wu had mentioned something about an attempted coup in Lietuvi a year before, rumored to have been staged by Iksuvi, but more likely financed by the Teleri. Who knew for sure? Even if these kings squabbled among each other, their countries remained ostensibly independent only through the tribute they sent to the Teleri Empire each year.

Kaiya shifted the outer gown over her shoulders, as if it would warm her from the frigid stares the young rulers exchanged.

"Such a beautiful dress!" Queen Ausra ran her hand over the silk, again demonstrating the Northerners' disregard for personal space.

Kaiya offered a gracious smile. "Thank you. Your gown is lovely, as well."

"Do you like it?" Ausra beamed. "We buy the silk from your country, and the dyes from Vyara City. Of course, it all comes in on Cathayi ships."

The First Consul brushed a hand over the table, which was carved from a single cross-section of a tree trunk. He met Kaiya's gaze. "Greywood trees, brought in from the Kanin Wilds. When we establish an easier way to bring them here, we will build a fleet of ships to rival yours."

Kaiya acknowledged Geros' impossible daydream with a curt smile, then turned back to the queen and their talk of fashion. "Yes, the Ayuri have an eye for vibrant colors. I bought several *sari* on my trip to Vyara City."

Ausra clapped once in excitement. "Vyara City is so beautiful. I went one time with my father, years ago. He exports the Nothori snow crab that the Ayuri so love. Those old memories are still so fresh in my mind! The Crystal Citadel is simply amazing, both in sheer size and design. The architecture is so beautiful."

Kaiya nodded. "As are buildings here in Iksuvius, which I could not help but admire last evening when I arrived. They are nothing like the ones we build in mountainous Cathay. Yours are constructed to withstand the bitter cold sea winds, and yet they are aesthetically beautiful in their simplicity. It is reflective of the Nothori people's practicality."

Lietuvi's boy King Arvydas snorted. "It is a practicality borne from centuries of combating bitter cold, both from the Heavens and our fellow man." He glared at King Evydas.

Iksuvi's king scowled back. "I could not agree more. The bitter cold causes crops *and* the human spirit to wither, especially in the absence of benevolent leadership."

Arvydas pointed his fork at his counterpart. "Though, as the famed Lietuvi historian Istorikyas wrote, *Nothing is more frigid than the cold corpse of a dead king*."

Evydas' eyes narrowed and his hand strayed to a butter knife. The soldiers of the three Nothori kingdoms edged closer, their hands resting on sword hilts. The First Consul smirked. Had he instigated the hostilities to keep his vassals divided and ruled? His smug grin suggested he would not be intervening any time soon.

Which left her, lest these boys come to blows, with her and Queen Ausra caught in between. *"Nothing is more frigid than the cold corpse of a dead king,"* Kaiya repeated. "One of my favorite quotes from the Chronicles of Vydas. From the twelfth chapter. A hundred years after the War of the Ancient Gods, when the great Vydas defeated a neighboring tyrant in single combat and founded the Nothori Empire. I have read that your royal families all descend from Vydas."

Arvydas' hands relaxed, fork returning to its place. Likewise, Evydas' bitter expression melted away. The table was momentarily silent, and all the kings' gazes fell on her.

Geros Bovyan, however, chuckled. "The Nothori *Empire*? I would not consider a rogues' gallery of petty princes and chieftains, held together by political marriages, adoptions, and hostage exchanges, an empire. Even your modern day *kingdoms*"—he spat the word in disdain—"would fall apart if your childish squabbles were not held in check by the protection of Teleri imperial order."

The table fell into an awkward silence, all the Nothori kings cowed by their powerful neighbor. Behind them, servants held trays, ready to deliver the first dish of the seven-course meal, but none dared approach the table after the First Consul's tirade.

Kaiya placed a hand over her mouth to cover a soft laugh. "First Consul," she said, channeling her most disarmingly sweet voice, "we in Cathay believe that brotherly love holds people and nations together more than fear of the sword. Was that not also the belief of your ancestors, the Bovyan Knights," she gestured with an open hand toward one of the stained-glass panels, "who protected the Arkothi states following the Hellstorm and Long Winter?"

The First Consul scowled, and Kaiya imagined his brain was overheating as he searched for a rebuttal to her question.

She forced her expression into serenity, even if her nerves were strained tighter than the coiled strings of her *guzheng*. Had she gone too far in confronting a man who could probably break her in half with his bare hands?

With a cold stare at her, he stood and raised a hand.

CHAPTER 12:
Distractions

Jie never made it to the table at the back of the hall.

She knew a set-up when she saw one, having engineered many in her life. The Teleri planned to embarrass the princess by isolating her from counsel and surrounding her with enemies. Ambassador Wu could protest until the vanquished Orc Gods returned to Tivaralan on their flaming chariots, but the dozens of armed Teleri soldiers would not be changing the seating arrangements any time soon.

Tian met her gaze, his nod conveying their mutual understanding. Any attempt to intervene would risk the princess' safety.

Jie looked toward the front of the hall, where the First Consul stood, staring daggers at the princess. Elf ears notwithstanding, the buzz of a hundred quiet conversations drowned out whatever Geros was saying.

He took his seat, and servants began setting down plates of food. It was a perfect opportunity for them to poison the princess. They had already tried once, after all.

Jie glanced at Tian, flashing a simple hand motion to convey her intent. *I handle it.*

She turned towards her usher. Rising on her tiptoes, she whispered in his ear. "Where might I go to freshen up?"

The young man craned back and gaped at her. His confused look might have been amusing if not for the urgency.

"The privy," she hissed.

His face flushed an interesting shade of red. "Oh. My apologies, miss." He gestured toward the right side of the hall. "Outside that door, to your left."

With a curt nod, Jie swept towards the door, taking note of its relation to the kitchen exit. In the corner of her eye, young General Marius di Bovyan was watching her.

He rose to his feet.

Jie had spent the afternoon modifying her gown to conceal weapons and tools in the sleeves and hems, but now regretted not doing anything about improving its mobility. Lifting her skirts, she quickened her pace.

She burst through the door and out into the cool night air with a sigh of relief, her admirer left behind. Jie took one step, only to stop and marvel at the banquet hall's exterior. The bright lights from inside sparkled through the stained glass, shooting colorful blades of light up into the night sky. It had to be a coincidental byproduct of the garish interior. No Bovyan would intentionally create such an aesthetic view.

"Mrs. Zheng," Marius called her from behind.

Jie cursed under her breath. The combination of his longer stride, her restricting gown, and a temporary distraction had resulted in a needless delay. She spun around in a swift twist more befitting a warrior than the lady she meant to portray. So careless on her part! Hopefully he wouldn't notice. Channeling her inner Princess Kaiya, she flashed her most alluring smile. "General Marius, shouldn't you be accompanying your comrades?"

"I am around them all the time. As I am sure you can imagine, the company of a dozen taciturn Bovyans becomes quite dull."

Jie suppressed a shudder. Being among a dozen Teleri would mean something completely different for *her*. "I guess you spend hours discussing the most efficient way to split a skull?"

He placed a hand on his chest. "You know us too well. But in all fairness, we are not all so one-dimensional."

Doubtful, but then again, the sparkling view of the hall supported his claim. She tilted her head. "I've been told a Bovyan's appreciation of art is limited to blood splatters. Yet I couldn't help but notice how beautiful this hall is from the outside. Did your people design it?"

General Marius' expression lit up like Wailian Castle's firepowder stores. "I am happy you noticed! Actually, the framing is quite ancient. Legends say it is the bones of the ancient dragon Venorax, who allied himself with the orcs in their conquest of Tivaralan five thousand years ago. The elves slew him with their Deep Magic on this very spot. The first Nothori king, Vydas, built his castle here. First Consul Geros personally redesigned it a dozen years ago, when he was still just Junior Consul Haros."

Right, the First Consul. There was a princess to rescue. Jie opened her mouth to speak--

"Of course you know the real reason I followed you. I'd hoped to reminisce about the old days." He flashed a broad grin.

Old days? And that smile. The man must think his appreciated but unnecessary rescue was worth reminiscing about, and that a month ago was the *old days*. Jie channeled her inner Kaiya, tilting her head. "I'd love to catch up sometime. Perhaps I can join you at your table?"

Marius' eyes widened, the corners of his lips curling up. "I would be honored."

"The stuffiness in there overwhelmed me. I will join you after I cool down." Jie's hand lingered on a throwing spike in her sleeve before withdrawing a sandalwood fan. She snapped it open and fanned herself, pausing for a beat to conceal part of her face, while she batted her lashes.

The general's cheeks flushed. Maybe it *was* possible to make a Bovyan swoon. Princess Kaiya would be proud.

His smile broadened. "I'll be waiting."

A long time. Jie watched as he disappeared down the hall. Finally. She turned and tottered towards the kitchens as fast as the gown would allow.

The activity in the outdoor space between the hall and kitchen resembled the entrance to an ant hill, with servants bustling back and forth with trays in their hands. Scents of roasting meats and unfamiliar, pungent spices hung in the chill air.

Jie crept closer and peeked into the hall, immediately locating the main table and identifying the young Nothori server assigned to the princess.

"Excuse me miss, are you lost?" An unfamiliar voice said from behind.

She turned around to find a short, blond servant. "No, no. I was just admiring the efficiency of the kitchen staff. You don't mind, do you?" She squeezed her chest between her arms, trying to conjure the feminine curves that the Heavens had thus far denied her. She tilted her head and looked up through her lashes.

The servant loosened his collar and gulped. "Uh, sure. Just be careful."

It was too easy. No wonder the princess got her way so often. Jie brushed a loose lock of hair behind her ear, just as she spotted the princess' server. Closely bunched with several others, he approached with choreographed precision, platter in hand.

"Of course. I'll be so careful, you won't know I'm here." She offered a shy smile and bobbed her head. Then, with a short step backward, she conveniently tripped on her inner gown and careened into the closest server in the phalanx.

As his tray slipped from his grip, Jie caught it in one hand. She spun and exchanged the platter with another servant, before lifting the dragonshell lobster on the princess' tray and swapping it out with the same dish from the second server. In a final display of dramatic clumsiness worthy of an accomplished stage actor, she launched herself into the princess' server. His tray clattered to the hard-packed ground, sending chunks of spiced red potatoes and stewed baby carrots tumbling in a cascade of color.

Ugh, the humiliation of it, even when planned. No need to put any more of an act than necessary. She caught hold of another servant's arm to keep herself from flopping into the mess. "I am so sorry!" she whispered in as distraught a tone as she could muster.

She squatted, picking up the vegetables piece by piece and taking surreptitious sniffs. Nothing. She rolled her eyes, stewing more than the carrots. Why worry? Even if something were poisoned, the princess wouldn't eat any of it anyway.

"Do not concern yourself, miss." A servant bent down next to her, offering a reassuring smile as he joined her in cleaning up.

"I'm so sorry." Jie bowed her head yet again.

A set of boots came to a halt in front of her and she looked up to meet the hard scowl of the kitchen manager. He pointed a finger towards the hall. "Begone!"

"I'm sorry." If Jie had to say it again with so much sincerity, she might actually convince herself that she meant it. She bowed her head a last time, her neck more sore than the time she'd wrestled an altivorc. Picking up her skirts, she took the service entrance back to the reception.

The hall was silent. At the front table, Princess Kaiya was locked in a staring match with the lobster. Spectators watched the duel enthralled, wondering in low voices if the princess was not so perfect after all.

With a snort, Jie stalked over to the main table, deftly avoiding a hulking Bovyan guard who tried to block her way. The princess clenched and unclenched her hands under the table, her face blanched. Across from her, the First Consul wore a gloating smirk.

Jie hurried over and bowed deeply at the princess' side. "Your Highness," she said in Arkothi so that all could understand, "you must not eat shellfish now." She turned to face the First Consul and bowed again. "Your Eminence, Princess Kaiya hoped to play the zither for you on this auspicious night. In Cathay, it is taboo to eat shelled animals before a performance. Too much of an imbalance between hard and soft, cold and hot."

Murmurs broke out among the guests.

Jie sucked on her lower lip. How ridiculous a lie was that? She could come up with better—

Geros' smirk disappeared. "Play for me? Yes!" He rose to his full height, towering over all. Even across the table, his presence was unsettling. He waved servants over. "Clear the dais."

This had to be a dream. It had actually worked. In the middle of a formal banquet, no less.

The princess offered Jie a frail smile. She floated to her feet and spoke, her melodic voice carrying across the hall. "Ambassador Wu, have my *guzheng* brought over and prepared."

Servants scurried to obey the First Consul and princess' command. As she fit silver picks on each of her fingers, the handmaidens brought forth an antique *guzheng*. A resonant half-tube wood cavity over five feet long, the instrument had thirty-six twisted silk strings with moveable bridges. They placed it on a carved wooden stand, and set a gold-embroidered cushioned stool behind it.

With the planned distraction in place, it was time for Jie to slip out. Now if only she could get Tian's attention.

From his seat at the back of the hall, Tian had ground his teeth as he watched the princess embarrass herself and Cathay.

Over a crustacean, of all things. Without Jie's intervention, the guests would still be chattering about the spoiled Princess of Cathay. Instead, they were now admiring the craftsmanship of the antique *guzheng* as the handmaidens set it up.

The princess glided across the floor to the dais. Settling on the stool with her back perfectly straight and hands resting in her lap, she raised her head and swept her gaze over the audience. Gracefully raising her arms, she extended her delicate fingers. The picks glittered in the light. The sleeves of her outer gown settled down around her elbows, revealing slender, porcelain-like forearms. A hush settled through the room, everyone's focus transfixed on the dais.

All except the altivorcs. With a look of disdain, the orc prince rose to his feet. Chairs rattled across the stone floors as his guards stood as well. The prince spun on his heel and stalked out the main door, his entourage in tow. Only a handful of heads turned at their blatant departure.

One of those was the Teleri general who'd been sticking to Jie like a wet leaf. He also rose and headed towards a side door.

The sound of the *guzheng's* first elocution yanked Tian's attention back to the front, as if the note had tangibly wrapped itself around his head and turned it. The slow, deliberate strum through pentatonic notes caressed his cheek like fanning fingers. The vibrato alternated between jubilant, short high notes and long, pensive low notes, eventually transitioning into a melancholy tremolo. He closed his eyes, basking in the sound's embrace.

Something hit him in the ear, jolting him from his reverie. Tian jerked his head toward the source. Jie scowled, motioning towards the mesmerized audience.

His logical mind awoke from its torpor. The song, *Between Heaven and Earth,* was a particularly long piece about man's smallness compared to the wonders of the Heavens above and the world around. If the First Consul understood that the princess was rebuking his ambition through the song's symbolism, he might become even more adversarial. And indeed, the Bovyan seemed less entranced by the rise and fall of the notes, and more by the rise and fall of the princess' chest.

Still, the length of the song afforded Tian plenty of time to reconnoiter before anyone missed him. He nodded at Jie, who slipped out a side door. With everyone else captivated, he stood and slunk out the front. The enthralled guards didn't move to block his way.

The cool night air greeted him. He crept through the shadows towards the rear, taking note of the compound's layout. At the back of the main residence, the jingle of chain armor sent him ducking behind a thick hedge. He peeked up from the bush.

The altivorc prince and his guards came to a stop near the building's back door. Apparently, Tian and Jie weren't the only ones using the musical distractions towards nefarious ends. He crouched, motionless. Hopefully, the bright moonlight would dim the altivorcs' heat vision.

Jie's Teleri general arrived next, approaching the orcs with a nod of his head. "Do we still have a deal?"

"Will you still deliver on your side of the bargain?" The prince bared his fangs as he grinned.

"Of course. The Teleri do not renege on their treaties and promises."

"Good," the prince said. "As we agreed, three thousand of my foot soldiers have descended from the Nothori Mountains and are heading up the main highway from the south. Five thousand of our men, garrisoning the southern border for Iksuvi, abandon their post as we speak."

What were the altivorcs up to? And how could they know troop movements hundreds of *li* away?

The general nodded, showing no sign of surprise. "Then you will allow the Lietuvi army to attack western Iksuvi?"

"The garrison will join in the assault," the prince said. "Another ten thousand of our soldiers have joined up with the Rotuvi army to invade Lietuvi while they are distracted attacking Iksuvi. If your First Consul wanted to destabilize the Nothori Kingdoms—and why, I cannot fathom, since you have them well under control—then you will get what you wished for."

Blood rushed to Tian's head. Jie had been right. The Teleri were staging an invasion. The princess was caught in the middle.

The general shook his head. "These pathetic wretches live in constant fear of their incompetent rulers. When the Nothori Kingdoms are no longer simply tributaries and become integral parts of the Teleri Empire, all will prosper from peace and stability. We are still under treaty with those petty kings until midnight the day after tomorrow. After the treaties expire, we will begin our attack. By the third day, the Kingdom of Iksuvi will be no more, and the other two will be in chaos. Now if only we could liberate Cathay as easily."

"You will control all exits to the city soon enough. Take their whelp hostage and watch her daddy sing." The altivorc prince shrugged.

Tian clenched his jaw. The princess embarrassing herself over a lobster now seemed trivial.

The general harrumphed. "Now is not the time. The First Consul has other plans for Cathay."

The altivorc laughed. "You may lose a golden opportunity. Just know that our king is amenable to assisting you, if you wish to assail their embassy."

CHAPTER 13:
Symphony of the Gods

Jie looked for a place to change. Sneaking around in a gown worked just about as well as hiding the moons on this cloudless night. The White Moon, Renyue, hung full and low in the sky, shedding a soft light over the compound. The larger Blue Moon tilted sharply, its rings at their smallest and dimmest for the year. The Iridescent Moon waxed towards half gibbous. Though their interplay cast enough shadows to hide in, the guards would be sure to see the flash of silken colors.

Blending into the deepest shadow, Jie withdrew a pouch from her silk sash. She pulled out a lightweight black shirt, pants, and mask. They would have never fit into such a small space if not for the enchantment placed on the pouch by the elf wizardress, Ayana. She shrugged out of her gown and shimmied into the outfit, then wiped a black cream over her face and the backs of her hands.

She crept towards the residence, pausing at the sight of a Teleri soldier standing guard at the main entrance. Not an easy access. However, a small balcony on the shaded side of the building offered an alternate insertion point. She slunk along the base of the wall and stopped right below. With spiked hand straps and feline dexterity, she scaled the wall and swung over the balcony.

The door was unlocked. She opened it a crack and slipped in.

The large, undecorated room was furnished with two single beds and a wooden armoire. Two sets of armor—each consisting of a chainmail tunic with a leather cuirass—rested on stands at opposite sides of the room. Large rectangular shields and longswords completed the set. The markings indicated that they belonged to high-ranking infantry officers. Nothing interesting here.

Jie opened the interior door and peeked out into the moonlit hallway. Empty. The muffled conversations downstairs didn't seem relevant. Most of the important people were probably attending the reception. She slid soundlessly through the halls, checking doors and sparsely furnished bedrooms. Nothing of consequence.

After several minutes, she came to her first locked door. Perhaps this room was more important. It easily yielded to the lockpicks from her pouch. Pushing the door open a crack, she peered in. Even her elf vision couldn't penetrate the darkness.

She slipped in, closed the door behind her, and produced one of her Aksumi beads. Her vision adjusted to the sudden change in light.

In the center lay a large table, over three times her height in diameter, its entire surface a scale model of the Iksuvi kingdom. Blocks of various colors dotted the map, likely indicating troop strengths and positions. Blues, the most numerous in and around the city, probably represented Iksuvi soldiers. The Yellows...

They corresponded with known Teleri troop locations inside the city. But there were many, many more just on the Teleri side of the Alto River. If each block denoted two hundred men, then there must be over twenty thousand in the border town of Altogrina. And who were the Blacks?

Someone outside the room pushed a key into the lock.

Jie stowed her light bead into a pocket and slid under the table, just as the door opened. Heavy footsteps paced across the floor. His weight and length of stride, as well as the type of boot, all betrayed his identity. General Marius, her admirer. A flickering candle approached the table.

His feet came to a stop. Several blocks brushed across the table top.

Not even her newly discovered feminine charm could convince him she was a simple handmaiden if he saw her now. Jie kept her breath slow and silent. As long as she didn't give him a reason to look under the ta—

One of the blocks clattered to the floor.

Was there enough light for him to see her? She crept back, deeper into the table's shadow.

He squatted down and plucked up the piece between two fingers, his head never dropping below the table line. Thank the Heavens for Bovyans' tall stature.

The block cracked down on a spot near the edge. He then turned and left. His footsteps trailed out and the door locked.

Jie ducked out from under the table and looked at the changes in troop positions.

She sucked in a sharp breath.

Tian waited until well after the Teleri general and the altivorcs parted ways, contemplating the situation. With the entire region about to descend into chaos, they had to get the princess to safety.

Picking himself out of the hedgerow, he brushed himself off and slunk back to the reception with his head swimming. The princess was still playing as he peeked in. There was no sign of Jie. Taking advantage of the captivated guests, he crept into a chair near the rear.

The melody trailed off and came to an end, and the princess bowed from her seated position. The audience rose to their feet, and thunderous applause swept through the room. Tian stood and joined in, even if his thoughts were elsewhere.

The princess made some adjustments to the bridges of the guzheng. She raised her arms, and the audience fell silent in anticipation of an encore performance. Her slender fingers danced over the strings, now plucking on a heptatonic scale reminiscent of Northern lutes.

It was a Nothori folk song, popular in the drinking halls Tian visited to trawl for information. It celebrated the perseverance of a nomadic Nothori tribe on the Eastern Plains, which had refused to submit to the Arkothi Empire three hundred years before. They outlasted the empire's attempts to wipe them out, surviving through the Hellstorm and ensuing Long Winter that led to the fall of the agrarian Arkothi nation.

The Teleri—who saw themselves as inheritors of the Arkothi Empire—would certainly understand the significance of the song. Tian had never seen anyone dare hum it in the presence of the Bovyans. Was the princess trying to encourage the Nothori kings? Or intentionally agitate the Teleri, not knowing that they were about to be entangled in a warzone?

Around him, the Nothori people responded with nods and smiles to the princess' unique rendering of an otherwise simple song. Even the musically disinclined Teleri grinned and bobbed their heads to the beat.

And then she began to sing.

If her speaking voice was melodious, her singing voice was nothing short of celestial. It resonated with clarity through the deep hall. Tian closed his eyes, as his heart floated. Perhaps this was like the music Guanyin sang when her consort Yang-Di presented the newly-forged world as a gift to her.

The princess' voice softened, and the *guzheng* took over again, repeating the refrain in different keys, becoming lighter and lighter until the hall reached complete, reflective silence. Time passed before deafening applause filled the room. Only the First Consul himself refrained, a contorted smirk on his face.

Kaiya lifted her head and cast her gaze across the room. Guests stood, applauding. She had won them back, after losing their respect with her hesitance to eat their food. She suppressed a shudder, remembering the dragonshell. The dead eyes had gaped at her from its stalks, controlling her much as she had captivated the hall with her entrance. Her stomach had rebelled, and it took all of her power to conjure a smile at the expectant faces.

Those faces now beamed, entangled in the magic of her song. She stood and bowed. Languid and fatigued, she took tentative steps towards the closest seat. After settling on the edge of a chair, she closed her eyes and listened.

There it was: the subtle but unmistakable resonance from when she'd first entered the hall. It sang louder than the Teleri ambassador's booming announcement of a dance, and the ensuing sounds of servants clearing tables and chairs from the floor.

The reception hall must've been built over a deeply magical location. The first hint had been the colors. As she had played, the music appeared as swirls of iridescence, wrapping radiant light around her audience. The circumstances of resonance and visible sound bore an unmistakable resemblance to her experience at the Pyramid of Ayudra, and later, Shakti's Hill in Palimur.

However, none of the dancing lights ever reached the First Consul. The curious metal pin on his chest absorbed all her music's luminescence before it could touch him. What did it mean? Her eyelids fluttered open.

And there he was.

Her heart lurched. Pushing through the crowd, First Consul Geros approached, his mouth curled into a smirk. The mismatched colors of his eyes made them look all the more predatory. He towered above her, his very shadow chasing away her bliss.

He clapped his hands together several times. "Absolutely amazing. You have surprised me time after time tonight. When I heard your father was sending you to meet with me, I expected nothing more than a pretty face to distract us. However, you are certainly no ordinary girl."

If only she were. She rose to her feet despite her knees' protests. "First Consul, my ambassador tells me that Bovyans do not care for art or music, but I am glad that you appreciated the zither tonight. We Cathayi believe that underneath prowess with a sword or technical knowledge of shipbuilding lie the cultivation of the spirit through creative endeavor. The arts form the foundation of our culture, and it is the hope of noble and commoner alike to honestly express himself through art. To do so allows us to find a quiet amid all of the background noise of daily life."

He cocked his head, eyebrows clenched together.

She gestured to the *guzheng*. "With this is mind, I would like to offer my zither to you as a gift, in hopes that you may find some peace through it. It is hundreds of years old, made during the Long Winter when the trees of the world grew slowly and densely, by one of our most famous craftsmen. Its value to our people surpasses even the fastest ship in the west, the *Golden Phoenix*."

The First Consul harrumphed. "You are correct. We care little for creative endeavor, because our austere lifestyle makes the Bovyans strong. Our contentment comes from the satisfaction of our basic needs, not from idle pursuits. A musical instrument may be beautiful, but it is easily smashed with a club. An artist's hands may create fancy things, but her fingers can be severed with a blade. The zither means little without the musician to play for me." Extending his hand, he added, "I wonder if this musician would join me for a dance."

Fear clamped iron claws around her heart. Forcing a demure smile, she said, "First Consul, the last time you took my hand, I was not sure when I would get it back. Although I am honored by your invitation, I do not have the energy after performing so long."

"Princess, the style of dance in the North requires no energy on the lady's part. All you have to do is follow the man." Geros took a step closer.

It took all of the willpower she could muster to keep from shrinking back. "I will meet you in two days at the appointed time to discuss more weighty matters than art. Perhaps after we establish our countries' eternal bonds of peace, we might celebrate with a dance."

The First Consul grinned. "If your terms for a dance are so stringent, I wonder if we will be able to negotiate an accord."

"Regardless of the outcome of our meeting, I promise to share one of our dances with you before I return to Cathay."

Geros' grin contorted into a frown. He raised a hand and motioned for some of his soldiers.

Tian and Ambassador Wu closed in behind her. But where was Jie?

Chapter 14
Plans Never Survive First Contact With The Enemy

With the First Consul intimidating the princess at the front of the hall, Tian reached into his sleeve. He palmed a stack of throwing stars as he took note of enemy numbers and positions. The closest escape path was through the door to the kitchens, and for the moment, no Bovyan blocked it.

He could hold the First Consul and his guards here long enough for the princess to escape the hall, but with his old knees, Ambassador Wu wouldn't be able keep up. Even if he could, he didn't have the skill with a sword to protect her against one soldier, let alone the entire Teleri embassy. He mouthed to the handmaidens, *Bring the imperial guard.*

And where was Jie? She didn't seem to be among the dignitaries who watched the face-off in silence.

The princess kept her chin up, her expression inexplicably calm. She must have been oblivious to the danger. If she gave the First Consul just one dance, they could walk out of there and then get her aboard the *Golden Phoenix.*

Six enormous Bovyans closed in, and Tian eased forward. If they took two more steps, he'd put throwing stars into their faces. Would Sameer come to his aid? His Paladin skills made him worth a dozen Teleri.

"Allow us to retire for the night," the princess sang.

Stern expressions softening in unison, the soldiers took two steps back and bowed.

Her legs wobbled, and she reached out and took Ambassador Wu's sleeve. She'd saved them for now, but it appeared as if the power she wielded came with a cost.

The First Consul's gaze shifted from his men back to her, his frown turning up into a calculating grin. "My men will escort you to your palanquin. I look forward to our meeting in two days."

Tian kept a grip around his throwing star. This was too easy to be true.

The princess nodded her head at a shallow angle. "Thank you again for the pleasant evening. I am sure our negotiations will bring new opportunities." Posture straightening, she beckoned the handmaidens to join her. She turned and glided leisurely towards the entrance and out the door. Heavens, she was confident, and thoroughly unaware that there were a thousand more Bovyans.

The cool night air prickled at Tian's damp neck. Had the First Consul called more men and barred their exit, there was nothing they could've done about it.

At the base of the steps, the Cathay procession stood at attention. Without protest, the princess took the ambassador's hand for support and ducked into the palanquin.

Her hand, previously concealed in her long hanging sleeves, trembled.

She did understand the danger. And she had the sense to hide her fear.

The entourage passed through the dark, quiet streets of Iksuvius without incident, their drums and lanterns breaking the sleeping city's tranquility. Upon their arrival at their own embassy, the princess shuffled through the halls toward her suite without a word to anyone.

Tian turned to Ambassador Wu. "Please meet me in your office. In a few minutes." He then headed toward Jie's room. Perhaps she had already come back.

There was no sign of her, so he went next door into his own office.

He hastily tacked up a few notes about the altivorcs and reorganized the relational positions of the three Nothori Kingdoms. Grabbing a map of the surrounding area, he went to the ambassador's office

Ambassador Wu slouched in his chair, sweat beading on his uncharacteristically pale brow. He let out a long sigh. "Little Tian, I was concerned back there."

Tian nodded. "So was I, Godfather. We have more reason to be. The Teleri Empire is plotting. To overturn the balance of power in the Northwest. They are no longer content to collect an annual tribute."

Ambassador Wu frowned and sat up.

Tian snapped out the map and spread it over the ambassador's desk. "They are pitting Rotuvi and Lietuvi against each other. They will gobble up Iksuvi for themselves. The altivorcs will help. Iksuvi will fall by the end of the month. Lietuvi within a year. Rotuvi will stand alone as Teleri's ally. Threatening our border."

The ambassador looked from the map to Tian, then back down. He pointed to the east. "The Teleri are too bogged down in their Eastern Campaign."

Tian nodded. "So we thought. But if I'm right, they will be a direct threat to us. In three years. Maybe even two. Then there's their monstrous breeding program. In fifteen years, they'll have produced enough troops. To fully subjugate the Northwest. And they have gained this city. The only deep-water port in the region."

Wu's eyes narrowed. "The embassy is about to be caught up in a conflagration. What is our best strategy? What do we accomplish with our meeting in two days? What about tomorrow, when the princess meets with Rotuvi? Perhaps we should delay until after the summit so we know where the Teleri stands in the Northwest. Or just send the princess away as soon as we can provision the *Golden Phoenix*."

"The summit is just a diversion," called a soft voice from the door.

Tian turned around to see Jie, her face black. Thank the Heavens she was safe. "Where were you?"

Jie smirked. "In the Teleri embassy war room, and I've seen their plans. An army of fifty thousand regular soldiers and another ten thousand of their homeguard are about to cross over the border. There is also a large battalion of altivorcs moving up from the south."

Tian tapped his chin. "That might be why they left the southern gate open—it's a trap to make the Iksuvi believe there's an escape route."

"That's not all," Jie said. "A Lietuvi army of forty thousand has already crossed the border into southwestern Iksuvi. The bulk of the Iksuvi army will be pinned down west of the mountains."

Ambassador Wu sucked in his breath. "Is our mission here in any direct danger?"

"No," Tian said. "I overheard their general. He said we are of no consequence. They have little to gain from attacking us." Except maybe a pretty princess.

Ambassador Wu stroked his beard. "Would it benefit us to tell the Iksuvi of the imminent threat?"

Tian shook his head. "The Teleri might take punitive measures. They could declare an embargo on our goods. Their influence is strong enough that it might hamper trade."

"It is our moral imperative to warn them." The princess' voice protested from the door.

Tian turned to see the princess dressed in a double-layered white sleeping gown. She looked weary but resolute. And alone.

He scowled at Jie. How could she make the mistake of leaving the door open?

The princess locked her gaze on him. "We know their process of subjugating a country. They will slaughter the male members of the royal family, and subject the women to rape. I like Queen Ausra, and shudder at the thought of her fate."

Tian bowed his head. "If I may, *Dian-xia*. That is Iksuvi's problem. Not ours. Our concern is your safety. We must put personal feelings aside. And look at the implications of an unsettled Northwest."

The princess' eyes glinted.

Before she could reply, the ambassador said, "*Dian-xia*, it is late, and you have a long day ahead of you tomorrow. Please, let us formulate a strategy, and we will present our recommendations when you are fresh in the morning."

"Whatever that strategy is, it must include assistance for the Iksuvi royal family, even if we will not aid the nation itself. That is my command." She turned on her heel and stomped back to her room.

"She is idealistic," the ambassador said in a low voice.

"And stubborn." Tian shook his head.

"And she has good ears," Jie said. "We have less than two days before the Teleri plot comes to a head. We need to demand Rotuvi turn over Lord Peng, and then get the princess out of here."

Their final plan ensured the princess' safety. Whether she heeded their counsel or not was another story.

After tossing and turning through the night, Tian rose well before dawn. He donned simple training robes and slipped out into the courtyard to practice a meditative martial form. Jie was already there, swimming through the very set of slow, deliberate motions that he planned on doing himself. No longer made-up as a handmaiden, nor face-painted for espionage, she was simply Jie.

What did that mean anymore? For so long, she'd been just a clan sister. A best friend.

She didn't pause in her form, even as she greeted him with a smile. Her long dark hair was tied back in a pony tail, fastened with a pink ribbon that dangled over her own plain white robes. As her hand stretched out to *Part the Wild Horse's Mane*, he approached and paralleled her position, his wrist crossing hers. She pressed her body structure into his stance, and he twisted his hips to redirect her force. He then turned to push his own energy back into her.

In this partner exercise of sensing intention, Jie had always surpassed him at harmonizing energy, even if he was better at planning attacks. Yet on this morning, their interchange was perfect, her *Yin* intermingling with his *Yang*. At a neutral position, with hands crossed between them, their gaze met for what must have been the ten thousandth time in their lives.

In that second, he *saw* her. For the first time. His image reflected in her half-lidded eyes, as if their lucidity had ensnared a part of him. She was more than just a skilled fighter and spy. More than a little sister. Perhaps—

Her other hand slapped down on his crossed hand as she first came forward. It landed with light force, though enough to knock him back half a step. A maelstrom of fluid strikes in the span of a second followed, and none of the set responses in the form prevented him from getting hit. Her leg slipped behind his as she twisted his torso, sending him tumbling to the ground.

He looked up. Where had that come from?

Her grin might have reached her ears. "It works, even on you!"

"Huh?"

"The princess gains the upper hand in her interactions because she knows how to use her body language. Everything from the tilt of her neck to the way she looks at you. You fell for it."

"Well, you cheated. You didn't use the motions. From the form."

"When did I ever play fair?" Jie raised an eyebrow, yet it was her eyes beneath that were captivating. "I bribed one of the princess' cousins to teach me their *Praise Spring* style, the one that all the noblewomen learn. It's simple and practical for those who don't have time to train anything in depth."

"Bribed her with what? You don't own anything. Nothing an aristocrat would want." Not that it mattered where she learned a new trick. He just continued gazing at her.

"Information. She's a gossip-monger, who would make a great *Black Fist* if she didn't talk more than she listened. Stop looking at me like that, it's distracting."

From his spot on the ground, Tian threw out his legs and caught up Jie's in a scissor kick. She stumbled on top of him. They pitched into the gravel, neither gaining the upper hand for a few seconds until Tian finally ended up on top, pinning her hands on the ground beside her head.

Their faces were no more than a breath away. Their gazes met again, her playful look melting into one of longing. She closed her eyes and parted her lips, inviting him. They'd walked the path that had been expected of them, brother and sister in a clan of warrior-spies. But a new path lay ahead, determined not by where they had taken the first step of the journey, but rather from where they chose to walk now. Tian leaned in.

"Minister Zheng, Ms. Yan." A male voice from the residence door called.

Tian's head jerked up before his lips met Jie's.

Standing next to the main entrance was the ambassador's young aide, his face red. "The princess will be ready to receive your briefing in a fifth of a phase of Iridescent Moon."

Tian pushed himself off of Jie and stood, brushing himself off. He extended a hand to help her up. When hers met his, something felt... different.

Standing in Ambassador Wu's office, Jie wistfully tugged out the wrinkles in her training robe. What had their face-to-face in the courtyard been about?

It couldn't be happening. Years of affection, never destined to go anywhere, now becoming something more? And just before she would be returning to Cathay. She reached over to give Tian's hand a squeeze.

Then Princess Kaiya glided in with nonchalant grace, wearing a light-blue, long-sleeved silk inner gown. A fur shawl covered her shoulders, and her hair hung in a ponytail. Even without make-up, she looked stunning. Jerking her hand back, Jie suppressed a jealous pout. All bowed low, holding that position until the princess ordered them to rise.

She alighted on the edge of a chair. "What plans have you considered, Ambassador?"

The ambassador bowed. "First of all, a messenger from Rotuvi arrived, insisting we move your meeting with King Gunvydas to Iksuvi's royal palace. He suggested it was a more appropriate venue for royalty than the Iksuvi Trade Ministry."

"Do you see any reason to deny the request?" The princess swept her gaze to each person.

"It's more heavily defended," Tian said. "If we needed to escape, it would be difficult." He then gave Jie a meaningful stare, his unspoken message clear. The princess would likely ignore the potential for danger, so it would be best to prepare.

Jie nodded at him. She'd review the palace's schematics after the meeting adjourned.

"I understand your concern, Young Lord Zheng," the princess said. "However, in this foreign land, we are never completely safe, even here in our own embassy. Furthermore, this is our one chance to demand Lord

Peng's extradition. Ambassador: relay a message to Rotuvi that we will meet at the palace. Now, what is your advice regarding negotiations with the Teleri?"

The ambassador bowed again. "With the Teleri Empire's intended power grab in the Northwest, the region will be embroiled in chaos. They will not pose a threat to us for the time being. We have no reason to meet with them."

"We should call off the meeting," Jie said, wondering if the princess would disagree. "It is safer that way, especially after the way the First Consul treated you last night."

Ambassador Wu raised a hand. "Little Jie speaks from her standpoint as head of your personal security. However, from my position as a diplomat, I must also consider Cathay's interest. Whatever else we may think of the Teleri, they take their treaties very seriously. Our mission here stems from our agreement with Iksuvi."

Jie peered at the ambassador. He'd made no mention of this the night before.

He continued. "In two days, this will be Teleri-occupied land. Since we do not have any formal relations with them, there is nothing to prevent the Bovyans from seizing this embassy. However, if you successfully negotiate a treaty with them, you will ensure our trade and information mission in the North continues unhampered. You bear the *Tianzi's* plaque. It is your decision to make."

Trade Minister Zhang nodded. "We must ensure that trade continues. If we anger the Teleri, they may pressure their allies and tributaries to restrict our exports. Also, this may be a good opportunity to sell our first-generation muskets. In times of conflict, there is profit to be made."

This, too, was a deviation from the script. Jie stared back and forth between Zhang and Wu.

"We should not be profiting from the misery of war." The princess' withering scowl caused Zhang to lower his head. "If anything, my meeting at the Iksuvi palace will be a chance for us to pass on the message about their imminent danger."

"Respectfully," the ambassador said, "we should not meddle in these affairs. We are neutral in these matters, and will only make enemies if our interference is discovered."

The princess shook her head. "Ambassador, Iksuvi will fall to a surprise attack, and Lietuvi will be weakened by underhanded scheming. The Five Classics—which you and your ministers mastered in order to join the ranks of the civil service—implore the ruler to act morally, even at risk to himself."

"We are far away from home," Tian said. "Would you put yourself at risk?"

It wouldn't be the first time. Jie sucked on her lower lip.

The princess' stare bore down on him, and poor Tian lowered his gaze. "Ambassador, during our visit to the Iksuvi palace, you will warn King Evydas of the impending invasion. Offer him and his family safe haven on the *Golden Phoenix*."

The ambassador bowed his head. "As the princess commands."

A slight smile formed on her lips. "Young Lord Zheng, your concerns are duly noted. Therefore, I will not meet with the First Consul." Though she kept her back straight, her hands trembled. "I will depart for Cathay as soon as the *Golden Phoenix* is ready to sail. It must be provisioned before the Teleri lock down the city.

I am told that you are an unparalleled planner, so you and Jie will make preparations for our early departure."

"As the princess commands," they said in unison, bowing.

All bowed as she rose to her feet. "I will be in my quarters preparing for the meeting with King Gunvydas."

Tian watched her drift out of the room, then shook his head. "She has a kind and just heart, but that is not an asset so far from home."

"Don't worry so much." Jie laughed. "She masterfully cornered the Maduran prince in her negotiations there. She is much sharper than you give her credit for." If only she felt as confident as she pretended.

CHAPTER 15:
Bait and Switch

Jie looked back towards the embassy as she followed the princess' procession of a hundred imperial guards towards the Iksuvi palace.

Tian, who was staying behind to plan the princess' escape, offered her a farewell smile from the gates.

She returned it with the tilt of a head a Cathay wife might use to send her husband off.

What had passed between them earlier that morning? As she walked at the palanquin's side, Jie thought back to the warmth of his body, the closeness of his lips. She'd let down her guard and surrendered to him.

Then, duty interrupted.

Whatever had budded between them was left unresolved.

How *unsurprising*. She frowned. Years of unrequited affection, about to be returned. Only to have responsibilities get in the way. And now, she might be leaving as early as tonight. The gods sure had a cruel sense of hu—

She looked up to see a palace of white stone and stained glass, looming high above the squat buildings surrounding it.

Several weeks before, Tian had shown her the floor plans and brought her here. Despite the aesthetic modifications made over the centuries, the original architect had intended it to function as a fortress. Even if elegant white stone walls and graceful towers now replaced battlements and anti-siege defenses, the interior layout of the main keep included bottlenecks, murder holes, and long halls with arrow slits. The defenses not only kept invaders out, but could also prevent *guests* from leaving.

Outside the entrance stood dozens of officials and armed soldiers in precise formation, all dressed in the light-blue and yellow livery of Iksuvi. Porters set the palanquin down, and Jie moved forward to open its doors. A distinguished-looking Nothori man of middle years, dressed in a long formal coat, stepped forward and took the princess' hand.

She wafted out of the palanquin with the grace of a dancer. A dark-blue silk outer gown, open in front to reveal a light-blue inner dress, trailed behind her. Held up with silver pins, her hair was wrapped upward and to the left into a coil, with the last feet of straight hair cascading to her shoulder. A dark-blue *qinghua* flower nestled on the left side. No matter how pretty Jie felt today, she could never compare to the princess.

"Princess Kaiya," the man said with a sweeping Arkothi bow. "I am Lord Jonyas, steward for the Iksuvi royal family. I bid you welcome to the palace. Please follow me to the throne room to meet with King Evydas."

She cast him a demure smile. "My thanks."

"You may bring two of your guards, while the rest wait outside in the palace courtyard." Jonyas licked his lips.

A telltale sign of nervousness. Jie shot a glance at young Cheng, disguised as the flag-bearer. The boy gave a near-imperceptible shrug.

"Of course." The princess motioned toward her two personal guards, Chen Xin and Zhao Yue. Excellent choices. Both were exceptional swordsmen who could best Jie in a fight. Or at least, in a *fair* fight. With confident strides, the pair fell in behind the two other handmaidens and the ambassador. The princess then nodded towards the steward.

With a flourishing bow, he turned and walked through the nine-foot-high, silver-gilt double doors. On either side of the entrance, two large guards in light-blue dress uniforms held stiff bows as the princess' entourage passed.

They were too big, their movements too awkward. Jie tugged the princess' sleeve. "We should—"

"Princess Kaiya!" Queen Ausra met them in the airy foyer, taking the princess' hands in her own. "I am so glad to see you! Come, come!"

Sweat glistened on the queen's forehead despite her broad smile. Behind her enthusiasm, her tone sounded forced. Jie pulled on the princess' sleeve again, and looked back towards the doors just in time to see them close.

The princess ignored the tug, and instead nodded. "Queen Ausra, thank you for personally greeting me."

"Oh. As we say in the Northwest: *a lady who greets her guests adds warmth to the home*," Ausra said with a giggle. "It applies to the queen in the palace just as much as to a peasant in her hovel. Come, come!"

As they passed through the halls, the queen's excitement bubbled into her stories about the palace décor. But while she was busy telling them that the colorful carpets had been imported from Ayuri lands aboard Cathayi trade ships, Jie's pulse quickened.

There were deep footprints spaced far apart in the plush wool rugs. Even though famous painters had rendered the Arkothi-style oil paintings of Iksuvi's past monarchs, two hung off-balance on the walls. They concealed interior arrow slits, if her memory of the castle floor plans served her well. And the musky scent of Levanthi incense? It *almost* covered the metallic smell of well-oiled weapons.

Even more concerning were the palace guards—all too large for their uniforms—who occupied strategic bottlenecks. Sweat gathered on Ambassador Wu's forehead, and both Zhao Yue and Chen Xin sized up potential enemies. Only the princess, still chatting with Queen Ausra, seemed oblivious to the warning signs.

Jie leaned in and whispered in the Cathay tongue. "*Dian-xia*, this is a trap."

Not breaking stride, the princess turned. "I know. I assumed you were coming up with an escape plan." She turned back to Queen Ausra and smiled. "My handmaiden was complimenting your taste in carpets. It helps muffle the sounds of soldiers' footsteps."

The queen blanched. Her smile looked forced. "It helps, but not when there are two hundred and thirty-seven inside clanking around in their chainmail. Thank the gods the other thousand outside didn't insist on coming in."

Jie sucked on her lip. There was no escaping. Now, was Queen Ausra threatening them? Or warning them?

They passed through heavy wooden double doors and into a windowless antechamber. Sunlight flooded in from the throne room, which lay directly across the chamber, through another set of double doors. Copper lamps with Aksumi light beads were shuttered in the corners. Antique tapestries of scenes from the Nothori

Empire's storied past hung on the walls, and a light-blue carpet covered the stone floors.

Why was King Evydas *here* in the antechamber, and *not* in the throne room? He glared daggers at young King Arvydas of Lietuvi, who sat at the opposite end of the room. Around them, ministers and soldiers of Rotuvi, Lietuvi, and Iksuvi stood, wearing the bright court colors of their respective countries. Hands squeezed sword hilts, eyes darted back and forth, and the air reeked of male sweat.

The voice of Rotuvi's ambassador echoed in from the throne room. He was pledging a long list of tribute: ten thousand bales of red wheat, a hundred barrels of red wheat liquor, a thousand pounds of salted fish, a thousand pieces of gold—the list went on.

Ambassador Wu's jaw dropped. He leaned over and whispered to the princess. "This is the Northwest Conference! The tribute list from Rotuvi is almost twice normal." Probably since they would be the last Nothori kingdom left standing.

The princess shot a glance back at him. "Ambassador, you were supposed to arrange our meeting before the conference."

Sounds of struggle erupted at the entrance. Jie turned around. One of the large palace guards seized Queen Ausra's shoulders and pulled her away.

The steward remained there, his attention first following his queen, then turning back to the princess. With a trembling hand, he motioned towards one of the velvet-upholstered chairs. He stuttered over his words. "P-please be seated."

"Lord Steward," Ambassador Wu said, "what is happening? We came today to meet with King Gunvydas of Rotuvi. We understood that the summit would be held tomorrow."

"Ambassador, please forgive the misunderstanding." The young Bovyan General Marius stepped forward with an unapologetic smile. "The First Consul had an urgent change in plans, and moved the conference up to today."

Jie sucked on her lower lip. No doubt those plans were nefarious; probably involving this trap.

Kaiya bowed her head. "Then we would not deign to interpose on these important proceedings." She turned to her retinue. "We shall be leaving now."

"It is but a small matter," General Marius said. "We hope you will stay." With one hand, he motioned the princess toward a cushioned arm chair, while with the other he made a not-so-subtle gesture. Behind them, chainmail clinked as half a dozen Teleri soldiers moved to block the exit.

The princess scowled. "General, are you detaining me?"

"Of course not, Your Highness," the general said. "We are merely providing protection for you. The palace is not safe right now."

Because it was infested by Bovyans. Two hundred and thirty-seven of them, if Queen Ausra was to be believed.

The princess met Jie's gaze with a raised eyebrow.

She shook her head. No, no way to escape. With only her knife and a dozen throwing stars and spikes, fighting the heavily armed Bovyans—even with Chen Xin and Zhao Yue's formidable swordsmanship in support—would only delay the inevitable. For the moment, they were trapped.

CHAPTER 16:
Demands Unmet

Kaiya's heart pounded in her ears, drowning out all other sounds. They'd been tricked into attending the conference, but why? Now they were trapped and separated from the rest of her guards. With no other recourse at the moment, she glided to the chair and perched on its edge. The Teleri general afforded her a curt nod before returning to his position by the double doors to the throne room.

Concealing her worries behind a calm façade, she sat serenely amid the two young kings' unbridled hostility. Like two grasshoppers locked in a duel, they ignored the bird waiting to devour them both.

King Evydas looked as if he were ready to leap across the room and choke his rival with his bare hands, not knowing that Teleri troops massed on their side of the Alto River, waiting for their treaty to expire. King Arvydas' smug grin revealed that he had no idea that his own Lietuvi would soon be invaded from the south by Rotuvi and their altivorc allies.

Kaiya turned her attention to the throne room, where the First Consul sat on the king's throne, looking down at Rotuvi's King Gunvydas and his ambassador. He was supposed to meet with *her* today, not the First Consul. And yet—

The king stepped forward to perform the sword presentation ritual, an old practice that dated back to the times of the Arkothi Empire. In an act which represented allegiance and obedience, he knelt with a bowed head and offered his sword with two hands. The First Consul received it with one hand and flipped it over. When he passed it back, King Gunvydas received it again with two hands.

"The Teleri Empire recognizes your allegiance," the First Consul said. "Our treaty shall stand for three years."

The Rotuvi entourage in the antechamber mumbled among themselves, while Gunvydas cocked his head.

Ambassador Wu leaned over and whispered. "Usually, their treaty lasts for five years. The Teleri must assume it will take three years to conquer the other two."

Weakened from their invasion of Lietuvi, and bankrupted by their tribute to the Teleri, Rotuvi wouldn't stand a chance when the Bovyan pointed their spears at them. Which would put the Teleri Empire at Cathay's border. Kaiya suppressed a shudder.

The First Consul dismissed the king with a wave of his hand. "Return to your seat and wait quietly until your counterparts have likewise submitted. You will not receive the Princess of Cathay today."

Kaiya's palms sweat. The First Consul wanted her here, and not to negotiate for Cousin Kai-Long's extradition.

"As the First Consul commands." Gunvydas bowed again before turning on his heel and marching back out into the antechamber. As he passed the threshold, his perplexed expression transformed into a grin. He paused to cast a haughty glance at the other Nothori kings. His two guards assumed positions around him as he took his seat.

It was time to get some answers from Gunvydas. Kaiya started to rise.

The Teleri general spoke. "The First Consul Geros Bovyan XLIII summons King Arvydas of the Nothori Kingdom of Lietuvi."

The young king rose to his feet and strode through the double doors. His ambassador stood and followed him.

Gunvydas could wait. Kaiya used the distraction to glide over to the chair beside King Evydas. Leaning over, she whispered in his ear. "Your nation is in grave danger, Your Highness. The Teleri will not extend your treaty. They plan to invade once it expires. We offer your wife and family refuge in our embassy."

He turned to her, mouth agape. Without a word, he bolted up and darted out of the antechamber and into the hall. The Teleri soldiers at the door made way while his soldiers stumbled out after him. Everyone in the room exchanged confused glances.

"What did you say to him?" King Gunvydas' eyes narrowed as he regarded her.

Kaiya ignored the question. How easy it had been for Evydas to leave! She stood and headed toward the door. Chen Xin and Zhao Yue followed.

The Teleri guards closed ranks, forming a cordon of steel. Her own guards strode forward, hands on their swords. Brave and skilled as they were, they were hopelessly outnumbered. Chen Xin and Zhao Yue would die, and she would be no closer to escape.

Kaiya drew upon the power of her voice, singing her command. "Stand aside." Heaviness crept into her arms and legs as her vital energy transformed into magic.

The Bovyans' blank expressions jumbled into confusion before all six opened a path to the door.

"Men!" the general barked from behind her.

Kaiya started towards the door, her listless limbs protesting with each step. Four more Teleri swept in from the hall.

They might succumb to the power of her voice as well, but how many Bovyans stalked the palace, ready to *protect* her? The draining effect would leave her exhausted before they made it halfway out of the castle.

Kaiya looked toward Jie, only to find the half-elf wasn't standing in her previous spot. Her eyes swept over the room. No sign of the Insolent Retainer. Kaiya fiddled with a lock of her hair. For now, the only recourse was to persevere. She returned to her seat.

In the throne room, King Arvydas now stood before the First Consul, bowing. When he lifted his head, he spoke in the ritualistic language of the defunct Arkothi Empire. "I, the embodiment of the Nothori Kingdom of Lietuvi, present myself to the First Consul."

Kaiya sighed. The poor boy didn't realize what was happening.

"King Arvydas," Geros said, using plain Arkothi, "the last time you swore allegiance to the Empire, you were a boy of twelve, with your regent playing you as a puppet. Now, five years later, you make your own decisions. Do you understand the ramifications of today's agreement?"

Arvydas bowed his head. "Yes, Your Eminence."

"Very well, then." The First Consul grinned, and returned to the old language. "It pleases the Teleri Empire to embrace the Nothori Kingdom of Lietuvi as brothers. What does Lietuvi present as goodwill to us?"

The Lietuvi ambassador stepped forward and bowed before unfurling a scroll. He began reading off a long list of gifts. With the comparable climates and geography of the Northwest, the annual tribute was similar to that of Rotuvi, though the amount was only about half. At the end, Arvydas stepped forward to perform the sword presentation ritual.

"The Teleri Empire recognizes your allegiance." The First Consul handed the sword back to the boy king. "Our treaty shall stand for two years."

Around her in the antechamber, the Lietuvi entourage exchanged glances and muttered their shock at the short duration of the agreement. If only they knew what was about to happen. Kaiya looked back into the throne room, where King Arvydas remained stoic.

Geros gestured him out with his hand. "Return to your seat and wait there until your counterparts have likewise submitted."

Counterparts? There was only one, King Evydas of Iksuvi. Unless that meant—

Arvydas bowed again and returned to the antechamber. He looked around the room, pausing momentarily on Evydas' vacant seat. He offered the princess a respectful nod.

General Marius gestured towards his men at the doors. "King Evydas should have been back by now. Do you see him in the halls?"

The soldiers shook their heads. He stepped into the throne room and approached the First Consul. Kaiya strained to hear his whisper. "King Evydas left and has not returned. How long shall we wait?"

The First Consul's own voice was barely audible, even to Kaiya's ears. "Perhaps he suspects something. Send your men to find him. Drag him back here if need be. In the meantime, send the Princess of Cathay in, so that the other kings will think she is here to submit."

Kaiya pursed her lips. So this was a game of image. Tricking her into attending the conference and make it seem as if Cathay was proclaiming its loyalty.

The general strode back into the antechamber. "Princess Kaiya, the First Consul is ready to receive you."

Kaiya stared at the wall. Let the Rotuvi and Lietuvi see she was being forced. "If the First Consul wishes to see me before our appointed date, he will have to come here."

Two Teleri soldiers squared their shoulders and strode towards her. Chen Xin and Zhao Yue stepped forward, hands on their sword hilts. Around them, the other kings jumped to their feet while their own guards formed up around them.

Kaiya raised her hand to stay the guards, and rose from her chair. As long as she got her message across, nobody needed to die. She glided into the throne room, Ambassador Wu stumbling behind her.

The room jutted out from the rear of the palace, and was well lit by windows that overlooked the bay to the west and the Alto River to the east. More light streamed in from the skylights, illuminating faded tapestries on the walls. She continued down a rich burgundy carpet that stretched down the center of the room, ending at Iksuvi's throne.

There First Consul Geros sat, his leer on her bosom.

She tightened her outer gown over her shoulders and met his gaze.

He was flanked on his left by a scribe, and on his right by his ambassador. A dozen armed guards in black-and-gold Teleri uniforms stood on either side, while another two stood by the entrance.

And somewhere in the room, there was an impossibly slow breath mingled in among all the others.

Jie's.

Kaiya smiled. She had extra protection.

The heavy blockwood doors closed behind her, muffling her guards' protests in the antechamber. She looked up.

The First Consul watched like a bird of prey, all the more disconcerting for his mismatched eyes. "Princess Kaiya, thank you for visiting. You are certainly much more pleasant on the eyes than those boring kings who came before you." He laughed before clearing his throat. "Today, for the first time, I am extending the Teleri Empire's cloak of protection over Cathay. What does Cathay offer in return?"

Kaiya smiled, even as she eyed the First Consul's pin. It would protect him from the power of her voice, as it had twice last night. That left only her wits and charm to extricate herself and her countrymen from the situation. "Most gracious First Consul, on behalf of the Heavenly Empire of Cathay, I thank you for your generous offer."

He started to open his mouth, but she raised a hand to stop him. "However, we owe allegiance only to the Sun God, Yang-Di, to whom my Father the *Tianzi* is but a faithful servant. Yang-Di's Jade Palace may be far away in the reaches of the Western Sea, yet that is where we deliver all of our tribute."

His grin melted. "I—"

She held up a hand again. "Under his watchful eye, we have remained at peace with our neighbors since the War of the Ancient Gods ended a thousand years ago. While Teleri protection comes at a steep price, our Great Wall and rifles are economical."

Geros gritted his teeth. "Your defiance comes as no surprise. However, this chance will only be offered once.

I advise you to give it some thought, since walls and rifles may not deter all of your enemies."

The enemies the Teleri sent. She smiled innocently. Let him think she misunderstood his threat. "Up to now, they have effectively deterred your friends in Rotuvi and Madura, who make noises at our borders. I believe if we can arrange a treaty of non-aggression, we can ensure lasting peace that will benefit all."

The First Consul crossed his arms over his chest. "I am afraid that the Directori would not approve of anything short of recognizing your country as a protectorate. However, in the interest of peace, I will use what little influence I have to persuade Rotuvi and Madura not to trouble you for a while. However, I do have a price for this."

Ambassador Wu stepped forward and opened his mouth, but the First Consul silenced him with a glare. "I do not ask much. Just one of your renowned dances that so enchanted Prince Dhanannad in Vyara City."

Kaiya's skin prickled at the name. The way Prince Dhanannad's eyes had roved over her still felt like a violation, half a year after the fact. She forced a reply. "Such a magnanimous gesture. Very well then. A dance, tomorrow afternoon, since your conference was moved to today."

"My guards will escort you to my embassy to stay the night." Geros' lips twitched into a slight smile. "For your protection, of course."

The audacity! Kaiya veiled her protest with an innocuous smile. "I would prefer to prepare for tomorrow in the familiarity and comfort of my own embassy."

The First Consul's grin broadened. "Since we simple Bovyans cannot master the delicate refinement with which you speak, I shall be blunt. I need an assurance you will actually come tomorrow."

Finally, the demand clearly stated. Yet why did he want to see a dance? With her focus locked on the First Consul, she used a tone of command. "Ambassador Wu, the plaque of the *Tianzi*'s office."

A gasp preceded his words, which he spoke in the Cathay tongue. "*Dian-xia*, if you give him the plaque, you cannot back out. It, like the Broken Sword, is the embodiment of the *Tianzi*."

As if she didn't know. "There is no other way. My virtue, your life, and Chen Xin and Zhao Yue's lives depend on it." She switched back to Arkothi, motioning him forward without ever looking back. "The plaque, Ambassador."

She extended both arms toward the ambassador, never breaking eye contact with Geros. The reassuringly cool jade met her hands, and she closed her fingers around it. She pressed her forehead to the surface, and then extended it towards the First Consul. "This plaque represents the *Tianzi* himself. My own word of honor *should* be sufficient, but this surpasses even that."

The First Consul glanced towards one of the tapestries, and Kaiya followed his gaze, listening. There was the extra breath from before. Geros nodded ever so slightly and his attention returned to her. Who was hiding there?

Not Jie.

"I accept this as a token of your word." He reached with one hand to take the plaque.

Kaiya did not let go. "First Consul, please receive it with two hands."

His smile twisted into a smirk, and he pulled a little harder. She stumbled a few steps forward. Her heart lurched. His manipulations and contempt for her, she could endure for the sake of her retainers' lives; but disparaging the embodiment of the *Tianzi* was insufferable.

He laughed and took it in two hands. No matter how important the symbol, a wave of relief washed over her as she released it.

With a last glance at the tapestry, she bowed her head. "Tomorrow morning, I will send word of the time and place for our meeting. I—"

The doors flung open, revealing King Evydas. Sweat glistened on his forehead, and his fair face looked even paler than usual. His hands tightened into fists. One step behind him, his foreign minister gripped a sheathed sword in trembling hands. A wall of Iksuvi guards held the outnumbered Bovyans at bay in the antechamber beyond.

What was he planning? Kaiya dug her nails into her hands.

Around her, the Teleri reached for their swords and started forward, but Geros raised his hand. The synchronized clop of boots echoed in the hall as his soldiers snapped to attention.

"King Evydas," the First Consul snarled. "You are late."

The young king strode forward, pausing at Kaiya's side. "It was a pleasure to have met you, Princess of Cathay." He then leaned over to whisper in her ear, "Please make sure my family is protected."

Her eyes widened. He didn't intend to leave the throne room alive. She grabbed ahold of his arm, just as he took another step. *Value your life,* she mouthed.

He offered a wry smile before continuing towards the First Consul.

Ambassador Wu tugged at her sleeve. Audacious. Urgent. At the throne room entrance, the imperial guards clenched their jaws.

She frowned and furrowed her brows to let her will be known.

They would stay.

Ambassador Wu loosened his grip and she turned to watch First Consul Geros and King Evydas.

The king stood several feet away from the First Consul, his posture stiff and dignified. He reached back with his left hand. After a second, he made an emphatic gesture.

The foreign minister, trembling and sweating, tottered forward and placed the sword in his king's hands.

Evydas held the weapon on either side of the sheath and lifted it. "This sword, *Tamskelti*, was forged by dwarven smiths in antiquity, and holds an edge imbued with elven magic so that they could oppose the armies of the ancient Orc Gods. My forefathers used it to protect our people against the expansion of the Arkothi Empire. Iksuvi will terminate our alliance with the Teleri Empire, and I present this sword as prescribed by ancient rituals."

Before he could take a step forward, the First Consul halted him with a raised hand. "By tradition, you must present the sword with the hilt on your left."

King Evydas froze for a second. Then, with a brusque nod, he flipped *Tamskelti* over, strode forward and extended it towards the First Consul.

As Geros reached to take the weapon, the king switched his grip and whipped it out with his left hand. The edges of the intricately etched blade glowed a luminous blue, and its hum resonated in Kaiya's core.

The sword swished toward the First Consul's midsection. Evading the attack, Geros ripped the grey metal pin from his shirt with a rasp. Evydas transitioned into a stab toward his chest. The Bovyan twisted away and used his pin to slap the blade with a muted clang.

A minute pulse of energy rippled out from the impact, percolating through Kaiya. The luminous glow of the blade went dull.

Evydas gasped.

Chainmail clinked as two of the soldiers on either side of the First Consul sprang into action, lowering their spears. Geros drew one of their swords with his left hand. The weapon whooshed as it cut toward Evydas' head. The king lifted his own blade, but it shattered with a clank on impact.

Iksuvi soldiers flooded into the room. A wave of jingling armor and rustling cloth surged past Kaiya as they joined in the fray. One of the Teleri charged and thrust with his spear at the king. Evydas evaded the stab with a quick spin, and simultaneously caught the weapon's shaft in both of his hands. The turn pulled the Bovyan soldier forward, into the foreign minister, and both went crashing to the floor.

Spear in hand, the king faced off against the First Consul. The Teleri guards at the door joined in, their own spears flashing. The one guard picked himself up off the minister, and a compatriot threw him a sheathed sword.

Having listened to the cacophony of crossed swords, Kaiya snapped out of her dread fascination.

Ambassador Wu was pulling at her arm. His voice was hoarse and insistent. "We must leave now!"

Her two guards Chen Xin and Zhao Yue shoved through the crowd to protect her, holding their *dao*.

Another dozen of the Iksuvi guards burst into the antechamber from the hall, heading toward the throne room.

The broken sword's shards vibrated, pulsing through her. Kaiya pushed past her own men. Pulling the hand-length *dizi* flute from the fold of her inner robe, she approached the throne. She played four melodic notes, which cut through the tense air more sharply than the flashing blades.

The king, his foreign minister, and all the soldiers on both sides lowered their weapons. Only the First Consul held a defensive stance, eyes darting around the room. He lowered his sword.

Kaiya edged forward. Brushing her gown down to her shins, she kneeled on the plush carpet. She spread her arms horizontally to straighten the sleeves, then brought two open hands to the front of her knees and bowed her head. Such a bend was two levels from the deepest bow in Cathay culture, those highest levels of respect reserved for their own royalty. "My Lords, please desist."

The imperial guards gasped. They dropped to a knee, right fists to the ground with heads bowed. Ambassador Wu pressed his forehead to the rug.

King Evydas raised his spear again. "I appreciate your consideration, Princess Kaiya, but this must end now. Please withdraw to your embassy for your own safety. And remember my earlier request."

She shook her head. "My Lords—"

"Forgive my rudeness," the king said. "Guards, remove her."

Iksuvi men darted in, putting blades at the Cathay imperial guards' necks and wresting the swords from their hands. A third soldier ignored her protests and pulled her to her feet.

Interrupted *and* manhandled! Kaiya tore her arm away from the soldier and lifted her chin. "Chen Xin, Zhao Yue, ambassador, come."

Iksuvi soldiers hustled the Cathay contingent out of the throne room, through the antechamber and into the hall, where Iksuvi and Teleri soldiers paused in their conflict to let them pass.

Turning a corner, they ran into a company of two dozen Cathay imperial guards with naked blades, General Zheng at their head.

"Unhand the princess," he demanded, his Arkothi heavily accented.

The Iksuvi palace guards, who probably wanted nothing more than to go back to their own king's defense, released her not unkindly and bowed. They returned the weapons to Chen Xin and Zhao Yue before racing back towards the throne room.

"*Dian-xia*," General Zheng said with a bow of his head, "please follow me."

He escorted them outside, where they were greeted by the bright light of late morning. The remainder of the imperial guards stood in ranks, ready to storm the palace if the need arose. There was not a single Iksuvi uniform around.

Ambassador Wu turned to face her. "There is nothing else we can do for the king; his fate lies in his gods' hands. We must hurry back to the embassy before we get caught up in the chaos."

Kaiya nodded. "Let us be gone from this hornet's nest as soon as possible. I hope the *Golden Phoenix* is provisioned. Where is Jie?"

The procession's flag-bearer stepped forward and dropped to his knee. "*Dian-xia*. My clan sister drew off the gate guards and signaled for us to go in and find you. She must still be inside."

"We shall wait a few minutes for her." Or perhaps it would be better to storm back in. Kaiya wrung her hands.

The ambassador sunk to his knee. "Jie can take care of herself. We must get you back to the safety of our own embassy."

All of the imperial guards dropped to their knee in perfect unison.

They were right. Jie could take care of herself.

Kaiya nodded, looking around for a horse. Seeing none, she cast her palanquin a frown before curling in.

The walls pressed in on her, suffocating. Her chest tightened and her heart skittered like a rabbit. Fighting to draw a breath, she slid the window open.

Horns blared from the palace, and their call echoed throughout the city. The procession headed east towards the embassy with the imperial guards' formation tightly packed around her palanquin.

Commoners frantically rushed through the streets. Several squadrons of Iksuvi soldiers marched towards the city center, their leaders ordering the citizenry into their homes. Gone was Ambassador Wu's typically calm and collected composure, replaced by trembling hands and quivering lips.

They arrived at the compound as the barely visible Iridescent Moon waxed to its first crescent. When Kaiya emerged from the palanquin, she found Tian waiting there to greet her on one knee, fist to the ground. "*Dian-xia*. We have urgent business. Come to the receiving room."

CHAPTER 17:
Price of Insolence

Tian searched the faces among the returning procession without satisfaction. He drew aside the flag-bearer, clan brother Cheng. "Where's Jie?"

"She's in the Iksuvi palace, I believe to latch on to that Teleri general."

Him again. For a Bovyan, the general seemed inordinately interested in one girl. And what about Jie? Surely she couldn't like him. Why put herself in so much danger?

Unless she was the mole who'd helped the Teleri the night of the princess' arrival. Jie was unaccounted for on another instance, as well—in the Teleri embassy. Right after the general had parted ways with the altivorcs. And of course, there was the mysterious past relationship between the two, which Jie repeatedly denied.

No, that couldn't be. His thoughts were drawing connections that weren't there. Tian sighed and hurried to catch up with the princess, who was nearly to the receiving room.

He waited outside as the doors opened, revealing Queen Ausra perched on a delicate-looking bloodwood chair. Evydas' two teenage sisters sat beside her. A wet nurse held the king's infant nephew, the next in line for the throne. All wore simple cotton traveling clothes, their satin gowns abandoned in their haste to flee the palace through a secret tunnel. Their escort of a dozen Iksuvi guards had also disguised themselves as commoners, though their swords would have marked them as soldiers to anyone who took a second look.

Queen Ausra stood and curtseyed as the princess entered. She stumbled forward, blinking away tears. "Princess Kaiya, I am so sorry to have betrayed you at the palace. We were forced."

The princess smiled and motioned for the queen to sit. "I understand, Your Highness. It is already forgotten."

So magnanimous. Tian buried a snort.

Queen Ausra bowed her head and sniffed.

The princess placed a hand on her shoulder. "I do not wish to be the bearer of bad news, but I am sure you would want to know. When we left the palace, your king and his men were fighting for their lives. He was very brave in ensuring that I escaped."

The queen crumpled back in her chair, her voice cracking. "I... " She wiped a sleeve across her eyes, cleared her throat and straightened. "Before we parted, my king asked me to convey his deepest appreciation. His brothers and uncles are preparing for war. However, he has asked that you shelter his sisters, for they will endure horrors if they are captured. And of course his nephew, the heir."

Tian tapped his chin as he watched from the entrance. This was not their problem. One of his spies slipped a note into his hand, and he glanced at it. The latest report.

"... and we are not at war with Teleri," Ambassador Wu was saying, "so you are safe in the embassy for now. Nonetheless, I suggest that you board the *Golden*

Phoenix tonight, under the cover of darkness. Although it is not as comfortable as our embassy, the situation here is dire. It may be necessary to make a hasty withdrawal to Cathay in the event that Iksuvius falls."

Iksuvius would fall, and Tian had little doubt who would be responsible for escorting the queen to the ship.

The princess nodded. "Please, make yourself comfortable. You must be tired from your harrowing escape. If you need anything, please let me or the Ambassador know." She rose to her feet, nodded to the guests, and glided out.

Tian dropped to his knee as she emerged. "*Dian-xia*, Ambassador. I have information from my brothers."

With the princess and senior embassy staff surrounding a map, Tian pointed out landmarks. "King Evydas was seriously wounded in the castle. He managed to escape. We are not sure of his current whereabouts. His younger brothers have taken command of the army. They have set up headquarters at the Ministry of War. The Teleri are sweeping throughout the city. Searching for the king's family. They don't know they are here. They've closed all the city gates. Except the southern gate."

"I imagine there are a lot of people trying to get out through that one gate," the ambassador said.

Tian nodded. "And into the hands of the altivorcs. They are coming up the southern road."

The ambassador turned to his chief of staff. "The sun will set in a couple of hours. If the princess is in agreement, send a message to the captain of the *Golden Phoenix,* informing him of Queen Ausra's arrival tonight. Also instruct the embassy staff to ensure the queen and her family are spared no expense for their comfort until then. After night falls, Tian and his men will take them to the ship."

Of course. Tian suppressed a snort.

General Zheng dropped to his knee. "*Dian-xia,* I suggest you board the ship as well."

All of the assembled officials and soldiers followed suit and knelt in a rippling rustle of robes and clatter of armor.

The princess shook her head. "I have promised to dance for the First Consul. To go back on my word, especially to the Bovyans, who value honor, would reflect poorly on Cathay."

"*Dian-xia,*" Tian said. "Your safety takes precedence. Over honor. I will take you to the ship. By force if necessary. When you are safely on board. I will cut my throat for my impudence."

The princess glared at him, but he raised his head and broke protocol by making direct eye contact. Her expression hardened even more. She motioned towards her imperial guards, Xu Zhan and Ma Jun. "General Zheng, have your men remove this insolent cur from my sight. If he dares lay a hand on me, cut it off."

General Zheng, still on his knee, removed his sheathed sword and held it above his bowed head with two hands. "When you are safely aboard the ship, I will cut my throat for disobeying your command."

All of the soldiers repeated his motion, while the unarmed officials dropped from one knee to two, foreheads pressed to the ground.

Ambassador Wu sighed. "She has given the First Consul a plaque of the *Tianzi*'s office as a guarantee."

The collective sucking in of breaths told him what he already knew: like the Broken Sword, a plaque was the embodiment of the *Tianzi*. Not to honor one would be tantamount to the *Tianzi* forsaking the Mandate of Heaven. The last emperor of the preceding dynasty had reneged on his plaque-bound obligations three centuries prior, and the gods had punished the world with the Hellstorm and Long Winter.

There must have been other options than using the plaque! "How could you take a symbol of state so lightly? There—"

"Little Tian, desist." The ambassador's voice was low. "What is done is done."

The princess glared at him. "I do not need to explain myself to an impertinent boor like you, but I will. We were surrounded with no chance of escape. By promising to meet with him later, I may have exposed myself to danger again; but I will do so at a time and place of our choosing, with an opportunity for the Black Fist to plan my defense. But perhaps I have overestimated your ability."

She afforded Tian a last scathing glance before whipping around and marching out of the office. Xu Zhan and Ma Jun hurried after her.

An apology was in order. Tian rose to follow, but the ambassador warded him off with a hand. "Little Tian, your intentions were noble, but you have made the princess lose face. Give her some distance."

Kaiya strode through the halls towards her suite, all trace of poise forgotten. Her imperial guard Chen Xin opened the door for her as she came to her room.

Handmaidens and servants were crating up her personal belongings, just as she had commanded upon her return from the audience with the First Consul.

"Out!" she ordered, her choking voice sounding wrong in her ears.

The servants and handmaidens' eyes widened, but they all bowed low and scurried out.

Kaiya slammed the door behind her. The Northern-style doors made the most satisfying sound.

She walked across the room and slumped into a chair. Using the imperial plaque had been a mistake. Had she waited just a few minutes, King Evydas' attack on Geros would have provided an opportunity for them to escape.

That didn't excuse Tian for scolding her like a child. He'd always been her support in all things, her confidante. Instead, now he publicly humiliated her. To think her eight-year-old self wanted to marry him.

Kaiya sniffed. She could order him to cut his own throat, but she did not want that burden any more than she wanted to risk herself by dancing for that brute of a First Consul.

If only she could leave behind the power of life and death, the traditions that placed honor over life, and the loneliness that only someone in her position could understand. She looked into the mirror, to see her reflection blinking away tears.

Tian poked his head out of the Cobweb several times to see if Jie had returned. By nightfall, there was still no word of her. Most of the other Black Fist brothers *had* returned, bringing strategic updates and the news of a mass exodus of citizens through the southern gate.

He sent some of his men back out to spy on Teleri positions, but organized six to escort the Iksuvi royalty to the *Golden Phoenix*.

When his team arrived at the receiving room, they found the queen and her retinue dressed in dark robes, ready to depart. A handful of servants milled about, attending to their needs, while the ambassador and princess bade their farewells.

She looked up as he entered. Her expression instantly hardened, as if she had found a raw turnip in her imperial soup. He dropped to his knee as protocol demanded, but she'd already turned away.

Perhaps there was nothing he could do to make amends. Their constant verbal duel over the last few days had cut through whatever childhood threads connected them.

That wasn't important right now, anyway. He rose and bowed before Queen Ausra. "Your Highness. We must leave now. Before the White Moon reaches its zenith. And brightens the night sky. My team needs your guards' swords. If we need to use force. It needs to look like part of the conflict. Between your nation and the Teleri."

Queen Ausra nodded towards her men, and they reluctantly surrendered their swords. Her smile was frail. "Please lead on. Our lives are in your hands."

Tian bowed. He and his Black Fist led them out of the compound through the warehouse tunnels. The secret passage went under the walls and connected to the city's sewers. Walking as quickly as possible through the muck, they emerged not far from the docks.

Eight Teleri soldiers stood at the head of the deep-water dock, checking the few people who passed. It would be impossible to sneak the Iksuvi royalty past them, and equally unlikely to draw the sentries away from their post. That left one option, expedient but distasteful.

Tian motioned for the queen and her family to stay back, then used hand signals to assign targets to his men. On his mark, his brothers slipped through the darkness in utter silence, hanging at the edges of the Bovyans' light bauble lamps.

As he strode towards the soldiers, Tian collected a few rocks and flung them at their heads. Once he came into their light, he drew an Iksuvi longsword and brandished it at them.

One of the men pointed. "Lucius, Cyril, Augustas, and Sciro, execute the rebel."

As if taking the life of a faceless enemy wasn't hard enough, their leader had to name them. Four of the soldiers lowered spears and approached in tight formation. Tian tightened his grip on the sword.

His own men slid in behind the soldiers holding the dock and slashed their throats with knives. They caught two of the advancing Bovyans from the rear and slew them as well. When the two living ones turned to see what happened, Tian came up from behind and ran one through. The remaining soldier quickly fell to a coordinated onslaught. As always, efficiency took precedence over honor.

Tian frowned. His master had told him that killing became easier each time, but that never seemed to be the case. "Arrange the bodies so it looks like they died fighting regular infantry."

After seeing the Iksuvi royals safely onboard, his team slunk back to the embassy without incident. There was still no word of Jie, so Tian went to his own room and threw himself into bed.

Maybe Jie *had* avoided kissing him in the courtyard that morning because she was the traitor.

CHAPTER 18:
Escape Plans

Tian's eyelids fluttered open as a red haze filtered in through his window. A blurred image came into focus.

Jie looked back at him, elbows on his bed and face propped in her hands. Her lips curled into a grin, reminiscent of the dolphin he had seen on the voyage over. She still wore the blue court gown from the day before, though it was as ruffled as her unkempt hair.

He bolted upright, wiping the gunk from his eyes. "Where've you been?"

Jie's lips twitched, and her gaze roved over what must be his disheveled hair, but her expression quickly transformed into one of seriousness. "I spent the night in the Teleri embassy. I entered on the arm of General Marius, then made sure he enjoyed a long slumber. I am sure he is waking up with a bad headache and a very poor recollection of yesterday's events."

Heat rose to his face. She couldn't have...

"N-no. I-I did not." Her face flushed bright red.

"Sorry," Tian said. He'd made too many assumptions. He'd even believed Jie was a mole. What was he thinking?

"Never mind. I learned from Marius that the senior-most Keeper of the Shrine of Geros is here, though I couldn't find out why."

Was she really on a first-name basis with the general? "The senior-most? Important. Was it worth it? Risking yourself and worrying me... us... all night? Why didn't you slip out earlier?"

Jie gesticulated in exaggerated stabs and circles. "I was hiding and got stuck in the war room as their officers came and went. The bulk of their army is less than a day away, and they are moving soldiers to strategic points in the city."

Tian rose to his feet, pulling the wrinkles from the sleeves of his stealth suit. "The noose is closing around the city. I'd hoped to get the princess aboard the *Golden Phoenix* last night—"

"Let me guess, she refused?"

If only his simple nod could convey what had transpired.

Jie sighed. "I also overheard the First Consul talking about her last night. He hates her for her defiance, and he wants to possess her. He told his officers to draw up plans for her capture once the city is secured."

"What? Does he not know we have guns? We have enough provisions to hole up in this compound. For a year if need be. Plus the imperial guards. We are safe here."

Jie shook her head. "What do we do after a year? They outnumber us here, and our homeland is too far away to be a credible threat."

"You're right. However, we are still more powerful at sea. Let's get her aboard the *Golden Phoenix*." Hopefully, the *her* didn't sound as acidic enough as it tasted in his mouth.

Jie shook her head again. "The Teleri have secured the docks with over two hundred men. They are allowing us to bring cargo aboard, but they are checking everything."

Tian sighed. They'd lost the one easy opportunity to get the princess aboard. Of course the Teleri would bolster security after his team's attack last night.

Jie sucked on her lower lip. "Our compound is under constant watch. If we raise suspicions that we know of their plot—"

"Time is short," Tian said. "Assemble the senior staff. In the ambassador's office. I will inform the princess myself."

After Jie left, Tian changed into robes and combed out his hair, then headed to the princess' quarters.

Even at that early hour, music emanated from behind the closed door. The short strumming sounds of the *pipa*, a Cathay lute, melded with the long hum of the *erhu*, a two-stringed bowed instrument. Not wanting to disturb the music, he quietly pushed the door open and slipped in.

In the corner of the anteroom, two of the handmaidens plucked at *pipa*s, while another played the *erhu*.

In the middle of the room, the princess glided through classical movements, seemingly lost in her dance. She wore a simple white sleeping robe, her hair cascading loosely over her shoulders to her waist. Even without her make-up, she was stunning.

Tian stood mesmerized by her grace, forgetting why he'd come.

Though the music continued, she froze in a perfect stance: back slightly twisted, neck tilted at a gentle curve, and arms above her head in a smooth bend. One bare foot was rooted to the ground, while she held the other leg weightlessly with her toes on the floor. A shapely calf peeked out from the slit of her gown.

The musicians stopped, all eyes on him as he gawked at the angle of her neck. The princess straightened from the pose, brushing her hair behind her ears. Her severe look locked on him. Her cold voice doused any fascination. "Yes, Young Lord Zheng?"

Tian dropped to his knee in salute. When he spoke, an *I-told-you-so* tone slipped out. "*Dian-xia*. Geros plans to take you hostage." And probably more. "We will be convening a meeting in a half hour. To discuss how to expedite your escape."

The princess backed up and collapsed into a chair by a window. Hair curtained her face, and her shoulders trembled. "How I wish I had never been sent to this godforsaken land. That I never met that demon of a First Consul."

Tian hadn't expected vulnerability. Perhaps his tone was too harsh. He bowed his head.

Pushing her hair back, her gaze met his, searching for something. Perhaps a word of consolation.

In that moment, she was the child he remembered, not the uppity princess she'd become. He took a step forward, hand outstretched to comfort her.

With a lift of the chin, her expression hardened, the cold look returning as if it had never changed. Her voice was icy. "I hope you have come up with a plan."

Kaiya couldn't forgive herself for showing weakness in front of Tian. She was too embarrassed to look at him when she came to the ambassador's office a half hour later. Let him believe it was anger.

More importantly, Jie was back. Safe. She knelt among the senior staff.

Kaiya paused to smile and clasp the half-elf's calloused hands as she glided towards the ambassador's desk. A map of the city lay unfurled there.

"*Dian-xia*," Tian said. "The *Golden Phoenix* is under tight guard. From eight soldiers last night. To two hundred now. We cannot get you aboard. Not if they choose to stop us."

Another reprimand, for not leaving last night? Kaiya squared her jaw and refused to make eye contact.

The captain of the *Phoenix* bowed his head. "*Dian-xia*, if we can get you aboard, the *Golden Phoenix* is provisioned and can be ready to sail in two hours."

Tian shook his head. "As long as they maintain that troop level at the docks, escape by sea will be impossible."

Kaiya snorted. Perhaps Zheng Tian was not such a great planner after all. "Can we charter a boat to take us to the ship?"

It was Jie's turn to shake her head. "Charter, no. Maybe we can steal one."

"The docks are crawling with Teleri," Tian said. He pointed to the Alto River on the map. "Captain, how far upstream can the *Golden Phoenix* go?"

"At low tide, we can pass under the Great East Bridge, maybe as far south as the docks at Aremarela." The captain pointed at a fishing town about twenty *li* south of Iksuvius, on the Teleri side of the river.

Jie gawked. "You can't simply sneak the *Golden Phoenix* up the river."

The captain laughed. "Who said we would sneak? *If* they even realize what we are doing, there is nothing they can do to stop us. They can't float anything larger than a fishing boat, and my hundred muskets will keep their heads down."

Tian's eyes darted back and forth across the map. "Speed will be of the essence. And a level of deception. We have to leave through the eastern gate. Pass through the crowds on the eastern bridge. Into the Teleri Empire. Then take the road to Aremarela."

"Into Teleri?" Kaiya covered her gaping mouth. Tian was supposed to be the second coming of his clan's fabled Architect, and this was the best he could do?

The captain nodded. "There are no other docks deep enough for the *Golden Phoenix* on this side of the river."

"However," Jie said, "we need a very good reason to leave the embassy compound. They have us surrounded."

Murmurs broke out, but Kaiya silenced them with a raise of her hand. "We have a good reason. I have promised to perform for the First Consul. Choose a time and place."

Jie sucked her lower lip and let it go with a pop. "Wait. We must reach Aremarela before sundown, because the Teleri western army will be passing through as they move to occupy Iksuvius."

The captain tapped the bridge on the map. "The tide will start coming back in, so we need to be on the northern side of the bridge not long after sundown."

Escape seemed less and less likely. Kaiya's chest constricted.

Tian placed several Cathay coins on the map. "The princess dances for the First Consul as promised. However, we move the time up to the Iridescent Moon's second waxing crescent. Move the location to the northern suburbs. We pass back through the northern gate. The wall is deep there. There is a long tunnel. We create a diversion. Stop the palanquin in the tunnel. We switch the princess out. Then she and an escort will take her through the eastern gate. We will need some fast horses waiting on the east side. You can reach Aremarela. One hour at full canter. In the meantime, the *Golden Phoenix* will sail out of the harbor. Up to the mouth of the Alto River. Then down to Aremarela. That will take three hours. So the ship must be ready to disembark by Iridescent Moon's waxing mid-crescent."

Several of the officers nodded.

"It's a variation on the Sword Saint and Night Fox story," Jie said. "From before the Yu Dynasty."

Kaiya shook her head in disbelief. It was amazing how quickly he calculated everything. Still, there was a one glaring problem. "The palanquin is narrow. You will need a long diversion and very simple clothing if you expect me to be able to change in there."

General Zheng cleared his throat. "How do we keep the First Consul from detaining the princess at their meeting?"

How could they? One answer immediately came to Kaiya's mind, though she wondered if she had the ability or will to go through with it. No, it had to be done, and perhaps it would avert the invasion of Iksuvi.

She took a deep breath. "I will kill him myself."

CHAPTER 19:
The Dance of Swords

In the momentary silence that hung over the room, Jie considered the possibility. The princess had never killed anyone before, at least not that she knew of. Then again, she had vanquished a *dragon* with her song. Not many people could say that. Only one other, in fact, in the history of Tivara. She exchanged a look with Tian, whose pursed lips almost distracted her from the slight shake of his head.

"*Dian-xia,*" he said, "forgive my impertinence. Have you ever killed anyone before? You need technique. You need resolve. King Evydas had both. He failed to slay the First Consul."

The princess nodded. "I will perform the *Dance of Swords*. I should be able to hold his attention until it is too late. Between then and now, I will find the resolve."

Jie chewed on her lower lip. A surprise attack. Hardly honorable, but practical. Perhaps being around Black Fists was rubbing off on the princess. Still... "The Eye of Solaris will warn him of an attack." She tapped beneath her right eye.

"Not if I disguise it." The princess stood. "Trust me with the dance. You will handle the small details."

All knelt in acquiescence.

After she glided out of the room, Tian and Jie again exchanged glances. All the things she wanted to say to him would have to wait.

Despite her bravado, Kaiya questioned whether she had the skill or resolve to kill the First Consul with a proverbial underhanded knife in the back. The procession departed the embassy as the Iridescent Moon waxed to its first crescent, with all hundred imperial guards escorting it. She rode astride a horse through the city, even as porters toiled at carrying her palanquin. In the hour it took to reach Iksuvius Heights, a sanctuary reserved for nobility, the doubts Tian had seeded in her mind grew to worry.

Kaiya dismounted and straightened out her maroon gown, while handmaidens fussed over an errant thread in its gold-embroidered borders. As planned, the colors coordinated with the tall wispy trees that flaunted their autumn raiment on either side of the white stone pathway. Her hair was pulled back and fastened with a golden comb, and her cheeks were lightly rouged by *danhua* flowers, her lips tinged a deeper red.

With her imperial guard taking up posts halfway up the hill, she accompanied her handmaidens to the white marble open-air pavilion whose columns crowned the hilltop. Her stomach twisted. Could she really do this?

She twirled around to drink up the panoramic view of the harbor to the west, the Old City to the south, and a long stretch of the Alto River as it twisted from the southeast to its mouth several miles to the north. Two of her ladies set up a *guzheng* outside the circle of columns, while another prepared hot water.

The tightness in her stomach juddered into somersaults.

Below, the First Consul and his contingent rumbled in on warhorses. Dismounting at the base of the Heights, he ambled up the hill. His white toga fluttered behind him. On his command, his retinue of a hundred guards halted halfway up.

Kaiya stole a glance at the Iridescent Moon, now waxing past its second crescent. The plan relied on a narrow window of time, one which Geros tightened more by his slow pace. Ignoring his mismatched eyes, she greeted him with a demure smile. "First Consul, you are late! Please, enter and sit. Unburden yourself from the weighty matters of state."

"You actually came." With a smirk, he presented the plaque.

Thank the Heavens. Bowing her head, she received it in two hands. After passing it to a handmaiden, she motioned toward a pair of plush blue cushions on either side of a low rosewood table in the middle of the pavilion. A hammered iron kettle of water boiled over a small, contained flame at the side of the table, a wooden ladle resting inverted on the kettle top. Next to the kettle, a silver tray held two eggshell porcelain cups, two matching bowls, a tea brush, a sky-blue silken handcloth, a silver tea scooper, and an eight-inch octagonal brocade tube. On the other side lay a pair of lightweight straight swords.

"I am sorry you had to witness the hostilities yesterday." His tone managed to be at once smug and flippant. "Sometimes, our vassals do not agree with the equity of our arrangements."

Kaiya frowned but said nothing, following the First Consul toward the cushions. From behind, his monstrous frame brought into question the wisdom of her plan. He rounded the table, pausing midstride to look at the swords. He glanced back at her, and then shook his head with a grin.

So dismissive, so rude. Her resolve strengthened. She brushed the gown down to her shins and settled to the cushion on both knees. With her left hand holding the end of her long right sleeve, she extended her open right hand in an invitation for the First Consul to sit.

He dropped into a cross-legged position, the thump of his weight on the floor causing the ladle to fall. Kaiya swept it up before it hit the ground and returned it to its position. Distasteful as it was to defer to the tyrant, she bowed low, as ceremony demanded.

The heavens, the acupuncture treatment an hour before kept her nerves settled, even if they left points on her hand and foot sore.

As she straightened, she cast a glance at the matching pair of ceremonial straight swords. The blades lay sheathed in a double scabbard on the marble floors, just within reach.

The instruments of murder. How could a musician, who'd never hurt anyone, become a cold-blooded killer? Her stomach twisted as all resolve faltered.

Kaiya lifted her gaze to the other side of the knee-high table, where the hulking dictator lounged. His white toga exposed sculpted arms and provided little protection from the cool breeze blowing through the gazebo. He yawned, his bored expression suggesting he didn't mind the cold. His eyes followed hers from the weapons, until they met. He snorted. Daring her to try.

So dismissive. And why not? He loomed a head and chest taller, his enormous frame at least twice her size. He'd likely killed hundreds of enemies in battle even before her birth. Her pulse skittered like a tentative rabbit. Forget resolve. Maybe she didn't have the skill to hurt him.

Still, she couldn't betray weakness to this despot. Kaiya closed her eyes, letting the gentle thrum of the handmaiden's zither settle her racing heart. Both his and her guards waited outside the hilltop gazebo, halfway down the slope. They could see everything, but stood too far away to intervene. In here, it was just her and two handmaidens.

And two ceremonial swords.

Without magic to balance out his advantages in size, skill, and experience, the odds looked bleak. No, it would be foolish to even try. There had to be some way to escape, without gambling on a desperate attack—one which would leave a stain on her soul even if she somehow succeeded.

Kaiya opened her eyes to find his leer on her. His wolfish grin left no doubt as to what he wanted. His gaze roved over her, as if formulating a plan of attack with her curves as the battlefield. Her only defense was a gown, and the gold comb which held up her hair.

And the two swords, which weren't meant for actual combat.

She was powerless and trapped. The calm she'd felt from the acupuncture all but slipped away. Maybe she should've asked Doctor Fang to sedate her, to keep her from embarking on this foolish endeavor in the first place.

Stomach hollow, Kaiya shook the terrifying thoughts of being pinned beneath this dictator out of her head.

Disguise strength in weakness, her ancestor had written. In these dire circumstances, it meant acting demure and deferring to the male ego. It was all part of her upbringing anyway. She could do this.

But first, he needed to lower his guard. What better way than to serve? With her left hand holding the end of her right sleeve, Kaiya leaned forward to the tea set on the table. She lifted the kettle and poured into his eggshell cup. "Please," she offered with a bow of her head. "Admire the tea's color and savor its aroma before taking a sip."

Eyeing the cup with a frown, the First Consul pushed it back across the table. "You first, My Lady."

Such vulgar behavior. Still, the situation required hiding her disgust and fitting his image of the weaker sex. Kaiya lowered her head while still maintaining coy eye contact through her lashes. She covered her mouth with a hand and softly laughed. "First Consul, it is not our custom to poison even our most hated foes when serving them tea. And while Cathay and the Teleri Empire have our differences, we are certainly not enemies. But if you insist."

Kaiya took up the cup in both hands, reveling in its warmth. She closed her eyes and took in a long sniff. Her shoulders relaxed and her concerns unwound. Bringing the cup to her lips, she took a sip. With a smile, she returned the cup to the table, with an unfortunate hint of red from her lip balm.

As Kaiya reached for the kettle to fill the unused cup, Geros snatched up the one she'd just sipped from. The contrast of his large, rough hands emphasized the dish's delicate lines. It was a miracle he didn't crush it between his stout thumb and forefinger. Holding her gaze the entire time, he emptied it into his mouth and gulped it down without so much as pausing to savor its scent or flavor. He wiped his mouth with his sleeve, and then thrust the cup onto the table.

Barbaric. To think such uncultured thugs ruled over the world's largest empire. Looking up from the two swords, she forced her expression into indifference. "First Consul, how can you enjoy the tea if you wolf it down like so? Appreciation of tea reflects our appreciation of life. Without simple pleasures, what is the purpose in living?"

The First Consul scowled. "As I told you, we have little use for extravagance. Ultimately, as your own ancestor said, *the world will be brought to peace and order by the sword*. I have studied him in depth, and highly doubt tea, or your haughty manners, could achieve the same results."

"Yet the Founder was highly cultured and known for appreciating fine tea."

He slammed his open hand onto the table with so much force that the cups fell over. Kaiya's stomach jumped into her throat.

"My patience wears thin, Princess. There are lands to bring under Teleri order. Enough of this idle talk. Let us see your dance so we can continue with more enjoyable endeavors."

Kaiya hid her sinking heart behind a pleasant smile. There were no redeeming qualities in this brute. No signs of repentance for his empire's evil deeds. His death would save countless others. Would Heaven take that into account when it judged her for the evil deed she was about to commit?

She waved towards her handmaidens to clear the floor of the table, cushions, and tea set. After bowing as etiquette demanded, she smoothed out her dress and picked up the scabbard.

The First Consul leaned forward and grabbed her forearm in an iron grip. His huge hand seemed large enough to wrap around her slender wrist twice. He yanked her toward him with a menacing glare, and she thrust her free hand down to keep from falling on her face.

With his other hand, he withdrew one of the swords to half its length. It was a thin, supple blade meant for ceremony and performance. Though it held a sharp edge, it lacked the tensile strength for thrusting.

Her calm façade slipped. He'd never intended to watch the dance. Heavens, he was going to take her now, before she could even attempt to kill him. Fear coursed up her spine like a spear of ice. Her arms and legs froze, ignoring every instinct which screamed to pull away and flee. Her words came out in a stuttered squeak. "Please, First Consul, you are hurting me."

The two handmaidens at the edge of the pavilion shuffled over in their own restrictive gowns, though not even the three of them would be able to overpower the man.

"Would you try to assassinate me?" He drew the sword to its full length and wiggled it with a patronizing grin. "With these toys? You have been eyeing them this whole time."

So he'd suspected a trap, despite her best efforts to disguise it. Kaiya's pulse galloped. Again she spoke, her voice sounding like an eight-year-old version of herself. "Please... I just need these for my performance, the *Dance of Swords.*" As if he cared about her plea.

Geros smirked. If he intended to intimidate her, it was working. Rising to his feet while forcibly dragging her up, he pulled her close. Her heart pounded up against his hard belly, while something unpleasantly firm pressed against hers. He brought his face down close. His breath burned hot against her face. "Very well. Dance!" He pushed her arm as he let go of her, and she stumbled back.

Her handmaidens came to her side and supported her by the arms. Her entire body shook of its own accord. Heavens, no one had ever manhandled her like that.

At least she'd been wrong. For whatever reason, he was letting her dance before proceeding with the worst kind of assault. She had to remain calm, if only to reassure her handmaidens.

She pressed two of the points Doctor Fang had needled, *Tian-tu* in the divot at the base of her neck, then *Dan-Zhong* in the center of her chest. Combined with a deep breath, her pulse settled.

"It's all right," she said in the Cathayi tongue. "Return to your places. Play the music on my signal."

Bowing low, they shuffled back. They'd share the same fate if she failed.

Her wrist ached from where Geros had seized it, and she rubbed the *Wai-Guan* point there. A wiggle of her pinkie toe stimulated *Lin-Qi.* The calming effect allowed her breath to slow, and was gentle enough to avoid causing damage to her Qi meridians.

She turned to face the tyrant, and gestured to the cushions on the eastern edge of the gazebo. "Please, First Consul, sit facing the west. That way, the harbor below and the autumn trees above may serve as a backdrop for my dance."

The Bovyan flashed a grin before strutting over to the cushion and dropping into a cross-legged seat. He crossed his arms. "Get on with it."

Kaiya motioned to the handmaidens. One strummed a slow, tremolo tune on the zither, while the other joined in with the plucking of a lute. Borrowing the music's vibrations, she forced her hands to stop trembling. She unsheathed the swords and took up a position in the middle of the floor. Curving her body like an elephant tusk, she held both blades behind her back in her left hand with an underhanded grasp. Even if she couldn't use musical magic against him directly, she could borrow it to lend her strength.

Her heart beat with the resolute rhythm of the zither, while her breath united with the plucks of the lute. With the energy of the duet coursing through her, Kaiya swept her arms up to meet one another and split the swords into either hand. Weightless as clouds, she twirled in an arc.

From this opening, Kaiya continued her dance, transitioning from position to position with graceful precision, orchestrated to the varying tempo of the zither. She never held a pose for more than a split second, making it appear as if she were in constant motion, moving and transitioning as if she were a wisp of smoke, seamlessly transformed by a gently shifting breeze.

Losing herself in the performance, she let the vibrations of the world propel her effortlessly through the dance. She was safe in this state, the fear and humiliation of the First Consul's physical intimidation melting away. The aches in her acupuncture points subsided. The blades became one with her, swirling and shaking in harmony with the music.

In the corner of her eye, the First Consul sat spellbound. Not through the magic of music, but rather through the connection between performer and audience.

For a few fleeting seconds, they shared that bond, where both found spiritual calm.

There it was, his humanity. Just a moment prior, he was an evil monster responsible for the misery of millions. One intent on violating her and her handmaidens. Now he was simply a living, breathing man. How could she kill him?

Him or her. He would have no reservations, but that was what separated them. Her window of opportunity was closing quickly. Time to make a decision.

Coming from a culture that considered women to be little more than breeders and objects of carnal pleasure, First Consul Geros Bovyan found Princess Kaiya to be an enigma. On the one hand, he found himself begrudgingly admiring her for her poise and quick wit; yet he despised the girl because she challenged all of his assumptions of the *weaker* sex. More than anything, he wanted to punish her for embarrassing him.

When he had seized her in his grip, he had broken her spirit. It was obvious from the fear in her eyes, the tremble in her hand. From then on, he assumed a bored expression, waiting for her to finish this silly performance so that he could get on with showing her just what a woman was good for in Teleri.

Yet now, as she willowed through her dance, Geros could not contain his respect for her. Though a Bovyan would care little for elegant style or intangible beauty, he found himself appreciating the martial aspects of the dance—the exacting cuts and thrusts, the sweeping parries and redirections, the elusive slips and weaves. The Eye of Solaris, usually reliable in predicting attack vectors with red lines across his vision, mis-identified movements on several occasions. It was so different from the brute power of the Bovyans' fighting style!

And yet, the subtlety so mirrored his own strategy of deception, which had broken the long stalemate with the Eldaeri Kingdoms and opened the Eastern Campaign. It would soon engulf the Northwest as well. Within a few years, it would put the empire on the doorstep of Cathay itself, which would be ripe for the picking because of the spy he had planted there years before. How ironic that these were the lessons he had learned from studying the military, diplomatic, and economic acumen of Princess Kaiya's own ancestor, Wang Xinchang.

The combination of the gentle strumming of the Cathayi musical instrument, the mesmerizing motions, and the warming sensation of the tea lulled him into a state of tranquility. For this brief moment, he forgot all about the world events that he was shaping, and cared little for his own ambitions.

Time seemed to slow. The princess and her swords flattened into the surroundings as if she were the moving subject of an oil painting. The wispy trees in the background gently waved at the clouds drifting above.

She lunged at him with her sword. Sun reflected off the blade, flashing into his eyes and blinding him. Though the Eye of Solaris adjusted, it was all he could do to scuttle backward out of her reach.

The blade tip in her right hand sword cut though the cloth holding his pin in place. With a surgical spin and reverberating shake, the blade sent the pin flying high into the air. The left followed instantly with a precise, shallow insertion of the tip into the center of his sternum. The right blade whirled in a circle, cut through his boot and nicked a spot on his left little toe; and the left arced back to scratch yet another spot on the outer part of his right wrist.

The entire sequence must have taken no longer than a second. The princess ended in a cross-legged squat, her left sword again held behind her back in an underhand grip, and her right blade tip planted shallowly in the divot at the base of his neck.

Time resumed its normal flow as she withdrew her right sword with a smooth flip and passed it behind her back into her left hand to join its twin. Gaze locked with his, she extended her right arm out again. His pin dropped neatly into her outstretched hand.

She'd attacked! Yet all he could do was focus on her elegant pose. Geros could not help but admire her. Had she been born a Bovyan man, perhaps she would be First Consul, soon to be Emperor, instead of him.

Nonetheless, she had disengaged, leaving him uninjured. Nothing hurt. Now to end this charade.

He moved to stand. His muscles refused to respond. He tried to clench a fist, to no avail. What was happening?

Geros looked at the areas her toy sword had struck. They felt numb and heavy, though there did not seem to be much blood. One more attempt to stand. Nothing!

He called out for his guards, but no words came out. Only a hissing whisper.

"I have spared your life today," the princess said as she spun to her feet. "I have closed off four energy centers of your body: your Yin reserves are obstructed and pooling at *Tian-Tu* on your neck and *Dan-Zhong* on your chest; your Yang vitality is locked and stagnant at *Wai-Guan* on your wrist and *Lin-Qi* on your foot."

It was all gibberish, but the effect left no doubt: he was helpless. Devious whore!

Her expression remained grave, devoid of satisfaction. "You will not be able to move, nor speak louder than a whisper, until you are treated by one who understands the *Dao*. There is such a doctor at our compound's temple. I suggest you make use of his services by sunrise tomorrow, or your injury shall likely be permanent."

Lying helpless, Geros envisioned all of his well-laid plans slipping from his grasp. This visit to the Northwest should have cemented his place in Teleri lore. The edict he had forced through the Directori, with pressure from the Keepers of the Shrine of Geros, would have crowned him First Emperor. These were now meaningless. He was an invalid, spared by the mercy of a girl.

"Treacherous bitch!" he croaked. "You had better kill me now, or else I will surely hunt you down and force you into a life of misery, fear, and humiliation. I shall make the crushing of Cathay my sole reason for living."

She shifted back a step, lips quivering and eyes wide. Her knuckles whitened around the sword hilt. Yes—he had intimidated her, sown the seeds of fear in her. Perhaps that would be the final pleasure he would enjoy in this life.

As quickly as it came, her fearful expression flickered away, replaced by a pity that only infuriated him more. "Until you cherish life, starting with your own, you will never truly find inner peace." Picking up the scabbards, she sheathed her weapons and motioned for her handmaidens. "Leave it all, we must make haste."

They walked past him, beyond his line of sight. Unable to turn his head, he lay stranded on silken cushions. Hatred stewed inside him, roaring louder than the Cathayi musket volleys from the slope.

CHAPTER 20:
Escape from Iksuvius

Shouts and jingling armor greeted Kaiya as she emerged from the pavilion. Her imperial guards were deployed in three ranks halfway up the hill, standing between her and the advancing Teleri phalanx. Spears protruded between the enemy's shields as they approached, trampling down the grass as they came.

She might not have an eye for strategy, but it was clear: the wider Teleri line could envelop her own men.

The imperial guards were all armed with muskets, which had been hidden in her palanquin. *Her* idea.

"Fire!" General Zheng's command was answered with a rumble of musket fire from the first rank. The volley tore through the wall of shields and into the Teleri line. Several gaps opened as men fell with grunts and screams. Kaiya shuddered, memories of her few brushes with combat roiling her stomach.

With the precision of a dwarf water clock, the Bovyans in the rear line lifted their spears. Wherever there was a hole, a soldier stepped forward to fill it, while several men on either side of the front line fell back to the back line. They reset their spears. Some injured men rose to form a reserve in the rear. Astoundingly, the wall's advance continued during the entire position shift.

At the same time, the front line of Cathay soldiers stood and retreated to the rear to reload while the second rank knelt and took aim. On General Zheng's command, they unleashed another volley and stepped to the rear.

Kaiya's heart raced. Would the imperial guards be able to stop the Bovyan advance? Hundreds of armies had fallen to their charge.

The continuous barrage of musket fire took its toll. The Bovyan ranks began to falter as the injured men slowed their approach. Smoke and the stench of gunpowder hung in the air. Bodies littered the ground. In just two minutes, half the soldiers lay dead or incapacitated.

A Teleri officer bellowed the order to charge. The Bovyans broke rank and surged forward. Kaiya's hands ran cold and clammy.

General Zheng's voice carried over the din as he raised his *dao*. "Fire and form a single bow!"

Kaiya watched in dread fascination. The first rank of imperial guards unleashed a final volley and fanned out into a half-ellipse. The third rank followed them as they formed a single curved line, with the second rank occupying the center as they finished reloading.

"Take aim!" General Zheng's voice boomed, and all the imperial guards lowered their rifles. As far as Kaiya could tell, only a third held loaded weapons.

The Teleri officer barked out a command. The remaining Bovyans halted their advance and formed up into a tight square, shields facing outward. Perhaps only twenty remained within the main group, while others littered the blood-soaked hillside. Kaiya blew out a breath. General Zheng's bluff had worked.

He now stepped to the head of his troops. "Brave Teleri soldiers, you are hopelessly outnumbered and outgunned. Do not needlessly waste your lives. Surely we will meet on the battlefield again so that you might have a chance to avenge your brothers."

The spears jutted out from the defensive square, and the formation resumed its advance, albeit more slowly. Even if General Zheng's trickery had deceived them, apparently they were willing to walk into certain death. Maybe not so certain, unless the imperial guards could reload.

Kaiya pushed through her men, fighting the rising nausea from the sight of blood and gore. She pointed back to the gazebo. "The First Consul lies at the top of the Heights, helpless and dying. If you die here, on this hill, he will certainly perish as well. Surrender now, and we will send someone who can heal him. You have my word."

A Teleri officer stepped forward, spear held aloft. "The First Consul would rather die than to live at your mercy."

Kaiya closed her eyes and listened. His voice carried across the hill, its strong resonance picked up by the steadfast beating of his men's hearts. Behind her, the imperial guards' heart rates stuttered. They might win with superior numbers, but not without serious casualties.

Gripping the ground with her toes through her slippers, she channeled the world's resolute pulse. Modulating her voice to interfere with the frequencies of the Bovyans' heartbeats, she sang her command: "Surrender."

The Teleri line wavered. The officer lowered his spear. "Stand down. Drop your arms."

Kaiya's shoulders sagged as she let out another sigh. In the three centuries since the Bovyans appearance in Tivaralan, had any ever laid down their spears or shields?

General Zheng turned to her. "*Dian-xia*, this is the first time the Teleri have seen our battlefield tactics. Though it pains my honor as a soldier, I recommend that we execute them to the man so that none can speak of it."

Eyes wide, Kaiya shook her head. "I gave my word."

"You gave your word to send someone to heal the First Consul." He stared at her feet.

If they resorted to such technicalities, they'd be no better than the Teleri. Kaiya shook her head. "You will spare them. Let them take their wounded to the Heights, and tie the able-bodied to the columns so they cannot follow us."

"That will take time."

Kaiya looked up at the Iridescent Moon. Her sense of morality clashed with her instinct for self-preservation. "Then I bid you hurry."

On the general's orders, the imperial guards helped the disarmed soldiers bring their wounded to the top of the Heights to join their Consul. Uninjured Bovyans were tied to the columns, while the imperial guards tended to the wounded.

Kaiya helped over the protests of her men since, as General Zheng had said, valuable time was slipping away. It was not until twenty minutes later, halfway between the Iridescent Moon's mid- and fourth crescents, that the procession was ready to return to the Old City.

Kaiya now rode in the palanquin, struggling in the tight confines to strip off her gown. Had they really hidden a hundred muskets in here? Her fingers trembled as she wrapped a broad cloth around her bosom several times to flatten it out as best she could. Lastly, she squirmed into the simple brown robes of the Cathayi monks who wandered the lands.

The light filtering in through the palanquin windows darkened. Her soldiers' footsteps echoed on stone floors. They must have entered the long tunnel through the northern gate. Shouts erupted from up ahead.

Then the procession ground to a halt.

Jie looked up at the ninety-foot watchtower above the northern gatehouse. She had snuck up there one afternoon and enjoyed the spectacular view of the northern coast.

Yet today, it cast a shadow over the bustling northern marketplace. She shivered and returned to the task at hand, wondering why the princess' procession had not yet arrived.

Jie had come at dawn to set up a stand selling pork buns, right by the side of the main road. It provided a good line of sight into the gatehouse tunnel, where Tian waited, dressed as a wandering monk.

The Nothori people apparently had little interest in pork buns, a favorite among the Cathayi. Even if hawking fattening snacks wasn't her real purpose in being there, the slow business was disappointing. It did, however, give her plenty of time to glance over at Tian. Once the princess had safely boarded the *Golden Phoenix* and he returned to the embassy, they'd have plenty of time to sort out whatever it was between them. Her heart fluttered.

They had to get the princess on the ship first, though, which meant focusing on the task at hand. Just after giving a repeat customer a generous deal, Jie's ears perked. The boots of marching men approached. At last! They were behind schedule. She craned her neck to get a clear line of sight on Tian.

There was his signal. Jie grabbed ahold of a citizen who had the misfortune of passing by at the wrong moment. Who cared if he had little interest in pork buns? "You! Give it back! That's eight copper *kroon*."

"What? What are you talking about?"

Jie shoved him. "The pork bun. You took one of my pork buns!"

The man stepped back, hands raised. "I didn't. I wouldn't eat that junk anyway! And it's not worth eight coppers."

Bystanders gathered around and pointed, while Iksuvi soldiers tried to clear the way.

Jie only argued louder. She deftly kicked out the legs of her stand, sending pork buns rolling into the road. Street urchins scrambled forward to capture the delicious prizes.

General Zheng marched to the head of the procession, now stalled by Jie's show, to snarl at her in the Arkothi tongue. "Clear the road, woman! Your princess is passing through."

Jie cursed him and all of his ancestors with Arkothi vulgarities that surpassed the limitation of Cathay's sterile language. A large crowd pushed forward to watch, pointing and laughing at the fracas.

Jie smiled. Mission accomplished. The Teleri Nightblade she'd been eyeing had missed the exchange.

Tian had waited in the northern gate tunnel with a real Cathayi monk, begging for alms as people passed. Both wore long, round straw hats whose brims sank down to eye level, though Tian's long hair made it difficult to secure. Besides a walking staff, the only other weapon he carried was a concealed dagger and several throwing stars and spikes.

Travelers were sparse, donations even sparser. If he had to wait much longer in the musty chill, he'd catch a cold. Not to mention the princess might not make her ship. She was already an hour behind schedule.

At last, her procession came through. It stopped and she stepped out of the palanquin. The monk handed her his hat, revealing his bald head. She put it on, tilting it forward so that her face was slightly covered. All performed with admirable precision.

When she'd finished stuffing her hair in the cone, she placed a letter in his hand. "Have this delivered to the ambassador immediately."

The monk nodded as he bent into the palanquin. Tian looked through the tunnel, into the city.

Just in time. Up ahead, the Iksuvi soldiers had restored order. With loud shouts and a little jostling, they cleared a path through the streets and the procession continued. As the crowds dispersed, Tian guided Kaiya through the northern gate and into the city.

He looked up at the Iridescent Moon, already waxing to its fourth crescent. They were running well behind schedule. Not a word passed between them as they walked toward the eastern gate, briskly heading south along the main road that ran from the northern gate to the southern gate. They turned east on a ring road that bypassed the city center and intersected with the main east-west road.

Tian stole glances at the handful of people they passed along the way. They didn't pick up any followers; at least this part of the plan was working. Not only that, they were making up for lost time. They would make it.

Waiting at the intersection of the ring road and the east-west road were the princess' five most senior guards, all dressed as wandering monks: Chen Xin, the leader, followed by Zhao Yue, Ma Jun, Li Wei, and Xu Zhan. They dropped to a knee, right fists to the ground.

Unbelievable. Eyes darting left and right, Tian beckoned them to their feet. Leave it to an imperial guard to expose their disguise. Luckily, the streets were nearly deserted.

Chen Xin bowed his head. "There are rumors that the Teleri western army is about to pass through Aremarela. If it is true, they must have moved their timetable up."

Tian shook his head. They couldn't risk crossing the bridge into Teleri and running into an army. Picturing the area in his head, he drew up a new plan. "Change of plans. We pass through the southern gate. There's a fishing village on the Iksuvi side of the river. About fifteen *li* south. Not far from Aremarela on the opposite bank. We can commandeer a fishing boat. Then row back up."

Xu Zhan growled. "We need to meet up with the stablemaster, who is waiting with horses outside of the eastern gate." Always pugnacious, Xu would likely prefer to test his sword against the entire Teleri division instead of running away from them.

Li Wei counted on his fingers. "It will take too long to row from the village to Aremarela. Our horses wouldn't be fast enough to ride from the eastern gate to the southern gate, and then down to the village anyway."

If there was anyone who expected anything and everything to go wrong, it was him. The unforeseen change only validated his bleak outlook on life.

The princess sighed. "Your plan has failed, Zheng Tian. We should just head back to the safety of the embassy."

Tian's mind ran calculations. "We can't hole up in the embassy indefinitely. The Teleri will lay siege. We must press on with this plan. Let's hasten to the Kanin Embassy. They're no friends of the Teleri. And the ambassador was impressed by the princess. If they loan us some of their horses, we can make it."

Ma Jun, the opposite of his best friend Li, was always optimistic. "*Dian-xia*, the idea is sound. We will make it."

All attention turned to the princess.

"We will never make it in time." Li Wei shook his head.

Tian pursed his lips. It was a sound plan. It would work.

The princess' eyes searched his. "Very well. To the Kanin embassy."

The Kanin compound was located just off of the ring road, in the southeast section of the Old City. It took fifteen minutes, and they arrived as the Iridescent Moon waxed halfway between its fourth and fifth crescents. Still more than enough time.

Except for the gate guards doubting that the ragged monk before their eyes was the Princess of Cathay. She removed her hat and shook out her hair, and the gaping guards allowed them entry. Tian glanced back at the handful of passersby. Hopefully, no one had seen her.

They were brought to a comfortable receiving room, where Tian planted himself by a window. The floors were uncarpeted stone, and oil paintings of scenes from the Kanin plains hung on the walls. The princess examined the portrait of their rugged king, whose likeness gazed over the entire room.

Tian fidgeted. Iridescent Moon was passing its fifth crescent.

This was taking too long. Perhaps Ambassador Manuwaya had already started drinking.

The old man shuffled in with a red face and a wide smile. Tian gritted his teeth. Suspicions confirmed.

"Welcome, welcome!" the ambassador said. "We are honored by your visit. Though you are certainly curiously dressed. To what do I owe this pleasure?"

The princess stood up and bowed. "Ambassador, I have some important information, and also a humble request of your great kingdom. The Teleri Empire will be invading Iksuvius with overwhelming force tonight, while the Kingdom of Lietuvi will cross the southern border in support. Iksuvi's days are numbered."

Ambassador Manuwaya stared at her, his eyes shifting to Tian.

Tian nodded. Of course the ambassador would trust him. They'd worked together many times. Now if only the princess would hurry up with that humble request.

"In addition," she said, "The Teleri First Consul is plotting to take me hostage, and plans for my escape have run into unforeseen obstacles. I beg you to please provide us with horses, since your great steeds are the only ones fast enough to reach our rendezvous point in time."

The ambassador nodded his head. "Of course, of course, my dear. We certainly cannot allow a precious jewel like you to fall into the hands of the Teleri! No telling what demands they will make of your father."

Tian shuffled on his feet. The First Consul probably had other plans for the princess. The leverage he wanted had little to do with politics.

The princess bowed at the waist. "I will never forget this. When I reach the safety of Cathay, I will ask my father to send me personally to Kanin to deliver a set of our finest teacups. I extend my deepest thanks and appreciation for your help."

The ambassador provided them with seven horses. The Cathayi packed away their monks' clothes, then donned black-lacquered leather jerkins and painted red Kanin symbols on their face. Armed with borrowed cavalry sabers, lances, and short bows, they would hopefully pass as a Kanin patrol.

It helped that the Cathayi and Kanin people looked similar to the untrained eye. Tian's were not untrained, however—to him, each difference was glaring as a noon sun. Someone would notice. And the Iridescent Moon had already waxed past its fifth crescent. Almost no margin of error.

"It is not too late to turn back to the embassy," Li Wei said.

Tian eyed his enormous horse, famed for its speed. "It's not too late to make it, either." Even with the time wasted at the Kanin embassy.

CHAPTER 21:
Personality Clashes

Kaiya's ears rang from the constant pounding of horse hooves on the paved highway. In fact, her entire body vibrated after an hour of hard riding. Their Kanin guide looked none the worse for wear, unlike her tired guards. He'd had to stop several times to allow them to catch up.

She cast a jealous eye at him as the journal of the famous Minister Deng Liansu came to mind.

In all my travels, I was aided by the Kanin and their thoroughbreds. Though trapped between the Ayuri and Arkothi empires, the Kanin empire has maintained its nominal independence through a series of shrewd, if brazen, switches of allegiance. None of Tivara's people can raise the horse like they, born in the saddle, learning to ride before they walk. A Kanin, it is said, stands on his own four feet.

Wherever this ride ended, she probably wouldn't be able to stand on *two* feet.

Despite Tian's concerns and Li Wei's pessimism, they didn't encounter any problems, either in the city or the fields and woods on the way to the village. A windswept wooden sign at the outskirts named the community as *Gaukaimos*. Dirt roads crisscrossed the paved highway, lined by some hundred squat homes with thatched roofs.

Kaiya wrinkled her nose. From what Tian had told her on the way, the locals farmed mollusks and fished for a living. The stink of shellfish left little doubt of that.

When they came to a stone bridge over a stream, Kaiya looked up. Iridescent Moon was waxing to half-crescent. Her hands ached from gripping the reins so tightly, and her heart raced. There was very little time left.

Tian led them down a dirt road to a stone-lined embankment. The top, some six feet above the water, gave a commanding view of the river. On the banks, children played and collected shells. Their laughter carried over the whisper of small waves lapping against the shore. Numerous boat landings jutted into the channel.

Kaiya gasped. Plenty of fishing boats plied the waters, but none were moored to the docks. No way to cross the river to Aremarela. Maybe there was a boat within earshot. She scanned up and down the river.

There, maybe five *li* southeast in Aremarela, the *Golden Phoenix* lifted anchor. With sails down and oars extended, it began heading downriver. Towards them! Sticking to the deep channel which cut unseen through the middle of the river, the ship's course would take it right by. Maybe more than a *li* away from them, and closer to the Teleri shore, but surely the captain would send a boat out.

Without waiting for her permission, Tian and her guards dismounted and ran down the closest dock. Kaiya's heart soared, though she kept her demeanor calm as she followed. As the *Golden Phoenix* approached, they waved and yelled. Someone onboard would just have to see—

Musket fire cracked, echoing across the water. Smoke rose from the ship. Another volley. Who were they shooting at?

Tian patted at his leather jerkin, then withdrew a spyglass. He brought it to his eye, but then lowered the instrument and examined it. He shook his head. "Broken lens."

Broken lens? How could the supposedly brilliant planner not check his equipment? Kaiya looked back towards the ship, now speeding northward. "Can the horses swim out?"

Their guide raised a hand. "No; even our best thoroughbreds would not make it before your ship passed."

"With the tide coming in," Tian said, "the *Phoenix* would be stranded on the river for six hours. By then, every Bovyan within fifty-two *li* will know of your attack on the First Consul. The captain has no choice. He has to escape to open seas. And use the last rays of sun to help navigate the deep channel."

Li Wei threw his arms up. "I told you this wouldn't work. Now they know we are here."

"No," Tian said. "Not necessarily. The *Golden Phoenix* fired at the Teleri side of the river. It was anchored at a Teleri town. They would assume the princess was there. If not already on the ship."

Maybe. Still, Kaiya watched in despair as her means of escape disappeared north through the river, racing against time. For now, they were stuck in this backwater, fetid village, caught between a city in turmoil and the contingent of altivorcs approaching it.

Sore all over, she sighed. They'd wasted too much time on the Heights, a half hour that could've been used to flee.

Her decision. Her fault.

A lone tear trickled down her cheek. She wiped it away, the coarse sleeve of the Kanin tunic scouring her skin.

It wouldn't do to let her retainers see her like this. Heavens, she'd confronted Avarax without melting into a quivering mass of tears. Straightening her back, she composed herself before facing them.

"Be strong, *Dian-xia*." Tian must have seen her crying. His encouraging tone rang with patronization, and his smile was forced.

Be strong. Easy for him to say. *She* was the one who'd almost been violated, just three hours before. Who still faced that risk. The memory of the First Consul pressing against her sent a shudder through her body.

Tian continued, inconsiderate and undeterred, "We should be safe here. For now. There was an inn. Near the entrance to the village. Let us rest there. Think of a new plan. At least there... we will avoid the chaos in Iksuvius tonight."

Kaiya bit her lower lip, fighting back more tears. Oh, to be safely home, where the food wouldn't make her sick. Out of the reach of a Bovyan tyrant who planned to take a very personal revenge on her. Tian couldn't understand. At least as a child, he would have tried.

She nodded at his suggestion, nonetheless. She couldn't summon a dignified tone, and her voice sounded childlike in her ears. "Lead the way to the inn."

The Kanin Rider swept his hand out from his heart. "I will take your leave and return to the city. Do you wish me to bring any message to the ambassador?"

She forced a brittle smile. "Please convey my gratitude to him."

"May the wind ever be at your back, Princess." Waving his hand out in an arc, he spurred his horse north at full gallop.

With Tian leading, they rode their borrowed horses towards the inn. Their motley crew attracted curious looks. They arrived as the sun winked out over the horizon.

In the fading light, the inn appeared to be a decent size—the only two-story building in the village thus far—and made of wood planks that had weathered years of brackish winds. A faded sign hung above the door: *The Hard Shell.* The Arkothi words were painted in a simple hand below brightly colored images of various crustaceans and mollusks.

Kaiya fought back the rebellion in her stomach. The name might refer to the food or the quality of bedding. Maybe both. Not much different from being aboard the *Golden Phoenix*, really, except for the danger of being captured and raped. Her insides twisted again. This danger... she'd invited it by doing the right thing and sparing Geros and his men. It was too unfair.

A second look at the sign evoked another obvious shudder, her vulnerability on display. She lifted her chin and hid fragility behind stubborn conceit. "I can't stay *there*. There has to somewhere else."

"*Dian-xia*. It's dark now." Tian shook his head, his tone reminiscent of a nursemaid. "The closest inn is back in the city. This will have to do."

Her shoulders trembled against her attempts to square them and suppress the sobs wracking her body. She let a cascade of hair hide her weakness.

Tian dismounted and came to her, extending his hand. "Please. Let's go in. Rest a while." His short sentences, so endearing as a youth, now sounded like a rebuke.

Refusing his hand, she clasped the reins tightly and turned to look down in the other direction. There had to be another option. Keep moving, find somewhere to hide. Just not here.

He seized her wrist firmly and tugged.

The impudence! Kaiya resisted and tried to withdraw her hand. Her despair transformed into anger, and she found her voice. "Guards!"

It was an unequivocal order, yet the five imperial guards looked among each other without moving from their places. Finally, Chen Xin bowed his head and his juniors followed suit. She was alone in this battle of wills.

"Please," Tian said.

A little late for a request. She'd already lost face. She pulled back away from him.

Tian's growl was nothing like his childhood sweetness, and he gave her a push.

The nerve! She leaned back towards him so as not to fall off the horse. A sudden pain bloomed in her wrist as he twisted it and caused her to lurch sideways. With a sharp gasp of protest, she tumbled into his arms. He dumped her unceremoniously on her feet and pulled her toward the door of the inn.

It was worse than when the First Consul had grabbed her. At least then, it'd been an enemy. At least then, her handmaidens had supported her. Now, even the imperial guards refused to intervene.

Humiliated and defeated, she surrendered and allowed Tian to drag her toward the inn. Hair curtained her face as she hung her head, but anyone could tell she was crying from the unconstrained sobs. So much for maintaining a dignified façade.

At least he could be less rude. If he only had a fraction of chivalry, like his sophisticated, charming brother.

Tian motioned toward the guards. "You four come with us. Don't show the princess any extra attention. Xu Zhan, you stable the horses. Keep guard outside the main entrance. One of us will relieve you. Soon."

The stench of steaming shellfish assaulted her nose as soon as the door opened. Her stomach churned. Kaiya covered her mouth.

The Hard Shell, despite its weathered exterior, was actually quite comfortable on the inside. About twenty round tables, each surrounded by several empty chairs, occupied the spacious main room. Covered in soot, a large unlit hearth stood at the far end.

A balding barkeep paced behind the smooth bar, drying off tankards and ignoring the four locals who sat there. While they laughed over mugs of red wheat beer and shared fish stories, a fifth man folded his arms on the bar and cradled his head face-down.

Kaiya didn't resist as Tian pulled her to a table close to the hearth. He motioned her to a chair so that her back faced most of the room, while he plopped down across from her. The four guards took up other chairs, two on either side of her.

"Let's eat something," Tian said. "I need to think."

He should have thought things through before. Kaiya gnawed on her lip.

An uncomfortable silence hung over the table until a barmaid came and listed what was on the menu for that night. Kaiya's skin prickled. All the main dishes included some sort of shellfish.

Without even asking her, Tian ordered a cheap clam dish and potatoes for each of them. She didn't have the energy to protest. Only Zhao Yue, who loved to eat, seemed pleased by the choice.

She beckoned the barmaid over. "Please bring a quill, ink, and paper."

The server shrugged. "Will you be staying the night?"

Tian's eyes flicked toward the bar for a second before turning back. He nodded. "What's available?" His gaze shifted back to the bar.

Kaiya focused her hearing in that direction, picking out the deep, slow breathing of one of the men. He was pretending to be asleep.

The barmaid's screechy voice interrupted her concentration. "We have two small singles, four doubles, and three large common rooms that sleep eight."

The jingle of Tian's pouch under the table sang of copper coins. There was disappointment in his voice. "We will take seven beds. In a common room."

Share a room with men? How could the son of a prominent family be so inconsiderate and uncultured? That, after he treated her like a child and ordered food for her. And he'd told her guards to ignore her. Who was *he* to punish *her*? She shot Tian a furious scowl.

He returned it with an aloof rise of his eyebrow, and then turned away.

That was too much. "Young Lord Zheng—"

Tian's livid glare bore into her, and his hand signal made it clear that she was not to talk.

Heat flared in her cheeks. Who was the princess, and who was the half-rate spy?

The barmaid grinned at them, muttering "lover's quarrel" under her breath. She thrust a charcoal pencil into Kaiya's hands. "Sorry, we don't have a quill or ink down here, though there should be one in the room."

Kaiya glowered at Chen Xin, sure that he would understand her silent order. *Go get the writing instruments, or there will be hell to pay later.*

Chen Xin looked from her to Tian and back before standing, bowing his head, and hurrying towards the steps.

Kaiya turned her head to watch him go. The sleeping man at the bar shifted on his stool.

An awkward silence hung over the table. Kaiya crossed her arms and turned her head to the side, while Tian leaned back in his chair and stared at the table. She would glance back at him, only to find his eyes on her, and jerk her head back.

Chen Xin returned and interrupted their battle of wills, placing a quill and inkwell in front of her with a bow of his head. His voice trembled. "There was no paper."

It was all she could do to keep from throwing her hands in the air. With a sigh, Kaiya withdrew the love letter from the dashing lord from her tunic.

Tian couldn't believe that this petulant girl had once been a stately and confident princess. When future historians extolled the legendary charmer of dragons, he hoped his own ancestors would be around to tell his side of the story.

The letter could have been an imperial heirloom, the way she gazed at it. She unfolded the rice paper coversheet, with her name written in a confident script. Flamboyant even. Whoever penned it was undoubtedly ambitious and vain.

Brow furrowing, she smoothed out the cover sheet and jotted a long letter in Cathayi script. She folded it in half twice. On the back, she signed her given name in lieu of the stone name chops that had been sent ahead on the *Golden Phoenix*. On the front, she crossed out her name and wrote *Ambassador Wu*.

She then unfolded the letter. As her eyes roved over it, a smile tugged at her lips. With a deep breath, she closed her eyes, and then tore it in half. On the back, she wrote another letter in Arkothi print. She folded it in half twice, and then wrote a second message on the other half. Folding it in half twice, she looked up. And scowled at him.

Tian cast his gaze down. Whatever she was up to, it was bound to get them in trouble.

She turned to Chen Xin and proffered the first letter. "After you finish eating, return to Iksuvius and deliver this letter to Ambassador Wu."

Chen Xin received it in two hands, head bowed until Tian cleared his throat.

The princess snorted and held up the second letter. "Take this to the Lietuvi embassy at first light tomorrow, and deliver it into the hands of King Arvydas. After he reads it, he will hopefully ask you to bring him here. Do so, unless you suspect treachery."

She then showed him the third letter. "If the king refuses to see you, then allow yourself to be caught by the Teleri with this letter. If you are caught before delivering the messages, do everything necessary to destroy the letter to the King of Lietuvi first, then Ambassador Wu's next; but make it seem that you are trying to destroy the third letter without actually doing so."

Bowing his head, Chen Xin received the three letters in two hands.

Still acting like an imperial guard! Surely even the yokels would find it amiss. Tian glanced at the bar, where the patrons ignored them. Thank the Heavens. Still, she was sending a soldier to do a spy's job.

Their food came. He and the guards virtually inhaled it, all propriety forgotten after a long, grueling day. The princess just nibbled at the potatoes.

More people entered and joined the party at the bar. At least some people here were enjoying themselves.

Chen Xin wiped his mouth and took his leave. Tian stood, too. There was no point in escalating tensions with her, but his instincts screamed to read the content of those letters.

"I will relieve Xu Zhan." Tian followed Chen Xin out. He quickly caught up. "Let me see the messages."

Chen Xin hesitated, his uncertainty so unlike the brash young imperial guard who'd brought his ten-year-old self before the *Tianzi* a decade before.

Tian extended his hand. "This is a matter of security. The princess might endanger herself. And in any case... she didn't seal them." Chen Xin probably wasn't so gullible as to believe such flimsy reasoning, but it had been worth a try.

"The princess didn't have anything to seal them with... but although I hate to say it, you are the more level-headed right now." Chen Xin handed Tian the letters and continued towards the stables.

Tian scanned quickly through the letter to Ambassador Wu, picking out the key points without actually reading it in its entirety.

... did not succeed in boarding Golden Phoenix... make sure sets sail for Cathay immediately... ensure safety of [obscure character for Iksuvi] queen... did not succeed in killing First Consul... will seek revenge on our country... Teleri probably believe I am in compound, use to your advantage, but do not sacrifice yourselves needlessly... [obscure character for Kanin] has provided aid, please extend thanks... am sending a message [obscure character for Lietuvi] king asking to meet... not revealing current location in case messenger intercepted... am entrusting Zheng Tian to protect me... will send word from safe location... inform the Tianzi.

A smile pulled unbidden on Tian's lips. She might be acting like a child, but the princess still had a clear head. She told enough without giving away too much, and it did seem she understood he was trying to protect her. But what about the letter to Lietuvi, who was complicit in the events that would unfold tonight? She could get herself in trouble with it. He folded up the first letter and unfolded the letter to the King of Lietuvi.

Your Royal Highness, King Arvydas of Lietuvi:

By now, you have probably heard that Cathay and Teleri are at war. We know that you have conspired with Teleri to occupy and annex the Kingdom of Iksuvi, and are therefore an ally of our enemy. However, Cathay and Lietuvi are not at war with each other, and it may be that we share a common foe. We also have information that may make you reconsider your agreement with the Teleri Empire. Please meet with me tomorrow morning at the fourth waning crescent, at a location that you will be led to by my messenger. The city should be in pitched battle in the east, leaving our position unguarded."

Princess Kaiya Wang of the Empire of Cathay.

Tian nodded. There was no denying her reasoning. She kept the door open to dividing the Teleri and Lietuvi alliance, thereby helping to protect Iksuvi. It might also provide a possible escape route for them. Finally, he read the third letter, the one which Chen Xin should reveal in the event he was captured:

Your Royal Highness, King Arvydas of Lietuvi:

As per our arrangement, we will be supporting your alliance with Iksuvi, which will ultimately envelop the Teleri western army. We have five thousand musketmen and twenty warships which will be sailing up the Alto River and landing at Altogrina. With this defeat, the Teleri Empire will lose its foothold in the Nothori region.

Princess Kaiya Wang of the Empire of Cathay

Tian blew out a breath. She'd planned better than him, especially with the instructions she gave Chen. If all went perfectly as she planned, then the young Lietuvi king would meet with her here. The princess would presumably tell him of the deal between the Teleri

Empire, altivorcs, and Rotuvi. They would make a new friend.

However, if Chen Xin was caught, it would make it seem that Lietuvi was in collusion with Cathay and Iksuvi against Teleri, and would at the very least cast suspicion on their alliance, if not completely divide them. Tian had started to fold up the letters when he again noticed the writing on the back.

The letter to the princess: it bore the red chop mark of Zheng Ming—his first brother and heir to his home province of Dongmen.

Tian had once idolized his brother, but it had been ten years since they last met. As a first son, Zheng Ming would most likely be married to the daughter of an important family. He'd been trained as one of the few remaining cavalry officers in Cathay. His skill at mounted archery had gained him fame during the annual Spring Festival tournaments held in Cathay. Flamboyant and charming, he was well known for his quick wit and oratory skills. A perfect match for the princess.

And this was a personal letter. It had nothing to do with either national security or the princess' safety. There was no need to know about her personal matters. Tian sighed. It was none of his business. He began to fold the letters back up and return them to Chen Xin in the stables.

Then, unable to contain his curiosity, he put the two pieces together and read.

CHAPTER 22:
Unexpected Visitors

Lying helpless on Iksuvius Heights, all Geros could do was watch the Iridescent Moon pass through two phases. His muscles tightened and joints locked up more and more as time dragged on. Around him, his soldiers shuffled and struggled to loosen their bindings, to no avail. He would miss out on leading his invading army tonight. Worse, he might never move or speak again, cursed to live out his few remaining years as an invalid.

Geros was about to give up all hope when a young Cathayi man dressed in yellow-and-red robes reached the top of the Heights. He wiped sweat off his forehead and bowed deeply. When he spoke, his accent was thick. "Your Eminence, my princess sent me to care for you."

Care for him! The thought of being indebted to her was demeaning. Geros opened his mouth, but only a croak escaped. He had been able to speak in a whisper right after the girl ambushed him. His condition must have since deteriorated.

The priest bowed, before kneeling down to examine his wounds. "The princess did this to you?"

Yes! The bitch! That priest wouldn't be grinning like that once Geros cut his head off and stuffed it on a pike.

He did his best to nod, but his head weighed more than a warhammer.

The Cathayi placed three fingers on Geros' wrist. His brow furrowed. "Show me your tongue."

His tongue felt like sand and barely moved. What could this priest do to undo the princess' craven attack?

"The princess has blocked the flow of your life energy. I will restore it." The priest withdrew several thin needles from a silk brocade box, and without ceremony inserted them in Geros' arms and legs. Each spot felt like a jolt of lightning racing up his limbs and into his core. The heaviness immediately diminished.

"Your constitution is strong. You will make a full recovery. Rest for now." The man turned toward the wounded Bovyans and began examining and adjusting their bandages. In some, he inserted more thin needles.

While the Cathayi worked, Geros' energy gathered, a drip at first, then a trickle. Relief washed over him. He would not be crippled for the rest of his life. Furthermore, despite this setback today, he could still move forward with his plans tonight.

He rose and shook out his limbs. Though languid, at least the feeling had returned to his hands and feet. In three steps, he bounded over to the priest and seized him by the throat. The effort nearly winded him. "Where is the princess now?"

The priest's eyes rounded and his voice choked. "Back. At. The. Embassy... "

Geros released him, shoving him back. He hid his wheeze for air, lest his men see him weak. "You saved my life today, and for that, I will spare yours. I suggest you flee the city now, because I will raze your embassy and kill everyone there."

The priest's face blanched, and he scuttled backward with bobbing bows. When he reached the edge of the pavilion, he turned around and fled in a flash of red and yellow.

Geros snorted derisively as the man escaped. Coward. Just like the princess and the rest of her ilk.

With no blades immediately available, he fumbled at untying his aide-de-campe. "Go to headquarters. Convey my order to surround the Cathayi embassy and kill any man who tries to leave."

In the fading sunlight, Jie counted the Teleri soldiers amassing around the embassy walls. Inside the compound, two hundred musketmen watched from the battlements, while imperial guards armed with repeating crossbows deployed behind a line of shields at the main gate.

Only a skeleton staff remained—just enough to give the guise that the princess was still there. The ambassador had ordered all non-essential personnel to flee, both for their own safety and also to reduce the number of mouths to feed in the event of a protracted siege. With the princess disguised as a wandering monk somewhere in the city, the temple priests had been sent out as decoys.

Jie returned to the main residence foyer. There, Ambassador Wu paced, with sweat trickling down his head.

"Godfather, you summoned?"

He nodded. "Little Jie, I know your primary responsibility is to the princess and not to the embassy. However, I need your help now. I am going to meet with a Teleri general who waits outside the main gate. Accompany me as I listen to his demands, see what you can pick up. Of course, we must maintain the deception that the princess is here."

Jie bowed her head. "As you command."

She followed a step behind him as he trudged towards the main gate, his slow pace seeming even more labored than usual. Yet he held his head high, like the captain of a sinking ship, the honor of his two decades of service in Iksuvius radiating in his dignified expression.

The imperial guard parted, opening a path for the two to walk. Up ahead, General Marius stood cross-armed on the other side of the gate, flanked by two gigantic officers. His eyes widened as he caught sight of her. Having shed a court gown in favor of utility clothes that she could fight in, Jie grinned at his shock. He probably still believed they'd slept together the night before.

Marius composed himself before they arrived at the gate, stiffening in his stance. "Ambassador Wu, the First Consul demands that you surrender the embassy and turn Princess Kaiya Wang over to us."

Ambassador Wu smiled grimly. "You know what our answer will be. You also know that your shields and armor cannot stop our firepowder. We have stores to last us a year."

"And what happens after a year, Ambassador?" Marius looked toward the princess' window. "The First Consul is patient."

Ambassador Wu laughed. "Do you think the Son of Heaven will stand for you holding his beloved daughter hostage? Within a couple of months, expect an armada of warships on your coast with a flight of phoenixes ready to extract her."

Jie sucked on her lower lip. Hopefully, Marius would believe the bluff. Although Cathay kept a handful of lesser phoenixes in the imperial aviary, they had limited endurance and range, and only flew during the New Year's parade. The highly sensitive birds would never survive a trip by sea.

Marius swept his arms outward. "We will flood the harbor with fire and fill the sky with enough crossbow bolts to blot out the sun."

"Then it looks like our negotiations have reached an impasse." Ambassador Wu bowed his head.

"I suggest you reconsider. I will give you until dawn." Marius cast Jie one last look, his eyes round and wounded. Was it a sense of betrayal? Or pity? Or even concern? It was hard to tell in the twilight, where her elf vision didn't work.

As he turned around, she caught a glimpse of his shadow shifting out of sync with his movement.

It was a Teleri Nightblade. And unlike the young men who failed to infiltrate the embassy, this one was very skilled. By the time she focused on the area, he was gone.

CHAPTER 23:
A Chance Meeting

Dearest Kaiya,

I never knew what it meant to be truly alive before I met you. During your diplomatic mission to Vyara City, when we were separated for a month, I felt so empty that the finest food and wine seemed flavorless, the most melodious music sounded flat, the most radiant painting colorless.

I promised I would always follow you and protect you, and it pains me that duties in my province prevent me from joining you on your trip to the Nothori lands. Not just because I must break my promise, but because you are like the air to me. Please be safe on your journey. I am consoled by the hope that each morning I awake brings me a day closer to being with you again.

Zheng Ming

Tian had never thought of his brother as being truly romantic, beyond the dashing façade he presented. Nor was it typical for Cathayi people to express themselves in such a... personal manner. Did the princess feel the same way? She must, since she had kept the letter with her all this time. And why had he not heard about this already from Jie or his cousin, General Zheng?

Tian could never expose his soul like that. If he *did* write something like that to Jie, she would probably punch him. Pondering the relationship between Eldest Brother and the princess, he went back to the inn.

The suspicious man who'd been sleeping at the bar was gone. Tian pushed past the drunken revelers, approached the barkeep, and pointed to the empty seat. "Where did that man go?"

The barkeeper looked around before beckoning Tian closer and whispering, "It was an altivorc. He went upstairs, where he's staying in a private room. I hear from our patrons that there have been several altivorcs passing through this last week. Though for all I know, maybe it's just one individual. They all look the same to me."

An altivorc! Likely an advance scout for the battalion, on its way to aid the Teleri in the subjugation of Iksuvi. While the Cathayi and Kanin peoples shared enough similarities that the locals probably couldn't tell the difference, an altivorc scout would. He might not know their identity, but he would surely think it strange that there were Cathayi people masquerading as Kanin horsemen.

Tian tapped his chin. If the altivorc knew about what had transpired on the Iksuvius Heights earlier that day... . No, impossible—the altivorcs were coming from the opposite direction.

He pointed at the stairwell. "Are there any other ways to access the second floor?"

The barkeep shook his head. "No, those steps are the only way."

"Besides us, who is staying here?" Tian produced a shiny silver coin to entice an answer.

The coin disappeared into the man's palm. "Besides your party in a common room and the altivorc in a private room, there is also a trifle guide and his three dark-skinned friends in two of the doubles."

Tian swept his gaze around the room to take stock of the patrons. *Trifle* and *halfling* were derogatory terms for the madaeri people, a short but good-looking race of non-humans. They were known to be excellent guides, scouts, and foragers, with ravenous appetites and something of an inferiority complex. Hailing from the Eldaeri Northwest, this one was a long way from home. As for the dark-skinned clients, could they be the mysterious Aksumi people? Or the pious Levanthi? Or perhaps the Ayuri? They probably wouldn't be in league with the altivorcs.

Tian motioned Ma Jun over. "There's an altivorc scout. Staying here. He might know who we are. Keep watch on the stairs. Let me know if he comes down. Or if anyone else goes up. The rest of us shall retire. In two hours, someone will come down to relieve you."

Ma Jun nodded. "We should allow the princess to sleep by herself."

So loyal. And impractical. Tian shook his head. Since they'd planned to board the *Golden Phoenix*— "We don't have much money. Not enough for a separate room. She'll have to make do."

"The men are willing to exchange our rings for their finest private room." Ma Jun held up a thick silver ring cast with the dragon crest of Cathay, the mark of the imperial guard.

Tian stared at the symbol, which a guard would never sell, even if he came on hard times. To think they would sacrifice it for the princess' comfort. Sadly, in Nothori lands where the significance meant nothing, their rings would be no more valuable than their weight in silver. Not to mention it would draw undue attention to them.

"That will not be necessary," the princess said, approaching from behind. The squeak in her voice was gone, replaced by a regal, albeit tired tone. "I would not sacrifice your badge of honor just for my own privacy for one night. I will retire for the evening. Please give me some time to myself before following."

The imperial guards, who had gathered around, reflexively bowed despite Tian's orders. She disappeared up the stairs, the graceful float in her step replaced by a defeated trudge.

There was still the altivorc up there. Tian gestured for Ma Jun to follow. "Stand guard. Outside the door."

The rest returned to their table, mood somber amidst the merriment of a growing crowd. Tian leaned back and watched the entire room, noting comings and goings, and paying particular attention to the stairs.

Before long, a short figure descended the steps. At first glance, a child; but on further observation, undoubtedly the madaeri guide the barkeeper had spoken of. The diminutive fellow climbed up to a barstool and ordered a long list of food. Patrons shifted away from him.

Even if his group had no relevance to their current predicament, a guide would know more about the area. Tian motioned for his companions to wait at the table. Withdrawing his map of the region, he slipped through the boisterous villagers and sidled up to the madaeri.

The little man was no different from most of his kind: fair, with short-cropped hair that emphasized his pointed ears. Light skin and sharp features gave him a passing resemblance to a certain half-elf. A long dagger was tucked into a broad leather belt, which held up black cotton pants. A greenish-brown traveling cloak draped over a dull brown shirt.

The madaeri turned and faced him. "I've walked from one coast to the other," he said in very loud Arkothi, "been to the icy rim in the far north and the sweltering heat of the deep south. Never in my life have I seen a Cathayi looking so ridiculous wearing a mismatched suit of Kanin armor. Even your sword is on the wrong side!"

Tian gaped, and then looked down at his sword, sheathed on his left. "Um, I'm left-handed," he said, his voice about two decibels lower than the guide.

The madaeri laughed from his belly. When he spoke, it was in a big voice that did not seem to match his size. "No, you're not."

Some of the bar patrons now looked in their direction.

Heat rose to Tian's face. Usually, it was *he* who prodded information out of people, either through trickery or by not-so-friendly means, not the other way around. "Please lower your voice a little. We are trying to keep a—"

"Low profile?" the madaeri whispered, lifting his shoulders and ducking his head. "You're not doing a good job of that, at least not to someone who has any amount of world experience. Luckily, I am probably the only one in this room with that. You could do better, but you would need some actual training."

Tian held back a retort. "My name is Tian. Come join us at our table. I have a proposition for you. I would like to discuss it in confidence."

"My name is Fleet, short for a much longer name that you won't be able to pronounce or remember, so we'll just keep it at that. Any chance I could get you to pay for my meal here?" Fleet jerked a thumb toward the kitchen.

Tian cringed. It would be expensive, but worth it. Madaeri were compulsive information-gatherers. Dangle some rumors in front of him and they would find out plenty in return. "Let's talk first. I have earth-moving information."

Fleet turned to the barkeeper. "Bring my food to this fine gentleman's table." He hopped off the stool and extended his hand. "Lead the way, friend!"

"So where are you taking your clients?" Tian asked on their way to the table.

Fleet's jovial tone turned grave. "I'm not allowed to speak regarding these types of business transactions. Wouldn't you expect your privacy protected if the roles were reversed? Perhaps you can ask them directly."

Arriving at the table, he looked around. "Interesting, Cathayi imperial guard, also in poor disguise. Which one of you is the dignitary?" He cast a glance at Tian, scrunched his forehead up, and then shook his head. "Not you, obviously."

The guards shuffled uncomfortably but remained silent, all glaring at the madaeri.

He pointed to the princess' untouched clams. "Anyone eating this?"

Tian nodded "Help your—"

The clams disappeared into the madaeri's mouth, shells and all. The entire table gawked at him.

"What?" With a wounded expression, Fleet scratched a scar on the back of his neck. "I grew up in a big family where we had to fight for the food. You learn to eat fast."

Tian waved off the madaeri's protests. "No, eat. We need to confirm the accuracy. Of a map. Your people are the best mapmakers." He unfurled the paper and spread it out on the table.

Fleet munched on potatoes, his eyes darting over the markings. He shook his head and looked up. "Was this map made before or after the Hellstorm?"

Tian scowled. The final episode of the conflict between the Ayuri and Arkothi empires, three centuries prior, had drastically transformed the landscape. His map couldn't be *that* bad. He opened his mouth to answer.

"It was a rhetorical question," Fleet said. "Your map is definitely outdated. I can certainly spruce this sad rag up... for the right price." The quill the princess had used now twirled between his fingers.

Tian pursed his lips. "We are short on funds. Is there something else?"

"A woman, perhaps? This quill sure smells nice." The madaeri took a long, deep sniff of the feathers.

All three guards sprang to their feet, hands on their weapons, knocking chairs over and startling all the patrons into silence. Fleet didn't flinch. Tian put his hands up, tacitly telling the soldiers to stand down.

Fleet chuckled and fanned himself with the map. "A dead madaeri can't fix this antique for your pretty princess."

"Princess?" Tian feigned shock.

"Why else would Cathayi imperial guard react that way?"

The madaeri was good. It was useless trying to hide anything from him. Might as well confirm it. Tian leaned in. "Our guards are devoted to their princess. I implore you. For your own sake. Don't speak ill of her." He motioned again for the soldiers to sit down.

Fleet scratched his head. "Alright, how about this: you tell me something interesting, and I'll make revisions to the map based on the value of what you tell me."

Tian nodded. "That's fair. Here's a tidbit: Teleri will invade Iksuvi tonight."

Fleet whistled. The guards gritted their teeth, probably because of the Cathayi belief that whistling at night attracted ghosts. Unfazed, he inked the quill with several blots, and extended a road that ran from Iksuvius along the coast of Cold Harbor.

Tian smiled. The road reached all the way to the head of the bay, which might be a place they could catch up with the *Golden Phoenix* if they rode hard enough. "The First Consul of the Teleri Directori. He's here himself."

Fleet nodded, and put a dot and notation on the map, in the woods they had passed through earlier today: *Good mushrooms here.*

"Come on! That information is valuable!"

"But something I'd already guessed." Fleet grinned and rubbed his hands. "All the Teleri activity, plus the amazing procession at the Great East Gate a couple of days ago... But you get the idea: the quality of your information begets the quality of mine."

The back-and-forth continued for a while, with the madaeri adding all kinds of notes, roads, and information to the map, while Tian shared intelligence about troop strengths and movements.

At last, Fleet said, "Look, I can add so much more to this map, but at this rate, we won't be done until the Orc Gods return on their blazing chariots. Stories say that the only daughter of Emperor Wang is an unparalleled beauty, who sang a dragon into a stupor. Let me see her face, and I'll update everything I know."

Was it worth the risk? There was little they could do to keep the madaeri from hanging around and seeing her anyway.

Something flashed by the staircase. Fleet's head turned, and Tian's followed.

Another figure descended the stairs. He wore a dark cloak which covered nearly his entire body, with a hood pulled over his head.

The madaeri and his requests could wait. Tian motioned towards the guards with hand signals. *Block exit, flank, I take.*

None of the imperial guards budged.

Of course not.

Fleet's jaw dropped. "No, no, that's my client. She's no threat to you." He beckoned her over.

The cloaked figure approached the table, lowering the hood to reveal an attractive young woman with a light chocolate complexion and piercing dark eyes. She had coarse, wavy black hair which fell to the middle of her back. Aksumi. They rarely left their city-states in the south, and Tian had never seen one before.

The imperial guards, however, rose to their feet. In unison, they each pressed a fist into a palm.

"Lady Brehane," Li Wei said.

"Wei," she said with a toothy smile and a thick accent. "And Yue."

Tian's gaze shifted from Brehane to the imperial guards. How could this be? From the way Fleet's eyes bolted back and forth, he must have been just as surprised.

The Aksumi woman counted on her fingers. "But where are Jun, Xin, Zhan, and Ming? And little Jie?" Her eyes locked in on Tian.

Such a piercing stare. Tian shuffled on his feet. Brehane extended her open hands towards him, and he looked at Fleet with a raised eyebrow.

"It's their custom to clasp hands at their first meeting." The madaeri encouraged Tian with a tilt of his head.

Tian tentatively took Brehane's hands in his own. "I am Tian Zheng. I am honored to meet you."

Brehane held his hands and showed no signs of letting go. "Mister Tian, the honor is mine. I trust you and your family are doing well?"

What a strange question. "We are all well," he said. Eldest Brother most of all, apparently.

Another smile bloomed on her face. "You are that scoundrel Ming's brother, aren't you? I can see the resemblance. Which means you're the one Little Jie... "

Tian's face flushed hot enough to fry an egg. Usually, he knew more about people than they did of him. And the unspoken part about Jie. He turned to see the imperial guards' lips quivering into half-grins. "Yes. Ming's brother."

"Better looking, too. I can see why Little Jie—"

Tian coughed. "How do you know my brother? And the imperial guards?"

She nodded in the direction of the men. "We shared an adventure not four months ago." She placed a hand on her chest. "I am deeply indebted to them. Their swordsmanship, Ming's bow, Wen's cleverness, and Little Jie's charm," she winked, "saved our mission."

Tian turned to the imperial guards. The smiles disappeared and they snapped to attention. There was a story here, one that he would pry out of the tight-lipped men. He looked back at her. "What brings you so far north? You are far from home."

Brehane sat down uninvited at the table and regarded him with curious eyes. She then turned to Fleet, who nodded. "What do you know about my people?"

Tian shrugged his shoulders. "Your people are the greatest magicians. You can bend the laws of nature. To suit your needs."

Brehane clasped a clear crystal that hung from a silver chain around her neck. "Some of what you know is true. Almost all of our women can sense the energy of the universe. Most only dabble. However, there are a very small number of truly wise and wondrous Mystics. I am an initiate into the Order of Mystics."

Her words sucked Tian in, the rest of the room and revelers fading into the background.

"Both my order and the Order of Ayuri Paladins have noticed that there are places in the world where our connection to the world's energy has weakened. My Paladin companion and I are charged with visiting the holiest places, where magic has always been the strongest—"

"The pyramids," Tian said. It all made sense, at least from what he'd learned at the reception the other night. "Your companion is Sameer Vikram."

Brehane nodded. "Yes, he is with me, along with the Akolyte Cyrus Estazadeh."

"A true Akolyte?" Tian kept himself from gaping. It was impossible. "Didn't they all lose their abilities to channel the divine magic of the gods?"

Brehane shook her head. "After the Levastyan Empire conquered Cyrus' homeland and took control of the pyramid there, the Akolytes lost their most powerful magic—but only in their homeland. The few who fled to other lands found their powers restored. When your friends and I infiltrated that pyramid, we found its font blocked."

Tian looked again at the imperial guards, then back. It would explain their camaraderie with Jie. "Where are you going now?"

"Fleet is guiding us to the ruins of a pyramid in the Kanin Wilds."

But how? Tian recalled the map. "Wouldn't it have been easier to go upriver from the Shallowsea?"

"Can I tell him?" Fleet jumped up and down on his chair. "Please?"

Brehane laughed. "Of course."

Fleet whipped a map out from who knew where and snapped it open across the table. It depicted the Kanin Wilds, with meticulous detail and all kinds of notations about landmarks, flora, fauna, and tribe names. He pointed to a ring of mountains right in the middle, which had several notes scribbled around it. *Tivorc City. Kanin Pyramid.*

Tian shook his head. "But how do you get there?"

"We will follow the north-south highway to the source of the Alto River, where the Nothori Mountains branch off into the Everwhite Mountains." Fleet traced a route on the map with his finger. "There is a secret pass near there, which will open into the Kanin Wilds near one of the branches of the North Kanin River." He pointed at one of the small tributaries. "There is an old, almost overgrown stone road that dates back to the first Kanin Empire over six centuries ago, which will go through the wooded hills before opening up to the mountains of the pyramid."

Tian considered the route. From here to the edge of the Wilds, it was two weeks by horseback on the main roads. If they found one of the ancient roads along the North Kanin River, they could follow it right to the East Gate of Cathay. It would take another two weeks, at most. At the latest, they would have the princess home not long after the Mid-Autumn Festival. "How safe is the area? Around the North Kanin River?"

"There are many tribes of Kanin hunter-gatherers there," Fleet said. "Nothing like their horse-riding brethren in the Kanin Kingdom." He jerked a thumb at their armor. "There is also at least one tribe of wild elves, as well."

"Wild elves?" Thoughts of Jie crept unbidden into Tian's imagination.

Fleet gesticulated wildly. "Those elves that did not believe Aralas was the angel from their prophecies, and therefore didn't rise up during the War of Ancient Gods. They are the least of your worries. Ogres, on the other hand... "

Plans formulated in Tian's head. The most dangerous leg of the journey would start now. They would have to stay ahead of messengers coming from the north, who would be spreading the news of the princess' escape; and also avoid the altivorcs coming up from the south.

He turned to Brehane. "May we accompany you? To the confluence of the North Kanin River and its tributary? We can provide six extra swords. We'll help pay for the madaeri's services."

She was about to answer, when Zhao Yue motioned to the stairway. The altivorc was coming down.

CHAPTER 24:
More Unexpected Visitors

As night fell over Iksuvius, Geros slouched on his throne in the Teleri embassy. His energy still guttered in his limbs, and it took significant effort to maintain the façade of strength. Patrols had taken control of several strategic points, yet had met with unexpectedly stiff resistance at others. Progress might have stayed on schedule had he not redeployed hundreds of troops from the eastern gate to the Cathayi embassy.

Reports came in, each relaying another objective captured. His western army was scheduled to arrive within an hour. Soon, very soon, his dreams would be realized.

First Emperor of the Teleri Empire. It sounded wonderful in his ears, no matter how many times he repeated it. Fulfillment of the prophecy of his virgin birth, begotten by Solaris himself.

An unexpected visitor spoiled his anticipation.

Through the throne room doors, an altivorc prince marched in, surrounded by an entourage of guards in chainmail. Like the Altivorc King, he was handsome, especially compared to his hideous minions.

Without so much as a bow, the prince spoke. "First Consul, we are ready to assist you in the siege of the Cathayi embassy. I have three hundred men inside the city at my command."

Geros forced himself to sit straight and glared at the prince, wondering where he got such strange ideas. "That won't be necessary. I have sent my most trusted general to negotiate their peaceful surrender. The princess is too compassionate and weak. She will surely sacrifice herself for her people. I will take that girl and punish her for her insolence."

The prince grinned, revealing his fangs. "That is unwise, First Consul. Mark my words, she will only bewitch you."

"I do not need your counsel. She is only a girl, one whose spirit I will crush with a night in bed."

The prince's grin froze on his face. "Do not be so sure. Despite my king's warnings, you take her too lightly. You do so to your own detriment."

"Be gone from my sight." Geros waved his hand at the altivorcs. Even that simple motion was tiring.

The prince shrugged and turned on his heels without further comment.

Once the mercenaries disappeared, Geros motioned towards an officer who stood by the door. "Has General Marius sent word?"

The officer bowed his head. "No, Your Eminence. There have been no new reports from the Cathayi embassy."

"Send a runner to convey my orders to the general. Master Feiying and his Nightblades will infiltrate their embassy to find out where the princess is hiding, and capture her if the opportunity presents itself. If there is no movement by dawn, commence the attack."

Jie and ten Black Fist brothers gathered in the Cobweb, though it no longer deserved its nickname. The intertwined strings which Tian had meticulously connected over two years now lay on the floor, the notes and evidence all boxed up and ready to be hidden.

Old Tong, now in command in Tian's absence, turned to her. "Sister Jie, you are the most talented at setting the *Tiger's Eye*. Use it on us now and take command."

Jie offered a bow. Such responsibility! The *Tiger's Eye* locked away all emotions and moral compunctions, and drowned out all perception of pain. It would transform a Black Fist from a deadly adversary to a heartless killing machine who wouldn't stop until he was dead or his assignment was completed.

The brothers focused on her as she arranged her hands in a secret sign. When all sense of humanity faded from their eyes, she issued her command. "Your mission is to protect the embassy until daybreak, whereupon you will return to this room at first opportunity."

They flashed the answering hand signal, one that only their subconscious minds remembered.

Gut hollow, Jie addressed the two youngest. "Fen and Cheng, relieve your brothers at the warehouse escape route and send them here." With the tunnel secured, there would be a means to flee if the embassy fell.

Both bowed their heads and slipped out of the room through the balcony doors. No sooner had they left than red peacock caws emerged from the warehouse. The fainter, more distant set of screeches stopped mid-caw, almost as soon as it had started, while the other faded away in the distance before getting cut short as well. Had an enemy discovered the escape route? Had she sent the boys to their deaths?

"Sheng, Lu, and Yang: go to the temple and protect the princess' decoy. The rest of you come with me to the warehouse." The shadows shifted as they drifted from the room, and Jie beckoned the remaining Black Fist to follow her to the balcony.

Cool, reassuring air washed over her as she stepped out. Along the outer walls, none of the musketmen had taken up defensive positions, nor had the Teleri moved from their own ranks outside the walls. If they'd penetrated the secret passage, why weren't they attacking from the outside as well? Or was it a diversion?

Leaping down to the ground below, Jie swept through the courtyard. The imperial guard remained motionless at the main gate. Maybe there was no attack, despite the bird calls. She motioned her brothers to continue towards the warehouse, while she paused and searched the ranks for General Zheng.

There he was, near the front gate. She sprinted over. "General Zheng, what's the enemy doing?"

"Nothing. They just stand like toy soldiers."

It made no sense. Attacking from inside and out would work better. No matter; if they wanted to use a stupid strategy, that was their choice. "There is a threat on the embassy, coming from the secret escape passage. Have some of your men defend the temple. We want them to believe the princess is there."

General Zhang nodded and bellowed orders.

Jie caught up with her brothers. They crept through the darkened warehouse, fanning through before converging at the hatch that dropped into the underground tunnels.

It was open. The clang of swords echoed from below. The passage was compromised.

Jie tapped orders on the men's backs. One went to warn the general, while the rest dropped down into the passage.

She trailed several steps behind, listening. The sounds of combat had been replaced with the pounding of heavy boots, their spacing much too close to be Bovyans, but too heavy to be Nothori humans.

Altivorcs. Her second encounter with them in defense of the princess, her seventeenth in all. Each time, they seemed to have a personal vendetta against her.

In the pitch black, the Black Fist would lose their blind advantage, since the altivorcs would see their heat signature. In these depths, her elf vision would be useless as well.

"Lights! Altivorcs! Lights!" She yelled down the hall, pressing her back against the roughhewn walls at a turn in the passage. Someone would have to be rear guard.

Up ahead around another corner, the passage lit up. Jie stayed in the dark, well outside the reach of the light, readying her throwing stars and spikes. Again, swords reverberated against each other, mixed with the inhuman grunts of altivorcs.

Tong and Cheng fell back toward the corner and into her line of sight. One of Tong's arms hung limply from his body by a strip of flesh, while the boy had suffered several deep gashes. Yet they took a stand at the corner, fighting on as altivorcs crowded the passage.

Blades flashed, and altivorc bodies began to drop at the sides; but at last, Tong fell from the slash of a broadsword. Despite his mortal injuries, he grabbed at the closest enemy and bit into his unarmored thigh. Cheng fought on with a shattered sword in one hand and a knife in the other, even as his lifeblood spurted from a cut to his neck. After a few seconds, he collapsed, unmoving.

Her brothers! Jie had not received the *Tiger's Eye*, and their deaths wrenched her heart.

There was no time to grieve their loss. The altivorcs crunched the light baubles under their boots, plunging the tunnels back into darkness.

She pushed herself off of the wall and hurled at least a dozen stars and spikes in the direction of the orc grunts. Several bellowed in pain. She turned the corner back towards the hatch and waited, her own *dao* now held in both hands. The boots thudded in her direction, punctuated by exclamations in their guttural tongue.

As she planned, a few paused to hack at the spot on the wall where she had been leaning. Jie turned back around the corner and cut through three altivorcs in a quick combination of deadly slashes. A fourth swung at her with a broadsword, but she ducked under its whistle, while slicing through his abdomen with her *dao*. Ahead, more heavy feet stomped in her direction.

So many bloodthirsty voices! Jie was vastly outnumbered. No way to hold the passage by herself. She turned and raced towards the hatch. Scrambling through the opening, she slammed the trapdoor shut and barred it with a heavy blockwood board. She dropped the smallest of her light baubles by the hatch and looked up.

Perfect. The light didn't reach the ceiling, some twenty feet above.

Jie darted towards the corner and pop-vaulted against the walls until reaching the worn rafters. Crawling inverted, taking care not to slip in the dust, she arrived at an overhead door, installed just for these kinds of emergencies. Below her, the hatch door buckled as the altivorcs below slammed into it.

A few minutes of pounding. The hatch held.

Jie blew out a sigh—no! With a last shove, the altivorcs crashed through and tromped up the ladder into the warehouse. They bloomed out from the opening, taking in their surroundings, but never looking up. Two hundred seventy-nine in all, crowding the warehouse, several wounded. Among them marched a prince, a begotten son of the legendary Altivorc King himself.

Just as she began to inch towards the escape door, a last figure emerged, taller than the altivorcs, but gaunt. He looked around and up, and would have seen her had she not been concealed by the dark.

Jie chewed her lower lip. He was a Cathayi man, much too small to be a Bovyan Nightblade, and certainly too old. A *dao* hung on his back, and he was dressed in the manner of a Black Fist. Yet he was no one she had ever seen in her three decades at the Black Lotus Temple.

When he spoke in Arkothi, he barely had an accent. "She will go to the most defensible position. I suspect that's the temple, but I recommend sending several of your men to sweep through the rest of the compound. I will wait here to guard the escape route."

The altivorcs stampeded towards the door, their boots and armor rumbling and clanging like an earthquake. After several dozen exited, the thunder of musket fire roared through the night sky. Jie waited patiently until all of the altivorcs had departed and the sounds of hand-to-hand skirmishes resumed outside.

Now alone, the man picked up her light bauble. Before she could react, he threw it in her direction and looked right at her. His eyes bore a hint of sadness. Whatever; no time to dwell on it. The roof would provide a better view of the battle. Jie popped out of the hatch.

In the courtyard below, a large group of altivorcs charged through musket fire towards the lines of imperial guards defending the temple. Another regiment was locked in mortal combat with a detachment of imperial guards at the main gate.

Yet a third force stormed the main residence. A reserve had formed by the warehouse, shooting black-fletched arrows at the musketmen, who in turn discharged their weapons and passed them back to their partners for reloading. Several lay at the base of the wall, felled by altivorc arrows.

Jie raced along the rooftop and leapt to the battlements along the outer wall, timing her jump with a lull in the volleys. She peeked out of the compound.

The Teleri still held their position, showing no signs of joining in on the attack. Their officers, however, argued among themselves.

No time to think about it. She continued along the wall, dodging several well-aimed arrows... they really must have a personal vendetta against her! She didn't recall ever insulting an altivorc before, at least none that lived to tell about it.

Reaching the closest point to the temple, Jie vaulted across the gap and caught the bottom edge of the pitched roof. After flipping up, she teetered along the edge to the sole entrance and swung down. One last glance at the courtyard.

Outnumbered, the imperial guards were losing ground to the altivorcs.

She passed through the double doors. Inside, she was greeted by bright light shining from the huge statue of Yang-Di at the rear of the temple, sparkling off the gold paint on the red ceilings high above. Kneeling there in prayer were Ambassador Wu and Meiling. The last of the princess' handmaidens, she was a stunning beauty in her own right, now serving as a decoy.

"Godfather," Jie said.

Ambassador Wu turned to face her. His shoulders slumped, and his eyes now betrayed his age. "Little Jie, what is happening?"

"The Teleri haven't moved, but altivorcs have stormed in through our escape passage. An older Cathayi man assists them."

The ambassador shook his head. His voice was calm and melancholy. "We cannot hold the compound against an attack from the inside. All is lost. When the embassy falls, make sure all the firepowder is detonated. Without a sample, the Teleri cannot study it, nor use the guns they will capture tonight."

Outside, the roar of musket fire stuttered to sporadic shots, then stopped altogether. Shouts and cries grew louder, and a dozen imperial guards backed into the temple as the altivorcs pressed their advantage.

"Hold the door, hold the door!" General Zheng yelled as he took a protective stance by the decoy's side.

Keeping two of her throwing stars in reserve, Jie drew her *dao* and charged into the fray. Around her, the imperial guards fought brilliantly, dispatching more of the altivorcs than they lost. But before long they were pushed back, as they succumbed to fatigue and overwhelming numbers.

Jie found herself not far from the door, isolated from her countrymen, forced to fight half a dozen altivorcs on her own. In fact, it looked like they'd intentionally isolated her.

As she evaded deadly slashes and struck back at her attackers, she shot a quick glance back. The imperial guard had formed a protective circle around the ambassador and Meiling. A contingent of altivorc archers stood at the door, arrows trained on the decoy and her protectors. The prince stood at the fore with a wicked broadsword raised, his head protected by a T-slot helm.

He snarled a few words.

Jie gasped.

The altivorcs loosed their arrows into the group. Imperial guards fell, and others rushed forward to take their place as their circle tightened. Meiling screamed.

Ambassador Wu's voice of command carried above the pounding in her ears. "Jie! It is lost here. Remember what I said!"

Remember. Remember. Rage at the altivorcs washed over her. Her pulse thrummed in her head. What was she supposed to remember?

The firepowder.

Jie lobbed her sword at the closest enemy and dove into a roll between two altivorcs, popping up in front of the prince with knives held in underhand grips.

He hacked at her with a two-handed swing, but she twirled around him while stabbing at his midsection. The prince turned just enough that his rib stopped her thrust, and he bellowed in pain as black blood oozed from the wound.

He tried to spin with her, but she abruptly stopped her turn, slicing upwards across the back of his wrist. With a roar, he cocked back to chop at her again, but she pressed her attack and slipped a knife into his neck.

He gurgled and choked on blood. Jie didn't stay to gloat, instead cutting her way through the archers that stood between her and the door. She stabbed and slashed at them in rage, killing all that blocked her way.

Cool air and the coppery stench of blood greeted her as she made it out onto the terrace. With a quick glance, she appraised the situation. Bodies—both human and altivorc—littered the courtyard. Outside the temple, the altivorcs ushered the surrendering musketmen and wounded imperial guards into a corner of the compound. A dozen imperial guards still fought another group of orcs, pressing their way towards the temple.

An arrow zipped by her head from behind her. Jie withdrew a flash-powder packet from her belt and hurled it against the ground. Hopefully, the bright flash and smoke would provide enough cover for her to make it through the courtyard to the armory without getting hit in the back.

Bounding through the courtyard, arrows buzzing by her head, she somehow arrived at her destination unscathed. The door to the armory was unlocked; she pushed it open and slipped in. At the far end, past the muskets, swords, and armor, sat a dozen kegs of firepowder. Heavens, this was just like the caves beneath Wailian Castle over two years ago.

Jie pushed and shoved the heavy barrels, to no avail. Gritting her teeth and squeezing her eyes tight, she thrust her heel into the midsection of the centermost keg. The wood yielded with a splintering crack. She opened her eyes, thankful not to have blown herself to oblivion.

Black powder gushed out from the hole. She grabbed a broom and swept the powder in a line towards the door.

A peek out revealed a fierce fight between the few surviving imperial guards and altivorcs at the temple doors. The rest of the Cathayi knelt with hands on their heads in the corner of the compound as the altivorcs trained arrows on them. One of the orcs barked a guttural order. Arrows flew into her unarmed compatriots.

Their screams filled her ears. Her chest tightened. Jie turned her head away, grief flooding over her. Why had she not been placed under the *Tiger's Eye* instead?

The same accursed orc syllable repeated, followed by more screams of Cathayi men.

A tear ran down her cheek. With a deep, choked breath, she opened her eyes to survey the situation again.

Nobody between here and the warehouse. Only one old man to fight there.

Despite her vast knowledge of weaponry, despite having almost blown up Wailian Castle, Jie had no idea how large of an explosion the powder would cause. She slunk as far as she trusted her aim, and hurled another flash packet at the line of firepowder at the door.

It caught. A fizzling flame tracked down the line.

She bolted toward the warehouse.

She crashed through the door and just barely avoided a barrage of throwing stars that came hurtling at her. Two knives were in her hands as the old renegade Black Fist charged with a *dao* raised above his head.

Jie twisted out of his chop. Slipped the follow-through stab. Slashed at his forearm, but he jerked his own blade up with a flick of his wrist, deflecting her cut. With a subtle twist, the sword sliced towards her throat. A killing blow.

Jie had presence of mind to jump forward. Pain bit at her shoulder. Just a nick, instead of decapitation. She wrapped one arm around both of his and cut towards his throat with her other hand.

The force of the explosion rocked the walls and floors. Her body lurched forward. Jie's ears rang and something slammed into her head. All went black.

CHAPTER 25:
The Resonance of the Universe

The altivorc shot a quick glance at their table before hurrying towards the door. Tian signaled the imperial guards to stay in place. Seeing their blank stares, he said, "Stay here. I'm going to follow. And watch the altivorc."

As he got up, Fleet also rose. The two trailed the altivorc out of the inn and around the corner. Tian paused at the turn. On the other side, the altivorc breathed lightly and rapidly, ready to ambush him.

Tian smirked. Even if altivorcs fought well, apparently subterfuge did not come as easily. Time to spring a poorly set trap.

Feigning carelessness, Tian turned the corner.

A knife flashed in a deadly thrust toward his side. It was a quick, well-aimed shot that would have passed between the ribs and punctured the lung of an unsuspecting victim.

Tian wasn't unsuspecting. He caught the altivorc's knife hand, pulled his arm, and twisted it upwards. The altivorc's fingers loosened and the knife slipped from his hands. With a spin on his hips, Tian drove him face-first into the ground and kneeled on him. "All right—"

Fleet smashed a ceramic plate over the altivorc's head, knocking him out and shattering the dish in the process.

Tian scowled. "What did you do that for?"

The madaeri meekly shrugged his shoulders. "I thought you were in trouble."

"Now we're just going to have to wait for him to wake up."

"It can't be helped, so let's see what he has on him." Fleet grinned, snatching up the altivorc's belt pouch and shaking its contents onto the stable floor. After stashing away a few silver *kroon*, he held up a crude, hand-drawn map. "Even worse than yours, though not by much."

Tian snatched up a finger-length metal tube just before the madaeri's hand could reach it. Popping off the cap, he eased out a piece of parchment and unfolded it. The strange runes bore no resemblance to any language he'd ever seen.

He handed it to Fleet, whose large round puppy eyes shifted into foxlike focus as he quickly glanced through it and shrugged. "Maybe Brehane can help us. What about the altivorc?"

Tian frowned. "We can't have him spreading news. Of our presence." *Hold the dragonfly with care.* Did it apply to monsters? And did the princess still believe it?

Did he? He took the altivorc's knife and brought it to his throat.

"Wait!" Fleet whispered. "If he goes missing or turns up dead, it'll raise suspicions. There's another way." Reaching into his pouch, he pulled out some dried red mushrooms, which he crushed into a coarse powder. "Open his mouth!"

Tian watched dubiously. "What will that do?"

"These fungi have a sedative effect on altivorcs and tivorcs. Legends say that before the War of Ancient Gods, the altivorcs enslaved my people to serve as watchdogs to warn against dragon attacks. What they don't say is that we also harvested these mushrooms so they could use them for leisure. After he eats them, he'll be out for hours with sweet dreams, and have only a vague recollection of what happened." The madaeri grinned. "So don't say my notes on your outdated map are useless!"

They drugged the altivorc, and then half-carried him back to the inn. Locals turned their heads, but most quickly returned to their socializing. At the table, the imperial guards seemed uncharacteristically... relaxed. Their usually hard eyes were softened, their gestures animated. And they were smiling.

Two newcomers sat on either side of Brehane, their backs to him. Zhao Wei made eye contact and tilted his head in Tian's direction. Everyone's attention, including that of the two recent arrivals, fell on him.

Sameer. Dressed in the Ayuri Paladin's traditional *kurta,* he stood and pressed his palms together in greeting. The other young man, dark of skin with a bald pate, remained seated, his posture straight. Likely the Levanthi Akolyte Cyrus, if he was with Brehane and Sameer.

Tian greeted them with a nod, and then sat their unconscious guest down at an open chair.

Cyrus' tone was harsh as he addressed the madaeri in what sounded like the Ayuri tongue.

Fleet grinned at the Akolyte and shrugged, while binding the altivorc to the chair with confounding knots. After he finished with his handiwork, he swept his gaze over the room. He grinned at the few patrons who gawped. "Our dinner guest."

Their stares awkwardly returned to their drinks, and Tian withdrew the altivorc's letter. "Miss Brehane. Fleet said you could translate this letter. Do you read the altivorc language?"

She shook her head. "I only learned a little about the magic they lost millennia ago. However, I may be able to help."

Tian handed her the letter, which she opened and placed on the table. Producing a crystalline prism from a pocket in her cloak, she set it atop the sheet. She then spoke a three-second string of guttural words, whose harshness did not match her appearance. The prism glowed, and the words on the paper swirled into a different script. The Akolyte and Paladin joined Tian and Fleet in crowding around.

The wavy script of the Ayuri was still just pretty gibberish. "What does it say?" Tian asked.

Brehane translated: "Have been watching activity outside Iksuvius... Cathayi ship docked at Aremarela... Cathayi here dressed as Kanin Riders... appears to be princess, six guards... await your orders... "

Tian looked at the altivorc, who was smiling in his sleep. "The scout saw through our disguise."

"We should kill it." Xu Zhan slashed a finger over his throat.

Tian tapped his chin. "He was going to pass this message on. We need to find out to whom. When will he wake?"

Fleet chuckled. "A couple of hours. Aren't you glad I didn't let you kill him?"

So much for restful sleep tonight. Tian turned to Li Wei. "We'll have to rotate watches. You take first."

Li Wei was just starting to stand when the miserable but beautiful tone of a flute floated down the steps. The princess! Clear and resonant, the melancholy sound pulled at Tian's heart, constricting his chest. Around him, the spirited conversations guttered to a hush. All the revelers' expressions contorted into sadness.

Brehane clasped her necklace. Her eyes closed, but then flapped open. "What magic is this? So beautiful and serene, yet I can feel the Resonance of the Universe."

"That's our princess," Tian said. "She came to Iksuvius in peace. Now she's pursued by the Teleri Empire. I failed to expedite her escape by ship. Let us travel with you. At least to the madaeri's pass. It could save us weeks of danger."

Brehane ignored him, turning instead to Sameer. "Is this the princess you spoke of, who transformed a dragon with her voice, and captivated kings and generals with her music?"

Sameer nodded.

She turned back. "Mister Tian, please introduce me to your princess."

Tian raised his eyebrow at the imperial guards. Zhao Wei shrugged, and the others remained expressionless. They were leaving it in his hands. At least they didn't object to it, and apparently they trusted each other. Sameer was honorable as well. And regardless, there weren't many other choices. If he were to take the princess over the land route, he'd never find the mountain pass without Fleet's help.

He rose from his chair and beckoned Brehane. He shot Fleet a warning glance as the madaeri moved to get up and follow them. Climbing the steps, they came to the cracked door to the common room. Ma Jun stood beside it, his eyes tearing and lips sagging as the despondent tune floated out from within.

Tian peeked into the small room. The princess sat on a chair by a writing desk between two windows, wearing the simple pants and shirt of the Kanin uniform. Poor girl. He'd been too harsh. This had to be the most downtrodden place she'd ever slept in her life. But there would probably be harder days to come.

Kaiya had trudged up the creaking stairs, unable to remember the last time her limbs felt so listless or her heart so heavy. All sense of imperial comportment forgotten, she plodded through the narrow hall to the common-room door and pushed it open. The sour stench of sweat blew over her like a wave. She cupped her mouth to fight back the rising bile and stumbled over to the closest of eight cots.

The bed jolted her tired body as Kaiya threw herself down on its coarse woolen blanket. Tears pooled in her eyes, unbidden. Not so much from the pain of the rock-hard bed, nor even the inevitable vermin that hid there; they only seemed like the final insult in the worst day of her life.

She allowed herself a moment of self-pity.

Having wiped the tears away, she sat up and looked around the room. The cots lined both sides like sarcophagi in an Arkothi sepulcher. A crude writing desk and chair encroached into what little open space there was. With the two windows shuttered, it seemed even more stifling than the ship's cabin.

The leather cuirass, though not actually that tight, contributed to her sense of confinement. Kaiya stood and struggled with its buckles. When her trembling fingers failed her, she tried squirming out of it. Designed by a man, for a man. She paused in her futile efforts and caught her breath. With persistent twisting and turning, it finally came loose. She flung her tormentor onto the cot and glared at it.

With a sigh, Kaiya inched through the room and collapsed into the chair. She withdrew her flute from a pocket and began to play, the memories of the day flooding back to her. Geros pulling her to him. The hopelessness of missing the ship. Tian humiliating her. Her own guards betraying her. And finally, this lice-ridden inn.

"*Dian-xia*." Tian's hated voice interrupted her self-pity, calling from outside the door.

Kaiya shuddered. She'd left the door open a crack. Had anyone seen her wallow?

"You have a visitor. She might be able to help us. Would you meet with her?"

Her? Had Tian brought some woman warrior like Jie to show just how useless she was in comparison? Very well, let him try to humiliate her more. She attempted to compose herself, straightening her carriage and lifting her chin. "Send her in."

Tian opened the door and fell to one knee, head bowed. "*Dian-xia*. I present Brehane. An Aksumi Mystic."

A chocolate-skinned woman strode in with the gait of a man.

"Leave us." Kaiya didn't even look at Tian.

He turned on his heel and left. When his soft footsteps lightened as they went down the steps, Kaiya turned back to Brehane. She'd never seen an Aksumi person so close. The woman's dark skin and coarse hair would be considered unattractive by Cathayi standards of beauty, but she was pretty all the same.

Brehane walked over to the desk. Locking a penetrating gaze on her, she extended her hands and clasped Kaiya's.

Such strange customs, rude by the conventions of the Cathayi court. Kaiya fought the urge to break eye contact, to pull back.

Brehane spoke with a heavy lilt. "I am Brehane, daughter of Dahnay of Bahir. I am honored to meet you. I hope that your health is well in this chill autumn air?"

Never before had a complete stranger addressed her so! And the Mystic's hands were so hot. Comforting, actually. Kaiya nodded.

"And your family is all well, too?"

How to answer such a question? Father's health worsened by the day, and her two brothers remained heirless. Kaiya rose out of the chair. "I am Kaiya Wang. My health, and that of my family are all well, thank you. To what do I owe this visit?"

Brehane smiled and released her hands. "My friend Sameer spoke of you, saying you were the most beautiful woman he had ever seen, and that your words alone disarmed a tyrant. I had to see for myself what kind of woman that was."

Kaiya's shoulders stiffened. As the old Cathayi proverb said, *Flattery is often followed by a knife in the back.* Cousin Peng and Avarax had proven the adage true. The Mystic's eyes searched hers, and she spoke again in a soothing voice. "Yes, your inner spirit is strong, strong enough to tame the Last Dragon. But a deluge of events beyond your control has crushed it. Even now, you deplete what is left in a tenuous maintenance of your mask. Let go; you are safe with me."

The audacity! Yet she couldn't deny the truth in the Brehane's words. Even now, it took all of her control just to hold back tears. She shook her head, all the same. "You are mistaken. Perhaps you should question the strength of your magic."

Brehane laughed. A sincere laugh, devoid of mocking or rebuke. "Miss Kaiya, my words have nothing to do with magic, and everything to do with being a woman who has also had her confidence shattered. As a girl, I was considered a prodigy. But my natural gifts could not surpass less talented people who practiced harder. That realization forced me to question my very understanding of my place in the world. Is that much different from how you feel?" She reached out with both arms, inviting Kaiya into an embrace.

Kaiya stiffened and took a step back. It would not do for the Princess of Cathay to show weakness, or allow herself the close contact that foreigners engaged in so freely.

"I've had my spirit crushed, as well. I lost the man I loved. I was forced to give up our child." Brehane beckoned her closer.

How reassuring it would be to confide in someone. Someone who would disappear from her life just as quickly as they had come. That someone was supposed to have been Tian, but now, perhaps it was this stranger. Her resolve faltered. She stumbled into the Mystic's arms. Empathetic warmth enveloped her, and tears flowed down her cheeks as the Aksumi stroked her hair.

Kaiya's shoulders relaxed. She drew away, wiping her eyes on her coarse sleeve and lifting her chin. The sisterly hug hadn't been too awkward or embarrassing. It was pleasant, even, though the last time she'd found comfort in a hug was with a dragon in man's clothing.

Brehane smiled. "You are not alone."

Kaiya nodded.

"Now, Miss Kaiya, might I ask you to play your musical instrument?"

Though it would be considered rude to make such a request in Cathay, Kaiya withdrew her flute. Why not? She had already *hugged* a stranger. She brought it to her mouth and started a peaceful tune, the previously melancholy sound all but forgotten.

"More emotion," encouraged the Aksumi.

Kaiya complied, allowing her renewed sense of serenity to float on the notes.

Clasping a jewel which hung from her neck, Brehane closed her eyes. "I can feel it. The Resonance of the Universe." She started a slow chant in a guttural language. It rippled through Kaiya's music.

The Aksumi intonated one last syllable. Several crashing sounds came from downstairs, followed by silence.

Kaiya lowered her flute, while Brehane came out of her trance and looked around.

"What was that?" Kaiya asked.

"As you were playing, I could sense the energy of the world coalescing, similar to the vibrations surrounding the ancient pyramids—though not as strong. I tried to help put you into a state of relaxed sleep with my magic, since I was so certain your scattered thoughts would prevent you from resting well tonight. Yet you are still awake. How is that?"

Kaiya's emotional armor reformed. The Mystic had tried to put her to sleep without her consent. She glanced at her pack on the bed, where she'd stowed the Teleri imperial crest. Certainly, it couldn't protect her from magic from so far away. And no matter how compassionate Brehane had acted, it was not worth the risk of revealing it.

"I do not know," she said. "Let us go downstairs and see what all the noise was."

Down in the main room of the inn, everyone from the revelers to the barkeep to the imperial guards slept; some on the floor, others at the bar, some at their tables.

Heavens. Kaiya turned to Brehane. "Did you do this?"

Brehane's eyes rounded. "My skill is not so powerful as to cause an entire building of people to fall asleep. I believe that your music amplified my spell. However, you remain completely unaffected. Where did you learn how to manipulate magic?"

"We do not manipulate it, as much as evoke emotion through our art."

Brehane waved her hand at the sleeping room. "This is more than just stirring emotions."

Kaiya shrugged. "It is a long story, which starts with an elf lord who serves as my father's advisor. He taught me to feel that all things vibrate. He also gave me a book explaining how music affects those vibrations."

Wonderment danced in Brehane's expression. "Do you have this text with you?"

Technically, it had not been a book, but rather a magic mirror which displayed text. Kaiya shook her head. "I left it in Cathay, with the elf lord."

"It is said that during the War of Ancient Gods, the elves taught us magic based on our peoples' natural affinity. But perhaps my people's sorcery and your artistic mysticism are not so different." Brehane clasped her necklace. "I would like to meet your elf, so that I might listen to his invocation of ritualistic Deep Magic. I have heard that it sounds almost musical. Maybe it, too, is similar to your own music."

If she ever made it home. Kaiya forced a smile. "I will give you the text and do my best to introduce you. I warn you, however, that he is a private person with strange whims, coming and going as he pleases."

"Then I will do my best to make sure you make it home. In the meantime, we should wake these people. Though maybe it would be better if we did not tell them what happened." Brehane winked at her. She spoke again in the harsh words of magic, and everyone started lifting their heads and rubbing their faces.

Tian, who'd been asleep with his head resting on their table, looked around through half-lidded eyes. "What happened? Is everyone all right?"

After his involvement in this horrible day, it was impossible to resist a petty jab. "Everyone is fine, thanks to your watchful vigilance." She regretted it as soon as the words passed her lips.

His expression blanked.

Brehane furrowed her brows at Kaiya before turning to him. "Mister Tian, considering your men's past assistance, we would be happy to escort Miss Kaiya to the Nothori Mountain pass. It will be a long, hard journey, so we had all better get some rest. Miss Kaiya will stay with me in my room; Fleet, you sleep with the Cathayi boys."

Fatigue crept back over her, and Kaiya did not bother to hide her relief. Not only did she have more protection, she would also not have to share a room with men.

Her relief was short-lived.

Tian looked around. "Where is the altivorc?"

CHAPTER 26:
Rude Awakenings

The pounding of a fist on a breastplate jostled Geros awake. His eyes fluttered open, and he dragged himself out of his slouch on the throne. His limbs felt listless and heavy, the effects of the princess' brazen assault still weighing on his energy.

All around him, officers stood at attention. A soldier stepped through the doors, and Geros acknowledged him with a half-hearted nod. "The city center is ours, First Consul!"

He had almost slept through his moment of glory. "What time is it?"

A general on his flank spoke. "The Iridescent Moon wanes to its first gibbous, Your Eminence."

Well past midnight. Geros frowned. "We are a phase behind schedule."

Another general thumped his chest. "Your Eminence, because of our redeployment of men to the Cathayi embassy, we did not have enough troops to completely secure the eastern gate. Even now, the Iksuvi soldiers are mounting a counter-attack along our flanks."

Cathay. The princess. Had Feiying captured her? Or at least located her? "What is the latest report from the Cathayi embassy? Did Feiying succeed?"

The first general shook his head. "No, Your Eminence. Feiying is unaccounted for."

"Unaccounted for? What about the Nightblades?"

"Also unaccounted for."

"Tivar take them!" Geros pushed himself up out of the throne, towering to his full height despite his tiredness. "Never mind that for now. Prepare my horse. We will set out for the eastern gate to greet our armies. In the meantime, move the cavalry from the northern gate to the eastern gate, and order them to prevent the Iksuvi from setting an edge on our flanks."

Fists pounded against chests as the Bovyan soldiers hastened to fulfill his command. Geros strode out of the throne room, his honor guard keeping pace behind him. It took all his will power to maintain the façade of strength. When he reached the courtyard, a column of cavalry awaited him. He mounted up on a horse, drew his sword, and held it aloft. "To the eastern gate to join our brothers! Iksuvius will be ours!"

His soldiers roared as they pounded their chests in unison, and followed his horse as he rode out. The streets were devoid of citizens, though the sounds of skirmishes carried from many different directions. On the eastern edge of the city center, a messenger caught up with them.

The soldier ran to the front of the column and saluted with a fist to his chest. "Your Eminence, the altivorcs attacked the Cathayi embassy from the inside."

Geros gripped the reins as he clenched his jaws. "What? After I told them not to? From the inside? How? What did Marius do?"

"We are not sure how they got past our cordon. Marius sent me to receive your orders."

Geros pounded his fist into his open hand. "Tivar curse them! Guards, come with me. The rest of you, keep up."

He wheeled his horse around and spurred it on, cantering in the direction of the Cathayi embassy. His dozen mounted guards followed him, with no semblance of their typically precise formation.

No sooner did he split off from the column than Geros regretted his impulsiveness. Their handful of mounted Bovyans would not be able to counter any more than a platoon of thirty. He could not afford to show any weakness now. He pressed his men onwards, and under Solaris' watchful eye, they rode unopposed.

Not far from the Cathayi embassy, a series of explosions rang out. Red and orange lights flashed above the squat buildings, and the ground shook. Geros yanked on his reins, though he hardly needed to as his horse shied at the loud sounds.

Their horses calmed and the Bovyans approached the embassy. Several of the buildings had erupted in flames, glowing in the night sky. Around the compound, Teleri soldiers stood in exacting lines, even as they looked on with wide eyes.

"The First Consul has arrived!"

Heads turned to face him and fists pounded on chests. The men parted in perfect synchronicity to create a path for Geros to ride through.

Young General Marius greeted him. "Your Eminence, the altivorcs appeared inside the embassy compound and attacked the Cathayi. We held our position, unsure of what to do in this unforeseen circumstance."

Geros dismounted with some effort and looked through the gates. The raging flames consumed the graceful Cathayi architecture, mirroring the anger that burned in his heart. "General, storm the embassy and take any survivors into custody. If you find any altivorcs, engage and kill them."

Marius bowed his head. "As the First Consul commands!" He turned back to the soldiers. "First, second, and third companies, prepare to breach the gates!"

The soldiers formed up in the center with drawn spears, just as dozens of altivorcs appeared on the other side of the walls. Their apparent leader flung open the gates and sauntered through. "First Consul Geros, I bring you a present."

With a wave of his hand, two altivorcs marched forward, dragging a limp body in bloodied, light-blue robes. Hair hung over her face. She yelped as they flung her down at Geros' feet.

His anger at the altivorcs' betrayal faded as a new rage at the princess boiled over. He grabbed her by the hair and jerked her head back.

Though beautiful, the girl was not Princess Kaiya.

"Fools!" Geros spat at the leader. "I have no use for this girl. Where is Princess Kaiya?"

The altivorc grinned and shrugged. "They all look the same to me. There were no other females inside, save for the half-elf girl who is burning in the flames as we speak."

Without breaking eye contact with the altivorc leader, Geros snarled orders to his men. "Enter the embassy, search for any survivors and bring them out. Collect their rifles and firepowder."

The altivorc laughed. "What do you think caused the explosion? All the firepowder was ignited, and the rifles destroyed. Maybe you can salvage some after the fire burns itself out."

"You. Get out of my sight before I change my mind and have you join the half-elf in the inferno." He looked down at the girl, whose teary eyes were wide with fear.

The sounds of stomping boots marched in perfect rhythm with the throbbing in Jie's head, jolting her awake. The straw mattress prickling her back beckoned her to sleep, but willpower pried her eyes open. The orange haze beneath her eyelids gave way to blurry sunlight, filtered through a small, partially shuttered round window. She went to rub her aching head, only to find her wrists bound tight above her head. Her ankles were likewise tied down with silk rope.

The stifling air hung in her lungs. She lifted her head to get a feel for her surroundings, realizing then that the only thing she wore was a bandage around the cut on her shoulder. Some dust in the center of her chest sparkled in the brittle sun. Jie regarded her nakedness with a detached apathy and returned to taking in her surroundings.

The cot barely fit into the tiny room, whose pitched ceiling and exposed rafters suggested an attic space of some sort. There was a familiarity to it, but why?

Her black clothes lay neatly folded by a trapdoor in the floor. Next to them, a crude ceramic cup on the floor taunted the dryness in her throat.

"You're awake." The male voice behind her was aged and hoarse, and spoke in the Cathayi tongue.

Jie craned her neck to get a better view, to no avail. "What happened? Where am I? What day is it? Who are you? Why am I naked and bound?"

The man cackled. It was a melancholy laugh, filled with contagious sadness. "I will answer the last two questions first, with a question of my own. If you captured a Black Fist master, how would you secure them?"

Sedated, naked, and bound, with no tool that they could use to escape.

The man's face came into view. It was the one who had helped the altivorcs assault the embassy. Up close, he was gaunt, with sharp cheekbones and sunken eye sockets. White streaked his thinning black hair. Rage should have welled up within her, but oddly, she didn't care.

He held her head up and brought the cup to her lips. She drank greedily, not caring if the cool water was poisoned.

"You are in one of the Black Lotus safehouses," he said. "They won't have use for it anymore. I brought you here after the explosion. It is the next morning."

A safehouse. The next morning. "What about my comrades?"

"As far as I know, dead to the last man, slain by the altivorcs."

Though her logical mind knew she should be angry, she felt nothing. "Why'd you help them?"

"I swore to avenge my broken heart. When I heard that you were so close, I couldn't pass up the opportunity. And when I saw you, you looked just like *him*. I hated you in that instant."

What was he talking about? Who did she look like?

"But after I knocked you unconscious, with your eyes closed in peaceful sleep, you reminded me so much of *her*. I couldn't bring myself to kill you."

Emotion broke through her apathy. Jie's heart raced, the urgency in her voice sounding odd in her ears. "What are you talking about? Who do I look like? Who do I remind you of?"

The man uncapped a bamboo tube, and the heavy scent of deer musk percolated through the small room. Everything came together now: the dust on her bosom, the subtly sweet taste of the water, and now the musk. A staged euphoria toxin, exactly the same as the one the Nightblades had tried to use on the princess, similar to the one she'd used on General Marius two nights before. Her captor could tell her the answer to the Unanswerable Riddle from Eldaeri folklore, and she'd never remember.

He brushed his finger across her neck. A pleasant buzzing replaced the aching in her head.

"Who do you remind me of? Why, your parents, of course. But as you've probably surmised, you won't remember much of this conversation anyway. Trust me, I am doing you a favor; you're better off not knowing."

"My parents?" The dead mother she never knew, the elf father who abandoned her. "You knew my parents?"

His voice no longer seemed tired, seemed to carry a lighthearted tone. "Oh yes, very well. Now, tell me about your father."

Who didn't have father issues? This guy, probably. She giggled. "He left me at the gates of the Black Lotus Temple with a letter asking for them to take me in."

The man inhaled sharply. What was *his* problem? It was *her* father, not his. So much tension in those shoulders. "So you never knew him?" he asked. "Nor he you?"

"No. Nope. Not at all." Hah! On a normal day, mention of her father would nudge her into a carefully concealed anger. Was she usually so uptight? It wasn't like she was the first one to ever be abandoned. Her face must've now been wearing the most ridiculous smile.

"Well, that changes things. Not only can I not bring myself to kill you, it wouldn't achieve anything anyway."

Kill? That would sound like a threat if the guy didn't look like a grandfather. Not like death was scary anyway. She'd always faced it with a sense of resignation to fate. She let out a sputtering giggle. "What did you hope to achieve, anyway?"

The renegade tapped his chin, almost like Tian. "It's said that loss of a child is the greatest pain. I thought I could hurt your father by killing you. But he must not care, if he abandoned you."

"Yes. I would kill him myself if I ever met him." Would she? Maybe. It seemed like the right thing to say. "Gouge his elf eyes out and cut off his manhood!"

"Now there's an idea... I do hope you will remember parts of what I am about to tell you." He grinned.

Good, a grin. This guy really could stand to smile a little more.

"So, enlighten me," he said. "How do you think your father delivered you to the gates of the Black Lotus Temple?"

The question jabbed into her euphoria. The temple was well-hidden, and nobody could truly find it unless they had been shown the way. Jie had asked herself this question time and time again, but trusted Master Yan's word so implicitly that she'd always dismissed her nagging suspicions. Her goofy smile dissipated, replaced by knitted eyebrows.

"This letter, what did it say?" he continued.

"I never saw it. Master Yan lost it."

The man burst out laughing, and Jie found herself giggling with him. He choked as he forced himself to stop. "When does even a Black Fist apprentice *ever* lose anything? Let alone the great Master Yan? What did he say was written in the letter?"

Jie stopped laughing. Yet another buried suspicion, vocalized by someone else. "That my mother died in childbirth, that my father cared more about his adventures than me. That I would just be a burden, so he left me there."

The man's eyes were wide now. "Well, it seems I don't have much to do here. Yes, your father was a selfish dastard who didn't care for you or your mother. He only cared about making a half-elf by bedding a human. You have every right to hate him."

Jie didn't hate him, at least not right now. She just smiled. "So who's my father?"

"Royalty, from what I understand. Master Yan knows better than I, in that regard. If you remember our little talk, do ask him about your birthright."

Royalty? She wasn't just an abandoned child, whose elf blood the Black Fist thought would come in handy? And how could Master Yan, her adopted father, *ever* deceive her like that? Despite her euphoria, she protested. "I don't believe you. You're lying."

"Hush, hush. It is true. And unlike your father, I loved your mother. We were in love, before that Turtle's Egg came along. Now that I look at you, you really do resemble her. The beauty." The man brushed his hand through her hair, which sprawled loosely over the bed.

Even through her euphoria, his touch felt wrong. Jie struggled with her bindings, but they were even more secure than she could tie herself.

"She loved me." Her captor came around the cot and leaned over her, his body heat and musky smell suffocating. He brought his face to her neck. His hand brushed up her thigh. She squeezed her eyes shut and turned her head.

No, this wasn't right. The rope dug into her wrists and ankles as she fought to free herself.

And then the hot weight above her drew away. Jie forced her heavy eyelids open again, and gasped for breath.

Above her, the man wore a sad expression. "You are not her."

She shook her head, wondering for the millionth time in her life what her mother must have been like.

He slid a finger into her mouth, bringing a touch of sweetness. "Sleep now, my dear."

Jie fought the fog that settled over her mind, and mumbled one last question. "Who was my mother?"

The sadness of his voice added to the heaviness in her head. "She was—"

And then blackness.

CHAPTER 27:
Last Details

Tian shook his head. The altivorc couldn't have gotten far, and yet their search proved fruitless. With no other recourse, he questioned the drunken locals for news of altivorc activity over the last several days, only to be greeted by blank stares.

Certainly they would've heard about the battalion if it were within a few days' march. If they didn't have to worry about a few thousand altivorcs, it was better to take advantage of sleep here, instead of moving to a different location. Especially since Chen Xin would be returning in the morning.

Yet even with rotating watches, Tian slept restlessly, waking at the slightest sound. At first light, he pulled himself off of the cot to prepare for their departure.

The chill morning air greeted him as he stepped out of the inn. With precious little money, he was pleasantly surprised to find the Kanin Rider who'd guided them the day before, waiting by the stables with gifts from his embassy: a month's supply of Kanin cornbread in backpacks, more feed for the horses, the monks' clothes they had left behind, and thirty gold *kroon*.

Just before the Iridescent Moon waned to its fourth crescent, Chen Xin returned. Beside him rode Arvydas, the young king of Lietuvi, with a contingent of twenty mounted guards. Tian scanned the road behind them. Perhaps it was a trap. Perhaps a hundred enemy soldiers waited in the tree line outside the village. It was surprise enough the boy king had come at all. Unless it was to capture the princess. If only she would listen to reason.

Keeping his gaze on the king, Tian bowed. "Your Majesty. Princess Kaiya will be pleased. That you came."

Arvydas' mouth curled into a lopsided sneer, the fuzz on his upper lip reminiscent of a caterpillar rearing its head. He spoke with a contrived brashness that did little to hide the insecurity of youth. "Make haste. I have important matters to attend to in the city."

Tian made eye contact with Chen Xin and tilted his head back towards the inn. The guard nodded and headed in that direction. While they waited, the king and his knights took in the surroundings.

The princess emerged from the inn, walking as regally and straight as if the day before had never happened. Her hair was tied back tightly, and she wore just the leather cuirass of a Kanin soldier. The uniform did nothing to highlight her physical perfection, yet she still carried herself as if wearing silken gowns.

Around her, the imperial guards held their sword scabbards, their free hands never straying far from the hilts. Their eyes evaluated the king's guards. Tian palmed several throwing stars.

For their part, the Lietuvi guards sat upright, hands on the pommels of their swords. Their gazes shifted between their king and the Cathay.

King Arvydas' jaw remained rigid, though his glare softened when her gaze met his. His lips twitched, and his eyes roved over her with the hot blood of early manhood. He raised a hand, and his knights drew their swords and fanned out.

Oh, no. Though not unexpected. Tian stepped in front of the princess while the imperial guards formed up around her.

Though she wore pants, she gracefully dipped into a shallow, Northern-style curtsey. Her voice remained calm. "Your Majesty, thank you for meeting with me. Please, be at ease."

The last four words warbled like the song of a nightingale, but Tian shrugged off the power of her voice as it rippled over him.

The Lietuvi contingent, however, relaxed in their saddles. The king's expression twitched again, settling into an obviously forced scowl. His tone was accusatory. "You do realize the risk I am taking to come here? Speak."

"Your Majesty, these are words privy only to your royal ears. Please, walk with me, alone." She sang the last three words, power radiating from them.

The king's brash façade melted. Motioning for his shocked guards to stay behind, he joined her in a stroll toward the river's shoreline.

The princess turned to Tian, her silent order clear: *do not follow us.*

Foolish. All it took was for the king to resist her voice once, and she'd be alone, defenseless against him. Tian fought the urge to trail them, and just watched as the two descended to the riverbank. He pulled Chen Xin away from the semicircle of knights. "Did you deliver all the messages?"

Chen Xin shook his head. "Our compound was completely surrounded, so I went to the Kanin embassy and spent the night there. Their ambassador pledged to send supplies to the princess."

The embassy. Hopefully, Jie was there, safe behind the compound walls. "What about the *Golden Phoenix*?"

Chen Xin frowned. "Rumors say she has gone out to open sea."

"Out to open sea? How could they leave the princess behind?"

"She ordered the captain to return to Cathay, even if it meant leaving us behind." Chen Xin sighed.

Selfless, but ill-advised. It was Tian's turn to shake his head. "And you let her?"

"When has she ever listened to us?" Chen Xin threw his hands up. "I went behind her back, but I couldn't convince the captain to disobey her order."

Tian sighed. Stubborn girl. Noble, stubborn girl. There was no point in blaming Chen. "Did the Teleri take the city?"

"This morning, the Teleri captured the eastern gate and occupied much of the eastern portion of the city. The Iksuvi army puts up a valiant resistance in the city center, but it's only a matter of time before the Iksuvius is completely occupied."

Tian lifted his chin at the king's twenty knights. "And so the Lietuvi agreed to meet. I don't trust them."

Chen followed his gaze. "Give the princess more credit. She may be stubborn, but she has manipulated older and more experienced rulers than young King Arvydas."

Perhaps. Tian looked down towards the river, where the princess and the king talked, just out of earshot. "Let us hope she finishes her parley soon. We need to stay ahead of the news coming out of Iksuvius."

The early morning sun danced on the ripples of the lazy river, while small white birds floated on the light breeze. Standing by the sandy riverbank beneath the weathered seawall, Kaiya scrutinized the king.

Younger than her by two years, and having just taken the reins of power after years of being a puppet king, King Arvydas took long strides with his chest puffed out. His own insecurities, youthful ardor, and brashness would make him soft clay in her hands.

His lips were pursed. "The First Consul sent a message to his allies, saying that you have committed crimes against the Teleri Empire. He offered a substantial reward for your capture. I wondered what offense would warrant such a bounty."

Kaiya flashed her most disarming smile. "I wonder as well. I am just a girl, defenseless and far from home. There is little that I could do to the great Teleri Empire."

He jabbed a finger in her direction. "You fled the city, so you must be guilty of something. Tell me, or our discussion is over and I will deliver you to the First Consul's bedchamber myself."

Kaiya tilted her head and placed her hand over her heart. "I did nothing more than defend myself. Perhaps the First Consul cannot accept that he was bested by an untrained girl a third his size."

Mouth agape, Arvydas lowered his hand. He looked at her, his eyes appraising more than her curves. He snorted. "So... why did you ask to meet me?"

She looked up through her lashes. "I wish to discuss your new alliance with Iksuvi."

His mouth again hung open for a few seconds before he burst out laughing. "Why would I ally with those weasels? They tried to set up their own puppet to usurp my throne. That snake Evydas will receive his comeuppance soon enough."

"I think you will rethink your position after you hear about an even greater betrayal." She edged closer and lowered her voice. "My informants have told us that the Teleri have made several deals aimed at conquering the Nothori region. While your troops move into the south of Iksuvi, the altivorcs guarding your border with Rotuvi have abandoned their post and have left your rear unguarded. Rotuvi has made a deal with the Teleri to invade you from the south, while you are preoccupied with your invasion of Iksuvi."

The king frowned and waved a hand. "Preposterous! Why would the Teleri double-cross us? They have nothing to gain, nor the resources to fight a war on two fronts."

Kaiya chose her words carefully to avoid offending Arvydas. "I am only a girl, with no mind for military strategy, but I wonder why the First Consul set your alliance for just two years instead of five. After they conquer Iksuvi, who will be next? How long would it take them to conquer your kingdom if you weakened yourself by dividing your troops between occupying Iksuvi and defending your southern borders from Rotuvi?"

Arvydas paled, though he still spoke with bravado. "You *are* just a girl. Old Gunvydas is a coward. But if Rotuvi *does* attack us, we have enough soldiers in the south to repulse an attack. Why are you telling me this now? What do you have to gain from us joining forces with Iksuvi?"

At least he was entertaining the idea. Her real reason—to cover her own escape—would remain unspoken, replaced by a half-truth. "I do not care to see the Bovyan scourge sweep through the Northwest, for that will put them at Cathay's border. Iksuvi and Lietuvi standing together have a better chance than either one alone."

King Arvydas cast a sly smile. "Are you so confident in your information that you would be willing to come back to our embassy?"

Diplomatic words spilled off her lips on reflex. "I am confident in our information, but not so assured in the safety of returning to Iksuvius, even under your protection. The Teleri are bringing a sizeable force, and could easily surround your embassy if they learn of my presence there. It would be unfair of me to put you in that situation."

The king's peach fuzz danced back and forth as he visibly pondered her words. "What do you plan to do now?"

Of course this question would come. She'd prepared more half-truths to gauge King Arvydas' trustworthiness. And protect them if he decided to betray her. "I am heading south to winter in Kalenai City, as far away from the invading army as possible. I do not care to share a bed with Bovyan soldiers. Come spring, my father will send warships to press the Teleri for my safe return."

The king shook his head and offered a smug grin. "You are cornering yourself. You do not realize how quickly a Teleri army conquers. The only way out of southeast Iksuvi is either across the river into Teleri itself, or through altivorc tunnels in the Wilds. You should turn west at the highway crossroads and head toward Laramies."

Right where his armies were heading. Kaiya nodded her head and smiled coyly. "Thank you, Your Majesty. I defer to your military mind. I have no eye for strategy or map-reading."

Arvydas beamed. "Laramies is close to the border of my kingdom. You will find safe haven with us."

It was too fast a change in attitude. Still, it was better to play along and preempt his next suggestion. "Thank you for your kind offer. We do not know the way. Would it be impertinent to ask that you send one of your men with me as a guide?"

Surprised satisfaction flashed across his face, as evident as the sun on a cloudless day. "We are pressed for able-bodied soldiers in these times of uncertainty. Nor can I give the Teleri the impression I am helping you."

She raised an eyebrow. "And what about your alliance with the Teleri?"

His feral grin returned. "If your information is wrong, then I will tell the First Consul where you are headed. If it is right, then we still have two years to prepare a defense against them."

Kaiya curtseyed again. "Then we will both be safe. For the time being."

Tian appeared at the top of the seawall. "*Dian-xia,*" he said in the Cathayi tongue. "We must make haste. A swifthorse relay messenger just passed through. Iksuvius has fallen. Bovyan scouts are headed this way."

CHAPTER 28:
A Journey of a Thousand Li Begins With Trouble

Once they passed the exodus of refugees on the first day, Tian knew his plan would work—as long as they stayed ahead of the news from the north. The altivorc column coming up from the south would have no reason to stop a small patrol of Kanin Riders if they didn't know about the disguise.

The first three days of the journey went smoothly, with sunny weather and unseasonable warmth for early autumn. The highway ran along the river through pastoral farmland, passing through several villages and a few small towns. Farmers and townsfolk afforded them only an occasional curious glance. Even the usually pessimistic Li Wei seemed to be less gloomy than usual.

Across the river, which narrowed to about a *li* in width, lay several Teleri towns and villages. Yet from what Tian could see, life went on as usual, with no hint of the war that raged to the north. Fleet, regularly rode ahead to scout, coming back with reports that all remained calm in the south. More importantly, there was no sign of the altivorc army.

They stayed in the swifthorse highway lodges, though the message relay system had ground to a halt in the last week after horses started falling ill. As a precaution, Tian insisted on paying farmers to stable their own horses, away from the swifthorses. Despite that inconvenience, easy access to food and soft beds made their journey feel more like an outing than an escape.

The change in terrain matched the transformation Tian saw in the princess. Now out of immediate danger, she seemed happy as she rode side-by-side with Brehane.

The two exchanged hairpins, declaring themselves sworn sisters. They chatted and giggled like farmers' wives with few cares in the world. The Mystic frequently spoke of the young son she so missed, while the princess provided empathetic encouragement. She began to actually resemble the girl from his youth. But on occasion, the princess caught him looking at her. She would lift her chin and turn away, dispelling any illusions.

Around noon on the fourth day, they arrived in the river town of Kalenai. The friendly faces from previous towns and villages gave way to suspicious glares, and the townsfolk refused to sell them food or feed.

Fleet frowned as they came to a stop in the middle of the town. "I've been here many times and have never received such a cold reception."

Tian tapped his chin. They were riding well ahead of the news out of the north. "No one could possibly know. That we're being pursued. And even if they did know... The people of Iksuvi wouldn't help the Teleri."

"You!" a loud, unfriendly voice called out in Arkothi.

Tian turned.

A burly town constable approached, pointing at them. "You there, what business do you have in Kalmies?"

Tian had prepared a story before they'd even set out, just for these occasions, and had rehearsed the long sentence over and over again in his head. He gestured towards Sameer and his friends. "The Kingdom of Tomiwa has asked these Southerners to investigate a haunting at our villa in Kalenai."

The constable regarded him through narrowed eyes. "You're going to have to come with me."

Tian frowned. "Sir, we cannot be delayed."

"You are foreigners on Iksuvi soil—"

Brehane chanted a string of guttural syllables, while crushing some flower petals in her hands.

The constable's expression softened, and he beamed with outstretched hands. "My friends! Forgive me for my rude behavior just now. These are unsettled times."

Brehane smiled back at him. "My companions have said this town was always warm and hospitable; but today, we get nothing but suspicious stares. What has happened?"

The constable shook his head sadly. "I'm so sorry. An altivorc came to our station yesterday. He said that a party of seven Kanin Riders might pass through. He also said that Iksuvi would soon fall to Teleri, and that whichever town captured the Riders would be spared the Mating indefinitely. An entire squad of my men are coming to detain you. You must flee now. Be careful. There's a rumor of a large regiment of altivorcs heading north along the highway."

Tian gritted his teeth. How could their escaped prisoner have spread the news so fast? "Thank you. Tell your comrades that we fled. North along the highway." He then turned to his companions. "We must move quickly."

As they cantered through the streets and out of town, the locals whispered and pointed. They didn't pause until the town was well in the distance, and the next village was just within sight. With tired horses, hungry humans, and a famished madaeri, they left the road, descending to the Alto River bank to break for lunch.

The river flowed lazily north, its glittering ripples reflecting the sun high above. Birds flew south against the flow of the river, heading toward their winter nesting grounds. For the first time since the onset of their journey, they had to eat some of the Kanin corn bread. An uneasy silence hung over the group.

Akolyte Cyrus broke the silence. "Brehane, our own mission is in jeopardy now. We must split and go our separate ways."

Tian would do the same if their roles were reversed. He kept his voice measured. "We won't find the pass into the Wilds. Not without Fleet's help. You'll be condemning the princess to capture."

Cyrus kept his voice equally level. "As cruel as it sounds, the nature of Brehane and Sameer's duty impacts everyone on Tivaralan. I'm sorry to say that your princess is—"

Brehane touched her head. "Here, you are right." She then covered her heart. "But sometimes, we must decide *here* what is right. I will not abandon my sworn sister in her time of need."

Cyrus tapped his head several times with his finger. "Consider this. From what we know, we must be at the Kanin pyramid during the full White Moon. If we stay with the Cathayi, we'll be slowed down as they ride around towns instead of through them. We also risk capture. Your own mission must take precedence."

The Akolyte's reasoning was sound. Still, there had to be a way to convince them. Tian looked from Brehane to Sameer.

Sameer intervened. "Our mission is important, but I'm honor-bound to help protect those who need it, especially when we assured them of our swords. Remember that the imperial guard, and Jie helped us in Levastya, too, when our magic failed."

Tian blew out a breath.

Cyrus sighed. "As long as you know where I stand. I hope we don't regret this."

The princess rose to her feet. "Thank you, my friends. Once upon a time, I would have been too proud to let my own problem impose on others. However, you have seen me as none have before; I can never be the resolute and unfailing princess in your eyes. I admit I am afraid. I truly appreciate your help." She bowed low.

The imperial guards all dropped to one knee in a salute.

Fleet piped up, his voice cutting through the reflective silence. "Does anyone have mustard seeds? This bread is quite bland."

The princess glared at him for ruining the moment, and he lowered his head in mock shame.

As they finished up their lunch, Tian gazed over the madaeri's map. They'd reach the crossroads of the east-west and north-south highways by the end of the day. Soon after that, they'd be able to see the northernmost mountains of the Nothori range to the west. The altivorcs must have come from that direction. After reaching the highway, their battalion would turn northward toward Iksuvius. How far away were they now? Who would reach the crossroads first?

Chen Xin said, "The altivorcs are looking for seven Cathayi disguised as Kanin Riders. If we change back to monks' robes, it might throw them off."

Li Wei shook his head. "Wandering monks don't ride warhorses, and nobody will confuse a Kanin charger for a farm nag."

Fleet jumped up and down, waving his hands. "We'll be able to see the altivorcs on the river basin well in advance. We can leave the highway and ride through the woods a few miles west of here."

"We should split up," Cyrus said. "The Kanin horses are faster anyway, and they're not looking for the three of us."

Tian tapped his chin. Maybe the Akolyte was trying to abandon them again.

Fleet shrugged. "Whether we are seven and four or eleven, we don't stand a chance confronting an army of altivorcs. But in smaller groups, it'll be easier to bypass them. We can meet in the town of Issemies, at the confluence of the Alto and Noto Rivers. It's about two days from here."

It made sense. As long as they saw the altivorcs first, they could avoid them. Tian exchanged glances with Chen Xin, who nodded his approval. All eyes shifted expectantly to the princess, who consented with a tilt of her head. With reluctant farewells, the Cathay rode ahead.

That night, they camped under the stars for the first time on their trip, not far from the crossroads between the two main highways. After eating a dinner of cornbread, they fed the horses with the feed they'd bought in Gaukaimas.

Despite the pleasant evening weather, the princess' cheerful demeanor tumbled into silent petulance.

Tian hid his scoff. Some people actually enjoyed the outdoors. He and the five imperial guards rotated watches, allowing the irritable princess to sleep.

He woke the next morning to find that the horses were bloated and refused to be ridden. They pressed on nonetheless, pulling reins and cajoling their mounts for a couple of miles before their pace ground to a halt.

Tian called for a break. Removing everything except the horses' saddle blankets and bits, they sat at the roadside and snacked on cornbread. After an hour, the horses' condition deteriorated.

"We might have to leave them behind," Tian said, fiddling with the straps to his armor.

Cornbread crumbs dribbled from Li Wei's mouth as he spoke. "If we do, it'll be the dead of winter before we reach the rendezvous point."

Ma Jun shook his head. "We can buy horses in the next town. We should have enough for seven."

Tian tapped his chin. They only had thirty gold *kroon*. Maybe enough for horses.

"What about riding gear?" Xu Zhan pointed at their sick horses. "We can't carry it all—"

"Altivorcs!" Chen Xin scrambled to his feet, pointing with his sabre towards the river.

Tian turned his head. Fifteen altivorcs surged up the riverbank, armed with curved broadswords and spiked shields. Apparently not even the princess, with her keen ears, had heard them above the water splashing among the rocks. The altivorcs fanned out, encircling them.

Kanin spears and sabers in hand, the imperial guards formed a protective circle around her. Taking up a horse bow, Tian came to the princess' side. It'd been years since he'd shot, and as children, she'd always been better. Had she ever shot at live targets before? Her hands trembled as she fitted an arrow to her own bow.

The enemy circled, using their superior numbers to flank each of the guards.

Tian nudged the princess. "Do that thing with your voice."

Kaiya shook her head. "They're resistant to it."

The leader spoke in thickly accented Arkothi. "Turn the princess over to us, and the rest of you will be spared."

"Set spears!" Chen Xin ordered. In response, the guards all took a step back to tighten their circle and lowered their spears.

With a laugh, the leader barked an order in a foul-sounding language. Five of the altivorcs broke away from the group and trotted towards the sick horses.

Tian and the princess both loosed several arrows at the pursuing altivorcs, but they lifted their shields and continued towards the horses. None of the arrows found their mark.

Tian lowered his bow. The enemy could wait them out until they tired or reinforcements came. If someone didn't act now, the altivorcs would be eating horsemeat tonight. He dropped his bow and vaulted into a flip over the protective line, drawing his saber with a simultaneous cut toward the leader.

The sudden attack caught the altivorc unawares, and his head rolled into the dirt. The other altivorcs froze and gaped at the black blood which rhythmically spurted from the severed neck.

Using their shock to his advantage, Tian slashed through the knee ligaments of the next closest.

The imperial guards, perhaps sensing the shift in momentum, surged outward in unison. Spears flashed towards the closest enemy. Just as swiftly, the men spun back into a protective circle around the princess. Their vicious coordination and efficiency was jaw-dropping.

Tian glanced around, evaluating the results of the imperial guards' split-second attack. Chen Xin's lightning strike had impaled an altivorc in the throat, while Zhao Yue thrust through the eye slot of another's helmet. Three altivorcs had suffered injuries.

Those three had no time to fall back. The circle flared out again, this time in a crossing burst of precise thrusts, before reforming around the princess. One second, three more altivorcs down. No wonder Jie had come to respect them.

Behind Tian, the horses cried out. He turned to see two of the altivorcs hacking at their mounts, while the other three rushed back to join in the fray. The princess wept, her fingers fumbling at fitting another arrow.

All-out melee broke out, with one-on-one duels, man versus altivorc. Spears flashed, sabers glinted. Red blood splashed against black. In the half-minute that it took for the other three altivorcs to arrive, the Cathayi had killed or incapacitated the first group. Tian, along with four of the imperial guards, set upon the last three and quickly finished them off.

The two surviving altivorcs, near the slaughtered horses, bolted. Ma Jun and Li Wei scrambled after them.

"Don't let them get away!" Tian yelled. Why hadn't the princess shot them already? "They will reveal our position. And bring reinforcements."

His orders seemed to unfreeze her. The princess let arrows fly. Even as her hands shook, her aim was true: one altivorc fell, shot in the back, and the other one was slowed as another arrow lodged in his leg. Ma Jun quickly caught up and decapitated it.

The princess sunk to her knees. She turned away from everyone and threw up.

Tian afforded her a quick glance. It must've been hard on her, being so close to combat. He turned his attention to his second victim, the altivorc whose knee he had cut in the opening seconds of the encounter. He knelt, brandishing his broadsword.

Tian disarmed him with a deft twist of his saber, and then wrenched the altivorc's arm back in a lock. "Why did you attack us?"

The altivorc's voice cracked. "We knew to be on the lookout for Cathayi disguised as Kanin Riders, and were ordered to capture you. We knew it was only a matter of time before your horses ate the poisoned feed, and that we would be able to catch up with you."

The sleeping altivorc back in the inn must have passed the message on. But how? "How did your message get ahead of us? How many of you are coming up the highway? Where are they now?" Tian cranked the lock a little more.

The altivorc chortled and sealed his lips tight.

"Speak, and I will spare you!"

The altivorc set his gaze forward, a grim look forming on his hideous face.

Spewing foul language, Tian placed more torque on his lock. The tearing of ligaments and the dislocating of a joint made a wet popping sound.

The altivorc unleashed a guttural scream. His free hand yanked a dagger from his belt and jerked the blade across his own throat. Black blood gurgled from his mouth, and he collapsed into the dirt.

It was suddenly silent, save for the princess' sobbing.

Tian turned to her. Poor girl. She must have never experienced this type of carnage before. He then realized how wrong he was.

The pounding in Kaiya's ears drowned out all other sound. How she wanted to spit out the sour taste in her mouth!

She'd watched in slow motion as an orc spear floated through the air. Had it been aimed at her? Or Chen Xin's back? It should have hit one of them. But then Xu Zhan was there, in front of her. He wasn't Tian or Jie, able to use some Black Fist trick to turn aside projectiles. He blocked the spear the only way he knew how.

With his life.

Now, through the tears in her eyes, his unconscious form was blurry, lying in a pool of his own blood. She knelt beside him, using her shaking hands to try to staunch the profuse bleeding from the gash in his neck.

She wiped away the tears and looked up as Tian approached. What did his tight lips mean? Disgust at her for their predicament? Scorn for Xu Zhan, whom he'd scuffled with when they first arrived in Iksuvius?

Kaiya looked back down. Less of Xu Zhan's blood slipped from between her fingers as his pulse faded. Though belligerent, he'd always been the first to step up to her defense in times of need. How sadly ironic that he loved fighting, and his passion had claimed him.

He was only twenty, twenty-one? She clasped his cool hand. Hopefully, that would warm his spirit as he returned to Yang-Di's embrace for a temporary respite. She whispered a prayer that he be reborn into a better world.

As she knelt with a heavy heart, Tian helped the guards bind open wounds. His expression never changed, the loss of a comrade-in-arms seeming more like an inconvenience to him than a tragedy. Words more bitter than the bile's aftertaste threatened to spill out of her mouth.

Chen Xin came forward and knelt. "*Dian-xia*. We must bury Xu Zhan. We cannot let carrion birds and other wildlife desecrate his body."

Kaiya nodded in solemn agreement, though it was clear calculations were running through Tian's mind.

His voice droned like a failed poet. "We must hurry. We can't waste much time."

Waste time! How could he consider honoring the dead a waste? Despite his cruel words, he grabbed an altivorc shield and dug into the soft ground near the river. Chen Xin, Ma Jun, and Zhao Yue joined him. Li Wei, even more somber than usual, helped her collect large stones along the banks to form a cairn.

"Let us create more cairns," said Ma Jun, "to make it appear as if we have lost more than one of our own. Since we don't have the horses anymore, we should disguise ourselves as wandering monks, as Chen Xin suggested earlier."

Kaiya shot a glance over at Tian, who in turn looked at the Iridescent Moon. Still thinking about time!

"Very well," he said. "Keep it simple."

They made two more shallow graves, stacked rocks in a ring around the mound, and placed a Kanin suit of armor and sword on top of each.

When they were finished, the imperial guards all bowed their heads.

Kaiya followed their lead, saluting Xu Zhan. "If we make it home, I swear we will one day return in force so that we can take you back."

They threw the rest of the Kanin armor into the river, and dressed in monks' robes with broad conical straw hats. They kept the spears in hand and packed away three sabers, as well as her pair of straight swords. Saying their final farewells to Xu Zhan, they continued south down the highway on foot, keeping a quick pace and drawing the curious stares of passing travelers.

Kaiya sighed. They stood out like a bride on her wedding day.

CHAPTER 29:
Sacrifices

The princess and her imperial guards trudged down the road in front of Tian. Xu Zhan's death weighed heavily on his mind, clouding all the other questions that raced through it. Pugnacious and curt from their very first meeting, Xu had nonetheless earned Tian's grudging respect over the past few weeks.

Indeed, all of the imperial guards had proven more mentally capable than he'd given them credit for: Chen Xin's recognition of King Arvydas' dissembling; Li Wei's observation about their mismatched disguises; Ma Jun's suggestion to mask their losses with multiple cairns. Their precise and ferocious attacks when defending the princess. How many more of them would perish from his failed escape plan?

With a sigh, he tried to focus on their current predicament. Without horses, they couldn't outrun the altivorcs if they encountered a large regiment. He would have to find a way to buy or otherwise liberate some horses in the next town. If there were any healthy horses there.

By dusk, they had only walked about thirty *li* in somber silence. Tian glanced at the princess again. Her jaw had been rigidly set and eyes focused straight ahead the whole time.

His stomach clenched. Did she blame him for the death of Xu? The loss of their horses? At this rate, it would take around three days to reach Issemies, while Brehane and the others would arrive in less than two. Would they pass each other on the road sometime tomorrow? If they missed each other, would Brehane wait, over Cyrus' inevitably vocal objections?

Mercifully, they made it to a town before night fell. They stayed at an inn and ate warm food. The mood was solemn, with the imperial guards' sorrow at the loss of their comrade drowned by the local ale. Tian abstained, instead concerning himself with the stares of the innkeeper and patrons as they pointed and joked about the Cathayi monks with long hair.

Early the next morning, Chen Xin and Zhao Yue set out to look for horses. Though they returned unsuccessful, they were able to procure larger packs to carry the supplies.

After a quick breakfast, the group set out as the Iridescent Moon waned to its second crescent. Walking in silence, it didn't take long for them to reach the town limits. Before the third crescent, it was well behind them.

When they took their first break around the fourth crescent, Tian worked up the courage to say what he had been thinking since the night before. "We're dressed like monks. But we still have hair. Even the locals can tell."

Ma Jun ran a hand through his hair. "What do you suggest?"

Tian braced himself for their reaction. "Shave it off."

Zhao Yue grasped a lock of his hair. "Only monks, newly inducted soldiers, and convicted criminals shave their heads."

Li Wei snorted. "Or have it shaved for them."

Tian threw his hands up. He'd expected resistance. After all, long hair was a badge of pride in Cathay. But this...

"For the princess' safety." Chen Xin stepped up and extended his hand toward Ma. "I will go first. Ma Jun, your razor."

Thank the Heavens someone saw reason. Tian glanced at the princess. Her arms were folded over her chest, her eyes set forward above her frown. This one would be harder.

Li Wei snorted again, but headed down the bank. "At least Xu Zhan got to keep his hair."

Tian descended the riverbank with the guards close behind. The princess tentatively followed. The imperial guards helped each other cut their hair with a dagger, while Ma Jun shaved everyone close with his razor. When it was Tian's turn, he watched as his hair floated downstream.

When the last guard finished, Tian looked expectantly at the princess. "Now you."

She turned her head like a petulant child. "Never."

Tian looked towards the imperial guards for support, but they all edged back and stayed silent. "*Dian-xia.* Locals have been staring. At least cut your hair close. To hide under your hat. You don't have to shave it."

She scowled at him with a glare sharp enough to shear steel. "I will *not* look like a slave or prisoner."

Perhaps she wanted to be the First Consul's bed slave. Tian clenched his jaw. "On foot, we can't outrun the altivorcs. We can't fight any more than ten."

"My hair will not be touched. That is my order."

Where was Jie when he needed her? Maybe the princess would have listened to her. "Xu Zhan sacrificed himself for you. The rest of us will do the same. Is your own vanity more important than our lives?"

The princess' face hardened. She spun around and walked back towards the road.

Tian opened and closed his fists. His life would be forfeit if they ever reached home. She would resent what he was about to do, but she would live to realize it was the right decision. He might be the villain today, but he would not be the fool in history.

Kaiya stood by the riverbank watching the waters drift northward. Though she wouldn't admit it aloud, she took greater pride in her hair than even her voice. Even when she'd been a woefully plain child, her hair had been beautiful. And now, the silky, lustrous locks could be pinned, braided, or curled. The very thought of cutting them made her heart seize up.

But no. The incompetent cur was right in this regard. For everyone's safety, it had to be cut short enough to hide under the hat.

Still, he could've at least let her save face. Or even been less insensitive about it. Running her fingers through his hair, Kaiya took a deep breath and turned to climb up the bank.

"Ma Jun," she said, "your raz—"

He wasn't there. None of the guards were. They'd already reached the road, a couple dozen feet away. When had they departed? And where was Tian?

Her head jerked back. She gasped at the burning pain in her scalp from the yank on her hair.

"*Dian-xia*, forgive me. I do this for you." Tian's voice choked, even as he seized a larger handful of her beautiful tresses. He used them to tug her along, ignoring every tearful threat, curse, and plea she could muster.

With her feet unable to grip the ground, the power of her voice died on her lips. All grace and martial technique forgotten, she twisted around and flailed at him. Her long hair allowed him to stay out of reach as he dragged her inexorably towards the river.

At the bank, he spun her hair into a thick coil around his hand. She frantically tried to hold on to her precious locks, but her hands only became entangled.

Holding the dagger in an underhand grip, he slid his arm up the coil, pushing her fingers back through the mass. With a lightning twist of his wrist, the blade slashed through her hair. The sudden cut sent her tumbling to the ground, butt first.

They both stared at the long, voluminous bundle in his hands.

Her hair.

He had cut her hair.

He hadn't waited to hear *her* decision

Kaiya screamed. Staggering to her feet, she lurched over to Tian and repeatedly battered him with her hands. In her rage and sorrow, she barely noticed that tears streamed unchecked down his cheeks as well.

Too late, the imperial guards appeared at the top of the bank and scrambled down. Where had they been?

Chen Xin lunged forward, seizing Tian's robe. Tears glistened in his eyes. "What have you done?"

Tian flopped to the ground when Chen Xin threw him down.

Still weeping, Kaiya turned around and clambered up the riverbank. She stumbled to the road and collapsed against a boulder. With short, ragged breaths, she ran her hands through the remains of her hair, finding the cut rough and jagged. Only a finger-length towards the back of her head, it lengthened to an uneven hand-width towards the top.

Her hair.

She was going to cut it, anyway, but at least he could've spared her this indignity.

Zhao Yue and Ma Jun staggered after her and bowed, watching in silence.

They pitied her.

She raised her head.

Both guards dropped to their knees, offering their sabers forth in two hands. "Forgive me, *Dian-xia*!" they shouted in unison.

Kaiya looked back down towards the river.

She was the daughter of the *Tianzi*. The blood of the gods coursed through her veins. A ruler should not shed a tear over personal loss. Tian did what he had to.

Setting her jaw, she wiped the tears from her face. The chafing fibers served as yet another reminder of how far she had fallen. With a deep breath, she rose and marched back to where Chen Xin and Li Wei detained Tian. Zhao and Ma trailed a respectful distance behind.

Choking on his own sobs, Tian knelt down, hands on top of his bowed head. His heart pumped guilt through his veins. It was surprising, actually. He shouldn't feel guilty for something that gave them the best chance of survival. So why did it feel so *awful*?

Better to die, here and now, than carry the shame of hurting his childhood friend.

Chen Xin and Li Wei both stood cross-armed in front of him, though neither held a weapon.

Tian barely recognized his own voice through its hoarseness. "I'm so sorry. It had to be done. For her sake."

Chen Xin let an exasperated sigh escape. "We are just as guilty for letting it happen. We're soldiers, and we understand the need. You may look down on her vanity, but it's her armor against what she faces every day of her life. Try to empathize."

Empathize. All the other women in his life were Black Fist. Practical. Like Jie. Who he'd probably never see again. If only she were here now.

"If you'd given her a little space," Li Wei said, "she would've come to the same conclusion."

"Here she comes now." Chen's eyes flicked behind him.

Tian looked up.

The princess approached, her carriage straight and regal as always, even if her scraggly hair didn't match the image.

He cringed. He'd done that to her. Already on his knees, he touched his forehead to the ground. "It had to be done, *Dian-xia*. I will take my life now. If you so command."

Her tone was icy, biting with a hatred that chilled his bones more than a Northwest winter. "I have already lost Xu Zhan. We will not sacrifice anyone else needlessly. But know that from this day, your life belongs to me, and you will give it when I ask."

"As you command, *Dian-xia*." Tian raised his head, not daring to make eye contact.

The princess took a few steps along the rocks and glanced down at a tidal puddle. Her face was frozen in composed perfection, like an alabaster statue, as she stroked the remnants of her hair back. She then turned to Ma Jun and extended a hand. "Your razor."

Ma Jun withdrew his razor and held it up to her in both hands with his head bowed. She took it and lopped off what was left of her hair. After shaving five heads already, it had dulled and it did not cut evenly. Every couple of seconds, the princess winced.

It was a ragged job. Ma Jun clasped her hand and took the razor. While he worked at finishing the task, she silently took up a long lock of her hair and started braiding it. She finished quickly and stashed the braid away into the fold of her monk's robe.

When Ma Jun stepped back and bowed his head, the princess stood and gazed into the river again. She took a deep breath and then let out a long sigh. She didn't look at any of them.

Tian gritted his teeth. His fault.

On her hoarse and rasping command, they resumed their trek. After two phases of brisk walking in silence, Tian called on the party to halt. In the distance, open farmland gave way to wooded hills, which stretched from the riverbank to as far west as the eye could see and would obscure any approaching threats.

Tian tapped his chin. They could hide off-road behind the trees if they heard armored Altivorcs traipsing through the woods.

As long as they got there quickly. He beckoned the others onward. "Come on. We need to hurry."

A hundred feet.

Fifty.

Twenty.

Twenty altivorcs emerged from the trees, resembling spears thrusting out between shields in an Arkothi phalanx. Oh, no.

Tian motioned for the imperial guards to stay calm. They were about to test their disguise.

With the precision of a dwarf-made clock, the altivorcs' long line merged into a three-man wide column that took up the width of the road. At the head, their leader bared his fangs at them. "Off the road, peasants!"

Tian waved the imperial guards and princess off the road. All bowed their heads as the column passed without further word.

Vindicated!

Tian blew out a sigh of relief. He dared a glance at the princess, but her hard expression hadn't changed.

When the sounds of marching altivorc boots faded in the distance, they resumed their journey, following the road through the woods. Tian scouted ahead, seeing only a couple of travelers and hunters. Before long they emerged on the other side into open farmland.

After a few phases, the clopping of three horses approached from behind, at a walk. Tian turned around.

It was their friends from the South, minus the madaeri. The three soon overtook them and passed.

Tian waved his hands wildly. "Brehane! Sameer! Cyrus!"

Sameer reared his horse and wheeled around. "By the ten thousand gods! What happened to you? Where is Xu? Where are your horses?"

"Our horses were poisoned. We were ambushed." Tian was loathe to tell the whole story.

Brehane's eyes sought out the princess', but the princess turned her head and refused to meet the Mystic's gaze.

"We must keep going," Cyrus said. "Now that the Cathayi don't have horses, they'll only slow us down. A full White Moon draws near."

The rapid pounding of hooves from the south interrupted Tian's rebuttal. He threaded past the horses to see Fleet coming down the slope in the road, bouncing in the saddle with his horse at full gallop. As the madaeri approached, he waved them off the road. Once he was within earshot, he started yelling. "Altivorcs! Thousands of them marching down the highway!"

Tian scanned the road ahead, but the rising ridge obscured his line of sight.

Yet as if to punctuate Fleet's warning, deep, ominous drums echoed from beyond. The madaeri pulled up and the clop of his galloping horse quieted. The sound of thousands of heavy boots rhythmically thumped on the hard-packed road.

Another series of drumbeats thundered up ahead, frightening dozens of black birds out of a tree on the downslope.

"It would be bad for us to be seen together," Cyrus said, his voice flat and emotionless. "Especially if news from the towns up north has reached that our group—which stands out in this land of the fair-skinned—is traveling with yours."

Brehane nodded in agreement. "Cyrus is correct. There is no way we can fight thousands of altivorcs, and the plains are too open for us to find cover. We'll withdraw to the north toward the closest farm and wait for them to pass. Princess, come with us. Fleet, hide and keep an eye on the Cathayi. You may be our only chance to link back up. We will meet at the next town."

Tian nodded. The princess should be safe with the others. With the altivorcs soon upon them, they could test out their disguise, but without risking her safety.

Chen Xin bowed deeply towards Sameer. "If something should happen to us, I humbly request that you deliver the princess to Cathay after you have completed your duties."

Sameer pressed his hands together and bowed his head, while Fleet slid out of the saddle. He flashed a grin at Tian and helped the princess up onto his horse with a little too much enthusiasm.

Where had he put his dirty paws? The imperial guards glared at the madaeri, but if the princess was offended, she didn't show it.

They knelt in salute, and she looked at them sadly. "Thank you for your service up to now. I am sure this will not be our final farewell."

Maybe it would be. And despite all their conflict now, they'd once been best friends. Tian tried to make eye contact with her, but she looked away. The Mystic, Acolyte, Paladin, and princess all turned and galloped north. It would make a great opening to a bad joke, if the consequences weren't so severe.

Fleet winked at Tian before scrambling down the riverbank and into some shrubs. Even Tian's sharp eyes couldn't find him among the brush.

He turned to the remaining four guards. "Continue walking. It will look suspicious. If we just stand here. Waiting for them."

They continued down the road. The altivorcs reached the crest of the hill and started the gentle descent. They marched in a tight formation, six abreast, shoulder-to-shoulder, taking up the entire road. At their head rode a single mounted officer. Their black flags hung lifelessly on the windless day.

They drew nearer and nearer in neat ranks, trailing each other like a line of ants. When they were about fifty feet away, the mounted altivorc waved them to the side of the road.

Tian and the guards complied, moving to the side closest to the river. They removed their hats and bowed their bald heads. He could see the altivorcs clearly now, with their chainmail, spears, and curved broadswords, looking straight ahead and marching in precision. The leader guided his horse—was it a horse? It was covered head to toe in armor, yet barely made a sound—off the side of the road to meet them, while his troops kept moving forward.

He spoke Arkothi in a thick accent. "You there. Have you seen riders from the southlands, riding large warhorses? Seven total, perhaps with a woman."

Chen Xin shook his head. "No sir. The highway has been more or less empty for about two hours, with the exception of a small group of your kind who passed by half an hour ago."

The altivorc officer turned and rode south toward the back of the column. Not long after, drumbeats emanated from that direction. Several seconds later, a series of drumbeats answered, echoing from the north.

They must be communicating with drums. Tian memorized the beat pattern in hopes that he could decipher the code in the future.

Minutes stretched into an hour, and at last the rear ranks passed. At the end of the line, an enormous packhorse, over twice as large as a warhorse and clad from head to hoof in plate armor, took deliberate steps like a dressage show horse. Despite all the metal, it moved quietly, pulling a train of wooden wagons.

The first dozen were no more than cages on wheels, several filled with young Nothori women. With wide, desperate eyes, some reached towards Tian. Others sat listlessly, resigned to their fate.

The first wave of rape victims for the Teleri breeding program. Was there any way to help them? Five men and a madaeri against an army of altivorcs? Maybe trail the column and raid their encampment at night? No; if they weren't careful, Princess Kaiya would be joining these unfortunate women.

He watched as the last wagon passed, bearing a huge drum, cut from the cross section of a greywood tree. "What was the count?" Tian asked.

"I counted five hundred ranks," said Chen Xin, "so about three thousand."

They looked among each other and confirmed the count with nods.

"All right. Let's keep moving south. The princess will catch up. They'll go around the altivorcs. On the horses."

Fleet picked himself out of the brush and rejoined them by the road. "Well, that was fun. Been a long time since I've seen one of those beasts." The madaeri pulled errant twigs out of his hair as they started up the slope in the road.

Once they reached the crest of the hill, Tian and Fleet took advantage of the higher ground to look back to where their companions had fled.

Fleet squinted. "Oh no... "

CHAPTER 30
A Bitter Homecoming

The sounds of heavy boots stomped in rhythm with the pounding in Jie's head, jolting her awake. A straw mattress pricked her back, further prodding her eyes open.

Feeble rays of sun trickled in through a shuttered round window, barely illuminating a stifling, narrow room. The sharply-pitched ceiling with exposed rafters told her she was in an attic space somewhere. But where? And how?

Through the quickly clearing fog in her head, Jie fought to recall her last memories. She'd been about to slash the renegade Black Fist's throat when an explosion unbalanced her. He'd head-butted her! A dirty trick she could appreciate.

Jie pushed herself up, despite complaints from her listless limbs. The plain brown cloak that was draped over her slipped, revealing her nakedness. She looked down and sighed at her boyish form, made even flatter by weight loss. The cloak found its way back up, covering a bandaged shoulder wound she did not recall wrapping.

She rubbed at her chafed wrists as she wobbled to her feet. Concentrate. This was one of Tian's hideouts. Above a warehouse near the west marketplace. She let out the breath she'd been holding. One of her comrades must have brought her here. Or... the renegade? That couldn't be right.

A ceramic cup filled with water beckoned her to a neatly arranged pile of supplies. She greedily quenched her thirst with the tepid water while examining the items. A hunk of cornbread. A single-edged knife. Brown woolen clothes, suited for a peasant. A knitted wool hat with flaps that would cover her pointed ears. Her black stealth suit, its tears well-stitched. Most importantly, her magic pouch. She picked it up, revealing a sheet of crinkled parchment underneath. Cathayi words were written with a quill in an unrecognizable hand.

Iksuvius occupied. Citywide curfew at sundown. Cathayi embassy gutted. Blend in with the locals. Don't do anything stupid.

A Friend.

When did she ever do anything stupid? That was Tian's job, especially when Princess Kaiya was involved. Maybe he was back in the city, looking for her. Her heart swelled.

Chewing on the cornbread, Jie teetered to the window and pried the shutters open a crack. The marketplace below, typically buzzing in the late afternoon with the chatter of young women and the laughing of children, was quiet. Shopkeepers edged back into their stores as a patrol of Bovyans marched through. Though it'd taken her some time to get used to the stink of the marketplace, she'd always appreciated the overall liveliness. Now it was just filthy.

The brittle light would soon give way to night, and darkness would allow her to venture out. In the meantime, she ate, rehydrated, and stretched out her muscles. The pounding in her head felt less like a hammer on a dwarf anvil now, and more like a dull ache.

She looked at the letter again. *Now why would a Black Fist use a quill and parchment?*

Dusk came. Dressed again in her black clothes, Jie ventured out, drinking in the cool night air. The White Moon Renyue's waning gibbous marked two days since the attack on the embassy. Tian *had* to be back by now.

In the marketplace, doors were barred and windows shuttered. It was so quiet she could hear the waves in the harbor lapping up against the seawall. The silence also allowed her to hear patrols well before they came close, and she slunk unmolested through the shadows towards the embassy.

The damage was obvious even from a distance. The main residence and temple, which had once vaulted gracefully above the walls, were now nothing more than burnt-out shells.

A hollow sensation settled in her stomach that had nothing to do with hunger. The embassy had been home for only a month, but it had been an enjoyable month, which *almost* culminated in a kiss.

A pair of Bovyans stood guard just inside the gates, ready to ambush anyone who tried to enter. Jie almost pitied their lack of stealth. She crept along the walls to the east side, where the bathhouse courtyard—if it was still there—would conceal her insertion.

The wall felt cool beneath her hands as her fingers found nooks between the stones. In short order, she made it to the top and peeked over. All clear. Creeping between the crenellations, she dropped down onto the walk. The vantage point afforded a wide view of the damage.

Where the armory had stood, there was now nothing but a dark splotch in her elf vision. The debris radiated out from the blast site, with blackened stones lying in a clearly-defined circle starting a dozen feet from the epicenter. Fire had claimed the warehouses, leaving only roofless, charred shells of stone. The main residence itself fared no better—flames must have consumed the wooden beams, leaving only the stone façade and western walls intact.

This place was where she had reconnected with Tian and almost fulfilled a decade of unrequited affection. Now rubble was all that remained. Jie swallowed the nostalgia and returned to her task of information gathering. There were the two sentries to interrogate.

Dropping down to the ground, she snuck along the walls toward the temple. It remained untouched by the destruction, probably due to its distance from the blast. Inside, the statue of Yang-Di still glowed. The green hues of her night vision burst into full color.

She almost wished they hadn't. The dark bloodstains stood out on the white stone floors and the red-painted walls. Memories flooded back: the slaughter of the ambassador, the imperial guards, and the princess' decoy, Meiling. Her scream was haunting— handmaidens rarely left the sumptuous confines of Sun-Moon palace, and none in the history of Cathay had ever been lost to violence.

Jie shook the thought out of her head and came to the long rope that sounded the temple bell. She gave it a gentle tug: light enough so that its ring would hopefully stay within the confines of the embassy grounds.

She then rushed to the entrance and peeked out. As expected, the guards looked up at the bell. One broke from his position, drew a longsword, and marched towards the temple.

With a silent prayer of apology to Yang-Di, she climbed to the broad beam above the main doors.

The Bovyan clambered up the steps and strode through. She pounced on him, jabbing her knife through his subclavian artery and possibly into his lung. His sword clattered to the ground as he buckled to his knees.

Jie glanced toward the main gate. Her ambush would've stood out like a stage play to the other sentry. Her friendly wave jolted him out of his blank look. She turned to her gasping victim, whose blood now spurted in rhythmic bursts. It joined the altivorc blood she'd spilled in the very spot days before.

"Why are you here?" she demanded, on the off chance that he might actually reveal something with his dying breaths.

"Die, Cathayi snake." The words tumbled out of his mouth with his last moments of consciousness.

Jie looked back towards his companion. He took the temple steps two at a time. She retreated deeper inside.

To her dismay, the jaunt up the steps didn't seem to tire him at all. She ran to the side of the statue to lure him in.

The soldier approached, pointing his sword at her. "Surrender."

He was taller than the other, and the suns on his collar marked him as an officer. With another quick apology to Yang-Di, Jie turned and pop-vaulted onto the statue's base, just at the edge of her adversary's reach.

"You're the female Black Fist spy! You're supposed to be dead!" He swung his sword at her, and she danced away from the blows.

She stopped and raised an open hand. "Shhh... Can you hear that?"

The man paused, but kept his sword raised. His brow furrowed. "What?"

She grinned at him. "Absolutely nothing. None of your patrols are within my very long earshot." She pointed behind him. "It's just you and my partner there."

The man turned his head. In the split second before he could turn back and raise his sword, she leapt down and slashed his wrist tendons. His sword slipped from his fingers. Before it hit the floor, she ducked low and severed the tendon in back of his heel. Working her way around to his other leg, she hooked his ankle and pushed into the back of his knee.

The Bovyan hit the ground face-first with a loud bellow.

Jie swung around and sat on top of him, still cranking his knee. "You won't live to see the sun rise. If you don't answer my questions, you will survive to just before dawn, but you'll wish you hadn't. So why're you here?" She added a little more torque, just enough to get him to yelp.

He spoke through gritted teeth. "We are rounding up all the Cathayi in the city as enemies of the state. Some come back here."

"Where are you keeping them?"

He didn't answer. She twisted a little harder, evoking a grunt.

His words spilled freely. "The men, in the city jails. The women, at the Teleri compound, entertaining us. That one girl, the treacherous princess' little bitch, she was real good."

Meiling. She must've survived. Jie leaned back a little, adding just a little more pain. "She's at the Teleri compound?"

"No, she's at the palace now. She's a noble, so she is servicing the officers. Her child will be part of your country's new ruling class."

Jie decided to punish his gloating with another sharp twist. Ligaments tore, the knee joint popped. She spun around on top of him, took control of his left arm and began wrenching it behind him. "Why are you keeping the Cathayi prisoner? What use are they to you?"

He laughed past his pain. "We torture one man to death each day, in public. If your princess weren't such a coward, she would come out to spare her people. Tell her that."

So they believed the princess was still nearby. "You deserve a slow, painful death, but I'm not so cruel."

Despite what she led others to believe, killing wasn't fun, not even a Bovyan or altivorc. With surgical precision, she slid her knife into the space between his spine and skull. His body went limp.

What a mistake! Even at full strength, it would be strenuous and time-consuming to dispose of the bodies. The Black Fist traitor—assuming he was still at large— would be able to identify her work. Her only advantage now was stealth and surprise. Sucking on her lower lip, and yet again apologizing to Yang-Di and the dead men, she took a longsword and began mutilating the bodies.

To take her mind off the unenviable task, she began plotting her next move: rescuing Meiling from the Iksuvi palace, where the Teleri officers had apparently taken up residence. And she knew one Teleri officer very well.

CHAPTER 31:
Off the Beaten Path

The wind blew over Kaiya's scalp as Fleet's horse galloped behind the Southerners. The sensation served as a reminder that her head had been shaved; the periodic booming of altivorc drums proved it had been the right move.

Before long, they came to a tree-lined dirt walkway that cut through vast rows of leafy green vegetables. It ended at a one-story farmhouse some five hundred feet up a gentle slope. Brehane pointed them toward the path.

They followed it to the weathered house. Behind it, broad fields of red wheat swayed a head above her. Kaiya turned back and looked down towards the highway, which stretched along the river. Back south the way they had come, the altivorcs seemed like a line of black, inching their way up the white road.

Brehane gestured past an empty wagon towards a wooden stable, next to a chicken coop. "We'll hide there till they pass."

"I don't suppose we have time to tell whoever lives here that we are squatting?" Sameer's shoulders rose in a shrug.

A smile formed unbidden on Kaiya's face. Sameer, polite even in a crisis.

"No time!" Brehane pointed down towards the army making its way up the river road. Still far away, but there was certainly a risk of being seen. She clasped Kaiya's clammy hand and pulled her along to the stable. Inside, they found four old plow horses.

Hiding with the animals. Kaiya instinctively went to twirl her hair, only to find it gone. She shrugged off her pack and crouched, watching as the altivorc column passed along the road. She peeked out. Cold sweat beaded on her forehead as the first ranks marched by.

An hour of waiting trudged by. The last ranks passed, trailed by an enormous armored draft horse, effortlessly pulling a train of wagons. All those young women in cages. No way to help them. That could've been her. A chill crept up her spine.

She was about to let a sigh escape when a mounted altivorc wheeled and pointed towards the farm. Six soldiers broke off from the rear of the column and hustled up the path.

At the entrance to the farmhouse, an altivorc rapped on the door. He yelled in heavily accented Arkothi, "This region now belongs to the Teleri Empire. We are taking a census and collecting tribute."

Kaiya pushed herself deeper into the stable, her heart pounding.

The altivorcs waited for a few seconds, and then one kicked in the door with a loud thud. Within seconds, the sound of furniture and dishes breaking mixed in with the crude laughs of the altivorcs. Kaiya bit her lip. Whoever lived there—

One of the altivorcs laughed. "No tribute? Then we will take your daughter, instead!"

A woman screamed.

Kaiya rose. Maybe they couldn't do anything about all those other women, but they could help this one.

At her side, Sameer sprang to his feet, his curved *naga* in hand.

Brehane urgently waved them down.

Cyrus hissed at him. "Remember the mission! Remember the princess!"

Kaiya glared at him. She would not be an excuse for not helping.

Focus set forward, the Paladin strode out of the stable and toward the farmhouse.

Brehane sighed. "Not again... "

Again? Kaiya searched the Aksumi's eyes. "We should help him.?"

Brehane clasped her necklace. "He will have no problem with six altivorcs. He may be a newly-minted Paladin, but they are easily worth ten trained men. We just need to make sure none of them escapes to tell their friends."

That, Kaiya could do.

She looked back at the road. The distance between them and the altivorc column increased at a crawl. How long before they would send someone to find out what happened to their comrades?

Grunts emanated from the house. Loud crashes followed.

Hopefully, Sameer was all right. Kaiya craned over the others at the stable door, just in time to see two altivorcs burst out of the house at full sprint.

What could she do? Altivorcs had always resisted her Dragon Songs.

Brehane jerked her head back, but then began a guttural chant. Streaks of glowing arrows appeared out of thin air and darted towards one of the fleeing altivorcs. He let out a shriek as the energy tore into his back. He stumbled into the dirt. The other dashed down the walkway, waving his arms and yelling.

Oh, no. Kaiya's heart pounded.

From the rear of the column, an altivorc turned his head in the direction of the farm. Brehane mumbled something in her language. The tone could only be a curse.

Six ranks—three dozen altivorcs in all—peeled off the back of the column and charged towards the path. The sound of drums echoed down the river.

Cyrus shook his head and drew his scimitar.

"Sister, your flute," Brehane said as she reached down to pick up some dirt. "Play the tune from the other day!"

With trembling hands, Kaiya fumbled for her *dizi*, which was tucked in the folds of her robe. Bringing the flute to her lips, she played.

The sound warbled out disjointed, without clarity or resonance.

"More control! More soothing!" Brehane's forehead crinkled as she rolled the soil between her fingers.

The altivorcs covered the distance quickly. They were no more than twenty feet away.

Kaiya sank her toes into the ground and took a deep, calming breath. What were forty altivorcs compared to a dragon? The flute's sound leveled off.

Brehane seemed to inhale the musical notes and started invoking harsh words, finishing her incantation by tossing dirt at the closing altivorcs.

They collapsed to the ground with a loud clatter of armor and steel weapons. All deep in slumber.

"How did you do that?" Cyrus stared at Brehane with rounded eyes. "I've never seen you affect so many."

Bent over panting, hands on her knees, Brehane nodded at Kaiya. Before the Mystic could open her mouth, a black-fletched arrow lodged into the stable wall, just a handbreadth from her head.

Kaiya lowered the flute and tracked the arrow back to its source. A line of altivorcs stood on the highway, loosing a volley of arrows.

Cyrus grabbed her wrist and pulled her back into the stable. Both huddled near the ground as multiple thuds rained into the walls outside.

"Quickly, get your things." Cyrus scrambled on all fours and grabbed his and Sameer's saddlebags. Kaiya and Brehane also shouldered their own packs.

Cyrus peeked around the corner. "We can't stay here, we'll be trapped! Brehane, can you create some sort of diversion?"

The Mystic shook her head as if it were an anvil. "I'm depleted. I need some rest before I can call on the Resonance."

"Princess?" Cyrus raised an eyebrow at her.

Kaiya bowed her head. "Maybe if I could reach the altivorc drums."

Cyrus snorted. "It would be easier to run in the *other* direction."

Kaiya stood straight and squared her shoulders. "I will surrender myself, and try to barter my freedom for yours."

Outside, Sameer's voice rang out. "Altivorc fools, your archery is horrible, see if you can hit me!"

Brehane peeked out and then turned back. "They are taking aim at Sameer. Run! Into the fields behind us! They will have a harder time targeting us in the wheat."

Kaiya opened her mouth, but Cyrus took her hand and pulled her along. Before they turned the corner, she stole a glance towards the front of the house, where Sameer stood.

Dozens of arrows streaked towards him. He moved inhumanly fast, a blur to her eye. His sword seemed to glow a light blue as he effortlessly weaved around arrows that should have hit him. It might have been unbelievable if she hadn't witnessed his master fight on the trip to Vyara City. To think Sameer was only a newly-minted knight of his order.

Cyrus pulled her into the rows of wheat, where the stalks growing above their heads would hide them.

Within minutes, Sameer caught up, grinning.

After a while, their running slowed to a brisk walk. In the distance, the muffled yells of the altivorcs grew fainter and fainter.

Cyrus breathed heavily. "We can run faster, but the altivorcs have better endurance. They'll catch up. We need to find a way to lose them."

Sameer nodded. "Beyond the fields to the west are some woods, and several miles beyond that, wooded hills that start to rise into the mountains. Those should provide cover from their arrows. We can find a place to hide there and then return to the main road in a couple of days."

Kaiya's lungs and legs burned, unaccustomed to long stretches of physical exertion. Discarding any notions of propriety, she dropped into an unladylike squat, one hand on the ground.

Each breath was a struggle. Afraid and useless, a burden on strangers. The pack slipped off her shoulders. "I can't go on. It's me they want, so I will wait here and try to buy you more time to escape."

Cyrus shook his head. His voice was flat, conveying no emotion. "No, Your Highness, they know of our mission. They will come for us, regardless of whether you are with us. There's another way."

He withdrew a gold disk that hung from his neck. The symbol of Athran, the Levanthi God of the Sun. She'd seen it during her visit to Vadaras, while searching unsuccessfully for an Akolyte to cure Father.

He placed his hands on her shoulder and began chanting in a musical language.

A cool wave washed over her, and the aching in her muscles faded. Her lungs lightened and the air felt cool and fresh. It was like waking from a peaceful night's slumber.

His dark eyes searched hers. "How are you now? Can you go on?"

She nodded.

He smiled. "Athran favors you."

"Let's keep moving!" urged Brehane.

From near the crest of the hill, Tian saw the altivorcs in the distance break ranks and advance on a farm. There was no way the Southerners could defend the princess. His plans had failed. Again. To think his Black Fist brothers once considered him the second coming of the Architect.

He motioned for the imperial guards. "Come on. We need to rescue the princess."

"Wait." Squinting, Fleet raised his hand. "Our friends are safe for the time being."

Tian strained his eyes. How could the madaeri know?

Fleet pointed. "They are fleeing west-southwest through the fields of red wheat, towards the woods beyond."

The other group should have never run into trouble at all. Tian threw his hands up. "We need to help them."

Fleet held his stubby fingers up, framing a spot in the woods. "If they're smart, they will start heading south once they enter the woods. If we head due west, we might be able to intercept them. If not, I can track them. Follow me."

The madaeri dashed toward the hills. Tian and the imperial guards hurried to catch up, setting a brisk pace westward through the Iksuvi farmland. Fleet would occasionally look towards where they had last seen the other group, but otherwise kept moving forward. After an hour, they neared the woods.

Fleet raised his fist, calling for a halt. "I think we're still slightly ahead of them, based on the speed they were fleeing. Wait here while I look for tracks."

The others squatted to catch their breath while their diminutive guide disappeared into the tree line. How did he have so much energy? Tian fidgeted. He had to do something. Not just sit here.

Fleet returned soon. "There were no fresh human tracks, and certainly not a dozen altivorc boot prints." He motioned them in a north-northwesterly direction into the woods, and they had to hurry to try to keep up. Despite his short legs, he moved swiftly and lightly through the underbrush, leaving the Cathayi behind.

Tian yelled, "Fleet, slow down!"

"No time!" the madaeri called back. "I'll whistle like this... " he let out a very shrill sound, unbelievable that someone so small could make it, "... every few minutes to let you know where I am. You do the same."

The whistles drifted farther and farther away over the next half-hour. The trees grew denser and denser, until they came to a clearing. Exhausted, Tian threw himself down on a fallen log. He motioned for the imperial guards to join him.

It was hopeless. They'd never reunite with Fleet, let alone the princess. He was a failure.

The madaeri yelled back through the trees. "I found them. Stay where you are."

Tian's heart soared. The madaeri was incredible.

Before long, the Southerners emerged from an animal path, with Fleet in the lead. The princess glided straight and regal, with no sign of fatigue. The Cathayi dropped to one knee in a bow. "*Dian-xia*," they shouted in unison.

Fleet shot them an annoyed glance, cutting his hand in front of his mouth.

"It is a miracle," Chen Xin whispered, "that we were able to find you in these woods."

"No miracle, just exceptional wilderness skills." The madaeri grinned.

Kaiya bowed deeply to Brehane. The Cathayi followed suit. "I am so sorry. Because of me, you lost your horses, and you will not be able to reach the Kanin pyramid in time."

Cyrus shook his head. "What is done is done. There is no point placing blame. We must just continue forward. The White Moon is full once a month."

Fleet pointed west. "The main road will not be safe for the next couple of days. I suggest we head up into the hills and keep heading south. About three days south of here, the river bends. We can descend there and return to the road. We travel by day, to take away the altivorc's advantage with their night vision." Without waiting for discussion, he started down a path heading southwest.

Tian tapped his chin. What other choice was there but to follow? At least for now, they were safe.

With about three hours of daylight left, the group forged ahead, following paths worn by animals. When they came across streams, Fleet insisted that they walk through them until they found new paths.

By the time the sun sank to just above the Nothori Mountains, they had reached the foot of the hills. The trees thinned. For the time being they found themselves well ahead of the altivorcs, with cold feet and in desperate need of rest. While the others stopped to catch their breath and drink some water, Fleet backtracked to cover their trail. How did the madaeri get his endless energy?

Upon his return, he reported that the altivorcs had lost their trail. Even so, it would be safer to keep up a fast pace and head into the hills where they might find shelter.

After spending the last hour of sunlight marching, Fleet left the party again to search for a campsite. He returned with the news of a small cave not far up a nearby hill.

Tian wiped the sweat from his brow and turned to the princess. In the low light, the princess' features twisted. What now?

They climbed a winding path to the entrance to the cave. The Southerners entered first. The Cathayi sank to their knees and waited for the princess to go in, but she turned her head to hide behind hair she no longer had. "I can't stay in there. If they come this way, they won't think to look up. I can stay outside."

Fleet shook his head. "The altivorcs have excellent night vision. Your body heat would be a beacon. Better not to risk it."

Chen Xin looked up. "*Dian-xia*, we should get a good night's sleep."

After all that had transpired between them, Tian was glad someone else was pressing the princess.

Nevertheless, she folded her arms across her chest and turned her back to the cave entrance. What happened to the strong and resolute princess from earlier?

Tian began to rise, when Chen Xin shot him a warning glance. No, somebody had to talk sense into her, and the imperial guards would only go so far.

"*Dian-xia*," Tian said. "You must get used to this. Our trip will take many months. You'll spend many uncomfortable nights. On hard floors. In tight quarters."

The princess pouted and her eyes welled up. Without another word, she stomped into the cave.

Exasperated, Tian shook his head. He peered through the cave mouth. Too dark to see. What was the princess doing? At this rate, they wouldn't survive the night, let alone rest of their journey.

Fleet gathered up some branches and brush to cover the cave entrance. "We need to set single watches. One-hour rotations. Let the princess have her beauty sleep. We should be moving at sunrise."

Tian's limbs screamed for rest. He ducked into the cave, which was barely large enough for them to spread out all of their bedrolls. The princess insisted on sleeping closest to the entrance, even if it meant that people would have to step over her when their turn to stand watch came.

Whatever. Tian fell asleep in seconds.

Zhao Yue jostled him awake. "You have this watch."

Tian rubbed his face. It felt like he had only slept for a few minutes. His body still ached. It would be a long day, unless they died early. He sat by the cave opening, thinking. Hopefully, Jie was faring better than they were. She must be safe and sound behind the embassy walls, worried about *him*.

Fleet crept past him. "I'm going to scout out the altivorc position. If I don't make it back by breakfast, head due south without me."

Disappearing again? Tian opened his mouth, but the madaeri slipped out of the cave and into the night.

When the ink-black of night gave way to black-blue hues, Tian woke the others. They rolled up their bedding and ate a breakfast of Kanin cornbread in silence.

Fleet poked his head into the cave. "The altivorcs are breaking camp, about two hours behind us."

Tian tapped his chin, now covered with stubble. The madaeri had been gone two hours; how did he know where the altivorcs were? "Have they found our trail?"

Fleet shrugged. "Hard to say. We have to keep constant watch to the west. This area is crawling with altivorc tunnels. Not even *I* know where they all are." He grinned.

Tian rolled his eyes. "We can eat while we travel. It will save time."

Fleet shook his head. "Eat first. I don't want you leaving a trail of cornbread for them to follow."

Tian kept his expression blank. The madaeri was regularly leaving the group, and now he was keeping them in one place.

When the sun peeked through the autumn foliage, they set off. The princess was testy, refusing help from the guards and refusing to talk to anyone.

Tian shook his head. To think this girl had bedazzled kings and generals just a week before. They would spend another few months travelling like this, assuming her attitude didn't first get her caught and the rest of them killed.

Barely an hour had passed before altivorc drums echoed through the hills. The faint sound from a smaller drum answered from the direction the party had come, well in the distance.

Tian glared suspiciously at Fleet, but before he could say anything, another drumming pattern answered the first, this time originating from the hills ahead of them.

Fleet's eyebrows furrowed. Was that steam coming from his ears? "Our pursuers have discovered our campsite. Another band in the hills above is descending on an intercept path."

CHAPTER 32:
Confrontations

More drums, echoing through the wooded hills. Tian glared at Fleet. Was he leading them into a trap?

The madaeri pointed to the line of mountains to the west. "The Nothori Mountains are dotted with entrances to underground altivorc cities. Altivorcs are all over the place."

Tian blanked his expression. No point in vocalizing his misgivings at this point. Otherwise lost, they had little choice but to follow their supposed guide.

Fleet led them to the southwest, taking them closer to the mountains and apparently out of the altivorcs' intercept course. Yet after an hour of hiking, they stumbled upon another patrol. After a brief but fierce engagement, they backtracked and followed a tributary of the Alto River upstream toward the mountains.

Tian scratched his chin. It seemed like they were spiraling into a smaller circle. If only he could see the Iridescent Moon through the trees, he could get a better sense of direction. The wilderness was a lot harder to navigate than urban environments.

The arduous path bent upwards, with the river rustling ever to their right. On their left, the terrain rose, the thick woods now thinning from spindly deciduous trees to straight, fresh-smelling evergreens. The only signs of animals were intermittent bird chirps. The princess wore complaints on her hard expression, but thankfully kept quiet.

After several hours, the gentle rise in elevation on either side jutted sharply upwards, forming a gorge. The cliff walls were rocky, with an occasional shrub breaking the monotonous white clay.

Tian eyed the entrance. "There might be more altivorcs. On the other side. We'd be trapped. We should turn back. Look for another path."

"There are no humanoid tracks here." Fleet pointed down to the ground. "This path was formed by animals, not by altivorcs. And even if we have a lead on them, they might still catch up to us if we turn back now. Our best chance is to forge ahead."

Tian looked up at the cliffs that now towered sixty feet above them, their tops lined with rocks and trees. Just like ambushes he had set from rooftops. They might be walking into the jaws of a trap. "Can we be sure the path continues? Might it dead-end?"

"There's always that possibility," Fleet conceded. "However, if you look at the freshest deer tracks, there are more going in than out."

How could the madaeri tell? The tracks were bewildering. Maybe he was lying. Tian stole a glance at the princess, who somehow maintained an air of elegance even as she squatted to catch her breath.

She met his eyes and stood. Her weary voice still sounded melodious. "Young Lord Zheng, I don't like this either, but we have no choice but to trust Fleet. We will continue through the gorge."

Tian kept his face from twisting into a scowl. She was right. Without Fleet they'd be wandering aimlessly into one altivorc patrol after another.

"As the princess commands," He said.

After a few minutes of rest, they refilled their water skins in the river and pressed on. Had there been no sense of urgency, the ravine would have been picturesque, with occasional waterfalls and deep azure pools among broad mossy boulders. The rustle of the water dancing over the rocks drowned out all other sounds.

The path, which had started off wide enough for four of them to walk abreast, narrowed as it rose high above the water line. Tian glanced at the others. They all wore concerned looks—all but Fleet, who merrily hopped along, undaunted by the prospect of a dead end.

The ledge abruptly narrowed to just a few feet at a sharp corner around a river bend. Oblivious to danger, Fleet effortlessly skipped around the corner. Tian and the princess, too, had little problem negotiating the left-hand turn. The ledge widened on the other side.

Yet for the rest of the party, it became a heart-stopping endeavor. Brehane, in particular, squeezed the hands of Sameer in front of her and Cyrus in back of her as she inched around the corner, face pressed against the cliff wall. "I won't make. I'll never see my son again."

Such dramatics. Tian assessed the position. A perfect bottleneck, easily defendable for a left-handed warrior. He looked at Li Wei, who was already passing his gear to Ma Jun. The two exchanged knowing nods. Tian bowed his head.

With sweat beading on her bald head, Princess Kaiya pushed back through the others. Ma Jun bowed low and allowed her to pass, and the rest of the imperial guard gathered up behind her.

"Captain Li," she said in a low but severe voice, "why have you stopped? Are you abandoning your duty to protect me?"

Li Wei dropped to his knee, fist to the ground. "Never, *Dian-xia*. I can slow the altivorcs' advance here, especially since I am left-handed and can attack them as they turn the corner."

She frowned. "Do not needlessly sacrifice yourself. I command you to walk at my side."

He bowed his head lower. "Forgive me, *Dian-xia*. The punishment for disobeying your command is death. I will accept that now as I hold this position to give you a greater lead."

"And if I say we will all fight together?" she asked. Her sincerity was touching, if misplaced.

"Then we will all die together," Li Wei said. "We cannot hold it indefinitely. They have superior numbers and will eventually come around the other side. I would not be able to face Xu Zhan in the next life if I let that happen."

Tian took her by the crook of the elbow. They had to go. For *her* safety. "*Dian-xia*. It is our highest honor. To die for you. Come, so that Li Wei's sacrifice will not be in vain."

She stubbornly struggled against his pull, tears in her eyes, while Li Wei remained bowed.

"Stop resisting and conserve your strength," Tian said. She would need it.

Finally, the princess allowed herself to be led away, casting one final glance at her loyal guard. Despite his pessimistic demeanor, Li Wei was well-liked by everyone. Tian would miss him.

The river's water rustled in Kaiya's ears as she walked wordlessly down the paths. Despair squeezed at her heart. All these sacrifices made by her guards, handmaidens, and others, for her.

Li Wei, despite his droning pessimism, had been the most chivalrous, helping her on and off of boats and carriages. If only she'd killed Geros when she had the chance, maybe he and Xu Zhan would've survived.

At the next break, she crouched on a rock, sighing as she studied her reflection in a mud-clouded puddle. Her once waist-length, lustrous black hair now bristled as coarse stubble, suited to a solider recently pressed into service. Dirt and blood streaked her pearly complexion. Instead of the finest, vibrant silk gowns that floated on her like mist, she now wore faded brown hemp robes whose coarseness chafed her milky skin. They did little to warm her in the chill autumn breeze.

In the puddle's reflection, the brilliant reds, yellows, and oranges of autumn foliage, and the azure sky above, provided a breathtaking backdrop to her tattered appearance.

What should have been an easy, week-long journey by sea had warped into a perilous trek that might take months—if they eluded capture and survived. They'd lost two already.

Her fault.

A lone ripple floated across the puddle, radiating out from a single tear she allowed to fall from her cheek.

"*Dian-xia.*" Tian's hated voice interrupted her moment of self-pity.

He thought he knew everything. Where was the sweet, awkward boy she once adored? She clenched her teeth and wiped her tears away. He would not see her cry, not see that she was anything less than a princess of Cathay.

Even if she no longer looked the part.

Rising, she lifted her chin, focused on him and forced a regal smile. No matter how ragged her outward appearance, command had been bred into her blood.

He instantly averted his gaze, showing proper deference. Yet when he spoke, his tone was patronizing, like a teacher admonishing an unruly child. "Fleet is back from covering our tracks. He says we need to keep moving if we want to keep a safe distance from the altivorcs."

Before it was over, even more would perish. Because of her. Guilt and despair threatened to overcome her voice, so she kept her words simple. "Then move." She bent down and gathered her pack before turning away from him so he wouldn't see her tears.

It took all of Tian's discipline to conceal his contempt for the princess. She was wallowing in self-pity again. That much was obvious from the smudged streaks across her filthy face. *Then move?* What was that supposed to mean?

His concerns about the madaeri could wait. "As the princess commands."

The trilling and chirping of birds ceased, as if in reproach for his cold voice interrupting their songs.

He'd been harsh, but it was for her own good. He turned so she wouldn't see his regret, his eyes finding the three surviving imperial guards. Gone were their stoic expressions, silk blue robes, and burnished breastplates, replaced by haggard sadness and monks' robes. Even if they didn't look the part, they'd still happily give their lives to protect the princess. It didn't make Tian feel any less guilty for putting them in this position.

His attention shifted to their diminutive guide, who slouched on a moss-covered log, munching happily on a chunk of cornbread. He sat up straight and looked around, furrowed brows and tight lips marring his usually jovial expression. Plotting something, perhaps. Yes, time to tell the princess.

"Dian-xia—"

He turned his shoulder and reached out to snatch the shaft of a black-fletched arrow that whizzed past the princess' head. It would have hit him in the chest had his reflexes been any slower. He looked towards the source of the shot, using the arrow in his hand to swat away another one with a crisp sweep of his arm. Above them, along a ridge just fifty feet away, several altivorcs fitted arrows to their bowstrings.

Sameer whipped his *naga* from its sheath and charged up the ridge. The imperial guards bolted up, forming a living shield in front of the princess.

Not like she needed it. They wanted her alive, unharmed.

The others scrambled among the boulders along the side of the trail. Tian glared at the madaeri. "You said they weren't far behind!"

Fleet jumped out from cover and loosed an arrow from his bow. It flew true through the eye of an altivorc. "It's not *my* fault." He ducked back behind a boulder to avoid an answering volley of deadly arrows. "These are *ahead* of us!"

Right. Tian drew his saber. He couldn't leave Sameer to fight alone. He stepped out and looked up the ridge.

The Paladin had drawn the altivorcs' fire. He nimbly, almost impossibly, dodged some arrows while cutting others out of the air with his blade. Such recklessness!

Tian followed him up the slope, albeit with more caution, picking his way around trees, boulders, and fallen trunks.

Behind him, Brehane uttered foul gibberish. Her chant concluded with a hard inflection. A thunderous blast of sound reverberated from the altivorcs' position. The shockwave nearly knocked Tian off his feet.

The deadly rain of arrows ceased.

Tian sighed. The unnatural sound would reveal their location to other pursuers, but at least they were out of immediate danger.

Sameer sheathed his sword and headed back down the slope, grinning and patting Tian on his shoulder as he passed.

Tian's gaze followed Sameer down. Just beyond, Cyrus' brow furrowed in concentration as he bound Ma Jun's wounds.

"The altivorcs will be incapacitated for several hours," Brehane called. Her voice sounded exhausted. "That will give us some time to gain more ground."

Hold the dragonfly with care. It'd be easy to permanently put the unconscious altivorcs out of their misery. They'd take great pleasure in doing the same if the roles were reversed. "I'm going up to collect some of their bows. They can't follow us that way. You all continue down the path. I will catch up with you."

He clambered to the top of the ridge. The trees around them stood splintered by the sound wave. Twelve altivorcs lay unconscious.

Going to the nearest, he bent the soldier's knee, locked it between his forearm and shoulder, and twisted. It let out an involuntary grunt. The torque would sprain the knee joint, thereby preventing it from walking for several days. Tian repeated the process on each of the altivorcs. He then picked up four bows and several quivers of the steel-headed arrows, and hurried to catch up with the rest of his company.

How many more such encounters could they survive? The others came into sight. The princess lagged behind, her shoulders drooped. She'd been too busy looking at her reflection, and hadn't eaten while they were resting. He suppressed a growl.

Yes, she was infuriating, but he could only blame himself for their predicament. The original escape plan had been his. So had several of the subsequent alternatives.

All failed.

His plans never failed. Perhaps it would've been better to fortify the embassy in Iksuvius while sending the *Golden Phoenix* back home to bring ships and musketmen. Maybe even ask for a real phoenix to fly the princess home.

Certainly, things would have been different had he finished off the altivorc spy in Gaukaimos. Now Xu Zhan was dead, Li Wei missing. As he caught up to the others, he quickly wiped his eyes. For the time being, lamenting the past would do them no good.

Kaiya trailed behind the others, though Chen Xin, who'd guarded her since she was a child, often slowed down to help her through the rough terrain. She'd always taken him for granted. She'd never truly appreciated the imperial guards' dedication to her.

Now, one had died to protect her, and another had probably shared the same fate. Even Tian would sacrifice his life for her, if for nothing more than pride. It wouldn't make her feel any less guilty.

And then, beyond her own people, there were the four others, who owed no allegiance to the *Tianzi*, yet assisted her to the detriment of their own quest. Tears blurred her vision. Maybe they'd all share the same fate as Li Wei and Xu Zhan. Heavens, she was pathetic.

She had little time to cry before Tian caught up to her. Their eyes met, and Kaiya was surprised to see that his were red and swollen. Had he been crying, too? Maybe he was a human after all. She forced a smile at him, which he returned, equally forced.

"*Dian-xia*. I just caught this in a stream." He held up a miniature lobster, still squirming. "Please eat it. It will help your endurance."

Her stomach churned. Kaiya recoiled and covered her mouth.

Tian scowled, all sense of propriety gone. He jabbed a finger in her direction. "The comforts that *you* have been asked to forfeit—your hair, a soft bed in a spacious room, the finest food prepared by imperial chefs—they are an inconvenience compared to the sacrifice that Brehane and her group have made. And nothing compared to the ultimate sacrifice that Xu Zhan and Li Wei made."

He was talking to her like a little girl. He'd never spoken to her like that, even when she *had* been a little girl. Kaiya raised her voice, loud enough that any altivorc within three *li* could've heard. "Zheng Tian, do you think I don't understand this?"

Up ahead, the others stopped. Chen Xin sighed and started heading back.

Kaiya lowered her voice just a little. "I don't mind discomfort, but I can't handle narrow confines... and that's your fault." She pointed at him. She never pointed at anyone, as Cathayi custom considered it rude. Her voice shook, dropping to almost a whisper. "Ever since you locked me in our swordmaster's armoire, years ago, I can't think or even breathe in tight places."

Tian gawked, eyes wide, and then hung his head.

Chen Xin rubbed his bald head thoughtfully.

Hot tears trickled down her cheeks. She sank down, her back to a large boulder, and drew her head to her knees. Her voice wavered. "I don't eat shellfish, not because of the taste, but because I'd be throwing up for hours. Even the smell of it brings on nausea. But as princess, I have to hide weakness."

Tian stared at the ground. He dropped to one knee and bowed his head. "I'm sorry. I didn't know."

Brehane came back and offered Tian a reproachful glance before sitting down next to Kaiya and putting her arm around her.

Tian bowed his head. "I am sorry."

Kaiya looked up from between her knees and smiled a bitter smile. "It is also my fault. I assumed I could confide in you like we did when we were children. But we aren't children anymore."

An awkward silence ensued, broken only by the shrill voice of the madaeri. "I'm all for sentimentality, but we need to get moving again and cover more ground before sundown. I hear altivorc drums in the distance."

CHAPTER 33:
First Consul No More

Jie spent a week regaining her strength. She avoided physical exertion, instead disguising herself as a Nothori peasant child and mingling with Tian's network of local spies. For once, looking like a kid came in handy.

Learning of Chen Xin's visit to the Kanin embassy, she surprised their ambassador with a midnight call. Ambassador Manuwaya, knowing of the roundup of Cathayi nationals, offered asylum to all of them, as long as they could be brought in without drawing suspicion. The old man also gave her the princess' letter, where Jie learned about her escape into the Wilds—with Tian.

Alone, stranded, and with no one to report to for the first time in her life, she made it her mission to rescue the princess' handmaiden, Meiling. She didn't doubt she could get *into* the Iksuvi Palace undetected, but getting *out* with an untrained and now traumatized girl would be another challenge altogether. She stalked General Marius, thinking he could be the key to her plan.

Marius di Bovyan had the strangest habits for a Bovyan. Whereas most of them spent at least some of their time in the company of unwilling women, the general never visited his assigned mating compound at the Iksuvi Palace. He kept regular routines, though Jie would swear that he seemed almost sad these days.

One late afternoon, she made her move.

As Marius led a patrol through the marketplace, she joined in with a gaggle of street urchins and ran across the Bovyan column's path. She stumbled, careening into the general and slipping a note into his boot. With a quick bob of her head, she sped away, ignoring the Teleri soldiers' reprimands.

That night, she returned to the eastern marketplace in hopes that he would accept her invitation to meet. Arriving early, Jie scouted out the area to ensure he hadn't laid any traps for her. She found none, and hid in a weathered wooden stall which provided a full view of the area.

Just as the Iridescent Moon waxed to its mid-crescent, exactly at the appointed time, Marius ventured in—alone, as far as she could tell. With the White Moon near new, her elf vision gave her the advantage.

Jie threw her voice to make it seem like a nearby goat had spoken. "General Marius, thank you for meeting me."

The general frowned as he approached the goat. "Miss Jie, I was intrigued by your letter. Why did you want to meet? I suspect it has nothing to do with two years ago."

That again. Before the invasion, he'd babbled something about how they'd shared some adventure in Arkos, but she'd assumed it was just the effect of the euphoria toxin she'd given him.

As he walked by, she jumped onto the stall's counter behind him. She yanked his hair back and stuck a knife point to his carotid artery. "Hands up and away from your sword. Slowly."

Marius lifted his arms at a safe speed. "This is not necessary. I came in good faith."

"I did not. Needless to say, I'm not too happy about my people being imprisoned and murdered."

"Miss Jie, your princess attacked the First Consul. What did you expect? That he would not exact justice?"

Justice, eh? She pressed the knife into his neck, ever so slightly. "My princess knew his plans to kidnap her and acted in self-defense. Now, tell me, why is her handmaiden being held separately?"

"This is how things have been for a hundred and thirty years, since the Bovyan Edict. The ruling class of the Bovyans—our Prospecti—mate with the ruling class of nations with which we ally and protect. The offspring become a bridge between our nations."

Occupied allies, rape as a bridge. Jie'd heard as much during her mission into the Teleri Empire. Still, she shuddered at Marius' rationalization. She leaned in and whispered into his ear. "What you call *mating*, civilized people call gang-rape."

"It is necessary, lest our race die out. Even if you hate him, the First Consul works to end Tivar's Curse so that our mates might bear more children, both boys and girls. Until then, the prophecies state that a Bovyan who knows his true mother and father will bring an end to the Teleri Empire. We can't let that happen. Without the order we bring, the world will plunge back into a darkness unseen since the Hellstorm."

More excuses. Jie scoffed. As for prophecies— thank the Heavens they did not govern *her* life. She released a little of the pressure on his throat. "I have noticed that you don't participate. Why is that? Injury down *there*?"

Marius sighed and eased himself into a seated position on the counter. He set his hands down on the edge. "Because I love someone. Someone I shouldn't. By Solaris, we aren't supposed to *love* anyone."

Heat flared in Jie's cheeks. He liked her. *Really* liked her. Not like she was particularly interested in a Bovyan, reformed or not. If only she could see his face, to read his expression. She kept her guard up, nonetheless. "I hope you do not mean me, because—"

"No, no. I've always been fond of you, since we met in Vyara City" Marius started to shake his head, but stopped, probably because of the knife point at his artery. "However, this one is *really* married. I tried to forget her by rekindling what we had."

Always second best. Jie sucked on her lower lip. Even if the only thing she'd want to rekindle was his head—ideally with another cache of firepowder—it was a blow to the ego. She pressed the blade a little harder into his neck. "Don't bring up our past again." Especially fictional pasts.

"Of course." Marius sighed again, wistfully. "Anyway, she is gone now, escaped like so many others."

"Did you force yourself on our handmaiden?"

"No! No. After my love, I don't think I could ever sleep with another, especially not through the Mating."

He sounded sincere enough. But trust a Bovyan? "Perhaps, then, you can fathom how much poor Meiling is suffering. I want you to help her escape." She lowered the knife, ready to spring away if he tried to attack her.

Marius spun around, hands behind his back, mouth agape. Jie tensed, but did not jump away. He did not make any move towards her, instead shaking his head. "I could never betray my people."

Jie snorted. "Then you are no better than any other Bovyan. If you don't do the right thing, how can you expect your comrades to do the same when your own love is captured? "

"I... I... " His lips sagged into a frown, and his eyes shifted. Then he sighed. "Very well, I will help you."

Jie offered him a smile, even though he probably couldn't be trusted. "In return, I'll help your own love escape."

Marius shook his head yet again. His head would probably wobble off before the end of the night. "There's no need. Your people have already helped her. She's aboard the Cathayi flagship, already beyond the reach of our empire."

Now Jie gawked. The only married woman onboard the *Golden Phoenix* was Queen Ausra. She recovered from her surprise, composing her emotionless mask. "I want to initiate a rescue as soon as possible. When would be the best time?"

"Tomorrow," he answered. "When most of the Teleri will be at the Temple of Solaris."

If only she had a cache of firepowder. "Whatever for?"

"The Keeper will coronate First Consul Geros as Emperor."

Geros stood at the entrance of the Temple of Solaris, ignoring the ceremonial blathering of the Keeper, who spoke platitudes in a long-dead language. On this day, he had forsaken his typical dress uniform in favor of a silk toga befitting of an ancient Arkothi emperor. He looked every bit the part in the Arkothi-style temple, whose ornate white marble columns supported a massive dome.

In the center towered a gilded statue of the god, anointed with a crown of sun and bearing a striking resemblance to the First Consul. Holding a sword aloft, its right arm stretched out of its robe, revealing rippled muscle. Its other arm nestled a book: the Last Testament of the Founder.

Geros fidgeted as the Keeper droned on. He remembered posing for the statue, basing it on an image his ancestor had sketched in the Last Testament. That had been ten years ago, when he had ordered the construction of the temple on this hill, razing the ramshackle hovel that had passed for the temple of the Nothori god Deivos.

The Nothori folk insisted that he would be struck down by the god's own hand for this transgression. He stifled a laugh, lest he taint the sanctity of the ceremony. Here he was, standing; just a little tired as he recovered from his closest brush with death—not by the wrath of a god, but at the sword point of a girl.

With the exception of that minor setback, the schemes he'd set in motion that day had all unfolded as planned, leading to his well-deserved reward. He looked up at the hole in the center of the dome.

A narrow blade of sun shone through; it would not be long now.

He swept his gaze around the temple, where Teleri officials and soldiers stood in solemn silence, forming perfect rows in their meticulously kept uniforms. Under the statue stood the senior-most Keeper of the Shrine of Geros, there to consecrate the rites unheard of in the three centuries since the end of the Arkothi Empire.

The Keeper switched from the archaic language to modern Arkothi. "First Consul Geros, approach the altar."

Chin held high, Geros marched towards the statue, down a central walkway formed by the Teleri ranks. He knelt and looked up to see the sun almost at the center point of the dome's hole. His attention shifted towards the Keeper.

The Keeper bowed his head. "The Last Testament of the Founder obligates the Bovyan people to the duty of bringing peace to the world, and ushering in an era of harmony and prosperity unseen since the Hellstorm and Long Winter ended the Arkothi Empire three centuries ago."

Yes, yes, old history. Geros forced himself to stay still. He'd soon make a new history.

"To these ends," the Keeper prattled on, "we have always evolved. Our First Ancestor and his sons defended the village of Lagrina, and the next generation was the palace guard of Tile. As our mandate grew, we remade ourselves into the Bovyan Knights. When we brought more lands under our protection, we became the Teleri Empire. We now enter a new era, one where we require stability in succession, as outlined by the Edict of Blood Inheritance, agreed upon by the Keepers and the Directori early this year."

All of this was known. Geros clenched his jaw. He had bent the Keepers and Directori to his will. Now hurry up and—

The Keeper looked towards the entrance. The Teleri soldiers broke into low murmurs. Geros fought the urge to follow the Keeper's eyes.

A boy from the Shrine came up to his side, holding a black velvet cushion. On top rested the antique crown of the Arkothi emperors. Made of a bluish-grey metal, its tip held a starburst jewel—an artifact used by the elves a thousand years before in their losing war against the orcs.

Geros grinned in spite of the solemnity of the coronation. Unlike the elves, he would not lose a war.

The Keeper lifted the crown from the cushion and raised it just as the sun reached its zenith, bathing the statue of Solaris in brightness. The rays caught the starburst, showering the dome above with pins of light.

At last. The Keeper placed it on Geros' head.

Despite its bulk, it weighed very little. A surge of excitement roared through him.

"By the power vested in me by the Keepers of the Shrine and the Imperial Directori, on this day of the Autumn Equinox in the year 913, I crown First Consul Geros Bovyan, Forty-Third of his name, as Emperor Geros Bovyan the First."

Geros rose.

The Bovyans chanted his name, over and over again.

The chorus continued until the Keeper raised his hand, calling for silence.

"Bring forth the consorts of the imperial harem."

From the entrance, three dozen young women dressed in Arkothi robes came forward, walking in unison. It was a mélange of pretty faces, chosen from the nobility of six of the ten human races.

The olive-skinned Arkothi girls, descended from the last Arkothi emperors, had been conscripted from within the Teleri Empire. Nothori princesses were never mentioned in the Northwest Summit, but were tribute all the same. Daughters of Estomari merchant signores were there as well, bartered as part of trade rights and protection of trade routes.

From Teleri's allies in Madura, Levastya, and the barbarian tribes of Kanin, Geros had secretly negotiated girls from the ruling families, with the promise that one day, grandsons might become Consuls in the Teleri Directori; of course, he foresaw them as rulers of their own ancestral realms.

It was like a Levanthi sultan's harem, to breed a pool of potential heirs. Each consort would be discarded and replaced after they bore a son, to avoid tempting the prophecies of the end of the empire. The boys would never know their own mother. Yet unlike the Consuls, who were elected by the Prospecti—or the First Consul, who was elected from the Consuls—the next emperor would be personally chosen by Geros from one of his future sons.

Unrepresented were the Eldaeri, who falsely claimed to be the chosen tribe of Solaris, and thus deserved extermination for their blasphemy; the chocolate-skinned Aksumi, despite Geros' efforts to secure their females by diplomacy and other means; and the Bovyans themselves, who had no females. The fourth, the Cathayi—well, Geros knew very well who he wanted to bear his son, even if it meant inviting prophetic doom.

The Keeper placed a circlet of silver on each of the consorts' heads; and they, in turn, knelt before Geros and kissed the back of his hand.

Once the rituals ended, an honor guard escorted Geros out of the temple, to lead a grand parade back to the Iksuvi Palace. Typical Bovyan disdain for flamboyance was momentarily forgotten. Teleri soldiers marched in perfect formation, holding black banners with the nine-pointed sun of Solaris aloft. Each of the consorts was afforded her own litter, curtains open to the chill autumn air to further boast the grandeur of the empire. Geros himself rode astride a Kanin black stallion, waving to the crowds who threw autumn flowers in his path.

Geros wore a smile, even if he didn't feel it. There was still the matter of Princess Kaiya, tarnishing what should have been a crowning moment. She'd be his. She would suffer for her treachery. But for now, she was out of reach.

The steward Jonynas, the Nothori man who had previously served the Iksuvi king, greeted him with a deep bow at the palace gates. "Your Eminence, your bed chambers have been prepared for your long afternoon. Which of your consorts will honor you with her visit?"

Geros snorted. "I want the Cathayi handmaiden."

A look of confusion bloomed on the steward's face. He looked back towards the litters, then opened his mouth to say something.

No, there were no Cathayi among the consorts. Geros scowled, silencing his unspoken words.

Jonynas turned back towards a servant. "Bring the Cathayi girl to His Eminence's bed chambers." He offered Geros a weak smile and bowed.

Geros pushed past him, taking his time as he made his way towards the king's former suite.

A servant met him halfway, his face pale and dripping with sweat. The man fell prostrate. "Your Eminence, the Cathayi girl is... gone."

CHAPTER 34:
Orc Gods and Flaming Chariots

After their confrontation, Kaiya tried her best to be civil to Tian, even rebuffing his suggestion to break away from Brehane's group without criticizing the stupidity of the idea. Even if the madaeri was acting suspiciously, they were lost without him.

Over the next three days, the weather was cloudy and chilly. Frigid nights forced them to huddle close together. Altivorcs seemed to be everywhere, but Fleet had taken them off the main path and through a wide stream, higher into the hills. Cold, wet feet put a damper on everyone's mood, tempered only by the miracle of avoiding their pursuers.

At dawn on the day before the Autumn Equinox, Kaiya unwrapped a pack of herbs prescribed by the enigmatic Doctor Wu. Cyrus watched with wide eyes as she soaked the twigs, roots, and dried flowers in Fleet's copper bowl.

Kaiya's nose scrunched up as she sipped the bitter draught, but she couldn't contain a laugh at Cyrus' contorted face after he insisted on tasting it. Tian offered her a mysterious look, but no rebuke for her laugh, which any altivorc within five *li* could hear.

Cyrus choked on his words. "What do you drink this for?"

"Poor Cyrus." She giggled, deflecting the question. "My doctor tells me that adding dawn-blooming everblossom would improve both the taste and the effect. Unfortunately, there was a shortage in Cathay because of the exceptionally hot summer."

Fleet grinned at her. "There's plenty around here. I'll point it out if we come across it."

After they at last set off, the day dragged on as they seemingly wound in circles. Throughout the day, Kaiya would swear she had seen a boulder or tree or other landmark that they had passed earlier. Fleet, however, was resolute in saying that they were headed more or less south. By nightfall when they set up camp under a large rock outcrop, they had encountered no enemies.

Tian sprang to his feet, sword sheath in hand, as a shout tinged with pain jolted him from sleep. He peered around the campsite, barely lit by the slivers of the White Moon and nearly-closed Blue Moon. The dark shapes where Chen Xin and Ma Jun had settled down for the night pushed themselves into seated positions. Sameer, Cyrus, and Brehane stirred on the ground. Where was Fleet?

And the princess?

"Wake up! Altivorcs!" Zhao Yue's voice mixed with the clang of metal on metal.

Tian shook off the tight grip of sleep as Chen Xin and Ma Jun rose. At the head of the path to the outcrop,

Zhao Yue was fighting off altivorcs, even as his left arm hung limply at his side.

Pulling a saber free of its sheath, Tian charged over to help the embattled guard. He stopped in his tracks. Arrows darted in front of him, shot from dark shapes by the trees. With his left hand, he took hold of two throwing spikes from his forearm strap and hurled them toward the attackers.

Behind him, Zhao cried out. Tian turned to see an altivorc yanking a broadsword out of him. Yet Zhao fought on, swinging his saber.

Brehane uttered a guttural syllable, and the area flooded with bright light.

Tian squinted as his vision adjusted. The altivorcs seemed even more blinded. Behind him, metal weapons clanged, and Cyrus' distinct voice called on his gods.

With everything now clearer, Tian worked his way toward Zhao. Drums rumbled somewhere to his side, but stopped mid-sequence. The altivorcs, no longer shading their eyes, swarmed in again. He shot a quick glance behind him. His companions were backing under the outcrop, with Sameer striking and retreating with inhuman speed.

Saber in hand, Tian deflected an incoming hack that would have finished Zhao Yue. He grabbed the guard by the shoulder, fighting off attackers as he dragged him back to the relative safety under the outcrop.

A sea of altivorcs surged around them, broadswords bared. Behind them, a new line formed with bows trained on them.

Brehane held Sameer back. She barked foul words in the language of her people's magic.

The altivorcs loosed arrows at her as she chanted. Tian leaped forward. He should be able to catch at least one. Instead, they slammed into a spot in the air and ricocheted harmlessly to the ground. More altivorcs shot from all around the semicircle now, with the same results.

A single foul syllable from behind the line of altivorcs carried over Brehane's chant. The barrage of arrows stopped.

What now? Tian tightened the grip on his saber.

The lines parted and a tall altivorc, in a black tunic and with a golden circlet on his head, strode forward. He resembled the altivorc prince from the Teleri Embassy, though he was even taller and more handsome. When he spoke, it sounded like honey spilling out of his mouth, in perfect Arkothi. "How long can you maintain your shield, Mystic? Even now, you are weakening. If you want to live to see your child again, surrender now."

Tian turned to Brehane. Her face contorted. Sweat gathered on her forehead and trickled down. The strength in her voice faltered.

So this was the end of their ill-advised journey. Tian bent down towards Zhao Yue. "You were on watch. What happened to the princess?"

Zhao choked on his words, blood pooling around his lips. "She and Fleet left camp, half an hour ago. Said they would be back by sunrise."

Tian looked up. The star-speckled blanket of night's black gave way to deep blue on the horizon. Where had they gone?

The altivorc leader drew a wand from a sheath at his hip and levelled it at them. He uttered a hideous word and a bolt of red lighting sizzled forth, outlining a flickering dome between their groups.

In the instant that Brehane collapsed, the leader barked again. Another energy bolt struck Sameer. The

Paladin buckled to the ground, writhing as his eyes rolled upwards.

The leader twirled the wand on his finger and shoved it back in its sheath. He grinned, baring his fangs at Cyrus. "Now, Acolyte, tell me where the Eye of the Pyramid is."

What? Tian lowered his weapon. They weren't looking for the princess?

Kaiya strained her eyes in the predawn dark, waiting for the everblossom to burst open. They would be the most potent if harvested in that instant. Fleet leaned up against a tree, yawning.

Deep altivorc drums rumbled in the distance. Heart leaping into her throat, she looked up. Fleet's ears twitched and his forehead crinkled.

There was a distinct rhythm to the beats. Signals. They seemed to be coming from the direction of their camp. She exchanged glances with the madaeri.

The beating stopped short.

"The altivorcs found our campsite," Fleet whispered. "And there are a lot of them, too many to fight. We need to get as far away as possible."

An emptiness crept into Kaiya's chest. It was her fault that the Southerners were facing capture. "No. There must be a way that we can help our friends."

"Your Highness, you should be more concerned about your own safety." The madaeri had never looked so serious, even when their journey had taken turns for the worse.

There had to be a way. Joining her music with Brehane's, they could put dozens of altivorcs to sleep. She shouldered her pack and started heading back towards camp.

Fleet darted in front of her, holding his arms out. "No, Your Highness. That would be foolish. Your men would want you safe."

Kaiya moved to brush him aside, but he deftly avoided her hand every time and managed to stay in her path. She glared at him. "If you aren't going to help me, at least get out of way."

He grinned, sending a wave of anger rushing to her head.

"Back off." She sang the words, using the power of her voice. Tiredness crept into her limbs.

Fleet yawned. "Save your energy for running. Come on."

Kaiya poked him in the chest. Heavens, that was rude of her. "Brehane and the others might just be clients to you, but I care about my people."

The madaeri sighed. Loudly. "You don't understand. Once I get you to a safe place, I'm going to go back and help them. There are much greater stakes here than a princess fleeing a tyrant. Even greater than wars between nations. When Brehane, Cyrus, and Sameer's story is told, you will be a footnote."

"What are you talking about?"

The usually jovial madaeri's jaw squared, his eyes intent. "Do you know how the saying *'when the Orc Gods return on their blazing chariots'* means something will never happen? Well, there are those who would very much like to see that happen. I, for one, don't want to go back to the time when my people were slaves to the altivorcs. When I decided to help the Southerners, it wasn't because I needed the money."

The madaeri's sincerity was surprising, but what was he talking about? She crossed her arms. "What do they have to do with the Orc Gods?"

Fleet offered her a bitter smile. "The pyramids. If the orcs ever control all of the pyramids again, they can summon their gods."

Kaiya listened in disbelief. "I'm well-versed in the history and lore of Tivara. I've never heard of such insanity."

He laughed. "Tall folk don't remember like we do, nor can you seem to put together all the small images to see the big picture. What was the last episode in the War of Ancient Gods?"

Kaiya shrugged. "Easy. The dwarves stormed the Temple of Tivar—"

"No, afterwards. The Elf Angel Aralas' Last Command."

The madaeri spoke in thousand-year-old riddles. Kaiya forced the impatience out of her tone. *"Keep well the Pyramids, reminders though they may be of your enslavement."*

"Exactly." He gave a triumphant nod. "What do you think that means?"

She sighed. They were wasting time, debating folklore and long-departed Elf Angels. "How should I know? I will ask him next time I see him."

Apparently, her sarcasm was not lost on him. Fleet threw up his arms. "Never mind. You don't have to believe me or my people's lore. Just know that I will find a way to free our friends, because it's that important."

Kaiya shook her head at him. "I can help."

Fleet scrutinized her, eyebrows furrowed. "All right, follow me. Tread as quietly as you can."

They picked their way back through the woods, the only sounds being bird chirps. When they came within eyeshot of the outcropping, the morning sun revealed their ransacked camp. A single body lay among the ruffled bedrolls, while several others sprawled in a disorderly circle around the camp. Kaiya's heart lurched into her throat. Who was it? Kaiya started forwards, but Fleet grabbed hold of her sleeve.

"It might be a trap," he whispered. "You wait here, I will investigate."

She nodded and he disappeared into the brush. Even her keen ears couldn't tell where he went. She kept her focus on the body.

It flinched. Still alive.

Kaiya fought every nerve that screamed for her to run to whoever it was.

After what felt like an eternity, Fleet appeared at its side. He looked towards her and beckoned.

Kaiya picked her way through the brush and dead altivorcs. It was Zhao Yue, face pale and lips wan. He opened his eyes a crack and offered her a frail smile. "*Dian-xia*, you should not have come back... flee... while you can."

She looked at Fleet, who shook his head. Another person to die because of her. Her chest constricted and she fought back tears. She had to be strong, for him.

She forced a smile at Zhao and clasped his cold hand. "I release you from your duty to the *Tianzi*. Rest."

"I will watch over you until I die and am reborn," Zhao answered. "It would be my honor to serve you in the next life."

Fleet patted Zhao on his bald head and looked at her. "You stay here; I'll track the altivorcs. Pay attention to your surroundings. If there's any sign of danger, flee back to the everblossoms. If you aren't here, I'll look for you there." With that he disappeared.

Zhao did not linger long. Kaiya held his hand until his soul drifted from its corporeal bonds.

Alone, Kaiya cried freely as she went to look for stones to build a cairn. Through her tears, she caught sight of a hip drum under an altivorc body. An idea began to coalesce. She kicked at the corpse to make sure it was truly dead; then, with some hesitation, pushed it over to retrieve the drum.

Fleet returned an hour later. "Our friends are being held uphill, at an altivorc campsite. I counted about thirty of them."

Kaiya showed the madaeri the drum. "How well do you know their signals?"

A devious grin formed on the madaeri's face. "Well enough."

Tian subtly worked at the ropes which bound his hands behind his back, even as an altivorc guard glared at him. His companions all sat in a circle with their backs to each other, with the exception of Cyrus and Brehane.

Though he couldn't see them, their screams emanated from the rocky clearing behind him. Brehane repeated the name *Fassil* over and over again.

Sameer's unconscious form slumped against Tian's back. Their weapons lay out of reach, but tantalizingly close, amongst their packs—which the altivorcs had emptied and now rummaged through. On occasion, the sounds of the Southerners' torture were broken by an unintelligible tirade from the altivorc leader, followed by one of his minions beating out some pattern on the large drum. Try as he might, Tian couldn't decipher the code.

Escape, though unlikely, was still possible. With the bulk of the altivorcs already departed, probably to search for the princess, the imperial guards and Sameer might stand a fighting chance... if only they could break loose and get to their weapons before the altivorcs hacked them to pieces.

A break in the screams was followed by the altivorc leader's heavy footsteps coming up behind him. Tian twisted and caught a glimpse of Cyrus and Brehane. They stood about thirty feet away, their hands bound above their head, suspended from a tree limb.

The leader kicked at Sameer's feet. Then he stomped around to face Tian. "So, how did you come to join the Southerners?"

Tian licked his lips, feigning fear, even as he loosened the bonds a little more. "We were just travelling and ran into each other. It is always nice to have company on the road."

The leader laughed, pointing at Chen Xin and Ma Jun. "Don't lie. These two wear signets of the Cathayi imperial guard. You were protecting your princess."

Tian kept a straight face, even as he let a stream of curses explode in his head. "We split up. To draw you away from her."

"So she is with the meddling little halfling?"

Maybe Tian had misjudged Fleet. "You'll never catch her."

The leader laughed. "She's inconsequential, beyond being bait to dangle in front of my friend Geros. Tell me which way she went, and I'll let you go. I'll let her go, too, even escort you through our cities into Rotuvi. That's close to home."

Tian gauged the possibilities. Even if he didn't trust the altivorcs—he and the guards would be dead the second she was captured—he could at least pretend to comply. He let his features soften. "They fled towards—"

A beating of drums from the south interrupted him, and the leader held his hand up. "Oh, too bad. It sounds like my men are already on her trail." He unleashed a barrage of harsh-sounding syllables. An altivorc beat on the big drum, while several others formed up.

The leader grinned at him. "Well, duty calls. Savor your last breaths. It won't be long now." With another snarling command, his soldiers followed him out of the camp.

The leader was gone. Tian craned his head to see that a dozen altivorcs stood guard. Their chances of escape began to improve, albeit just slightly. He continued to fiddle with the ropes. If only Sameer would awaken.

Kaiya crouched at the edge of the clearing, Fleet by her side. She counted fifteen altivorcs: one by the large drum lying on its side, not far from them; six surrounding her people and Sameer; two where Brehane and Cyrus stood with hands bound above them; and six standing guard at points around the perimeter.

Fleet shook his head, likely seeing what she did: their friends were split up and the altivorcs were too dispersed. It would be impossible for the two of them to rescue both groups of their companions before their enemies slaughtered them.

Kaiya pointed to her drum. Maybe they could draw more altivorcs off.

Fleet shook his head violently. He pointed downhill, in the direction that the other group had departed. They would also hear any drumming.

Minutes passed. Fleet's scrunched-up forehead and suggested he was either at a loss for plans or, like her, suffering from menstrual cramps. More likely the former. It was up to her. She pointed him towards Brehane and Cyrus, and gesticulated. *I will break for the big drum, you rescue those two.*

His jaw dropped, but before he could protest, she rose and ran.

Altivorcs lifted their heads, their gawps as wide as the madaeri's. She made it halfway to the drum before they even started towards her. The drummer lurched forward and caught up her sleeve in his huge paw.

Her Praise Spring fighting style reflexes took over on contact.

She coiled her hand back on her sleeve, changing the angle of his grip. As he gave her another sharp yank, she drifted forward into his pull and swatted him with *Silk Whips Like Thunder* palms. The altivorc staggered back. The sharp rasp of ripping stitches and the sudden cool air on her bare arm indicated he'd taken her sleeve with him. She kept driving through his stumbling form, landing a chain of straight punches to his face.

He swiped at her again, but she slipped under his swing. He might have seized her hair had she still had any. Coming up on the other side of him, she reached the drum.

Rooting herself to the ground, she listened to the altivorc heartbeats. She couldn't affect them with her voice, but with an instrument, maybe...

One ferocious palm strike in the middle of the drum hide sent a sound wave reverberating outward. She raked her gaze over the clearing to see the effect. Everyone, save for Fleet, cowered.

Straightening her spine and digging her toes into the ground, she summoned ferocity in her heart. She pounded out a combination of beats worthy of the best war drummers in Cathay. It echoed through the hills, shaking the ground with its resonance.

Birds scattered from trees. Altivorcs fled. Fleet tentatively held his ground.

Kaiya changed the beat, softer this time, channeling all of the courage she could muster in hopes that it would hearten her friends. Without stopping to catch her breath, she ran towards her bound guards and picked up a knife from their scattered belongings.

Tian looked at her, eyes rounded in awe. "Well done," he murmured.

She leaned in and gingerly cut through the ropes behind his back. As soon as he was free, he snatched the knife from her. With swift strokes, he cut through the others' bindings.

Kaiya looked towards Brehane and Cyrus and realized the hole in her hastily drawn-up plan: Fleet was too short to easily reach the ropes above their heads. The madaeri was climbing up Cyrus like a tree, putting a foot in his face as he reached out and cut the bonds. As the two Southerners crumpled to the ground, Fleet leaped down and landed on his feet. He arched his back, tilted his head backward, arms raised in victory.

Such theatrics. Kaiya looked down towards her knuckles, where pain blossomed. Red blood—hers, not the altivorc's black blood—trickled over her hands. Yet she had little time to think about her own wounds as her companions hastily gathered their belongings and stuffed them in their packs.

Cyrus clasped his gold medallion with one hand while grabbing Fleet by the collar with the other. "Do you have them?"

"Relax. Of course. All accounted for." Fleet opened his bag and withdrew a clear gemstone. It resembled the Lotus Crystal from the pyramid of Ayudra in size and shape, except a grey metal coated its flat top.

Kaiya's eyes widened. It was the same strange material as the First Consul's pin. Which was in her... "Where's my pack?"

Chen Xin presented it, but looked in Fleet's direction. "We helped the Southerners recover that from the pyramid in Selastya."

So that was the story no one was telling her about. Still, there was no time to find out more now. Once the altivorcs recovered from their initial shock, they'd be coming back in force.

CHAPTER 35:
End of the Highway

Kaiya clenched her sleeves with clammy palms as she watched blades flash faster than her eye could see. Only her keen hearing picked up on the otherwise indistinct clinking of blades as Sameer's *naga* clashed against Tian's saber.

Metal flashed. Tian tumbled to the ground. His sword clattered across the clearing in the woods.

Cyrus, Chen Xin, and Ma Jun all laughed, though none of them had fared any better.

Sameer grinned and offered Tian his hand to help him up. "Best four out of seven, then?"

By Jie's accounts, Tian was one of the finest swordsmen in Cathay, yet he could last no more than a few seconds against Sameer's extraordinary speed.

"One more time," Tian said, his expression sour. If nothing else, he was persistent. Failures didn't seem to discourage him from trying again.

Kaiya rolled her eyes. Brehane shared a knowing nod.

Men. Their ego grew in proportion to the size of their sword.

It had all started over the last several days. After a week of tension-filled marching with little rest, they'd finally managed to escape altivorc pursuit. They eased their frenetic pace, and their spirits rose as much as they could, given their losses. Danger gave way to monotony. With little else to do, Fleet pointed out the flora and fauna to Kaiya.

Not to be outdone, Tian taught her strategies for improving her observational skills. Gone was the cold and unforgiving automaton. He even smiled on rare occasions, with the innocence of his younger self.

The lessons in awareness escalated into occasional knife-fighting practice, which in turn got Sameer involved in theoretical discussions of swordplay.

By Kaiya's reckoning, on Cathay's Double Ten Day—twenty-four days since they began their escape—they descended the mountain path by moonlight and set up camp. The ridge overlooked the walled city of Kalenai, the administrative seat for the southeastern region of Iksuvi, at the terminus of the north-south highway.

In the morning, while they waited for Fleet to return from scouting out the city, Sameer and Tian decided to test their martial theories out. All of the men were eager to join in, and yet, Sameer nonchalantly dispatched them all without any signs of fatigue. Tian had come the closest, though only with the use of trickery to clinch up with the Paladin.

He still lost.

Just as Kaiya began to worry Tian would hurt himself in a fourth bout, Fleet returned to camp and provided a welcome distraction. He reported that the city was still under Iksuvi control, and that neither altivorc nor Teleri soldiers had come this far south. It would be safe to rest there for a night and buy provisions for their trek into the Wilds.

After these weeks of slogging through the wilderness, sleeping outdoors, and eating bland rations, Kaiya's excitement rose as they approached the city. Nestled in the nook between two mountain ranges, the scenery was beautiful year-round, according to Fleet. Numerous hot springs attracted visitors from as far north as Iksuvius, and aristocrats from the capital kept hillside villas here.

Farmers jostled alongside the group, bringing in the final harvest. Fishermen clogged the streets with carts of Nothori toothfish, which were now making their annual pilgrimage up the river to their spawning grounds.

They made it to the northern gate at mid-morning. The city garrison greeted them with stares, but allowed them to enter.

Fleet guided them through the streets, which bustled with citizenry preparing for what was predicted to be a particularly long, harsh winter. Before long, they came to a secluded hot-spring inn. The madaeri forewarned them it was upscale and expensive, but no one complained—least of all Kaiya. Accustomed to daily bathing, she hadn't enjoyed a bath in weeks.

A wave of warm mist enveloped Kaiya as soon as Tian opened the ironwood door for her. Lit by Aksumi baubles, the spacious common room seemed even brighter than the early afternoon sun outside. Fleet strode up to the bar, where the rotund and balding Nothori innkeeper favored the rest of them with a curious eye.

"Welcome back, Master Fleet. The Life Spring is always happy to have you. I see you have brought more... guests."

Fleet produced a silver coin, which he sent dancing through his fingers. "Two rooms—one large one for the men, a smaller one for the ladies."

"Very good, very good," the man replied with a toothy smile. "Though it seems strange that wandering Cathayi monks would enjoy the earthly pleasures of fine food and a luxurious bath."

Another silver *kroon* appeared between the madaeri's fingers, and Kaiya looked at her own hand, wondering if she could spin two coins. "As always, I appreciate a level of anonymity."

The innkeeper shook his head. "And what about the red-haired beauty's horses? I've stabled them for a few months now."

Red hair. Kaiya reached to twirl hair that wasn't there. Hadn't Jie found a strand of red hair on Prince Aelward's ship, over half a year ago?

A third coin joined the other two, twisting through Fleet's digits.

"I know you like information, and there is some that your friends might be interested in." The innkeeper tilted his chin towards her.

The silver coins disappeared, replaced by a single gold *kroon*. Fleet slapped it on the counter. Where did the madaeri hide his money?

The innkeeper flashed a greedy smile and leaned forward, beckoning them closer. "News is, the Teleri stopped their advance at the highway crossroads and won't continue their offensive until spring. Rumor has it that they will head west towards the interior instead of coming south."

If true, that would hopefully keep them safe.

Though the common room was empty, he lowered his voice to a whisper. "However, I have it from a good source that there are a few spies wandering around the city. Also, there is another Cathayi monk hanging around here. Arrived about a week ago. He was asking for others of his kind." The innkeeper nodded in her direction.

"Thank you," Fleet said. "We'll bathe now. If you would, send your boy out to fetch us some clean winter clothes, preferably wool." He tossed another gold coin onto the counter.

"Very good. You can get your noon meal from the kitchens whenever you're done."

Kaiya couldn't reach the baths soon enough.

Carved out of rock to a depth of three feet, it looked like the pools could accommodate ten or more people at a time. They weren't much different than the bathing pools that were loved by the Cathay people, from inexpensive public baths to the *Tianzi's* exclusive hot spring on Jade Mountain.

Kaiya scrubbed off the dirt, sweat, blood, and tears that had accumulated like moss. Already slender, she was now almost gaunt, exposing muscles toned from constant marching. Thank goodness for the high ironwood fence that separated the men's and women's bathing areas.

As they soaked together in the warm water, Brehane commented that she looked much more the part of a wandering monk now, even if her hair had already grown a thumblength.

Across the fence, the men, except for Cyrus who waited to bathe by himself, soaked together. They bragged about their scars, with Ma Jun and Sameer telling colorful, almost unbelievable stories about their war wounds. Compared to their embellished battle of one-upmanship, Chen Xin sounded like a farmer recounting his daily weeding.

An hour later, all emerged from the baths pink and refreshed, and met in the common room for their first hot lunch in a long time: chicken and potato stew with a side of bread. It had been too long since they'd eaten something other than cornbread.

They changed from the monks' robes to the heavier woolen shirts and pants. Though not nearly as fine as the silk gowns Kaiya was accustomed to, the clothes still felt comfortable after weeks of wearing coarse hemp. When the inn's servant asked if they would like the monks' robes washed, Kaiya thought she would just as soon see them burned. Tian had other ideas.

For the rest of the day, they split into pairs to procure provisions for the remainder of the last leg of their journey. Tian accompanied Kaiya, who'd volunteered to find fur-lined travelling cloaks.

As they wandered the streets, perhaps looking like a couple as they peeked in stores, a handsome young Cathay monk with a walking staff rushed up to them. Even without his red and yellow robes, Kaiya recognized him up close. A disciple of her own Doctor Wu, Fang Weiyong was a palace physician who'd travelled with her on the *Golden Phoenix* to Iksuvius. Now that she was clean, her nose wrinkled at his gamey odor.

He dropped to his knees, drawing curious stares from the locals. "*Dian-xia*, I have been looking for you."

"Your Holiness, please stand," Tian said with an edge in his voice. "You're attracting too much attention."

The doctor rose, brushing the dust from his knees. "My apologies. I should have known better."

"What news do you have, Your Holiness?" Kaiya asked.

"Unfortunately, not much. I treated the First Consul, as you commanded. When I returned to the embassy compound, the ambassador ordered all Cathayi to flee the city. In my travels, I heard that you were also heading south. The Teleri offer a substantial bounty for your capture. I do not think it is safe for you here, even this far south."

Tian rolled his eyes. "Then don't draw attention to her again."

The doctor started to drop to his knees when Tian caught him. He bowed his head. "My apologies."

Kaiya nodded back. "Come, Your Holiness, join us for a bath and hot meal."

Tian's lips tightened, but he said nothing.

That evening, they gathered over a hot supper of roasted elk with seasoned potatoes and steamed vegetables. Watching their new companion eat, Tian wondered if the doctor didn't attack the food with as much vigor as the madaeri. He barely paused to breathe, answering questions with grunts.

Had he seen any other Cathayi? Grunt no.

Had he encountered any altivorcs? Grunt yes.

Nearby? Grunt no.

Could he wield a sword? Grunt kind-of.

Great. The last thing they needed was another mouth to feed and another body to protect. If only they had run into Cathayi soldiers instead.

Fleet had the unique talent of speaking clearly with food in his mouth. "Enjoy the hot food now, because it'll be Kanin cornbread again soon."

The princess shuddered. "I never want to see or taste that bland stuff again."

The madaeri chuckled. "And be sure to enjoy the warm bed tonight. It'll be a long time before you enjoy that luxury again."

Tian tapped his chin. The princess was probably up to the task. She'd weathered the journey better than expected. Proven her mettle.

Before retiring for the night, Tian beckoned her aside. "The doctor will be a burden. In the Wilds. We need swords."

The princess shook her head. "He might not be able to heal with the divine power of the gods like Cyrus, but a doctor may be useful in the Wilds once the Southerners go their own way."

Tian shrugged. Perhaps she was right, and even if he disagreed, she probably wouldn't change her mind. Despite his misgivings, he slept well that night.

The next morning, the air was decidedly colder, despite the bright sun. The princess gave the innkeeper a silver coin and two letters, signed with an alias and addressed to the ambassador in the Kanin embassy in Iksuvius.

The group left the city from the southern gate, where the road became nothing more than a worn dirt path heading south along the rocky section of river. After several miles of pasture where the farmers worked hard at their harvest, the road rose into wooded hills. It followed the bends of the river, which became noticeably narrower and narrower along with the road itself.

On the night of the second day, they camped by a lake, which was flush with spawning Nothori toothfish. While Tian and Ma Jun tried their hand at spear-fishing, Fleet taught the others how to make fires, with the expectation that they would soon be on their own in the Kanin Wilds. The princess learned quickly.

Toward the end of the third day, when the river shrank to a rapidly flowing stream, they split off the main road, which Fleet said continued to the Alto River's main source and the old, closed-off pass.

Instead, they walked through a rocky feeder stream, with the madaeri nimbly skipping from rock to rock without watching where he was going. Tian followed close behind. And the princess... with amazing balance and unbelievable grace, she darted among the uneven stones.

He stood gawking as she passed him, and she flashed a mischievous grin. Just like when they were children.

No, that wouldn't do. His clan would never let him forget it if he let a dancer beat him. He redoubled his efforts, speeding over the rocks.

Just as he was about to catch up to her, she pulled up short. Crouching, she rubbed her ankle and looked up at him. "I think I twisted it."

Oh no. Tian leaned over to look and—

Oof.

He picked himself out of the stream, his shoulder stinging from where she'd shoved him. He looked up.

Far ahead, she sat on a boulder with Fleet, both laughing at him. Yes, just like the little girl he had once known.

After several *li*, they arrived at an old trail with lush overgrowth stabbing through the cracks between ancient stones. According to Fleet, following it for two days would take them through the hidden mountain pass and into the Kanin Wilds. With winter fast approaching, they had little time to complete the last leg of their journey.

CHAPTER 36:
Into the Wilds

Kaiya listened to the wind in the evergreen needles and the rustling of a nearby stream. The three Southerners, along with Fleet, Tian, Doctor Fang, and the two surviving imperial guards, sat with her in a circle around the crackling campfire in the madaeri's secret pass.

The last few days of travel had been pleasant as they chatted and hiked at a leisurely pace through idyllic woods. She frequently walked beside Tian, who could keep conversations going with insightful questions. Perhaps it was just his training as a spy and interrogator, or maybe he felt guilty and was forcing himself to be nice. Nonetheless, he seemed more and more like the childhood confidante he'd been a decade before.

Shared memories, current court gossip, philosophy, poetry: they'd talked about anything and everything. Well, everything except his brother, Zheng Ming. It should have been an easy topic to broach, yet it felt awkward to bring it up. And really, she hadn't thought much about Ming in the last month.

They reached the pass on the evening of the seventh month's full White Moon. Crisp, cold air and clear skies provided a spectacular view of the heavens, framed by the mountain summits above. Surrounded by countless stars, the White Moon Renyue shone larger and brighter than usual, bathing the pass in a soft light. The Blue Moon, Guanyin's Eye, hovered half-obscured by the mountaintops. Caiyue joined the others, its colors swirling in its eternal spot low in the southern sky.

With a renewed friendship and beautiful scenery, Kaiya should've been happy.

Yet this was the night of Cathay's annual Full Moon Festival, her second-favorite celebration after the New Year's Spring Festival. Had the escape by sea worked, she would've been home already. At this moment, Father must be hosting a grand party for the hereditary lords on the shores of Sun-Moon Lake, where the placid waters mirrored the night sky.

Kaiya sighed. No fireworks, no mooncakes, no singing songs in tribute to Renyue this year.

"Here." Tian offered her a cube of moistened cornbread.

Yuck! Hopefully, he had used *water* to wet it. She raised an eyebrow and took it with two fingers. "What is it?"

"Try it." He grinned.

Locking a suspicious eye on him, she took a tentative bite. The subdued sweetness of the softened cornbread mingled with the sinewy zest of smoked elk. He'd made an imitation mooncake.

How considerate! So what if it was unladylike to smile while chewing?

Tian spoke up, breaking through their companions' conversations. "Shall we sing?"

All eyes turned to him, and they offered encouraging applause.

Kaiya politely clapped at his best rendition of a Cathayi folk song, even if she shuddered inside. This was why he was a spy and not a court singer.

Everyone took turns, even the Southerners who didn't celebrate the Full Moon Festival. From Sameer's Paladin Canticle to Cyrus' hymns; from Doctor Fang's herbal medicine mnemonic rhymes, to the imperial guards' chorus of drinking songs. Kaiya outshined them all, holding her friends entranced with her voice.

It was good to sing again!

This was the best Full Moon Festival ever. She'd been isolated in the Cathayi court, yet here in the Wilds, with people who'd shared the same perils, there was a sense of belonging. Like when she was a child, with Tian. And unlike their first reunion, he was so considerate and sweet now.

And handsome.

Heavens, did she just think that?

With Brehane's tribal tune as a backdrop, she looked across the fire. The flickering light danced across his features. The defined jawline and high-bridged nose. And those eyes, so intelligent.

And looking right at her.

Heat flared in her cheeks. She cast her gaze down. Heavens, it must be the full moon addling her better judgment. She peeked up through her lashes.

He was on his feet now, working his way around the others.

Toward her.

With an adorably timid smile, he sat down by her side. She fought the inexplicable urge to lean into him. How nice it would be for him to drape an arm over her shoulder. Bad girl, to even think this! It *had* to be the full moon.

He leaned in close.

Her heart pattered. What was he doing?

His hand reached out and plucked a stray twig from her short hair.

Her cheeks warmed. It might've been the first time he'd ever touched her without serious reason. She met his gaze. His normally expressionless mask contorted into self-admonishment, but she flashed him a reassuring smile.

His attention awkwardly shifted to the ground between his feet; but in that brief glance, she imagined a kindness in Tian's dark eyes. They were beautiful eyes, at least in that moment when he wasn't assessing a threat or planning an attack. Maybe that was what Jie saw in him.

If her cheeks burned any hotter, they might not need a campfire. Kaiya turned her head away. Beautiful eyes or not, he'd been thoughtless during the frantic escape from Iksuvius. Yelled at her. Humiliated her. Butchered her hair. No, she must just be conjuring up a resemblance to Ming.

Her musing did not last long as, one by one, the companions settled down for the night and let sleep overtake them.

The low light before dawn woke Kaiya from a restless, dream-filled sleep. It took her a few seconds to remember that she was in the pass straddling Iksuvi and the Wilds. Her breath misted, discouraging her from abandoning the warmth of her blankets.

Rolling over, she looked at Tian, who slept just a few feet from her. No, he didn't look like his brother.

She pressed a hand to her heart, realizing that for the first time, it didn't flutter when thinking of Ming. Asleep, without carrying his worries, Tian might be more handsome.

What *was* she thinking? She banished the thought and forced herself up.

Ma Jun paced the campsite, sometimes stopping by the fire to warm his hands. He dropped to his knee at her approach.

Kaiya nodded him out of his salute. Stretching her legs and arms out to get the circulation going, she strolled over to the southern end of the pass to scan the path ahead.

The sun had just risen. Countless evergreens in the valley below stabbed up through the thick morning fog. Unlike the thin woods behind them, the lands ahead consisted of dense forest, teeming with life.

She had little time to enjoy the view.

Fleet returned from scouting ahead, as was his habit, and greeted her with a cheerful grin. "You're up early this morning. I've collected some bark from the sweet evergreen trees below. When brewed into a tea, it'll warm you up and give you energy."

He boiled some water in his copper pot over the campfire and added the bark. A sweet, aromatic scent wafted from it. After a few minutes, he filled a wooden cup and offered it to her.

She thanked him and took a long sniff. Fresh and fragrant, it sent her nostrils tingling. "It is wonderful! The aroma seems familiar."

"We drink this tea in Cathay during the winter," Ma Jun said as he joined them. "Some people venture out of the Great East Gate into the Wilds to collect the bark. Maybe you had some at the palace."

That didn't seem to explain the eerily nostalgic scent. Perhaps—

"At least you only take the bark, and not the whole tree," Fleet said. "The sweet evergreen, which only grows on this plateau, has always been prized for its straightness and sweet smell. During Kanin imperial times, the Kanin emperors had the lumber hauled to their cities in the plains below to build great temples, castles, and fortresses. Much of the plateau was deforested and tilled for farmland."

Kaiya waved at the forest below. "It doesn't look like farmland to me."

The madaeri rubbed his hands together, maybe because they were cold, or perhaps because he simply liked to tell stories. "In the Long Winter that followed the Hellstorm, the land bore no crops. Many humans migrated off of the plateau and into the warmer plains. Those that stayed became hunter-gatherers by necessity. In the three hundred years since, nature has reclaimed the area with astonishing—some say mystical—speed. These forests stretch to the edge of the plateau."

Kaiya breathed into her hands. It must be difficult to live in the Wilds, away from any trappings of civilization. "What became of the people who stayed?"

"There are several tribes of Kanin folk who live here. They don't necessarily get along with each other, but will unite to fight an outside invader. They did so thirty-three years ago, when their plains-dwelling cousins invaded."

Kaiya nodded. Ambassador Manuwaya had bragged about fighting in those wars.

"However," he continued, "the density of the forest made it difficult to move troops in formation. The locals repelled the invaders."

Thirty-three years ago. A lot had happened then. The secret Black Fist mission to recover a book of songs. The dragon Avarax's awakening. Jie was thirty-two, her parents must have... Kaiya shook *that* thought out of her head and turned back to the forests. "Could the Teleri invade?"

Fleet shrugged. "The Teleri would have difficulty with their supply lines. Heavy snows starting in the middle of next month will clog the paths, closing them down until early in the new year."

Kaiya tried to picture a map in her mind. The Wilds stretched to Cathay's northeast border. "Then the terrain, climate, and inhabitants make the Wilds a safe buffer between Cathay and the Teleri."

Fleet met her gaze. "Cathay can't afford to remain neutral and trade with everyone. The Teleri won't rest until they conquer the world. The Wilds can't hold them back forever."

"How could they move soldiers through it?" Ma Jun asked.

"In the old days, the few large stones in the Kanin region were used to build highways." Fleet pointed into the forest below. "Not even the mighty greywood trees can grow through those old roads. I know these paths, and will show you one that goes to the East Gate of Cathay. However, it's only a matter of time before the Empire discovers the same route if they continue westward expansion. Maybe not for decades, and the resources required to restore the old highway might not make them a threat in your lifetime. But you can never underestimate the ambition of the Bovyans."

The tone of his voice sent a chill through her. Memories of the First Consul seizing her wrist and pulling her against him surfaced, unbidden. She suppressed a shudder, and quickly changed the subject to something more lighthearted.

From where he feigned sleep, Tian watched the princess warming her hands over the fire, bantering with the madaeri.

This Kaiya was much more likable than the princess. She was like the girl from his past, whom his ten-year-old self had childishly promised to marry. Her genuine smiles and girlish giggles had a charming appeal to them, even more so than the elegant courtly smiles and covered laughs that she'd used to win over kings and generals.

It was almost like Jie, but without the sarcastic sense of humor. Which was the real Princess Kaiya?

That morning, they began their descent into the Kanin Wilds. The next few days consisted of winding along worn animal trails, covered with the browning needles of the sweet evergreens. The forest was alive with the sounds of fauna, and a sweet aroma from the evergreen bark hung in the air. Nothing that Tian had ever seen in Cathay or Iksuvi could compare to these pristine woodlands.

On the third day, they came to a stream. Beside that ran another trail, where flat rocks peeked out from under the ground. Lines of small broadleaf weeds marked their borders. In some places, the roots of the huge, spindly-leaved greywood trees had pushed some of these ancient stones up and exposed them to years of wind and rain.

Fleet pointed to the markings on one, noting that it had been cut by dwarves, and that this road once crossed through the original pass between the Kanin Empire and the Nothori Empire, now the Wilds and Iksuvi.

They followed the hidden road for five uneventful days, until the stream widened significantly into rocky river rapids. Fleet explained that it was a tributary of the North Kanin River, and following it downstream would lead to the East Gate of Cathay.

Tian's home province. He hadn't returned in a decade.

They continued south along the overgrown road, which ran along the western side of the river for another five days, until the road turned towards the southeast. It was at this bend that they parted ways with the Southerners.

With their own mission to pursue, the Southerners would continue along the old road towards the Kanin Pyramid, while the princess' group would follow the river. It was a tearful farewell. Against all cultural norms, Tian and his compatriots warmly embraced their traveling companions.

"Remember," Fleet said, "Continue following the river south until it meets up with the North Kanin River—it will also flow south at that point. Be sure to stay on the eastern side of the river to avoid hill ogres! Eventually, you will come to this overgrown road again. Follow that road west until it ends, then continue along the river. If you're lucky, you might even see wild elves."

"Wild elves?" Kaiya cocked her head. "How are they wild?"

Like the last time Fleet explained, in the *Hard Shell* in Gaukaimos, an image of Jie appeared in Tian's mind.

Fleet grinned. "Well, *wild* isn't necessarily fair. It's just a label given by their kindred in the two *civilized* elven realms. During the War of Ancient Gods, the ancestors of the wild elves didn't share their brethren's belief that Aralas was an Elf Angel, prophesized to lead them in their uprising against the orcs. After the orcs' defeat, the wild elves refused to acknowledge Aralas' heirs. They stayed in these forests, making their homes in treetop villages."

Elf matters. It had little bearing on Tian's current mission, except... "Are they dangerous?"

Fleet chuckled. "They'll be the least of your worries. In all likelihood, you'll probably never see them. No, the greatest danger is from the hill ogres in the northwest. As long as you avoid that area, your journey should be safe."

The madaeri handed Tian a brightly painted, thumb-length woodcarving, of a bird of prey with its wings tucked. "This is a token of the Kanin Tribal Council. Present it to any of the tribes, and they'll provide food and shelter. From here, you're less than a month away from home. It might be faster if you can trade for a canoe, though the waters may be too shallow this time of year—ask the natives. They're simple, honest people, especially in the western reaches of the plateau. Hurry, because once the snow starts falling, it'll become virtually impossible to travel."

Tian repeated the instructions to himself several times before bowing low. "Thank you. For guiding us. I hope we meet again. So we can repay you."

The madaeri just smiled. "I'm sure our paths will cross. Your enemy is mine, and I have no doubt that the winds of war will blow us back together. Remember, stay in the east. Ogres are in the west."

The princess bowed low as well, and all of her retainers dropped to one knee. "I thank you for your generous assistance, especially as it has slowed your own mission. If your travels take you to Cathay, rest assured that you will be given a warm welcome."

She then turned to clasp Brehane's hands. "You will always be a sister to me. I hope you will be reunited with your son soon. Please bring her to Cathay when you have a chance. I will be sure to introduce you to our enigmatic elf lord."

From a pouch in her robe, Brehane withdrew a small glass ball with a soft white light glowing inside. "Aksumi cities are all lit with these lights. It is the first incantation we learn, so there are plenty. I have made countless in my life. It will never go out, unless dispersed by magic. I hope this will help you on the rest of your journey. Be safe, Princess Kaiya!" She took her up in a long, warm embrace, finally releasing her with a heavy sigh. Both wiped away tears.

The Cathayi waited and watched as the other group continued down the road, waving as they disappeared into the trees. Now it was just the five of them: Tian, the princess, the doctor, and the two imperial guards, Chen Xin and Ma Jun. Tian hoped that Fleet's assurances of safe roads would hold true.

"It looks like we are on our own now," Chen Xin said.

"And we will be finding out just why the Wilds are so wild, I'm sure," muttered Ma Jun.

Hill ogres in the west, Tian repeated to himself.

CHAPTER 37:
Hill Ogres in the East

Kaiya awoke to Tian's gentle shakes. The sound of the babbling river next to their campsite coaxed her head to clarity.

The crackling fire sent flickers across Tian's face, the dancing shadows emphasizing his eyes. *Your watch,* he mouthed.

In the three days since they'd parted ways with the Southerners, the men always insisted she take either first or last watch, allowing her uninterrupted sleep. If not for her command, they would've taken longer intervals and let her slumber through the night. Kaiya smiled back at him as she abandoned the warmth of her bedroll.

He cast his eyes down, and then looked back up. His lips, glistening in the flames, formed the words, *Goodnight.*

Heavens, staring at his lips? Kaiya gazed at the nearly pitch-black sky, with the White Moon shining as a thin sliver, the Blue Moon almost hugging the horizon. When she looked down again, he'd settled into his bedroll. Shaking her head, she paced over to a boulder, just inside the dim circle of wavering firelight.

A cramp clenched her belly. If only she had more herbal medicine from Cathay. Massaging her stomach, she closed her eyes and listened to the chorus of the night.

Gentle wind sang, set to the beat of crackling fire. Nocturnal animals danced in tune. The river rustled...

No.

Something was wrong with the sound of the waters. All the animal sounds fell silent.

The ache in her belly went from wail to whimper, almost forgotten as a chill crept up her spine. Gathering up her two straight swords, she crept toward the river to investigate. She held up Brehane's magical bead toward the inconsistent sounds, but the soft light only extended about thirty feet out into the dark waters.

Which meant that if something was out there, she stuck out in a mantle of light. Kaiya closed her hand around the light bauble, sending the surroundings into darkness. Eyes shut, she listened.

Something sloshed perpendicularly across the flow of the river, almost rhythmically... a dozen sets of sounds. Coming closer. Maybe fifty feet away.

She turned and raced back towards her sleeping companions. "Wake up! Something is coming!" Her voice rang frantic in her own ears. Behind her, the splashing footsteps sped up.

Tian woke first, having just fallen back to sleep. Saber in hand, he leapt to his feet and kicked at Chen Xin, who was closest to him. "Wake up, wake up!"

Chen Xin groggily rose to a seated position. Kaiya reached Ma Jun. Behind her, heavy steps crunched over sweet evergreen needles and dry greywood leaves, and fanned out around them. She desperately shook Ma Jun out of his deep slumber. What was Tian doing? She looked over her shoulder.

He was prodding Doctor Fang. Chen Xin was now standing, naked saber flashing in the guttering firelight. He rushed to her side. Ma Jun sat up and fumbled for his weapon. Kaiya took up a bow and a quiver of arrows.

A huge figure stepped into the firelight. Wearing a fur-lined shirt and loincloth, he stood about seven-and-a-half feet tall. In the low light, his skin appeared mottled grey. Long, dark hair sprouted out of his head in all directions.

Pointing a gigantic, spiked club at them, he barked in halting, heavily-accented Arkothi, "You drop weapons. You surrounded."

A hill ogre! Fleet had said they stayed on the western side of the river! Kaiya held up Brehane's bauble. White light radiated out in a thirty-foot sphere all around her.

Fifteen ogres encircled them along the edge of the clearing, all dressed and armed the same as their leader. Many shielded their eyes from the sudden bright light.

In that split second, Tian leaped in the direction of an animal path, swiping at the closest ogre with his saber. The blade cut across the ogre's throat, and the creature stumbled to his knees, clawing his neck.

Kaiya considered using a magical command. No, the ogres might not all understand Arkothi, while all her men did. Instead, she dropped the bauble, nocked an arrow, and let it fly. It hit the leader in the right shoulder. He shrieked, and the club slipped from hand.

Brandishing swords, Ma Jun and Chen Xin guarded her flanks. She fitted another arrow, took aim and shot at an ogre closing on Tian's back. It lodged in the ogre's spine.

Tian deftly rolled under the clumsy swing of another ogre, simultaneously cutting through his knee tendons. A gap opened in the ring of attackers. Tian beckoned her. "Run, this way!"

Chen Xin grabbed Kaiya's wrist and pulled her in that direction. Ma Jun backed up, keeping the other enemies in front of him. Tian ran toward her.

A high-pitched whistling sang from behind. Chen Xin collapsed, dragging her down with him. Kaiya staggered to her feet and tried to pull him, but he was too heavy.

Tian grabbed her by the shoulder. "Leave him. We must get to safety!"

"No!" She tugged at Chen Xin's inert body.

Tian reached under her arms and across her chest. He pulled.

Her sweaty grip slipped from Chen Xin's arm.

Tian's tone was insistent. "We must go! We can outrun them. In the dense woods."

Kaiya looked toward the fire, where Ma Jun and the doctor stood back-to-back, fighting valiantly. Four of the ogres turned and lumbered toward her.

Heart racing, she turned and ran, letting Tian pull her along through the darkness. Despite what he believed about the dense woods slowing them, the ogres loped with longer strides. The footsteps gained on them.

Tian pulled her down into thick brush with no warning. He threw himself on top of her, his hand on her mouth. His heat and weight smothered her. Images of Geros leaped into her mind. Her heart seized. She struggled for a split second.

No, this was Tian, trying to protect her. With conscious effort, she took control of her fevered panting.

The footsteps approached. Faster. Louder.

Then ran past them.

She held her breath, too scared to let it out. Her vision adjusted to the darkness and Tian withdrew his hand. All was silent, save for the ogres' pounding feet in the distance and the rustling of the river.

Motioning for quiet, Tian helped her up and guided her back towards their camp at a brisk pace. His hand on hers felt reassuring.

Then he dragged her down into more brush. In the far distance, the ogres spoke in their harsh-sounding language. Soon, that too faded.

"I think they're gone," Tian whispered. "You wait here. I'll go back. To check the camp."

She shook her head emphatically. "We stay together. We might get lost and separated."

He nodded in acquiescence, but his pursed lips, silhouetted against the dark, betrayed his opinion on the matter. He pulled her to her feet, and they crept back toward the sounds of the river.

When they reached the path by the water, the flickering of their campfire shone in the distance to the south. The sky had started to lighten, dark blues on the horizon merging with the black above. Slinking back as quietly as they could, they reached the site.

There, Chen Xin lay face-down. She stifled a gasp. He was bleeding from a horrific wound in the back of his head. Their gear had been taken. There was no sign of Ma Jun, Fang Weiyong, or the ogres.

Sobbing, Kaiya ran over and sank to her knees. She rolled Chen Xin over and nestled his head in her lap. Within seconds, his warm blood seeped through her pants. She stroked his short hair, and his eyes fluttered open.

Squinting at her, he offered a weak smile. His voice rasped in a strained whisper. "Princess Kaiya, it has been an honor to serve you all these years. I have seen you grow into a fine woman... I'm so... ." He choked on his words and fell silent.

Tian knelt down beside him to feel his pulse. He looked up at her and shook his head.

Tears trickled unheeded down Kaiya's cheeks. Chen Xin had been with her for as long as she could remember, had borne the brunt of her forceful personality without complaint. Now he was dead, at just thirty-eight. Her fault.

Tian eased her up and folded his arms around her. She leaned in, draping her arms around his neck and burying her face in his chest. The warmth of his body was comforting, filling the emptiness in her heart. He stroked the back of her head.

"Poor human," a mocking voice said from the shadows. "Stupid human, come back for friend."

A trap.

Tian's body stiffened as he muttered some unintelligible curse.

She was running, Tian's hand wrapped around her wrist and pulling her on a mad dash down the river bank trail. When had he grabbed her?

An ogre stepped in front of them, only to be cut across the neck with a swift draw and slash of Tian's saber.

Jumping over the body, Kaiya looked back. Two ogres shambled behind them in close pursuit.

Despite her improved physical conditioning after two months of hard travel, her lungs burned. She panted as the path sloped upwards. Below, the river descended, the roar of water suggesting rapids.

A whirling, whining sound swooped in behind her. Something tangled her legs. She fell hard into Tian's ankles, knocking the wind from her.

He tripped over the ledge and into the river below with a loud splash.

"Tian!" Kaiya sat up and struggled to free herself from the bola entangling her legs. Her fingers trembled, her heart raced. Was Tian all right? She squinted. Dozens of feet downstream, Tian's inert form bobbed among the rapids.

A dark shadow appeared above her. Heart pounding, she looked up.

"Girl need help?" an ogre cackled. His huge, six-fingered hand wrapped around both of her wrists and jerked her onto her entangled feet. He smirked, revealing sharp yellow teeth. Rubbing some of her short hair between his fingers, he grunted.

Then, he reached toward her face. No! He lifted her chin in a tight pinch between his thumb and index finger and fixed her with a dull gaze. "Girl got ugly hair, but pretty face." His breath reeked of rotten raw meat, stirring her stomach to rebellion.

She tried to turn her head through his strong grip, to no avail.

He laughed. His hand strayed from her face and down her back, then around toward the front.

Oh no. What was he going to do? All her muscles seized up, fear freezing her in place. The horror of this situation surpassed her encounter with Geros, swallowing up her attempt to use the power of her voice. Unlike altivorcs, who found humans to be hideous, ogres had a well-known appetite for human women. In human societies, one might sometimes encounter one of the few half-ogres born to women who survived the experience.

A male behind her barked in an unintelligible language. The hand on the side of her ribs withdrew. Patting her on the cheek, he mumbled, "Chief say we go. Maybe us do fun later." He winked, sending a shudder wracking through her.

He lugged her up over his shoulder, still holding both of her wrists in his hand, and shambled towards their camp. Incoherent thoughts bounced through her head.

When they arrived at the campsite, three more ogres leered at her. Chen Xin's body lay there, though they'd taken his boots. Why, considering their feet were so much larger?

With a deep breath, she settled her racing thoughts. "Put me down," she sang. Power, held back by fear, sputtered inside of her. Energy drained out of her arms and legs.

The ogre's expression blanked and he set her on the ground.

Kaiya stumbled away, her limbs weighing her down like dwarf anvils.

She did not get far.

An ogre tackled her from behind, sending her careening face-first into the ground and knocking the wind from her. He scrambled up and straddled her, his weight crushing into her back.

Her captors exchanged a few more words in their language and then flipped her over. One gagged her with a stinking rag, which must have been used to wash a goat. Two others bound her wrists and ankles with rope. The frayed fibers bit into her skin. They ran a long pole through the ropes, and then hoisted her up like a deer carcass between two ogres. Kaiya's rattling heart bounced all rational thought from her mind. She wriggled and writhed, only to be rewarded with cruel laughs. Finally, all energy spent, she wilted.

The sky above flushed pink, as the crown of the sun glanced through the tree tops. The beasts began their march back through the river. Where were they taking her? At the deepest point, the water reached to the ogres' waists. Their massive bodies resisted the strong flow of the current.

Kaiya wiggled upwards as best she could, to keep from getting her back wet from the splashing waters. After several minutes, they emerged from the river onto another path through the forest. They came to a clearing, where Ma Jun and the doctor lay bound to poles, just like her.

Ma Jun's left eye swelled shut, flushing an ugly shade of purple. He looked at her with his good eye and shook his head. Another seven ogres sat there, slurping on some food. Four ogres lay dead.

The largest one's arm dangled in a sling, with a black splotch seeping through a clumsy bandage on his shoulder. The leader. The one she'd shot. He glared at her and stood. He lurched over, drawing a wicked, serrated metal knife with his good hand and yelling foul gibberish.

His words needed no translation. The knife announced his intentions. He was out for revenge, coming to cut her throat here and now. Then they would do horrible things to her body, robbing her of dignity even in death.

She squirmed to free herself. The other ogres lifted the pole off the ground, setting gravity against her. Before the enraged leader could reach her, two of his companions interceded, stammering with wild gesticulations. He snarled and sheathed the knife, spitting on the ground. He came closer and aimed a kick to her side—not strong enough to break anything, but sharp enough to send pain flaring through her ribs.

She yelped. Ma Jun resumed his struggle, only to be punched in the jaw.

The leader leaned in and yanked her head back. "You lucky you pretty. You bring good money. Else I gut you." He released her and stomped away.

Good money? Were they to be sold into slavery? Kaiya let out a long exhale. Warm tears flowed freely over her cold cheek.

After a while, the ogres hoisted her and the two others back up and resumed their march through the forest. Where were they headed? There couldn't be a slave market in the wilderness. Could there? Fleet had never mentioned anything about the tribal peoples keeping slaves.

The sounds of wildlife fell silent as they passed. The brutes lumbered on, and the sun rose higher, peeking through tree branches as the morning progressed. After three hours, they arrived at what appeared to be a permanent campsite in a large clearing.

Kaiya's arms and legs ached from the strain. Hopelessness overcame her.

Evergreen needles and greywood leaves covered the ground. Several large tents circled a bonfire. A couple of ogres milled about, but the loud sound of snoring from the tents suggested there were a few dozen more.

And from one tent came the sounds of a woman, crying and screaming. Kaiya's heart leaped into her throat. She fought against her bindings. It was no use. She looked to see where the ogres were taking her.

Four fifteen-feet poles were secured horizontally between trees. On either side of each pole, alternating from left shoulder to right shoulder, dark-haired humans sat quietly, their wrists bound so that the pole passed between their arms. There were thirty-eight in total, about ten to each pole.

The ogres carried them over to the other prisoners. Black-haired with ruddy skin, they were Kanin tribespeople, dressed in deerskin clothes and furs. All young adults, mostly men. No children or elderly. Some looked up, craning their necks and meeting her gaze. Eyes widened and murmurs passed through the lines.

Kaiya sucked in a breath. There were several sets of twins.

The ogres untied her feet, and then added her to one of the poles. They secured Ma Jun and Doctor Fang to different poles. One ogre stood guard while the rest stomped back to the center of the camp.

How could they possibly get away? She looked over at her countrymen. Fang Weiyong was talking to a tribesman, or at least trying to. Ma Jun met her eyes and nodded. He must be making a plan of some sort.

Several hours passed. Mouth still gagged, Kaiya looked at each of the prisoners within her line of sight. They must all have some sad story. Like her, caught by ogres for some nefarious purpose. And why so many twins? If not for the stinking gag, she would've asked.

When the sun shone high in the sky, two ogres approached. One looked fairly intelligent, his eyes seeming to comprehend things more deeply than the average ogre. His comrades all nodded respectfully at him.

The chief, probably. His companion was the one she had shot, arm still in a sling. Perhaps a lieutenant of some sort.

Behind them, the chief dragged a comely young woman, tears streaked across her face. Her deerskin dress was torn, partially revealing her breasts and legs. The blood staining her thighs left no doubt as to what had happened to her.

Poor girl. Kaiya drew her knees to her chest. It probably wouldn't be long before she shared the same fate.

The other prisoners muttered and wailed. Others sobbed as the ogres tied the girl to a pole.

The chief came up and inspected them in a cursory manner. When he paused at Kaiya, her heart almost stopped. He bent over and clutched her chin in an iron grip between his thumb and index finger. Try as she might, she couldn't turn her head. He peered at her through sleepy eyes before turning to his lieutenant and grunting something.

The other ogre nodded and grinned.

Her entire body trembling, Kaiya scuttled back as best she could. The prisoner beside her yelped.

The chief snorted and released her, then stood and yelled back at the camp.

One ogre brought a sloshing wooden bucket and lifted it to each of the prisoners' mouths.

Water! It dribbled out the sides, and tantalized Kaiya's dry mouth.

Another ogre hand-fed them small chunks of some foul-smelling meat. The stench quelled the gnawing in her stomach.

The ogres approached. They would have to loosen the gag to feed her. And then the power of her voice... No. There must be at least thirty here, and without a musical instrument, she'd be exhausted after three or four commands. Her flute, in the fold of her robe... gone.

The Teleri imperial crest, too. Nothing to do now but wait, rest, and look for another opportunity.

And hope.

When offered, Kaiya gulped the water down. Its coolness ran down her chin and neck. The meat, on the other hand, stank so bad that she just turned her head. Those ogre hands were filthy, and what kind of meat was it, anyway?

The chief addressed them all, speaking in heavily accented but fluent Arkothi. "Rest well. You will be travelling in the late afternoon."

Then he turned to Kaiya, grinning. "Except you. We will keep you until our next group is ready. I'm sure the big bosses won't mind if we have some fun first."

Big bosses? Fun? Her heart resumed its pounding, but she nonetheless glared back at him in defiance.

Another several hours passed. Kaiya's wrists chafed from trying to loosen her bonds. Eventually, she gave up and closed her eyes, letting sleep overtake her. In what seemed to be minutes, loud clanging jolted her out of sleep.

Night had fallen, and the ogres were back with food. Again, she drank the water but refused the meat. After half an hour, the leader appeared again. "Now, get ready to leave. Stand up."

As the prisoners shuffled to their feet, he ambled over to Kaiya. "All but you." He laughed as he motioned his lieutenant to take hold of her. He pulled out a large knife and cut through her bindings. Kaiya kicked and struggled, but the ogre effortlessly lifted her in the air, far enough away from her flailing.

It wasn't long before she tired.

Ma Jun twisted and turned, disrupting his pole, but another ogre came and punched him squarely in the kidneys. Everyone cringed at the sound of cracking bones. He collapsed, almost bringing the entire line of prisoners down with him. The leader angrily barked at the offending ogre, who then yanked Ma Jun to his feet.

Kaiya's wrists were retied in front of her. An ogre shoved her to her knees, holding her down with enormous paws while the ogres prepared the others for departure.

A dozen ogres marched the prisoners out of the camp on a path to the south. Ma Jun stumbled along, slowed by his injury. Exhausted from her struggle, Kaiya could only watch them leave before the chief half-dragged her towards a tent.

CHAPTER 38:
Rescue with Red Hair

He lay flat on his back. The chill of the hard ground seeped through his wet clothes. Tian opened his eyes. Everything was blurry. He blinked to clear his vision, and listened. There was the rippling of the river, birds chirping, wind blowing through the trees... and talking.

His vision came into focus. Above him, the tops of sweet evergreen trees, swaying in the breeze, framed a bright blue sky. The Iridescent Moon was hidden from where he lay, but the sunlight suggested it was either early morning or late afternoon.

Where were those voices? He turned his head, sending a blazing pain searing through his temples.

Ignoring his body's protests, Tian pushed himself to a sitting position. With great effort, he looked from side to side, but the voices came from behind, in elegant, accentless Arkothi. His hand inched toward his saber, only to find that it, and his dagger, were missing.

"Well, well, General Shaotyan rises from the dead!" It was an unfamiliar but melodious male voice, butchering the name of the Wang Dynasty founder.

Tian twisted around, gingerly, fearing that any quick motion would cause his brains to leak from his ears.

Six people huddled in a semicircle on the ground, about ten feet away from him. Four men, most likely Arkothi from their olive skin and dark hair, nodded at him in turn. They wore camouflaged leather cuirasses and bore shortbows and longswords. Some sported short beards. Most looked to be in their twenties.

A fifth man, shorter, slimmer, and younger than the rest, regarded him curiously. He had pointed ears, fine features, and shiny golden hair, and wore a poncho of forest-green.

An elf. Perhaps a wild elf? A delicate-looking bow was slung across his back and a long, thin sword hung at his side.

"We were worried about you," he said. The accent, like the lilting of songbirds, marked him as the one who'd referenced the first *Tianzi*.

None were as striking as the sixth person: a young human woman about his age, she had tanned skin. Dark red hair cascaded in waves of curls down her shoulders. Her almost almond-shaped eyes twinkled a light green, and her beautiful features seemed to have an elvish refinement to them. The smile she directed at him was devoid of any warmth. Like the elf, she wore a forest-green poncho.

"Yes, thanks," Tian said, stumbling over the Arkothi words. "Where did you find me? And who are you?"

The elf pointed toward the sound of running water. "In the river, unconscious. You're lucky to be alive. You shouldn't go swimming in the rapids, you know."

As if he had planned it. Tian forced a smile.

The woman peered at him. "Who are you? What is a Cathayi doing in the Upper Wilds?" Her soft voice might have been cute, if her tone didn't cut like a knife.

"I… " What *was* he doing here? The princess… "What day and time is it? Where am I? Who are you?"

She pursed her lips. "I asked first, so you answer first."

There was no point wasting time in an argument. "I am Tian Zheng. From Cathay. I work in Iksuvius. I am escorting someone. Back to Cathay. Please tell me who *you* are."

Her bushy eyebrows rose. "Back to Cathay? Wouldn't it be faster and safer to take one of your ships?"

She was avoiding his questions. Meanwhile, the princess was out there, in need of help. "Yes. But we had no choice. We weren't able to secure passage. Now, can you answer me?"

The woman yawned. "Unable to secure passage on one of your own ships?"

He could lie convincingly enough to fool most people, but his half-truths didn't convince this woman. Tian stood up. His head pounded, but it didn't matter. "Am I your prisoner? Because if not, I must find my traveling companion. She may have been captured. By hill ogres. At least tell me what day it is."

"You aren't a prisoner." The elf shook his head. "It is the second day of the eighth month. However, given how clueless you are, I wonder if you even have a chance of tracking down your friend. Maybe you should tell us what happened. Perhaps we can help you." He turned towards the red-head. "Look, Allie, if his friend was captured by the ogres, then he is not our enemy."

Allie glared at the elf. "*If* he's telling the truth. The Cathayi are only interested in money. Who knows who the bastard has sold his sword to? Perhaps he works for our enemies and is tracking us."

Tian growled. As if anyone would send *him* into the woods to track experienced rangers. And the girlish voice did not suit her foul mouth. "I am guessing, Allie, that you are Eldaeri. That means the Teleri's imperial ambitions concern you. They declared war on Cathay by trying to take our princess hostage. I need to find her now."

The six exchanged glances. Of course, out here in the wilderness, they couldn't have heard the news.

The elf scratched his head. "I've seen your princess before, half a year ago. Describe her to me."

Tian bit his lip. Where to start? Banishing all the negative things that immediately popped in his head, he gave his most objective evaluation of the princess. "Voluminous hair. With a vibrancy of its own," at least before he cut it. "Doe-like eyes. A high thin nose. Full lips," a perfectly symmetrical face, really. "Graceful like willow branches in—"

"You sound like a man in love," Allie said.

Heat stirred in Tian's cheeks. "A voice that could charm a dragon."

"And did charm a dragon, for which I owe her a personal debt of gratitude." The elf turned to Allie and nodded.

Allie flicked hair over her shoulder. "If the stories are true, she's beautiful beyond compare. We'll help you. Be warned, if it turns out you are lying, we will nick your fucking intestines and tie you up to a tree. The Kanin brushhogs will come and eat your shit."

Tian hid his cringe, not so much at her threat but at her dirty mouth. "I'm not lying."

Allie smiled without the least amount of sincerity. "In order to find your princess, you need to tell us everything you remember about how you came here."

Tian paused to recollect the order of events. "We camped on the eastern bank of the river. We were running south when I fell off a ledge. It was just before dawn this morning."

Allie nodded. "The trail should be quite warm, then. It's now near the fifth waning crescent, and we are not far from where the river starts to drop and the east bank rises. Hurry up."

They all stood and collected their gear. Within minutes, they were swiftly marching toward the river, with Allie in the lead. The peaceful chirps of birds and the rustling of animals in the brush did little to assuage Tian's anxiety.

Arriving at the river in ten minutes, he scanned the surroundings. The ledge on the opposite shore was about ten feet higher than this bank, which in turn was level with the water. They turned north, walking uphill with the river at their side. Tian regularly checked to see the height of the opposite bank.

After an hour, they came to a stop at a wide trail that ran perpendicularly to the river.

"Ogre tracks." Allie pointed to the markings in the muddy ground. The others fanned out to look for clues.

Tian fidgeted, though noting how they operated. "Any human tracks? She's only this high." He held his hand at his nose. "Small feet. We also had two other men. About my height."

The elf shook his head. "If they were captured by ogres, they would have been carried."

"There were ogres." Tian pointed at one of the large, deep footprints in the mud. "We should follow this trail."

The elf again shook his head. "There are ogres all over this region, and we don't want to recklessly traipse into one of their camps. By the way, it is always safer to travel on the eastern side of the river, especially at night."

Just like Fleet said. Tian rolled his eyes. They *had* camped on the east bank. Apparently, the ogres didn't get the notice.

One of the men pointed. "A braid of human hair, coarse and black, about thirty centimeters."

The princess' braid!

Another one chimed in. "Blood on this leaf, red and fresh."

Tian looked at the elf and Allie with an urgent, forced grin, silently prompting them.

Allie tilted her head down the path. "Follow the trail. We're now entering dangerous territory. Keril, you take point; Rami, you have rear guard. You, Zheng, stay close to me and try to keep quiet."

One of the men padded to the front with a bow in hand. Although he didn't even seem to be watching his feet, he made no sound as he stepped through the needles and around the dried greywood leaves. The rest fell in behind him, all walking with equal stealth. Allie took the middle of the line and motioned Tian to follow her.

After a few minutes, Allie looked back and smiled at him, this time quite genuinely. She pointed at his feet and gave him a thumbs-up signal.

It wasn't *that* hard, considering his own stealth training. He smiled back.

Before long they came to a clearing. Keril raised his hand in a fist, and they all stopped. After scanning the perimeter, he motioned for them to enter. The sun now sat high overhead, providing radiant warmth in the clearing. Allie motioned Rami to continue down the trail and the others to fan out.

The scout came back in a few minutes and whispered, "Clear."

A torrent of whispered observations erupted.

"Ogres were here, probably about three hours ago."

"Looks like about a dozen, four dead among them."

"A human was bleeding here, the shape and amount suggests blunt trauma."

"Another human was set down here. Probably a woman, with six centimeter black hair. There's a flute here."

Tian hurried over to look at the flute, with Allie close behind. "This is our princess'."

Allie knelt down to sniff dried blood on a leaf. "Then it seems we are on the right trail. Let's break for lunch and rest."

Tian grabbed her shoulder and spun her around. "We must keep going."

All of the men grinned at him. One shook his head in a '*he's in for it*' look.

Allie lifted her arm to lock Tian's and started to push at him with her other hand. She slid a leg behind his.

It would have dumped an untrained man flat onto his behind, but Tian's reflexes instantly took over. He reversed her throw by pressing a hand into the small of her back, stepping laterally and twisting his own hip.

She fell backward, but with catlike grace put a hand down and rolled back into a stand. In the same motion, she drew her dagger and set it at his throat.

Tian turned and seized her hand, then twisted her wrist and swiped the dagger away.

Her companions reached for their weapons. The elf already had an arrow nocked and aimed at him.

Allie raised a restraining hand and flashed Tian a lethal smile. "You're more than meets the eye."

Tian pursed his lips. So, he'd gone from being the rear end of a mule to the front side of a male prostitute.

Tone softening, she added, "You remind me of another Cathayi. One I consider a friend, and to whom I owe a debt of thanks. If what you told us is true, you've not eaten breakfast, and since we're all hungry and tired, you must be even hungrier and more tired. How do you plan on rescuing your princess from a dozen angry ogres on exhausted legs and an empty stomach?"

"I'm sure you know... what the ogres will do to her." And it would be *his* fault for bringing her into this Heavens-forsaken wilderness.

Allie placed a hand on his shoulder. "Your woman is safe for the time being."

His woman? "How can you know that?" He flipped the dagger and offered it to her hilt-first.

"You'll have to trust me on this." Refusing the weapon, she flashed a wry smile. "Ogre superstitions will protect her."

Tian threw his hands up. "What does that mean?"

She rolled her eyes. "If you want to continue on your own, please feel free to get yourself fucked. It would certainly free us up to continue on our own mission."

Tian sighed. She was right. He *was* hungry and tired, and even at full strength, there was little chance he could defeat a dozen ogres in their home territory by himself. Defeated, he dropped into a seated position.

Something cold and hard bit into his butt. He popped back up. All heads turned to him, amusement dancing in their expressions. He looked down. A round piece of strange grey metal, a thumblength in diameter, lay partially hidden in the leaves. Picking it up, he turned it over in his hands and traced the etching: a circle surrounding a curious emblem of squiggly lines. A precisely cut scrap of black cloth was still attached.

Allie gasped. "The Teleri imperial seal. How did it get here?"

Tian furrowed his brow, trying to recall where he had seen it before. "I think the Teleri First Consul wore this."

Allie chuckled. "Of course he did, idiot. It's the heirloom of the Bovyans, passed down from the first Geros to every First Consul. If it's real. Let me see it."

Tian handed it to her.

After a cursory glance, she drew her sword and held the two objects close to each other. She sucked in a breath.

Tian craned over her shoulder. Both pin and sword seemed to be made of the same mysterious metal.

She handed it back to him. "I believe it's real. Both the seal and my sword were made from a falling star. There's so little of this metal in the world, and the skill for etching into it was lost long ago. It's impossible to counterfeit."

Tian nodded. "I remember now. When the princess faced the First Consul, she mentioned this pin. She must have cut it from his uniform." He stashed it in his lockpicking tool pouch, and put that in his pack.

Allie sighed and looked to Thielas. "So the First Consul still lives. Our plan to have mercenaries attack his entourage in Iksuvius must've failed."

Tian tapped his chin. It all made sense now. The Eldaeri repeating crossbows his team had found in Larusso's Iksuvius warehouse must've been ordered by Allie, to kill Geros. Yet another mistake Tian had made.

He looked to Allie, who'd already set up he bedroll at the other end of the clearing and was fast asleep.

The elf came and sat down beside him, offering him some bread and dried fruit. "Forgive my rudeness for not introducing myself earlier. I am Thielas. Allie is right, you know."

Tian nodded, chewing on some of the fruit. "Who are you people? What're you doing in the Wilds?"

"That's not my place to say. I leave that up to her to tell you, but you have to earn her trust first. Still, she does seem to have taken a liking to you." The elf's smile looked forced, his friendly tone masking jealousy. "She has a wild spirit; that much I can tell you. Even more so than your average human."

Tian nodded again. There must be something between these two. "I've been rude, too. Sorry. I should've thanked you. For helping me."

"With the appearance of this pin," Thielas said, "this rescue may be tied up in our own cause. In any case, you had better get some rest."

Around them, the five others had finished eating and unfurled bedrolls. Sighing again, Tian leaned up against the back of a tree on the other side of the clearing, in the shade, and closed his eyes.

He was awoken just minutes later by a gentle shaking. He opened his eyes.

Allie hovered over him with a smile. "Wake up, Tian. You were the one in the rush." She giggled like a girl. Everyone else appeared to be ready to go.

"How long have I been asleep?"

"About two hours," she said. "You looked tired, so I sent Kori and Rami ahead to scout, to make sure we were on the correct path. There are hundreds of ogre tracks passing through here, but I think we have the right one." She extended a hand to help him up, which he gratefully accepted. Her fingers were coarse and her grip strong, so unlike the princess' smooth, delicate hands.

Thielas looked up at the sun. "It is midday, so we should be safe from the ogres for a little longer while they enjoy their beauty sleep. We can be a bit less careful for another several hours. Let's make the most of it."

They started down the trail, with Keril taking point.

As they walked, Tian started probing as only a good spy could. "I don't often see ladies with such good wilderness skills."

Allie laughed. "How would you know what good wilderness skills are? Yours certainly need some work."

Tian laughed nervously, and prodded her to continue with a raised eyebrow.

Allie said, "My parents wanted me to be an elegant lady, but I preferred to run in the forests. When I was twenty-four, I met Thielas, who taught me woodcraft. Then, I was sent to live with a distant uncle, in hopes that I'd learn proper etiquette. After eight years, no success!"

She was least thirty-two! And obviously Eldaeri, whose traces of elf blood caused them to age more slowly. Time to coax more information from her. "I guessed you were Eldaeri. I've not met many." Except for two princes, both quite arrogant. "It seems odd. To be this far away from home. In this wild land."

She skidded to a halt and stared at him. "You talk like a stalking predator. Know that I am elusive prey. You won't learn more than I want you to."

Tian snorted. Smart woman. Who cursed like a sailor. No need to continue with the roundabout questioning. "What *can* you tell me?"

"You look smart." She flashed a feral grin. "How much have you already deduced?"

"The Teleri Empire expands to the east. Into the lands of the former Arkothi Empire. It will soon be on the border of the Eldaeri Kingdom of Serikoth."

Allie sighed. "Yes, my homeland. They have already captured Thundercloud Fortress, which guards the pass between the mountains and Bullhead Lake."

Capturing Serikoth would put the empire closer to Tarkoth and all of its resources, like... "Teleri wants shipbuilding lumber. And deep-water ports." Cold tingled up Tian's spine. Tarkoth wouldn't fall easily, but here in the Wilds... "That's why they captured Iksuvius."

"What? Iksuvius has fallen?" Allie came to a stop with a gasp, startling the rest of their group. She looked at Thielas and shook her head.

"Yes. That's why we took this route." Tian kicked a small rock. "The Teleri troops cut off access to our ship."

Allie's gaze followed the rock. She bent over and picked it up. "How would you know to take this route? The only pass between here and Iksuvi is very-well hidden."

"A madaeri scout guided us."

"Fleet." Her face relaxed, and she fell silent for a few steps. "You have more to worry about than he realized when he sent you this way. The Teleri have discovered the ancient highway through the Kanin Plateau. The bastards are using local slave labor to build fortresses and restore the roads. The terminus is a one-week march to Cathay's borders."

The web of correlations formed a clear picture in Tian's head. "You can't afford to have Teleri gain easy access to these forests. They will get wood. They will build ships. Challenge you at sea. That's why you are here. To assess the danger. Who are you? You lead men. Even at a young age. You must be of some importance."

Allie whistled. "I've already said too much. Perhaps, when we meet your princess, I can explain more."

They continued down the path. After an hour, the sun descended beyond the Nothori mountain range, casting long shadows. Allie gave the order to maintain silence. After another two hours, with dusk fast approaching, the trail opened onto the eastern side of the hill ogre camp.

CHAPTER 39:
Mixed Feelings

Despite his urgency, Tian knew it would be foolish to try and attack an enemy camp without getting an idea of their strengths and weakness. Just as he could do with his own network of spies, Allie issued several silent orders with her hands. Her men fanned out in admirable silence.

Allie motioned for him to follow her up a tree. The sweet evergreens grew straight and limbless to the height of two men, but the trunks' proximity to one another allowed him to spider-climb between them. At a height of about twenty feet, he and Allie perched themselves on branches, with a good view of the entire camp.

The clearing was about ninety feet in diameter, with an additional trail leading out to the southwest. Twelve large round tents, all ragged and dirty, surrounded a bonfire. Four long poles lay on the ground on the southern edge of the camp. Outside of the ring of tents, ogres worked at making rope, rendering meat, tanning skins, and sharpening rocks.

Tian counted eight ogres in the open. He named them based on their distinguishing features: Mop Head, Big Brute, and the like. After an hour, he identified thirty distinct individuals, all male, with one obvious leader and two secondary leaders. One of those lieutenants, shoulder bandaged and arm hanging in a sling, looked like the one who'd led the raid on their camp.

Allie signaled for him to come down. The other rangers rejoined them, and she motioned them deeper into woods, out of earshot of the camp.

In the darkness, she whispered, "What did we learn?"

"Thirty ogres," Rami said, "though the number of tents suggests that more live here."

"No prisoners. They must have already left with an escort," said Keril.

Thielas scuffed his foot in the dirt. "They leave a guard by the supply tent constantly."

"There's a tent," Tian said. "That none of them entered. Or left."

Allie nodded. "We can't attack now. They'd have the advantage with their night vision. Let's get some sleep. Two-hour watches, one person observes the camp, while another guards here. We'll strike at dawn."

Tian frowned. No telling what they'd do to the princess in that time. But Allie was right. A bad plan would get them all killed, without helping the princess at all.

They laid out bedrolls on the forest floor. Thielas took reconnaissance duty first, while Allie stood guard.

Tian couldn't sleep. His mind buzzed with thoughts. All the mistakes he'd made that had led to the princess' capture. He stared up into the sky, barely able to see the stars through the dense tree cover. Thick clouds rolled in from the west, completely obscuring his view.

He sat up and let out a deep sigh. Something hit him lightly in the back of the head, and he turned.

Leaning up against a tree, Allie beckoned.

He crept over.

"Can't sleep?" she whispered.

"Can't stop thinking. Everything that could go wrong went wrong. It's my fault. I've never failed at anything. I'm not used to this feeling." Why had he said so much to a stranger?

She patted him on the shoulder. "The first failure is the hardest."

Tian shrugged. "I feel so out of place. In this forest. In the wilderness. None of my talents serve me."

"Sometimes, you just have to... surrender." She reached behind his head and drew his face closer to hers.

Tian's heart pounded. His obsessive thoughts blurred out of focus. Surrender. Allie was beautiful, something that he'd missed behind her strong and commanding nature. Or maybe it was because her rugged exterior was so unlike the classical Cathayi beauties.

He closed his eyes, and their lips met. It was intoxicating. All his worries and concerns melted away. He pulled her closer to him, savoring her intriguing combination of toned muscle and feminine softness. Her lips parted, inviting him deeper.

Images of the princess crept into his mind. Heavens, here he was, losing himself in a stranger's embrace, while the woman he was responsible for faced untold violation and humiliation. Waves of guilt careened over him, dousing his fire. He opened his eyes and pushed Allie away.

She searched his expression.

"I'm sorry," he whispered. "I can't... surrender." Or maybe he was crazy about the princess.

There! He admitted it. How foolish. She hated him, anyway. And even if she didn't, he wasn't an appropriate match. She was courting his brother, for the love of Heaven.

Allie shook her head. "No, I'm sorry. It wasn't fair of me, to take advantage of you when you were feeling weak. Forget this ever happened."

If only he could. Tian hung his head. "I'm sor—"

Thielas appeared without a sound. "Ogres, coming this way, fifteen of them, about three minutes behind me."

Thoughts of princesses and brothers and ranger girls blinked out. Tian snapped into ready alertness. Allie handed him a dagger, then woke up the rest of her group. Though they were too far off the path for the ogres to accidentally stumble upon them, the rangers all took up arms and pressed themselves against trees.

Tian squeezed the dagger hilt, sweat beading on his forehead. The eight of them didn't stand a chance against twice as many ogres, except by surprise. He peered through the trees.

Shadowy figures lumbered by on the path, making plenty of noise. Several carried the long poles from the campsite.

The sounds disappeared into the distance. Allie beckoned the group together. "I know we're all exhausted, and we wanted to wait until dawn. However, this might be our best chance to strike, now that half of the ogres have left the camp."

Thielas nodded. "From their activity, I'd guess they've gone out to capture more slaves."

Allie nodded, drawing a rough schematic in the dirt with a twig. "We need to take either their leader or his lieutenants alive so that we can find out where they've taken Tian's princess."

His princess? He clenched his teeth.

She pointed with the stick. "We'll form a ring around the camp, placing ourselves so that we have a line of sight on the bonfire between each two tents. On my mark, take down as many targets as you can with your arrows. Every time one is killed or incapacitated, yell out the count."

Eyes following Allie's stick, Tian looked for possible flaws. What if several stayed in the tent? What if they didn't have a full count? There were just too many uncertainties to come up with a good plan.

"Once they sound the alarm," she continued, "we can expect them to head into the tents to arm themselves. If there're eight or less at that point, we will close in on the perimeter of the tents, and only engage hand-to-hand if necessary. If there're more than eight, I'll enter into the camp and try to get as many of them as possible to chase me down that southern trail. The rest of you will engage the remainders. Any suggestions?"

Tian tapped his chin. Not the best plan, but he couldn't have made a better one with their limited information. At least Allie's made the best use of the terrain and resources... Wait. He raised his hand. "All I have is a dagger. What am I supposed to do?"

Though cloaked in the darkness, Allie's smile was clear in her tone. "Your job is to check out the tent near the northwest corner that nobody goes into. Make your move in the ensuing confusion, and with your stealth, I am sure you will be fine. If you can, take out the guard on the provisions tent, right next door. Everyone give him your dagger."

Tian stuffed a few sheathed daggers in his belt, and one in each boot. He followed the rangers back to the campsite and continued around to the opposite side while the others fanned out.

He counted six dark ogre shapes along the outside of the tent ring. Cloud cover obscured the starlight, making it darker still. He waited for the signal, visualizing the path he would take between the supply tent and the unknown tent.

Allie's shrill call echoed in the night sky. Bowstrings twanged. Arrows thwipped through the air. Chaos broke out. Ogres bellowed in pain.

Shouts erupted around the perimeter.

"One down!"

"Two down!"

Crouching low to stay below the line of arrow fire, Tian broke towards the tent.

"Five down," called Keril from the east.

Disorganized ogre wails.

"Six down," Thielas yelled from the south.

Arrows whizzed above him.

"Seven down," another ranger called, again from the east.

Allie shouted out orders.

"Eight down," came Rami's yell from the west.

Now inside the tent ring, where firelight evened the odds between ogre and human, Tian assessed the threat. Fifteen feet away, the sentry at the provisions tent made direct eye contact.

Tian hurled the dagger in his hand, and immediately followed with another at his belt. The first hit the brute in the throat, the second in the head.

"Nine down," Tian called.

Directly ahead, the injured lieutenant ogre ducked into the supply tent. The leader waved a huge two-handed sword, barking out orders from the front of his own tent. Two ogres emerged on the northern and southern side of the ring, both armed with spears.

"Ten down!" Allie's voice called from outside the tent ring.

Five enemies remained, one of them unaccounted for.

Tian threw himself towards the entrance of his assigned tent, staying low. Hopefully, the bonfire would obscure the ogres' view of him. He slipped in through the flaps.

Pitch black.

He listened carefully, trying to filter out the clashing sounds from outside.

"Eleven down!"

"Twelve down!" called Allie.

Only three threats left. This fight was won.

Inside, near the center of the tent, was quiet breathing. Human breathing. Probably a woman trying to hide the sound of her breath.

Please let it be the princess. No, it couldn't be, not this long after their capture. "*Dian-xia*?" he ventured.

Whoever it was in the center of the tent burst into sobs. "Tian!"

Tian let out a sigh. He crawled toward the middle to avoid tripping over anything. Halfway there, his hands found a thin cotton carpet. Past that, a fur blanket which covered the smooth skin of the princess' crossed legs. He jerked his hand back. He'd touched her.

"Tian." Her voice was choked, laced with uncharacteristic pleading.

He rose up onto his knees and wrapped his arms around her, and she rested her head on his shoulder, softly crying. Her upper body was clothed, and her hands were bound behind her back, tied to the tent's central pole.

He stroked the back of her head. "Are you okay?"

Her only answer was gentle sobbing. He traced a hand down her arm to her wrist, where he found the cold metal of manacles. He felt at his belt for his lockpick pouch.

The tent flap opened, casting a flickering light throughout. Tian turned, making out the silhouette of an ogre with a huge sword in one hand.

A glaring light flashed from the other hand, washing Tian's eyes in a bright haze.

He sprang to his feet, simultaneously taking two daggers from his belt and throwing them. One clanged against metal, the other whirled out of the tent and tumbled across the ground. He squinted. A large blurry figure lurched towards him. It raised a sword with two hands to hack him in half.

Tian side-stepped the chop as he bent to pick up the blanket. The sword smashed against the dirt where he'd just stood. The blade then whistled towards him on an upstroke, rising at an angle with enough force to sever his head. Tian swept the blanket up into the sword's path while diving headfirst under its trajectory, into the ogre's knee. He seized the back of the ogre's ankle with both of his hands and thrusting his shoulder into its shin.

The leverage caused the brute to fall backward. The sword pitched across the ground. Tian finished with a forward roll, ending straddled on the ogre's chest.

He swept another dagger from his belt and stabbed downward with an overhand hold. The ogre caught his forearm in a powerful two-handed grip. Undeterred, Tian twisted his wrist, slashing the blade across the ogre's left wrist tendons. The grip from that hand went slack, and blood sprayed.

Tian bounced into a crouch and used his left hand to grasp his opponent's right arm—which still held fast to his own dagger hand. He twisted around and leaned back, hyperextending the ogre's arm in an armbar. He arched his back. The tearing ligaments and rubbing bones made popping and grinding sounds. The ogre roared.

As his vision adjusted to the light, Tian gave the ogre a sharp kick to the side of the head, knocking him out. He climbed back up to his feet, blinked his vision clear, and looked down.

The leader.

"Thirteen down." Tian turned to the princess. Her eyes burned red from crying, and tears left dirt streaks down her cheeks. With the blanket gone, her perfectly-shaped legs were bare. His gaze involuntarily lingered, and she twisted her body in an attempt to conceal herself.

Ashamed of himself for so many reasons, Tian turned his head. He picked up the blanket and covered her. "I'm sorry... " he mumbled. "I, uh, will see if he has a key."

He leaned over and searched the unconscious ogre. A ring of four keys hung on its belt. The smallest one fit into the princess' manacles.

Hands free, she wrapped the blanket around her waist and held it together with one hand. She extended her free arm, tacitly asking him to help her up. Her legs wobbled as she stood, and she threw herself against him, burying her face in his chest. He embraced her warmly, protectively, as she pulled him closer and wept.

What could he say? There were no words of comfort he could offer. Maybe the clan's *Tiger's Eye* mind-block could blunt the emotional trauma. No—no telling what it would do to someone not trained in Black Fist ways.

"I'm so sorry, *Dian-xia*." He stroked her head. "It's my fault... that this happened to you. If only we'd gotten here sooner."

She looked up at him with furrowed brows. "We?"

Tian looked down at her with an equally perplexed expression. "We... Some friends I met. I wanted to storm the camp hours ago. We could've spared you... you know... "

She lowered her head, pressing her ear to his chest. Her words shook through the shuddering of her shoulders. "They didn't."

"But your... " He pulled her closer. It was too awkward to continue. Maybe Allie would say something appropriate. "Never mind."

Outside, the sounds of battle died down to only an occasional ear-wrenching death keen. The ranger Rami burst into the tent, nearly tripping over the ogre. He stopped in his tracks. "Sorry to ruin the moment." He turned around and jumped out.

Heat rose to Tian's face. What must Rami be thinking?

A couple of minutes later, Allie spoke in an exaggeratedly loud voice, just outside the tent opening. "You men, wait a few minutes so the lady can make herself presentable. Zheng: be a gentleman—if that's possible—and come out here."

Tian gritted his teeth and stepped back.

The princess looked up again, this time with a demure smile. "You heard her. Out you go." She turned him around and pushed him in the back towards the entrance.

A blast of cold night air greeted him. Allie's expression wasn't much warmer. Thielas stood by her side, while the other rangers investigated the tents.

"Your lady friend okay?" Allie asked.

"Traumatized. But it looks like you were right about... that... "

Allie chuckled and pushed past Tian into the tent. "Don't come in until I tell you."

Thielas shrugged. "Curious creatures, women. Especially human women."

"Especially human women?" Tian cocked an eyebrow. "Do you know this from experience?"

"More than you'd expect." The elf grinned back.

"Are all the ogres taken care of?"

Thielas held up two fingers. "There are two unaccounted for: the leader and one of his seconds. That one has an injured arm, so he's not an immediate threat beyond his ability to bring reinforcements."

Tian tilted his head towards the tent. "The leader is incapacitated in there. Did you check the provisions tent?"

"Yes. It looks like a lot of the possessions they took from captives, as well as a locked chest."

Tian produced the key ring from his belt. "Perhaps one of these will fit."

Allie's muffled voice called from inside. "Okay, you can come in now."

Kaiya felt exhausted to the core, her legs barely steady enough to support her lithe form. She'd used the power of her voice several times to fend off the ogre's repeated attempts to violate her, and it took a physical toll.

At first, when she realized how thoroughly she could control him, it was almost amusing to watch him approach, only to be cowed by her command to back away.

She looked down at the unconscious leader and shuddered. Each time she'd used her voice, it drained her in alarmingly increasing increments. The effect of her command took longer to take hold and lasted shorter. As her fear grew, she found it harder to even find her voice.

The last time, he had managed to rip her pants off, and only the hook of her thumb kept her undergarments from going with them. She shuddered to think what would have happened if he had had another chance.

She pulled her pants back on. After this torment, she'd never look at a male the same way again.

That changed when the tent flap opened.

Tian entered. A sense of relief washed over her. When had that happened? In two months, he'd transformed from an uncaring oaf to the dear friend she remembered from childhood. His embrace had felt... good.

Behind Tian followed the most gorgeous man she'd ever seen, with delicate features and large violet eyes that could've been the essence of a dawn cloud concentrated into a rich liquid. Vibrant golden hair tumbled down his shoulders. He seemed familiar.

Kaiya ran her hand through her own short hair, suddenly feeling naked again despite the warm woolen pants.

Tian's attention shifted to the semi-conscious ogre. Kaiya shivered. Its rough hands had rubbed her face. Even now, after Allie had tightly secured those same hands around the pole, behind his back, Kaiya edged away from the brute.

"Greetings, Your Highness. It has been a while." The elf's voice sung like the symphony of gods. Oddly, it sounded familiar, even if she'd never seen him before—and she'd certainly not have forgotten meeting someone so beautiful.

"Have we met?" She tilted her head at just the right angle and smiled.

He nodded. "At the time, we were not properly introduced. I am Thielas Starsong."

The name didn't sound familiar. "I am sure I would have remembered you." Heat rose to her cheeks. Had she just said that?

Thielas' grin was captivating.

Embarrassed, she turned to where Allie and Tian knelt over the ogre leader.

"Nice handiwork," she was saying. "I don't know many people who could defeat an armed ogre with just a couple of daggers." Allie put a hand on Tian's chest.

An uneasiness sloshed in Kaiya's stomach. Jealousy? She shook off the thought, trying to replace it with more important matters. "We need to find out where they took Ma Jun and Fang Weiyong. They left the campsite around dusk, bound to poles."

Allie nodded. "That means they can't be traveling that fast." She gave the ogre a light kick in the leg. "Where do you take your prisoners?"

The ogre shot her a confused look and mumbled something long and drawn-out in his own language.

Allie scowled at him. "The people you captured."

"Me no speak you words."

If Kaiya didn't already hate the beast, she did now. "You do. Tell us where you took our friends."

The ogre chortled. "Whore, I won't tell! Since you'll kill me, I have nothing to gain. Unless you let me stab into your depths with my man-club!"

Kaiya winced, and he roared out in laughter.

His tone turned demeaning. "Of course, it'll have to wait until your girl-bleeding is finished."

Her face flared hot. All these men, learning her secrets. She fled the tent and stopped outside.

Inside, Allie whispered, though still loud enough to hear. "Don't follow. Just pretend you didn't hear or understand it."

The tent flap opened, and Allie emerged. "You okay?"

No. She nodded all the same.

Inside, the ogre bellowed. What was happening?

Tian's voice rose. "Poisonous fiend. You're right. You will die. Either quickly tonight. If you cooperate. Or very slowly overnight. If you don't."

Silence. Was the ogre considering the—

A roar of pain blasted out of the tent. Kaiya shuddered again.

Tian stomped out, Thielas close behind.

"It's no point in torturing the ogre." Tian shook his head with a look of frustration. "He won't tell us a thing."

Kaiya peered at him. "Get him to talk. Ma Jun and the doctor, and all those captives rely on that information."

Tian turned towards Allie. "Will you be able to track the others?"

"Not until daylight. Until then, I suggest that we get some rest. The tents reek, so I'm happy next to the bonfire." She beckoned her men over. "Two-man watches, two hours each. We'll let the princess sleep through. We should get moving before dawn, before the other ogres come back."

Sleep! After this horrific day, her body screamed for it, even if she was sure to have nightmares. Kaiya eyed the bonfire.

Tian headed towards one of the tents. After a short while, he emerged with their bedrolls and other supplies. He laid out Kaiya's bedroll for her, and then tightened the blanket around her, insulating her from the chill air. He really was like her childhood friend again.

A friend who might provide protection and comfort tonight. She pointed her chin towards the space not far from her and cast a shy smile. "Sleep there."

Tian's eyes widened, but he offered a tentative nod. He placed his bedroll where she indicated and settled in.

As she drifted into an exhausted sleep, she could hear his heart pounding.

CHAPTER 40:
Pursuit

At dawn, pins and needles skittered through Tian's left arm. He shifted slightly to relieve the pressure when Allie shook him out of sleep. He was lying on his side, something he never did.

Allie grinned as she pointed at his numb arm.

It was lying under the princess' neck, and wrapped around her shoulder. She also lay on her side, her back pressed to him, separated only by the thick blankets. His other hand... It rested on her hip.

Tian's eyes opened wide and he jerked his arm back. The princess rolled onto her front with a soft sigh.

His face burned hot, probably redder than the horizon. He'd just committed a capital offense, far worse than locking her in an armoire.

Allie chuckled. "She was crying in her sleep, and you reached over to comfort her. It was quite sweet, actually." She flashed him a sarcastic grin. "Your princess *is* very beautiful, though the legends of her luxurious hair are definitely overstated."

Tian's throat tightened. If only she knew. "Our secret, okay?"

"Another one?" Allie puckered her lips and grinned.

His face burned hot.

"Anyway, we'll need to get moving soon." She nudged her head back. "The others are getting ready."

Which meant they probably all saw him with his arm around the princess.

"After waking your princess from her beauty sleep," Allie continued, "I suggest you take what you need from the provisions tent. Find something warm. It'll snow today."

Was that a tingling in his chest, where the princess' back had pressed into him? He shook the thought away and crawled out from the bedroll, his body reluctant to abandon the warmth. The air seemed much colder this morning, and clouds greyed the sky. He gently shook the princess, and her eyelids fluttered open.

Hands clenched, she frowned. Her gaze shifted back and forth until it settled on him. The scowl melted into a beautiful, innocent smile, one that sent his heart skittering. "Is it already time to get up? I had horrible dreams all night, and it seems like I only slept for a few minutes."

"Yes, *Dian-xia*. Allie says it will snow today. They need to start tracking. Before we lose the trail. Get ready. I'll bring you some hot water."

The rangers prompted them to go within half an hour. Tian retrieved the Kanin sabers, Kaiya's straight swords, two bows, two quivers of arrows, and their own packs from the supply tent. Most of the other items belonged to the native tribes: bows, stone-headed spears, furs, and the like.

One of the keys opened the locked chest. Inside were Teleri-coined gold *draka*s. They had little need for them in the Wilds, but he took two large handfuls just in case. He also retrieved Chen Xin's and Ma Jun's silver rings.

Rami discovered a rough map in the leader's tent. Some locations were marked in green, others in red, though no one could decipher the code. A small island at the confluence of the North Kanin River and the nearby tributary was circled in blue.

Markel and Kori had examined the tracks and concluded that the prisoners had been taken down the southern path. They set the tents ablaze, leaving only the supplies and the leader's tent untouched.

Which left the leader. They could've avoided this entire journey had they killed the altivorc in Gaukaimos. Tian didn't plan to make the same mistake again.

Surprisingly, the princess insisted on letting the ogre live. Allie added that a crippled ogre would face torment among his kind for the rest of his life. He'd never admit to having been defeated by just eight humans.

The rangers departed down the path, with Thielas at point and Rami taking up the rear. Tian walked near the front, the princess staying near his side. Her closeness sent a shiver up his spine. What was he thinking?

Within a couple of hours, light flurries began to fall.

Allie gave the sky a dubious look. "It doesn't usually begin to snow this early in the season. This might be a long winter."

Snow already? Tian started to look up when Thielas pointed at the ground. "A large amount of human blood here. I'm guessing it was vomited, maybe three hours ago?"

With a flash of Allie's hand signal, the rangers fanned out.

Markel knelt by the head of a trail. "The trail of blood heads east down this path toward the river, but everyone else continued south on the main path."

Kaiya placed a hand on her chest. "The ogres beat Ma Jun before they departed, when he tried to protect me. He could barely walk."

Four imperial guards, already dead or unaccounted for. Tian sighed. His fault.

Allie came up beside Markel and pointed at the ground. "We'll follow this trail of blood. Based on the ogre map, we're not far from the river, and there is a red circle here."

Tian tapped his chin. So much stubble; something he'd never allowed before this journey began. He followed Thielas as they veered off onto the smaller path. The rangers pointed out drops of blood. The sounds of the river grew louder and louder. After half an hour, the path opened up into a clearing by the water.

An irrigated field. They pushed south through a narrow field of corn, its crop past ripe and now rotting on the stem.

On the other side, the princess covered her audible gasp.

Tian shifted on his feet. The red circle on the map marked death and destruction.

Dozens of simple wooden frames, charred by flame, were all that remained of lodges. With no evidence of doors or windows, there was no way of telling the orientation of the burnt-out structures, but it looked as if they circled outward from a huge fire pit. The soft rustling of the river interrupted the otherwise eerie silence.

Tian picked his way through the huts towards the center of the abandoned village. The place stank of death. Hairs stood on the back of his neck.

Heart pounding, Kaiya clasped and unclasped her hands as she followed Tian past the scorched huts and into the center of the village ruins.

With a sharp breath, he jerked to a halt. He turned around and put a hand over her eyes.

Too late.

Around the fire pit lay nearly two dozen bodies, their advanced stage of decomposition preventing identification of gender. Crushed skulls suggested the manner of their horrific death. Several smaller bodies could only belong to young children.

Kaiya's stomach lurched into her throat. She seized hold of Tian's arms so tightly that her knuckles went white. He drew her in close, pulling her head to his chest. His comforting warmth did little to melt the ice in her limbs. After a few seconds, she looked up at him.

Tears trickled down his cheeks as he looked past the gruesome scene. He hadn't shown so much emotion since their reunion. "Dragonflies," he whispered.

Dragonflies? Kaiya searched his eyes. He still remembered the old proverb she'd told him when they were children.

Allie came up beside them. "The ogres raid these villages for slaves, capturing healthy men and women, but taking savage delight in murdering the sick, old, and very young."

Horror and grief gripped at Kaiya's throat, choking her words. "But why? What do the ogres need slaves for?"

Allie tugged on her sleeves. "They sell slaves to the Teleri soldiers who have infested these woods."

Teleri? They weren't supposed to be in the Wilds. Kaiya shuddered. "How did the Teleri get here?"

Allie peered at her. "They spent years searching for the ancient roads from the Arkothi Empire into the Kanin Empire."

Which led right to the East Gate of Cathay. Throat dry, Kaiya swallowed. "Who thought up such a plan?"

"First Consul Geros."

The First Consul. Kaiya's blood froze. He had seized her, pressed himself up against her. She hugged herself now, as if that would protect her from the memory. She could've killed him.

Allie nodded. "Which brings us back to the Kanin. Since Teleri soldiers are only good at war, they need hands for construction, food preparation, and other services. In their satellite states, it takes the form of fair trade contracts—if you consider the Mating a fair part of the deal. But here, where there is no centralized rule to enforce Teleri law, their goals can only be accomplished with slave labor."

Kaiya's heart ached. All the unfortunate tribal people, subjected to the cruelty of an evil empire. For too many years, Cathay had enriched itself through trade with the Teleri, turning a blind eye to those it affected. Like Madura before. This needed to change. It would change, once she returned home.

From the distance, Keril called. "I think I've found your man."

Kaiya and Tian hurried in the direction of Keril's voice, on the eastern edge of the village, at the river's edge. He was there, kneeling over a human, who lay face up.

Alive? She gritted her teeth and looked down.

It was Ma Jun, her last imperial guard. His eyes were closed, and blood flecked his lips. Complexion wan, he breathed in rapid, shallow pants.

Kaiya knelt over him and stroked his cheek. He couldn't possibly survive.

Keril sighed. "He's bleeding internally and has lost a lot of blood. He doesn't have much longer. Unless Thielas can save him."

Kaiya looked up from Ma Jun. "Is he a doctor?"

Keril shook his head. "He can channel the divine power of the gods."

Like Cyrus, who'd given her energy when they fled the altivorcs. Kaiya nodded. She looked back toward the center of the village.

The elf knelt near the mass grave, head bowed in prayer.

She placed a hand on Tian's arm. "Please, bring Thielas here."

With a nod, he raced back toward the elf. She leaned over and brushed cold sweat from Ma Jun's forehead.

Thielas appeared at her side, his handsome features twisted into a melancholy expression.

Kaiya bowed low. "It is my fault my guard is mortally injured. Keril says that you have the power to heal. Would you please try?"

Thielas smiled wryly. "Only the gods have the power to heal; I am just their conduit into the realm of mortals. We can see if the gods have use for him in this life, or if they are ready to recall him to their bosoms." He closed his eyes, placed a hand on Ma Jun's forehead, and sang a prayer in the musical language of the elves. His chanting voice sounded familiar.

Inspired, Kaiya hummed with him.

The color returned to Ma Jun's face, and his breathing deepened.

Miraculous. Nothing Cyrus had done rivaled Thielas' healing powers. Kaiya reverently bowed her head and pressed her palms together. "Thank you."

Thielas smiled at her. "Thank Ayara, whom your people name Guanyin. Her compassion and grace restored him. He is safe now, but will require several weeks of rest in order to recover full strength."

"We still need to rescue the other prisoners," Kaiya said. "Will he be able to walk?"

"I am well enough to help, *Dian-xia*," Ma Jun answered in a weak voice.

Too weak; but conscious, at least. She looked down.

His gaze met hers and he tried to sit up.

Showing a surprising gentle side, Tian placed a hand on his shoulder.

"He needs to rest for another two hours," Thielas said. "Even then, he won't be able to keep pace with the rangers."

Tian lifted a water skin to Ma Jun's lips. "What can you tell us about the other prisoners?"

Ma Jun nodded and licked his lips. "Around dawn, the ogres caught another man. Since they needed more room on the pole, they released me since I was slowing them down."

"Was Doctor Fang all right?" Kaiya asked.

Ma Jun shook his head. "He struggled to help me, and the ogres beat him."

Allie appeared behind them. "The bastards will want to sleep during the day, and they'll be slowed by transporting the bound prisoners. It's been three hours since dawn. They can't be but so far ahead of us."

Hope rose in Kaiya's chest.

Allie pulled out the map and pointed. "Princess Kaiya, stay here with your countryman and make him rest for two hours; then both of you head back to the main trail and turn south. Once we've taken care of the ogres, some of us will come back for you."

Could she do it? One girl, untrained in the ways of the wilderness, protecting an injured man?

Tian shook his head. "It's too dangerous. The ogre camp could house forty, maybe fifty ogres. We only eliminated fifteen. Fifteen headed west at dusk. Another dozen are escorting prisoners. There might still be some around here."

Memories of the leader's gigantic hands sent a shiver down Kaiya's spine.

Keril shook his head. "Ogres don't like to venture out during the day. It should be safe until at least the late afternoon."

Allie nodded. "We'll need your help, Zheng, to fight this group we are pursuing."

"My duty is to protect the princess." Tian crossed his arms.

Kaiya put a hand on his shoulder. "No, our duty is to protect the defenseless. Zheng Tian, just as they helped me when I needed it, we must help them. And remember, the doctor is with them."

He opened his mouth to protest, but she shot him a stern look that silenced him. She straightened, invoking her tone of imperial authority. "That is my command."

Tian dropped to his knee. "Forgive me, *Dian-xia*. I cannot obey your command."

She took his hand, so large and calloused compared to hers. "Will you obey my request?"

His eyes widened and searched hers, his pupils darting back and forth as if debating each other. He dropped to his knee. "As you... request."

Allie chuckled. "You have him well-trained."

Heat flared in Kaiya's cheeks. She caught sight of Tian in the corner of her eye.

He was blushing, too.

Pretending to ignore the comment, she sat down and laid Ma Jun's head in her lap. "It is settled then. We will meet you in a few hours."

Tian thought it foolish to leave the princess and an invalid guard behind. Still, she made no threats of punishment. No use of the power of her voice. Only a request—one which he now regretted acquiescing to.

The rangers marched quickly to try to catch the ogres, until the snow started falling harder and began covering the tracks. But as Allie had pointed out, there was only one direction they could possibly be heading at this point.

After another two hours, they stumbled upon the ogres and their prisoners.

They must've settled down for the day earlier than Allie expected.

Clad in deerskin clothes and furs, the prisoners sat in a square. Each side was formed by a pole, to which all their wrists were bound. A dozen ogres were laid out wherever they could find space. Two stood watch.

The rangers nocked arrows and shot. One of the ogre sentries yelled out. Screaming captives awkwardly jostled each other on their poles. Some, including the doctor, kicked at their captors. Thielas danced into the fray with his thin elven sword.

Tian gaped. The elf moved with a blurring speed, not unlike the Paladin Sameer. Recovering his sense of the present, Tian dashed to a groggy ogre and slashed his throat before he could stagger to his feet.

With most of the ogres bleary-eyed from sleep and slowed by the daylight, the fight ended quickly. None of the rangers or prisoners suffered injuries.

Tian picked his way through the captives, cutting bindings while searching for the doctor. Many patted him on his back, speaking words that he assumed were thanks. There were so many twins! One dignified-looking man hurried north up the trail without saying a word or waiting for company.

Young Doctor Fang's eye was swollen shut. Blood flecked his lips and chin. His words came out hysterically. "The ogres kept the princess at their camp! We have to rescue her before they do horrible things. Ma Jun, too, was dying somewhere back there." He gesticulated wildly to the north.

Tian rested a reassuring hand on his shoulder. "We already rescued her. And Ma Jun. Both are at a village. Back the way we came."

Doctor Fang glared at him through his good eye. "You left her alone?"

"She ordered me to."

The doctor's eyebrow shot up. "Since when did you start obeying her orders?"

Tian waved the comment off. "Are you well enough to travel? We'll race back. To rejoin them." Tian looked around for Allie.

The other rangers were busy binding wounds. Markel spoke some halting Kanin language and found out that the prisoners were all part of the same Maki tribe, though they came from three different villages. Ogres lived much farther north, and historically had not bothered humans this far south.

Tian nodded. It explained why Fleet had not known about the danger. The ogres had come to this region just six months ago and started raiding smaller villages. Survivors sought refuge with cousins and distant relatives in other communities. Some of the larger villages now burst at the seams, stretching resources thin. Though these were relatively safer, the fear of capture generally kept people from venturing out in small groups, further straining the food supply of these hunter-gatherers.

More concerning to Tian was the news of the Teleri. Rumors from other tribes to the south and east told of a race of Metal Men, using the natives as slave labor to build new fortresses. Although there had been talk in the Kanin Tribal Council of allying to fight back, generations-old blood feuds and the upcoming winter season—predicted by their shamans to be the coldest and snowiest in years—had put those plans on hold.

At last, Tian found Allie, distributing what food they could spare. Other rangers were using their metal blades to sharpen crude spears from long, straight branches, so that the refugees could defend themselves on their return journey.

Tian placed a hand on her shoulder. "We should head back. To the burned-out village. The princess awaits us. Undefended."

She pointed to the blue circle on the ogre's map. "No, we're going to continue south, to find out where the ogres were heading. You escort the natives back north, at least until you meet up with your princess."

Undernourished and injured, the locals would slow him. Tian bowed his head in acquiescence, nonetheless. "Thank you for your help. I have learned so much. From your example. About playing our role in the world. Thank you again."

Allie wrapped him in a tight embrace.

So strange, so uninhibited, these Northerners. Tian tentatively returned the hug.

Then she brought her lips to his. All he could do was freeze in shock, while bystanders pointed and whispered. The doctor grunted.

Releasing him, Allie flashed a feral grin. "I would like to say that is sufficient payment, but you aren't particularly good at it."

From the heat in his head, he must have been glowing an interesting shade of red.

Her coy tone turned serious. "So instead, remember that our nations share a common enemy, and that we may one day have the honor of fighting side by side. In these woods, I am Allie, but know that my true name is Princess Alaena of Serikoth, heir to the Kingdom of Korynth."

Royalty! She was royalty. Tian kept his face blank and nodded.

She continued, "The fate of my people, your people, and these people, may very well rely on the bridges we build today."

Tian nodded.

She winked. "Be sure to practice your kissing, and you may win your princess' heart yet."

The doctor gaped at him, his good eye wide and his mouth wider.

What could Tian say? The heat from his flushing reached his ears. All he could was stare as Allie—Alaena—disappeared south down the trail with Thielas and her rangers. He turned to the Kanin people and motioned them to follow him north.

CHAPTER 41:
Opportunities

From her spot at the edge of the western marketplace, dressed as a street urchin, Jie eyed a dark-haired man with a cutlass concealed under his cloak. In a nation of farmers, occupied by a land army which confiscated anything longer than a knife, the typical sailor's weapon stood out to her trained eyes.

The bulge should have been obvious to Teleri patrols, and the man was a fool to be packing in the mid-afternoon sun. Maybe the Bovyans had grown lazy since Emperor Geros departed the city a month before with his concubines, leaving General Marius as governor.

When the stranger stopped by a nearby fruit vendor, Jie sidled up to him and began testing the apples. She'd learned—by some trial and plenty of error—that late-harvest apples this far north tasted better soft. Yet the man selected several hard ones with his worn, calloused hands. His face, from what she could tell from his profile in her peripheral vision, was tanned and weathered, punctuated by a stubbly dark beard.

"Don't go touching every last one and not buy anything." The vendor favored the two of them with a suspicious eye, though he wouldn't be running down any thieves with his clubfoot.

Poor man. His pretty daughter, who enticed customers with her flirting, had been taken by the Teleri not long after the occupation began. The thought of the poor girl saddened Jie, reminding her of her ambitious—and perhaps foolhardy—plan.

"Looks like a cold rain," the stranger commented in Arkothi. His voice was deep, his accent perfect.

Jie stole a glance up. There wasn't a cloud in the sky.

The vendor nodded, almost imperceptibly. "Oh, not for some time now."

Even more curious. A code, even. Perhaps an underground resistance forming? There hadn't been any acts of sabotage or attacks on Bovyan patrols.

Jie's instinct to find out more drove her to a hasty decision. A quick glance around the market revealed no Teleri patrols. Taking a deep breath, she tugged at the stranger's coin purse, yanking it free with enough force to let him know. She bolted off.

"Hey! Stop! Thief! Help!" The stranger ran after her.

Obviously a stranger. Though vendors might try to stop a petty thief, most of the locals left the street children alone.

Jie looked back to gauge his distance before turning into an alleyway between houses on a lazy street. With a pop-vault, she suspended herself a dozen feet up with outstretched arms and legs.

The man turned the corner.

She pounced, grabbing his cloak and wrapping him in it as they rolled on the ground.

She whipped a knife out and pressed it at his throat. "Quiet. Understand?"

Anger burned in his eyes, but he nodded.

"Now, who—" Jie cut herself short. She recognized the man.

He was one of the marines aboard Tarkothi Prince Aelward's ship, when he had transported Princess Kaiya to Ayudra Island, many months ago.

"Never mind. I know you're a Tarkothi marine." Easing the knife back to prevent him from trying to attack her, she pulled her hat off, revealing her ears. "I am Princess Kaiya's handmaiden. I'm going to let you get up, but do so slowly."

When a look of recognition bloomed in his expression, she sprung back out of cutlass reach, just in case he tried to attack.

He rose slowly, rubbing his lower back, where the cutlass had probably dug in during his tumble.

"Sorry about that." She grinned meekly. "Now I know who you are... or at least *what* you are. Is there a name to go with the beard?"

"Ciro." An Arkothi name. The marine glared at her, sizing her up as he extended his palm.

"Oh, yeah." She tossed his purse, which he caught with a quick snatch. "What are you doing here?"

His eyes remained narrowed. "I would ask you what *you* are doing here. Where is your princess?"

Jie looked him over. It wouldn't hurt to tell him generalizations. "She fled the attack on the city. I am stranded here."

"Well, maybe we can help each other."

Jie's ears perked up. "Go on."

"We are here—"

"We? Who is *we*?"

Ciro scratched his beard. "The TRS *Invincible*, captained by Prince Aelward, is off the coast. We are here looking for a band of rangers, led by a red-headed woman. Have you seen them around the city?"

Jie shook her head. He was undoubtedly referring to Alaena. Tian had had a strand of red hair dangling in his cobweb, but they hadn't uncovered the mystery before the Teleri invasion. She'd never even considered it could belong to the feisty ranger.

More exciting was a friendly ship, somewhere off the coast. Perhaps it was a way home. After she'd personally saved Prince Aelward from an assassin's arrow, he owed her a favor. "I would like to meet with the prince."

He scratched his beard some more. "On what business?"

"Mutual benefit, just like in the past." Jie imitated the princess' best smile.

Ciro looked at her for a few seconds. "Meet me on the coastal road, at the first cove outside the walls, when the Iridescent Moon waxes to half."

About three hours. Jie nodded. "Until then."

With little time to continue reconnaissance of the rape center as she had originally intended, Jie worked her way towards the coastal road. Well before the appointed time, she arrived at the meeting spot and descended on a path down the rocky embankment to a gravel beach. The waves roared as they came ashore, drowning out all other sound.

She hid herself among the boulders as the sky darkened, the setting sun giving way to the feeble light of the nearly-new White Moon. Her elf vision would surely give her an advantage if this meeting turned out to be a trap.

Not long after, Ciro arrived alone. Once he reached the beach, he looked around before peering out to sea and holding aloft a shuttered light bauble. He fiddled with it, sending flashes in long and short bursts.

A code. Jie tried to memorize it. She looked back towards the city walls and scanned the area. No threats.

Ciro paced, also squinting towards the walls. Before long, he took his cutlass scabbard in hand. He must have been quite nervous, but she would keep him waiting.

After a while, the dark shape of a boat came to shore, rowed by two men.

One of the men spoke. "Any word from the princess?"

Ciro shook his head. "No, our eyes and ears inside the city have not spotted her or her rangers."

"Then why did you call us ashore?"

Ciro sighed. "The Cathayi princess' handmaiden wanted to meet with Prince Aelward. However, she hasn't turned up."

Their conversation was reassuring enough. Jie used a *Ghost Echo* technique to throw her voice from a boulder. "I am here."

Ciro and both men jumped, startled.

Jie grinned. She emerged from her hiding place and approached.

"Hands up," Ciro commanded. When she complied, he patted her down, politely, finding two knives but missing her throwing spikes. He gestured toward the boat.

She turned to him. "Are you coming?"

He shook his head. "No, but you are in good hands with these sailors."

Jie saw the other men also had cutlasses at their side. She sucked her lower lip. On firm ground, she could dispatch a pair of armed men. In a boat, on the other hand...

She took one last look at them. Deciding they looked familiar, she boarded. One pushed the boat out into the water before jumping in himself. Ciro and the shore disappeared into the distance, the rhythmic sloshing of oars mixing with the roar of the surf.

Caiyue, never moving from its heavenly seat in the south, waxed to its first gibbous as the *Invincible*'s shadow ballooned. Before long, it loomed above them, even larger than Cathay's own trade ships. Jie looked back to see the tiny dots of light in Iksuvius.

Climbing to the deck, Jie remembered how much she detested the rocking. All of the sailors looked wide-eyed at her.

Prince Aelward approached, his long dark hair becalmed on the peaceful seas. His slim build and sharp features betrayed the hint of elf blood that flowed in Eldaeri humans' veins. She was about to extend a greeting, when he walked past her to the returning sailors.

"Where is Alaena?" Aelward's voice seeped with a longing that didn't take Black Fist training to notice.

Poor Aelward. Though he and Alaena had enjoyed each other's company while Jie travelled with him, Alaena wasn't the type to settle down with just one man.

One of the sailors crossed his arms in an X over his chest. "Your Highness, there is still no news of her." He then nodded towards Jie. "Ciro bade us to bring this one aboard."

Jie removed her hat and attempted her best curtsey. "Your Highness."

"Jie?" Aelward cocked his head, favoring her with a raised eyebrow.

"The same." Jie held her clumsy curtsey, waiting to be released.

He clapped her on the back, nearly knocking her to the deck. "I barely recognized ye through all the grime. I thought ye were some boy the men recruited."

Jie channeled her Princess Smile, even as she stewed inside at the blunt reference to her curveless figure. "That's not the nicest way to greet someone who saved your life."

He laughed again. "True enough. So, handmaiden, what brings you aboard?"

"A favor. I need you to take urgent news to Cathay."

The prince's smile melted. "I can't do that, I must stay in these waters to retrieve... a friend. But fear not, we spotted a veritable armada from your homeland not one week ago on our way here. I would gauge from the prevailing winds that they will be here soon."

Jie sucked on her lower lip. Of course the *Tianzi* would retaliate for the assault on his daughter. However, what could warships realistically do that would affect the Bovyans? And with the princess escaping into the Kanin Wilds, the ships here did her no good.

At the very least, Cathayi ships offered Jie a means of getting home to deliver the news. And perhaps she could get Meiling to safety as well.

Meiling. The girl suffered in the throes of morning sickness. From what she said, Emperor Geros had kept her to himself, and hadn't allowed any other Bovyan to take her. Which meant she carried Geros' child.

The Teleri prophecy came to mind: a Bovyan who knew his true mother and father would bring an end to the Teleri Empire. If Jie could get Meiling home, they might have something to bargain with.

CHAPTER 42:
Little Friends

In the devastated village, Kaiya waited patiently as Ma Jun slept. With nothing else to do, she listened to the laughing of the river, the twittering of birds, and other sounds around her. The tall greywoods towered high above the forest floor, devoid of leaves. Across the river, cliffs rose some twenty feet above the banks, their white-colored faces crisscrossed by tangles of green vines. Prickly-leaved shrubs with large, bright-colored berries grew along the banks. Birds and squirrels chattered at one another as they ate the juicy treasures.

Kaiya's stomach rumbled. Laying Ma Jun's head on her pack, she rose and walked over to the shrub to try the bite-sized berries. Their pleasant aroma was reminiscent of cinnamon. She washed them off in the river before taking a bite. A sweet flavor exploded in her mouth, followed by pleasant warmth percolating through her.

A sniffling sound carried almost imperceptibly over the rustling of the river. Children's cries? Kaiya followed her ears, walking down the river, though occasionally looking back to see that Ma Jun rested undisturbed. The sobs grew louder.

Colors flashed by a grove of berry shrubs. Kaiya padded over.

Two children huddled together by the river. With their backs to her, they were oblivious to her approach.

Kaiya paused, composing herself. Using her most gentle voice, she addressed them in Arkothi. "Hello."

The children jerked around, startled. One was a boy and the other a girl, both about six years of age, and looked so alike, they had to be twins. They wore unadorned deerskin shirts and breeches, and had the ruddy skin tone of the Kanin people. Shoulder-length dark hair framed their little faces, the girl's braided in an unkempt queue behind each ear. Red berry juice stained their petite mouths.

Both jumped to their feet, eyes wide as they gawked up at her. The boy clutched his sister's arm and they turned to run.

It wasn't the reaction Kaiya expected. What *had* she expected? She couldn't even remember the last time she'd been this close to a child. Lacking even a drop of maternal instinct, her smile was probably more suited to manipulating a man. And men were probably far more gullible than children. She caught ahold of the girl's other arm.

The girl cried uncontrollably. The boy tugged at her.

Such dedication. Like Kaiya's own two brothers trying to protect her when she was young. Squatting down to eye level, she reached out to take the boy's wrist, and pulled them closer. "It's okay, I won't hurt you."

The boy let go of his sister's hand, and now swatted at Kaiya's arm. The girl wailed. Kaiya sunk lower, kneeling, and drew them close, wrapping her arms around them. The girl went rigid, but the boy continued to struggle.

The Dragon Charmer, confounded by two kids.

She sang a Cathayi lullaby while gently rocking the two in her embrace. Feet rooted to the ground, she projected the calm of the light wind.

The boy stopped struggling. The girl melted in her arms. After a few minutes, she shifted her weight back and returned to holding the children's hands. Maybe this was what it was like to be a mother?

She smiled at them. Not a contrived court smile, but more like those she'd shared with Tian a decade before. And again, not long ago. She spoke slowly, carefully annunciating each word. "Are you lost? Where are your parents?"

The children looked at each other and then back at her, heads cocked.

They clearly didn't speak Arkothi. She placed her hand over her heart, and said, "Kaiya. My name is Kaiya." She extended her open hand towards them. "What is your name?"

The girl's eyes brightened and she clapped her hands together. A smile creased her face. Pointing to herself, she said excitedly, "Nadi." She gestured back and said, "Kaiya."

"Yes." Kaiya smiled again. "Pleased to meet you, Nadi."

The boy, now bouncing on his toes, pointed at himself. "Waka." Both children giggled.

"Nice to meet you, Waka. You must be hungry." Rubbing her stomach, she put a finger to her mouth.

They both nodded eagerly while speaking in their own language, their trepidation now apparently forgotten.

Trying to pick out words, Kaiya took their hands and walked them back to where Ma Jun slept. Flakes started to flutter from the skies.

They looked at him with wide eyes, and then up to her. "*Kane ma taichoupu tezuga?*" the boy said.

Though the words might have been gibberish, their sounds and cadence seemed familiar. She kneeled down next to Ma Jun and covered him with her cloak. She took some cornbread from her pack.

The children eyed it. When she offered the bread, they snatched it and plopped down cross-legged to devour it, crumbs scattering onto their clothes. So cute! She handed them some dried fruit, which immediately disappeared into their little mouths.

At least for the moment, they were content. Kaiya watched them eat. What would she do with these two? She pointed at them, then toward the burnt-out village. "Did you live here?"

The boy tilted his head inquisitively. He asked something of his sister, and she just shook her head. He met Kaiya's gaze and shrugged.

A few more attempts at gesticulating, making faces, and otherwise trying to ask questions all met with the same frustrations. Perhaps her time would be better spent trying to learn some of their language.

It helped that many words sounded vaguely similar to the Cathayi court language, spoken only by the Imperial Family. Her new little friends were enthusiastic teachers. By the time Ma Jun woke up a phase later, her vocabulary consisted of body parts, animals, and geographical features. Fast learners, they had also learned the corresponding Arkothi words.

Ma Jun eased himself into a sitting position and bobbed his head as she brought a water skin to his lips. He took a few tentative sips before beginning to swallow large mouthfuls. He then shifted to his knees and pressed his head to the ground. "*Dian-xia*, I am mortified to have you serve me like this."

She ruffled through her pack and withdrew his imperial guard ring. "In Cathay, I am the daughter of the *Tianzi*. Out here in the wilderness, we are just fellow countrymen, leaning on each other to survive. Think nothing of it. Are you well enough to walk?"

Receiving the ring with a bow of his head, he rose on wobbling legs and hobbled over to his pack. She lifted his arm over her shoulders to help him walk, and motioned for the children to follow her back down the trail to the west.

The boy and girl shook their heads violently. Refusing to follow, they pointed across the river, speaking animatedly. From the hour-long lesson in their Kanin dialect, the gist of their concerns seemed to be *there bad... river good.*

Kaiya looked up and down the bank. Her two new friends might know the forest better, but there was no way to cross. With the snow now falling fast enough to gather on her cloak, it would be wiser to head for the cover of the trees. Tian expected her at the head of the trail, anyway.

She emphatically motioned the children to come with her. After a few refusals, they reluctantly complied. Like ducklings, they pressed close, virtually tripping her as they clutched her pant legs. At their plodding pace, with Ma Jun's weight hanging on her, and slowed even further by the light accumulation of snow, it seemed like a full hour passed before the dead village disappeared from sight.

On, they trudged. In the distance ahead, someone approached, their form partially obscured by the falling snow.

Kaiya's heart lifted, her worries about progressing too slowly now melting away. Tian must have already reached the rendezvous point and was now heading up the trail to meet them. She called out to him. Was that *longing* she heard in her voice?

No reply.

What if it wasn't Tian?

The person drew closer, picking up pace. Too big. Much too big to be Tian.

Ma Jun pushed forward, saber in hand. His voice rasped. "It's an ogre... holding a shortsword in its left hand."

Left hand... Kaiya's heart skittered.

The children cowered.

Ma Jun shoved Kaiya in the back. "Run! Back to the village! I will stall him here."

Kaiya's palms sweated. At full strength, Ma Jun *might* be able to handle an ogre. In his weakened state, he didn't stand a chance. And the children. Even if she knew their word for *flee*, they could never outrun the loping monster.

Pulling Ma Jun behind her, she unslung the bow from her back and quickly let two arrows fly in succession. The first grazed the ogre's right arm as he shifted out of the way, while the second lodged in his thigh. He staggered forward.

His arm hung in a sling. The ogre lieutenant from two nights before. The one *she'd* hit with an arrow. The one who'd promised vengeance. Not enough time to take an aimed shot.

Kaiya threw down the bow and slid her double straight swords from her sheath. One, she held underhanded in her left hand behind her back, the other in her right hand pointing forward. "Stop," she sang with her voice of command.

The ogre skidded to a halt and glared at her. His expression glinted with hatred. "Girl give up, others go. Or me kill all."

Ma Jun tried to step past her, but Kaiya, never turning her eyes from the ogre, swept her right-hand sword into his path. "Stand down, Ma Jun. Protect the children: they are your first duty now."

He was in no condition to protect anyone. Ma Jun bowed his head and backed off.

Kaiya turned the sword point towards the ogre. "You are injured and alone, and our friends are coming back this way. You cannot defeat all of us, but you can live to rejoin your own kind. I will command my people not to pursue you."

The ogre, whose grasp of Arkothi was probably not much better than the two children after her one-hour lesson, laughed. "No come, you die!" Holding the shortsword underhanded like a dagger, he lunged at her with a clumsy stab.

A sequence from the *Dance of Swords* came to her, unbidden. She glided to his left. Her right sword slashed into his attacking hand, and she turned her shoulder so that the left sword cut under his attack and across his gut.

As he tried to recover, she turned and stabbed back at his exposed left flank with her left sword. The blade slid with precision between his ribs. In the same turning motion, her right sword cut across his left shoulder, and the point thrust through his neck. Before the ogre hit the ground with black blood spraying from his wounds, she had withdrawn and flipped her left behind her back.

Had she really just done that? Behind her, both children sobbed.

With a quick flick of her wrists, Kaiya shook the swords, vibrating the black blood off before she sheathed them. She knelt down and wrapped her arms around the whimpering children, hushing them with her voice.

Ma Jun dropped to his knee beside her, head bowed. "I'm so sorry to be useless. I couldn't fight the ogre, I couldn't even comfort the children."

She pulled him into the group. "All that matters is that we are all safe. Let's find Zheng Tian."

The snow now fell heavily, clinging to branches like cherry blossoms. Despite the cover provided by the tree canopy, nearly a finger-length of snow accumulated on the trail. After another half-hour, they came to the trailhead. Kaiya pointed south, following Allie's instructions.

The children exchanged a few lively words. Their shaking heads and the numerous times they said *bad* suggested that neither liked the idea. They followed nonetheless.

Before long, another solitary figure approached, slogging through the snow. Though it was not large enough to be an ogre, Kaiya had learned a lesson from their last encounter. She eased Ma Jun down, unslung her bow, and fitted an arrow.

The man trudged closer.

"Stop. Who are you?" Kaiya drew the bowstring. If he took three more steps without announcing himself...

The newcomer knelt and stretched out his arms. The two children dashed out from behind her, crying excitedly.

Their father?

Kaiya lowered the bow and wiped away the few snowflakes that clung to her face.

Ma Jun nudged her. "That is the man whom the ogres captured before releasing me."

Kaiya nodded. Let the father and children enjoy their tearful reunion.

The boy and girl chattered with broad smiles, gesticulating wildly. On occasion, the tall, handsome man would look up and favor her with a penetrating gaze. Like the children, he wore beige buckskin breeches and shirts, with a heavier fur cloak about his shoulders. His long black hair fluttered in the breeze. A necklace of animal teeth and shiny rocks hung around his neck.

He approached, placing his right hand over his heart and bowing his head. A dignified pride radiated from him. He spoke in halting, heavily-accented Arkothi. "Thank you. You save my children."

She spoke slowly, hoping he would understand. "I am happy they could be reunited with you."

Nodding, he favored her with a curious eye. "Nadi say you beat beast. I think you too skinny for warrior."

"I am not a warrior. He was injured and I had superior weapons. Otherwise, you and I might have never met, and you would have never seen your children again."

The man nodded solemnly. Maybe he understood. "We wait, you friend, close to here. What you name?"

Her friend... Tian? She bowed her head. "Kaiya. This is Ma Jun."

He placed his open right hand in his left. A greeting? "I am Yuha. You already meet Nadi and Waka. We are Maki."

Kaiya nodded. Maki must be the name of their tribe.

"Why you here?" His eyes narrowed.

The short version would have to do. She pointed toward what she hoped was west. "We travel toward our homeland."

Yuha shook his head. "Land now very dangerous. Many beasts, many Metal Man build... big house. This season, snow very hard. Many White Moons can't pass. But, you save us. Please, come to village."

Beasts and Metal Men—ogres and Teleri, perhaps. And many White Moons... were they stranded here for *months?* She imitated his gesture of thanks, putting her right hand over her heart and bowing her head.

Faced with the prospect of wintering in the Wilds, she decided to learn what she could of the local language. Piecing together words she'd learned from the children, she said, "When my friend come?"

Yuha beamed. Using Arkothi, he returned her feeble attempt at conversation in the Maki dialect. "You try speak our mouth. Not like Metal Man. They take all, give none."

She continued in his dialect. "Your mouth, how say *man?*"

"*Odogo.*"

Odogo. It sounded like the imperial language for male. After half an hour of picking up new words and listening for grammar patterns, Kaiya looked up to the sounds of footsteps crunching in the snow.

Shouldering the doctor, Tian was leading a large group of natives up the path. Fighting the urge to run to him, she just stood there. His gaze met hers and his lips curved into a crooked smile.

Why did her heart flutter? Every step brought him closer, but seemed to last forever.

He sank to his right knee, fist to the ground. "*Dian-xia*, we have freed the captives."

"Where's Allie?"

"She headed south."

The doctor, too, tried to kneel, but almost fell. Despite his obvious pain, he still felt the need to salute, for nothing more than her title—one that meant nothing here in the Wilds.

Kaiya stepped towards him, and Ma Jun limped forward as well.

Fang Weiyong straightened. Still a doctor in spite of his own wounds, he pressed along Ma Jun's ribs, causing the imperial guard to wince.

"He might have a broken rib," the doctor said.

Kaiya sighed. "Ma Jun and Fang Weiyong are both injured. This man, Yuha, says the snow will fall heavily. He offered to let us stay in his village. It seems that the Wilds are also rife with dangers that we did not expect. It might be wise to rest well and consider our options there."

Tian nodded, though he did not hide his dislike of the idea. "Very well."

Kaiya turned to Yuha and tried speaking the dialect. "We go with you."

He nodded and pointed them back down the path towards the gutted village.

The entire band of Maki tribespeople joined them, helping the injured as they pressed down the snow-covered path. Large, wet flakes fell. What had taken Kaiya half an hour earlier lagged out to a full hour now. When they passed the ogre's corpse, the children chattered. Everyone favored her with wide eyes.

Tian turned to Yuha. "It's so dangerous. You travelled. With your children alone. Why?" The question *she* wanted to ask.

"I... healer... I visit holy place with two child. Take ten days. On way back, beast attack. I tell children run home."

Kaiya looked at the two young ones, clasping their father's hand. They were so brave, to flee on their own!

When they reached the burnt-out village, many of the Maki turned somber.

"Belong to same tribe." Yuha's face darkened. "Maki. Our cousins. Many missing."

Kaiya shuddered.

Coming to the eastern edge of the village bordering the river, Yuha led them south along the banks. Everyone picked the berries growing in the bushes. He lugged out three canoes from where they were hidden in the shrubs.

They were nothing like the planked hulls of Cathayi boats and ships. Dug out from the trunk of a sweet evergreen, each canoe held four people. Several of the men talked animatedly, pointing at various points along the river. It seemed most of their homes were downstream.

Kaiya studied Yuha's body language and inflection. Despite his foreign words, he radiated charisma. His opinion apparently carried weight, for the natives all complied with his decision to cross. After an hour of ferrying people back and forth, all four dozen had reached the east bank.

They hid the boats among the shrubs before continuing south in the shadows of the cliffs. Narrow and dotted with huge rocks, the banks made for a treacherous journey. Yet Yuha indicated that, not far to the south, they would find a path leading up to the top of the cliff. He let others take the lead, while he held his children's hands to help them jump from rock to rock.

Kaiya and Tian also helped them negotiate the stones, made slicker by melting snow.

At the top of the cliff, the group took a short break—just enough to rest tired legs and catch their breath. With words of farewell, they broke into three groups, each heading toward a different village. Standing at the head of a dozen tribespeople, Yuha motioned for Kaiya to follow him.

They walked until nightfall and camped off the path, where the trees provided partial cover from the falling snow. Kaiya couldn't remember ever feeling so cold. She leaned against Tian for warmth.

In the mid-afternoon of the third day, with the snow accumulating to her knees, several lodges thankfully came into view. Villagers pointed and yelled at their approach. Several came out to join them.

A stately older gentleman with long white hair fluttering in the breeze held his excited people back. Flanked by a dozen warriors armed with stone-headed spears, he marched forward. Like the others, he wore a buckskin shirt and breeches. A necklace of shimmering river stones hung around his neck, and bright feathers adorned his head. His wise eyes, which spoke of many winters, met Tian's before shifting to Yuha. Anger creased his already time-worn features as he pointed at them, barking out words that did not hint at a warm welcome.

Metal Men came out especially frigid. Kaiya's throat tightened.

The warriors lowered the spears at them.

CHAPTER 43:
Village Life

Tian gauged the warriors' skill by their stances and the way they held their spears. Hand drifting towards his saber, he spaced them out in his head, plotting a path to their grey-haired chief. The Founder's treatise on warfare espoused targeting leaders: cut off the enemy's head, and the body would surely fall.

The chief's brow scrunched up, adding lines to his withered skin. He barked out a string of syllables, the unfriendly tone leaving little doubt where the Cathayi stood with the natives.

The princess placed her right hand into her left and bowed her head. The natives' dialect spilled from her mouth, flowing in her distinctive voice.

Tian gaped. How had she learned it so quickly?

The chief cocked his head, the furrows in his brow smoothing and his frown softening. He turned and exchanged words with the shaman Yuha, and nodded.

Behind the chief, the villagers surged forward, greeting their lost fellows in warm embraces. They were so relaxed with affection, in stark contrast to the more rigid Cathayi decorum. Physical contact in the form of pats, hugs, and hair-rubbing seemed a natural complement to verbal exchange for these people.

The princess edged forward and rested her hand on the inside of his elbow. She leaned towards his ear. "The chief doesn't trust outsiders, but it seems he will allow us to stay."

For how long? Tian turned to her. "You speak their language. How?"

"A woman has her ways." She cast him a mischievous smile.

His heart skipped a beat, even if her deflection lacked conviction. He raised an eyebrow.

She rose to her tiptoes and whispered in his ear again. "All members of the Imperial Family learn a secret language, passed down from the Founder. The words are similar to what the natives speak here. The grammar is different, though."

He pulled away, reluctantly. "It sounded convincing enough."

"The chief probably thought I sounded like a cute toddler." She flashed a playful pout.

Cute, yes. He tore his eyes away from the swell of her lips. Definitely not a toddler.

Yuha beckoned them closer. "Meet Chief Nuwa."

The old man placed his right hand in his left hand and said something.

The princess responded, naming herself, Tian, Ma Jun, and Fang Weiyong, gesturing with an open hand towards each of them in turn.

The chief smiled broadly, though the friendliness seemed reserved only for the princess. He spoke again and gestured towards the village.

Tian turned his attention to Yuha and his children. They huddled in the collective embrace of an older man and woman, and two attractive twin girls about the princess' age.

Wearing a glowing smile, Yuha looked up from his family and gestured him over. "Follow me."

The village itself lay in a large clearing on the eastern side of a wide stream, not far from the North Kanin River. They passed through broad cornfields, which lay fallow for the winter. Only chickens tended the fields now, foraging with precise pecks reminiscent of Tian's master snatching flying insects with his chopsticks.

On the other side of the fields, he counted thirty domed lodges laid out in a circle. Framed in thick sapling trunks, with walls and roofs made of smaller branches, mud, and grasses, they looked to be about sixteen feet long, twelve feet wide. Animal furs covered the entrance and windows. Rustic, primeval—hardly practical for the cold.

Near the center of the lodge circle, a wooden platform rose to a man's height above the ground. On it sat two magnificent drums, set on their sides and facing each other.

Yuha gestured towards the larger, which was even wider than a man was tall. "*Gogorowa.* Heart of Village." He then pointed towards the smaller, which was just a little shorter than the princess. "*Gamiwa.* Soul of Village. Hundred winters ago, one big tree here. After fall, messengers of gods carved into drums for us."

Tian stared at the drums. Just who were the messengers of the gods? The princess pulled him along.

Not far from the platform burned a bonfire. Coming to a lodge facing the flames, Yuha pulled the fur door open. "Welcome my house. Bring friends here to heal."

The two children skipped in, and the rest of them followed. Tian's nose wrinkled at the pungent odor of dried herbs as he entered with Ma Jun's arm around his shoulder.

Thick poles supported the roof, which had a hole near the center. Several furs covered the lodge floor, surrounding a small fire pit lined with stones. Dried herbs dangled from the roof in one corner of the lodge, while clothes and other personal effects hung from the walls. Contrary to Tian's initial doubts, the interior was quite warm.

Yuha motioned them to sit, and Tian watched as an old woman stirred the simmering contents of a large but crude ceramic pot.

With a few words, Yuha sent his kids out. He then examined Ma Jun and Fang Weiyong, and applied a poultice to their injuries. Doctor Fang watched with curious eyes, sniffing and tasting the herbs.

Presently, the children brought the pretty twin women in. Ma Jun and the doctor lost all interest in the herbs.

"My sisters," Yuha said. "Lana and Lahi. Kaiya stay with them. Men stay at other house. Now, we eat. Tell me your story."

The fire pit's flames crackled in the lodge that Kaiya shared with Lahi, Lana, and a few of the female refugees. She sat cross-legged, wearing a doeskin dress the twins had given her, watching as Lahi braided a queue behind each ear. The double queues marked her as unmarried.

As the village beauty, every unmarried man vied for Lahi's attention. Statuesque and elegant, she carried herself in fur and animal skins like a Cathayi lady would in silken gowns. In public, she played the boys off of each other with a demure act that belied her sharp mind.

Kaiya closed her eyes and recalled the entry of the famous Minister Deng Liansu in the *Encyclopedia of Peoples*:

The red-skinned barbarians on the Kanin Plateau, unlike their more organized cousins on the Plains, are beyond civilizing.

It is hard to believe that before the Hellstorm, they were part of an empire, even if that empire lacked the enlightenment or sophistication of Cathay's contemporary Yu Dynasty.

Though some of their tribes live not far on the other side of the Great Wall, they did not warrant my visit. They have nothing of value to offer us.

She stared into the fire. Half a White Moon had passed since their arrival at the village, and her observations in those two weeks suggested that the late Minister Deng had been unfair in his assessment. If nothing else, these people had a vibrant culture. When she made it home, she'd write her own treatise, so that her future daughters would look at the Wilds with different eyes.

Yuha poked his head in through the flap. With her fluency in their language improving, he spoke in his native tongue. "Kaiya. Chief Nuwa invites you and Tian to his lodge for dinner."

She had a good idea why. Maki storytelling had a way of evolving; perhaps only they knew where their myths ended and history began. And one new legend was already in the making.

With each retelling of the captives' rescue, Tian had risen from minor participant to single-handed vanquisher of dozens of ogres. Apparently, his reputation had found its way into neighboring villages.

Kaiya rose and found him waiting beside Yuha, outside the tent.

"*Dian-xia*." Tian bowed his head. Old habits had died hard, and though he no longer dropped to a knee, he remained stubborn with these salutes.

She suppressed the urge to roll her eyes, and lifted her chin toward the chief's tent. Yuha grinned and led the way.

Just outside, in the village center, the chief's handsome seventeen-year-old son Hati and another young man practiced spearwork with the blunt ends of their weapons. Several other men surrounded them, watching and cheering.

They weren't the only ones. When she turned and looked at Tian, his eyes were shifting with the clashing spears.

The combatants paused and looked up.

Hati tossed the spear horizontally at Tian, who caught it. He then took the spear from his friend. "I hear you are a good warrior. Show me!"

Though Tian had supposedly picked up some of the Maki dialect, he turned to her, mouth agape. "Did he say I have a nice rear?"

Heat flared in her cheeks. He *did* have a nice rear. "No, he wants to test his skill."

Or more likely, Tian's skill. He raised his spear.

"Be careful." Kaiya sighed. Tian's competitive streak dated back to her childhood, when she could beat him in swordplay and archery. It had gotten him in trouble before.

The old chief appeared at her side.

With a falsetto cry, Hati lunged forward with a stab.

Tian twisted out of the thrust and swept his own spear in an arc into the back of Hati's knees.

The youth tumbled to the ground, but leaped back onto his feet. He pointed the blunt end at Tian. "Now!"

He attacked again, and five other men surged in. To Kaiya's untrained eye, Tian moved like a blur, catching some weapons and using them to deflect others. He always positioned himself so one of his opponents shielded him against the others. Some, he threw to the ground, while others he knocked out of the ring.

Chief Nuwa leaned towards Kaiya. "Our tribal territories are well-defined and the resources are plentiful. There has been no armed conflict since our horse-riding cousins from the plains invaded a generation ago. Our weapon skills come from hunting, but downing a wild boar is different than fighting an ogre."

Kaiya met the chief's gaze. Had he arranged this confrontation?

The chief clapped his hands once, and the warriors backed off.

Tian extended his hand to help Hati up, and the young man hesitatingly accepted it.

Chief Nuwa placed a hand over his heart. "Young Tian, you are as good a warrior as Yuha says. Will you teach our men so that they might defend the village against ogres and the Metal Men?"

Tian looked to her, eyebrow raised.

She grinned. Even if his linguistic skills left a lot to be desired, he spoke the language of combat well. "He wants you to teach them."

After dinner with the chief, Tian walked the princess back through the snow. She leaned into him, huddling against the chill air. She must be cold. That's all it was. He tightened the fur around her.

"Don't let it go to your head, Tian." Her breath clouded in front of them.

Yes, she couldn't possibly feel the same way. He nodded. "Of course, *Dian-xia*."

She stopped in place, not far from her lodge. "Just because you beat a boy with a spear doesn't mean you can defend a village."

What was she talking about? He shook his head. "Oh, the training."

"What did you think I was talking about?" She raised an eyebrow.

"Nothing. I was going to recruit Ma Jun. To teach them about fighting in groups."

She resumed walking. "I saw him earlier today. Is he well enough for that?"

"He's improving. With Lana and Weiyong's attention." And especially Lana's. Whether it was her skill with medicinal plants and setting bones that did the trick, or her smile... Tian wiped the grin off his face. "Why don't you come and see?"

The princess turned her head and covered her mouth. "Visiting a man's lodge at night? I'm not sure that is appropriate."

Tian bowed his head. "Of course not, *Dian-xia*."

"I was joking." She pushed him in the chest.

"Oh."

With a small laugh, she took his hand and pulled him toward the lodge he shared with Ma Jun and Weiyong.

His hand tingled the whole way.

At the entrance, he pulled aside the flap.

Ma Jun sat by the fire pit, his chest bare. Lana stood behind him. Ma Jun's face flared in the firelight.

Had the princess seen? Tian closed the flap and turned to face her.

Blushing, she covered her mouth with a hand.

Tian stroked his chin. "I, uh, let me walk you back."

Ma Jun's voice called from inside. "Come in, it's not what it, uh, looks like."

Lana popped her head out and spoke. Even if Tian didn't understand the words, her tone carried no sign of apology. She beckoned them in.

The princess nodded and turned to him. "She was applying medicine to his ribs."

Tian grinned. Like her older brother Yuha, Lana had a knack for spiritual magic, and might have been a shaman if she were male. With her unabashed flamboyance, so different from her twin, the young men shied away. Ma Jun didn't seem to mind, though.

Kaiya turned her head from the chill wind, which rustled bare tree branches and sang its song to the babbling stream. Thank the Heavens her hair had grown back so quickly, protecting her from the chill. Like the other unmarried girls, she wore it behind her ears in two braided queues. Simple, compared to the lavish hairstyles in the Cathayi court. Just like everything else in the rustic village.

She looked down at the wild carrot in her hand. Dirt was caked in the creases of her fingers and clung beneath her nails. She smiled and set the carrot in a basket with some turnips and red-skinned tubers. Life here was easy, carefree. No need to worry about appointments and appearances. Her next responsibility today would be to check the village chicken coop for eggs.

And they said the winter months would be harsh.

"Kaiya." Lahi's pronunciation of her name sounded cute. The village beauty nodded her head sideways toward the forest path.

With the chief's son Hati playing the role of patient teacher, Tian tried walking through dry leaves.

Crackle, crackle.

While none of the tribesmen could touch Tian with a knife or spear, they had a lot to show him about the life of a hunter. He looked over to her and bowed his head.

Even here, where people admired his martial prowess, he felt subordinate to her. She smiled and waved.

Lahi giggled. "He likes you. Were you matched back home?"

The heat in Kaiya's cheeks made her forget how cold her toes were. "We were best friends." Were they again? Small, but considerate gestures brought out the adorable boy he'd been.

Lahi rubbed her belly. "Maybe you can make some babies, like Waka and Nadi."

Babies? Heat flared in her cheeks. Just a month ago, the twins had confounded her. After playing with them daily, she wondered if maybe she'd make a decent mother after all. Kaiya pointed at Lahi, such a rude gesture in Cathay, but an essential part of the nonverbal communication here. "Maybe *you* have a better chance with Hati."

That was no secret. Lahi could choose any man she wanted, and while she made them all believe they were special, in private, with her sister Lana, she left no doubt that she liked the chief's son.

Lana's curt voice cut in from behind them. "Kaiya's still too skinny. You need more berries."

As if she hadn't eaten enough of them. Harvested throughout the winter months, the red berries supposedly increased virility. They found their way into the stews, along with rabbit, wild turkey, and other small game. The men would occasionally bring down a deer. With this diet and the relaxed lifestyle, she had already regained the weight she'd lost in their flight from Iksuvius. Apparently she still wasn't fat enough for this baby-loving culture, though.

Lana grinned. "Well, I must be getting back. Miwa just started labor." She headed back to the village. If Lana couldn't be a shaman, she would make a wonderful midwife.

Kaiya waved goodbye. The first birth she'd witnessed were twins, common in the autumn months, according to Lana. The next three were all singles. Miwa's would be the fourth, and like all the others, a cause for celebration. The entire village would erupt in day-long festivities. They doted on new mothers, with each household taking turns cooking for her.

Kaiya wanted to contribute this time, even though she'd never really cooked before. She looked up to where Tian had been, only to find him gone. When he came back from hunting, he would be the first to try her dish.

Even if it tasted bad, he wouldn't complain.

Tian returned from an unsuccessful hunting trip—unsuccessful because of his poor wilderness skills. The chief's son Hati had taken special interest in him, helping him to build on the tracking and stalking he'd learned from Allie and her rangers. Still, it left a lot to be desired.

It also left a lot of animals alive, and for this, Hati just patted him on the back. The Maki had a great reverence for life, and whenever prey was killed, they thanked its spirit for the nourishment it provided. They used every part of the animal, nothing wasted. Yuha explained that all life was a treasure, and that the energy of all living things contributed to the balance and energy of the universe.

Just outside the village, he rounded the bend in the path and skidded to a halt.

The princess sat on a stump near the path by herself, sewing deerskin. He marveled at her delicate fingers dancing gracefully through the motions, reminiscent of her playing the *guzheng*.

She'd probably never sewed in Cathay. What a stark contrast to the image of imperial perfection she projected before! Also so different from the spoiled girl he thought she'd become, oblivious to the danger she and her retainers faced during their escape.

Still, a princess of Cathay doing menial labor was unacceptable.

Tian hurried over and dropped to a knee, fist to the ground. "*Dian-xia*. Let me do that for you."

The princess looked up from her work, and her lips curved into an innocent smile. It was so genuine, unlike the contrived mask she wore in Iksuvius, and Tian's mouth went dry.

She twirled the queue behind her right ear. "We aren't in Cathay. You don't have to be so formal. Call me Kaiya, just like when we were children."

Tian looked down, mouthing the name to himself, silently tasting it. No, it wasn't appropriate. He looked up, arranging his face in Black Fist blankness. "I will try, *Dian-xia*."

The princess' lips quivered, eyes laughing. With a tilt of her head, she beckoned him to a log, the beginnings of a dugout canoe. An unfinished pair of pants laid there, the seams of its legs unsewn. "Those are yours. You can finish them."

How embarrassing. And improper. The princess had been making *his* pants. Tian bowed his head low, the words tumbling out of his mouth automatically. "As you command, *Dian-xia*."

She smiled at him. "I have another command. I am cooking lunch for Miwa in a few days. I'm experimenting tonight. Will you eat with me?"

Tian kept his expression blank. Was she inviting him to a meal? They ate together frequently, though usually with Yuha's family, or occasionally the chief. Never just the two of them.

In the meantime, he had some pants to stitch. And a secret pocket to sew into his long-unused lockpick pouch.

Kaiya listened to the thin layer of snow crunching under their feet as she and Tian went fishing for the first time in their lives. A frigid breeze bit at her ears as they stepped out off of the forest trail and onto the bank of the river's pool.

Her attempt at cooking a stew had met with failure. Even if Tian praised the meal, his tentative chewing and forced smiles spoke volumes. Fish, at least, she'd roasted in the mountain pass between Iksuvi and the Wilds. And he'd devoured that fish.

Her excitement had made her forget about the bitter cold during the half-hour walk from the village, but now she looked dubiously at the flat boulder where they'd sit.

It looked freezing, jutting out over the expansive pool—famous for its large, succulent greyfish. The dozen tribespeople found places to sit, letting their legs hang over the edge.

Wait, they were broken into couples. Had Tian noticed that, too?

She studied his face.

He stared at the ground, chewing on his lower lip. He *had* noticed.

She glanced at Hati, who'd invited them along. From the spot where he sat with Lahi, he waved and flashed a broad grin. She smiled, too.

They knew, for sure, and must've planned this.

Kaiya looked over her shoulder. Tian laid out a fur blanket for them to sit on. She suppressed a giggle at the uneven stitching of his pant legs, deciding that the only things he'd ever sewn before were battle wounds.

They cast their lines and waited.

And waited.

The cold air bit through her doeskin and furs. Kaiya edged closer until she eventually huddled against his left side. He tensed up at her touch.

Tian inched away as he reached for another fur. "*Dian-xia—*"

"Kaiya."

"—your legs will get cold." He draped it over her lap.

Nothing would make her cold now, not with the warmth rising in her chest. It was so hard to imagine this thoughtful gesture came from the duty-driven, emotionless wizard's automaton who had forcibly shaved her head.

She leaned back into him and sighed, her breath hanging in the crisp air. He'd exacerbated her fear and sense of vulnerability months ago, but now provided nothing but a reassuring sense of safety.

Was it because he'd saved her from the ogres?

The fishing should've given her plenty of time to consider the question, but instead, his comforting nearness addled her thoughts. She stole a glance up at him through the corner of her eye, memorizing the angle of his jaw. He seemed to have achieved a meditative state, oblivious to her presence.

Pouting, she turned her attention to the dissonant interplay of noises around her: the river splashing lazily by, its waters low in the winter months; the drumming of a woodpecker; the rustling of underbrush as small animals foraged for food; the frequent chattering of birds.

Yet beneath the cacophony was a primordial harmony, an unrealized symphony of sounds that lacked a glue to hold them together.

She began humming her own tune, linking the various sounds into a concert of nature. Her hum built up confidently, the undertone taking over as the main sound. As it reached its crescendo, all other noises stopped as if the wildlife had stopped to listen, leaving just her voice.

Her fishing pole jerked.

Kaiya fell silent and stared at the rod. She struggled to her feet, her legs wobbly from the long hours of sitting. The particularly resilient fish took advantage of her poor balance, and she found herself plunging into the icy waters.

She floundered wildly in the water. "I can't swim!"

No sooner did the words leave her lips than Tian jumped in after her with a splash. The water only came up to his waist. His mouth gaped.

The Black Fist spy, gullible like when he was a child. Laughing, Kaiya stood and waded over.

The villagers' looks of concern transformed into laughs.

Shivering, she clasped his hand. "Are you all right?"

With a grin, he put a leg behind hers and twisted, dumping her completely into the water.

It was freezing! She let out a cry of surprise, which came out as bubbles. Getting her head back above the water, she wrapped her legs around his and twisted him back into the water as well.

Chortling, Hati urged them out of the pool. He held out dry furs. "Take off your clothes, or you really *will* freeze."

While Lahi built a fire, Kaiya wrapped the fur around herself and peeled off her wet clothes.

Tian apparently had no compunctions and stripped off the tunic clinging to his body. His belly was toned into six hard squares, his sculpted chest and arm muscles rippling as he flexed against the cold.

Her stomach fluttered like a dragonfly's wings, and heat flared inside of her.

Lahi winked at her, pausing before she draped a fur over Tian's magnificent body. Kaiya turned her head and loitered over to the warm flames. She held the furs tight around her as she sat.

Hati walked Tian over and pushed him down next to her. He pressed them close together. "You have to sit close, share each other's warmth."

Tian's face flushed an interesting shade of crimson. Hers must have been equally red. Beneath the fur blankets that separated them, they were naked.

Neither said a word while their clothes dried.

The walk back to the village was awkward, even as they huddled close together for warmth. With no fish in hand, only one thing had come from their fishing expedition: Yuha scolded them for getting their heads wet in the dead of winter.

She looked at Tian out of the corner of her eye. Maybe something more had come of it.

CHAPTER 44:
Wrestling

Normally skilled enough to slip through Hati's wrestling guard, Tian found his face pressed into the dirt ring, his arm twisted into a simple hammer lock. Not hard to get out of with patience and tenacity, but his heart wasn't in it today. He tapped on the ground, indicating his surrender.

Hati loosened his hold. "You're unfocused."

Tian accepted the chief's son's hand and clambered to his feet. Though his grasp of the language was improving, he still stumbled over some words. "Sorry I can't give you a better fight."

"You teach me a lot of tricks." Hati grinned. "Maybe I can teach you something."

Tian raised an eyebrow. The Maki excelled at wrestling. As one of the favorite pastimes among the men, they used it to impress women and settle disputes. Even so, his foreign Black Fist grappling techniques always gave him the upper hand. "A new hold?"

"Yes." Hati puckered his lips and mimed hugging. "You will concentrate better."

The instigator of the fishing trip fiasco!

Despite his knack for sniffing out ambushes, Tian had been caught flatfooted. Pressed up against the princess, with nothing more than two fur blankets between their bare skin, it had taken all of his discipline to stay calm. How mortified the princess must have been!

He glared at the youth. "You don't understand. Where we are from, she is the chief's daughter. I am her... " How could he explain? The Maki had no word for *servant* or *retainer*. "... piglet."

Hati swirled a finger around the side of his head, a Maki sign of confusion. "What's there to understand? Here, I am the chief's son. It doesn't matter who my favorite girl is."

With a sigh, Tian threw his hands up. If only things were that easy. "She only sees me as a piglet."

Hati puffed out his chest and pounded it with a palm. "I am an expert in these matters. Let me teach you."

Not that it would do any good. Tian pointed in the direction of the Iridescent Moon, obscured by the clouds. Hopefully, Hati wouldn't look. "It's almost time for weapons training."

Scrape, scrape. Kaiya sharpened stone arrowheads with Lahi. The Metal Men's encroachment into the forests had turned this man's job into everyone's responsibility. Though no hostilities had broken out, Kaiya's own experience with the Bovyan scourge told her it was only a matter of time.

She held up the arrowhead and ran a finger across its edge. Sharp. Dangerous enough to take down game, and even the ogres whose ambushes had dwindled during the winter. Teleri armor posed a greater challenge.

"You have to hit the heart." Lahi tapped on her chest.

Kaiya shrugged. "It has to get past the armor first."

Lahi laughed. "Very easy."

Was it? The Maki hadn't gone to war in thirty years, and even then, their opponents wore leather jerkins. Hopefully, they'd never have to test their stone weapons against steel. "I hope so."

Lahi peered at her. "You're a beautiful girl. His armor will melt with a smile... " She cast an alluring smile and twirled one of her braids. "... and body language."

Oh. That, Kaiya could do, and do well, probably better than Lahi.

It wouldn't work, though—not on Tian. Even though he'd warmed up, too much damage had been done in Iksuvius. She was still his burden, and would be lucky if he considered her a friend again.

But why did she *want* it? Want more?

And yesterday! It should've been embarrassing, being naked with nothing but a blanket between them. Instead, her heart fluttered even now, just thinking about it. Whatever she felt, it was real. More real than Ming's smooth words sending her head spinning, or Rumiya beguiling her with magic.

If only things were so simple. She was a princess, he was a spy.

Snow flew in her face. Lahi leaned back, laughing. "You look hot. Your face is red. You make too much of it. You are a girl. He is a boy."

Kaiya's eyes widened. Of course. In the Wilds, away from Cathay's customs and conventions, they were just Kaiya and Tian. All it took was a Maki girl to remind her.

Pacing the village field, Tian scanned the young Maki men facing each other in two lines, all holding cloth-wrapped stone knives in a defensive stance. Like the last lesson two days before, a handful of new faces had appeared, likely from neighboring Maki villages.

After Chief Nuwa's test, Tian had immersed himself in teaching combat to the males. Besides their superior wrestling skills, the natives also excelled at archery, perhaps more than anyone back home, given Cathay's shift from bows to muskets.

With no armed conflict since their cousins from the plains invaded a generation ago, their skill with spear and knife left a lot to be desired.

"Now," he barked.

The pairs all engaged in a fixed-pattern drill, quickly closing and disengaging. They were improving quickly, none more so than the chief's son. If not for the cloth wrapping around the knives, it might have turned into a bloody mess.

Clapping pattered from the edge of the field. Tian turned to look.

Ma Jun, ostensibly there to help teach tactics based on formations, leaned back against a fallen log, smiling and chatting with Lana.

Whatever she'd clapped about had nothing to do with the training. She wasn't even paying attention. Meanwhile, her twin Lahi craned to watch the men. Or like as not, one man: Hati.

Definitely a distraction.

Though none more than the impromptu swim the day before. Tian returned his wavering attention to the training. "Again."

The pairs repeated the same pattern several times, getting better each time.

"Good. Let's... " What was the word? "... spar." Tian circled his finger in the air and his students all sat cross-legged in a ring around him. "Who wants to go first?"

Hati jumped to his feet and pointed at Tian. "You and me!"

Tian smirked. Perhaps the young man thought his luck from the morning would continue.

The two circled and engaged in a furious exchange of cuts and stabs. Tian evaded or blocked all of Hati's attacks, while raking his knife across the young man's neck and wrists. When the opportunity presented itself, he poked him in the armpit.

Hati stepped back, bent over with his hands on his knees. Despite the thorough beating, he grinned.

Unwrapping the knife, Tian swept his gaze around the ring. "These knives will shatter on the Metal Men's... " They had used the word before, when describing the Bovyan's chainmail. Even now, the men scowled at mention of the big men whose voracious taste for meat had ravaged the large game supplies. "... skin?"

Hati shook his head. "*Roroi.*"

Right. "Backs of knees are open. Sometimes their hands are unprotected." He pointed at his face. "And their metal hat's openings. You must be fast and accurate."

One of the new men threw his arms up, speaking a mix of familiar and unfamiliar words in a strange order. Tian looked to Hati and raised an eyebrow.

"Our cousins, the Omiki," he said. "Their words are similar. He says it's impossible."

"Difficult, not impossible." Tian stroked his chin. "Use distractions."

A wide-eyed youth, Kosa, waved his hand. "How?"

How indeed? Tian opened his mouth, but then said nothing. Dozens of different ideas came to mind, yet none seemed practical given the tribespeople's resources.

Hati pointed toward the edge of the field. "Kaiya."

Heads turned. Tian ventured a glance. The princess stood next to Lahi... smiling? After their fishing misadventure, it should have been days before she so much as glanced at him. Yet here she was...

Tian hit the ground, with only his reflexes preventing the wind from getting knocked out of him. A heavy weight rested on his chest.

He looked up.

Hati sat on top of him with a grin, knife blade at his neck. "Distraction."

The men all laughed. Lahi clapped.

The chief's son learned well. Tian could have twisted past the knife and put Hati in an armbar, but decided against it. Let him savor his victory; let his people see him as a leader.

And Tian would save the technique for the village wrestling tournament.

The wind howled outside Yuha's lodge, reminding Kaiya that winter had yet to loosen its grip on the Wilds. Around the fire pit, the children Waka and Nadi held bowls of stew, chattering with their grandparents and aunties Lahi and Lana about the upcoming wrestling tournament.

Conspicuously absent was Tian, who always accompanied her when she ate with the shaman's family. He'd avoided her all day. Probably still embarrassed from the fishing trip. Kaiya looked up from her own bowl of stew.

Yuha was staring at her.

Returning his gaze, she raised an eyebrow.

"The world acts in cycles, guided by the spirits." He twirled his hand in a large circle. "In ancient times, even before the sky rained fire, the Turquoise Men enslaved our people."

Kaiya nodded. He must be referring to era before the War of Ancient Gods, when all humans were slaves to the Tivari. Still, it had nothing to do with village life or the upcoming tournament.

"And then, the Star Spirit, motivated by his love for the Willow Beauty, liberated us." He pointed up to the smoke hole. "The time will come again. The stars say in a year, when the Eye of Kannon greats the White and Pearl moons. The spirits have spoken to me."

Kaiya followed his finger up to the night sky. Lord Xu had said as much, that the dance of the Heavens mirrored events among mortals. "Why do you tell me this?"

"I—"

The door flap opened. Kaiya turned.

Tian. He gawked at her, eyes wide. The flap started to close.

"Come in, come in." Yuha jumped to his feet.

Tian froze in place and stared at the ground. He must've been really horrified by their catastrophic fishing experience. He might need an imperial order to forget about it. With a tentative step, he crossed the threshold and looked up. "Why are the Omiki coming?"

With a laugh, Yuha motioned for Tian to sit. "They live south of the river, it's easy for them to paddle across and visit us."

"That's not what I meant." Tian plopped down next to the fire, about as far away from her as possible.

Yuha stroked the feathers in his necklace. "The spirits carry news on the winds. The Metal Men expand. The tribes are worried. But now, there is hope. Since the Warrior From Beyond the Wall arrived, the ogres have retreated."

Kaiya covered a giggle. Tian *would* get the fancy nickname.

"Of course." Tian threw his hands up. "It's winter and the trails are snowbound."

Yuha shrugged. "Perhaps. But rumors of your skills spread far and wide. Many wish to learn from you. Many in this village believe you are our tribal guardian. Like the Star Spirit a thousand sun cycles ago."

At last, Tian's eyes met hers. "I'm one man. There's little I can do. To stop the tide of Metal Men."

"One man can bring hope. Sometimes, to an entire people." Yuha's gaze shifted to her. "Sometimes to a woman."

Was Tian blushing? Or was it the play of firelight on his face?

Kaiya's face was probably just as hot and bright as the flames.

Yuha grinned. "I think that man should prepare himself for the wrestling tournament."

Nothing brought out village enthusiasm like the winter wrestling tournament, which Tian had entered at Hati's urging. Held under a new White Moon on the Winter Solstice, two months after their arrival, it would determine the village's representatives for the tribal tournament held in spring.

As was the custom, single women dipped their hands in berry juice and marked their favorite competitors with palm prints. Wearing a dozen handprints like a leopard wore its spots, Hati flexed his muscles to rampant cheers. The defending village champion's toned physique glistened in the flickering bonfire lights.

Lahi came last, claiming her spot over Hati's heart.

No other woman would dare make such a statement, on any man, let alone the chief's son. Tian grinned for his young friend. He looked around at the dozen competitors, all boasting a handprint or two.

Only his bare chest remained unmarked.

Not that it mattered. Even though the Cathayi had all been accepted as members of the tribe, most of the village held him in awe. The girls were all too timid.

And, there was only one girl that mattered.

A firm hand clamped on his shoulder and spun him around.

Hati stood there, smiling. He wrapped an arm over his shoulder. "Do your best. I want to fight you in the last round."

"I hope so." Tian grinned back.

"You might need some luck," the princess said from behind him.

Hati turned him around.

The princess stood there, a shy smile gracing her face. Looking down, she pressed her palm over his... heart. Around them, the tribe erupted in whoops and cheers.

Her hand lingered there, warm, sending tingles through him. Her dark eyes looked up through her lashes. "Win."

His heart pounded under her hand. He bowed his head. "As you command, *Dian-xia*."

"Kaiya," she corrected, dropping her hand and backing off.

Blanking his expression, he turned to watch the first bout.

After weeks of him participating in impromptu duels, Black Fist joint manipulations had worked their way into the Maki repertoire of wrestling techniques. In his own first face-off, it took longer to defeat the man than it had in all previous meetings with him. By the bout with his third opponent, weariness began to creep into his limbs.

As Hati had hoped, he and Tian met in the championship. The chief's son looked just as winded, yet practice fighting through exhaustion would be important if the young men ever had to face an enemy on the battlefield.

At Chief Nuwa's signal, Tian and Hati circled each other.

Tian had tricked Hati time and time again with a wide arsenal of techniques. Tonight, Hati didn't bite on any of his feints.

Hati lunged forward for a two-handed grab, exposing his knees. An opportunity!

Tian shot in, taking hold of both of Hati's legs. He meant to drive his head into the young man's chest for leverage, but Hati turned his torso and caught Tian up in an underarm choke. As the two tumbled to the ground, Hati wrapped his legs around Tian's body, then arched his back to tighten the grip.

A technique he'd taught Hati!

Blood rushed to Tian's head. He couldn't breathe, and his neck felt like it was being stretched a foot. Nonetheless, he held on. It was nothing compared to the strenuous training he'd endured as a youth.

Hati cranked his choke.

Something popped in Tian's neck, sending a flaring pain shooting down his arm. He tapped on the ground several times.

People cheered, drums beat.

Hati helped him to his feet. With his head tilted at a funny angle, Tian exchanged hugs, patting the victor on his back. Maybe they'd get a rematch at the spring tournament.

The princess beckoned him over and gestured for him to sit. As they watched the closing dance, a muscle spasm wracked his neck. He tilted his neck to take the pressure off.

"It's all right, you can't win *all* the time." She knelt behind him and massaged the knot in his neck.

She was massaging *him*. He started to pull away, but she wrapped her other arm around his bare chest. Her kneading fingers seemed to relax the muscle, but Fang Weiyong's acupuncture would work better.

She continued to twist into the knot. "You are becoming too predictable. Hati could—"

The drumming picked up, drowning out her words.

Tian turned his head awkwardly towards her. "I am sorry, *Dian-xia*. I couldn't hear."

She leaned in close, her soft voice tickling his ear. "Hati could guess what you were going to do. He gave you that opening on purpose." Her soft bosom pressed against his back.

Tian's heart hammered in his chest. What was she saying? Something about some match? Was that *her* heart, pounding against his back?

Her lips brushed the back of his neck; first low, then a little higher and more distinctly.

Her warm lips sent a cold shiver down his spine. She was no longer the adorable little girl, or the haughty princess.

Here, she was just a woman. Sweet and smart and playful. More than he deserved.

Yet despite all of the barriers between them that had fallen in their months at village, his willpower and control would have never allowed him to say or do anything to act on his feelings.

Now, her soft body melted against his, her kiss warm against his neck. Ignoring the pain flaring in his neck, he turned and drew her to him. Her lips parted, inviting him.

The drums had stopped. Everything was quiet. Two hundred gazes hung on them. Their adopted tribe exploded in a cacophony of excited murmurs and cheers.

It didn't matter.

Sweet and intoxicating, her taste and smell overwhelmed his senses. She was the only one in his world.

But for how long? The specter of duty hung over his heart.

CHAPTER 45:
Obligations

Kaiya's pattering heart beat a dozen times for each of Tian's hot breaths brushing across her ear. Straddling him near the village stream, she lavished a kiss on his neck, marking him as hers for the hundredth time in the last two weeks. His arms enveloped her, pressing her body to his.

Wet with the heaven's dew that came each full White Moon, sweltering from months of longing, she drew her knees up, rocking against the hardness beneath his pants. She guided his hand to the hem of her undergarments.

His fingers froze in place; his breath hitched. The hand drew away.

Again? She raised her head and searched his eyes.

Lips tight, he refused to meet her gaze, instead looking past her.

Predictable. Kaiya pouted. "We aren't going any further than the other unmarried couples."

"We aren't like other unmarried couples, *Dian-xia*."

That title, again. She rolled off him and pulled the dress hem down over her knees. Apparently, someone hadn't bought into the Maki's lack of social hierarchy. Even if she were no longer the perfect princess, he was still the practical spy. She stared up at Guanyin's Eye, now opening to one-quarter angle.

He turned to his side and draped an arm across her.

An empty gesture. She brushed it off. She was the one always initiating affection, guiding him to what he should want. She might as well have been a whore.

He propped himself up on an elbow and brushed an errant lock out of her face. "Yuha says that the snows should slow down by the end of the year. We may be able to go home at that time. We could probably paddle down the river with the spring melt and make better time."

He was in such a rush to get home. She sat up. "What about Ma Jun?" What about her? "He's doing better, but I don't know how well he could handle the trip. In any case, I'm not sure if he wants to leave." Because of Lana.

And her, because of Tian.

Tian stared at the ground. "Ma Jun is a member of the imperial guard. His duty comes before love."

Duty. The memory of that cage sent a shudder down her spine. She pushed away, almost afraid to ask the question that gnawed at her. "Is that how you feel? What about *your* duty?"

His jaw locked, silence conveying his thoughts louder than words. With him, responsibility first.

"Answer me."

He sighed. "These last months have been wonderful. But eventually... we will have to return to our duties."

She turned away from him, pouting, coming up with every rationalization to prove him wrong. "What about our obligations to these people? Think of the Teleri's advance into the Wilds and the burdens that will place on them. They've adopted us into their tribe; they are as much our people as the Cathayi."

Sitting up, Tian shook his head. "Even though I love them like my own brothers, my first responsibility is to Cathay. You are its princess. You have your commitment to our people. I am a spy, and I have mine. No matter how I feel about the Maki, about you... I was born in Cathay and owe allegiance to it."

Even if he spoke the truth, Kaiya wasn't ready to hear it. Not now, when she'd thrown off that yoke for the first time in her life. Her voice cracked. "What about *us*? If we go home, we could never continue like this, never marry."

A long silence.

"Answer me." She shoved him with a hand.

Tian blew out a long breath. "Then we must cherish the time that we have left. When we return, we can only treasure the memory of our short time together." His next words came out flat, emotionless. "Marriage to a suitable husband is also your duty."

Kaiya leaped to her feet, tears blurring her vision. Within an appropriately arranged marriage, she'd not relive the excitement of falling in love. Had she never known what it felt like, it might not have mattered. She might have eventually come to love her future husband.

However, now that she'd experienced it, she despised Tian for allowing it to happen if he were so quick to abandon it. She tried to keep her voice steady, her words coming out as a whisper. "I thought you'd changed."

"I am sorry, *Dian-xia.*"

"Stop calling me that." She turned and ran back to her lodge, leaving a trail of tears in the snow.

Watching the princess escape, Tian regretted his words. How he wanted her! More than anything. What man wouldn't, if he got to know her beyond her façade?

But no. There was no hope for them to be together. Cathay's princess *had* to return to Huajing, and this banished spy was not allowed to step foot in the capital. Banishment would be nothing compared to the punishment he'd face for touching her the way he had.

Better to end things now before leaving even deeper scars.

For the next two days, the princess avoided him. If they were going to pass each other on the village paths, she would turn away without even making eye contact. When he sought her at her lodge, one of the women told him she was busy.

What had he done? Food tasted bland and he lacked the energy to even go through the training drills. Feeling more and more depressed in her absence, Tian sat down to eat dinner one night with Ma Jun and Fang Weiyong.

Still unaccustomed to using his hands to eat, Tian fiddled with his makeshift chopsticks. "How do you plan on telling Lana we are leaving?"

Ma Jun looked up from his meal, putting his own chopsticks down. "I've tried not to think about it." After a long pause, he amended himself. "That's not true. I've considered asking her to come with us."

"But you don't want to leave," Tian said.

"I know she'll refuse to come, and I'll miss her more. No, I'd far rather stay here, if I had the choice." Ma Jun's long sigh might have deflated the entire lodge. "I almost wish I had died at that burnt-out village. I would've never met her, never had to deal with the sadness of our inevitable parting."

The optimistic Ma Jun was channeling the spirit of his fatalistic friend, Li Wei. Tian gritted his teeth. How shallow their concerns were compared to Li's sacrifice.

A moment passed before Ma Jun spoke again. "What if we just stayed? By this time, Cathay will assume we are dead."

His hopeful tone, obvious to Tian's trained ear, suggested that this question had fermented in the back of his head for a while.

Outrageous.

Yet tempting. Tian tapped his chin. He'd never fit in with the hereditary lords back home. He felt needed by the Black Lotus, but their disregard for life never sat well with him. But in this rustic village, among a different race of people, he *belonged*. "Can we abandon our duty? Just for our own selfish desires?"

Fang Weiyong snorted. Easy for him; he had nothing here.

Ma Jun poked at his food. "It goes against everything I was ever trained to believe in. Yet somehow, it seems that with the Teleri starting to expand on the plateau to Cathay's doorstep, we can help both these people and our own by staying here."

Tian sighed. "The princess said the same thing. It sounded like rationalizing. I finally understand what the poets wrote. When they talked about lost love and lost hope. These last two days, without her. I've been walking in a fog... I'll be completely useless when we return to Cathay."

He closed his eyes, envisioning their approach to the Great Wall. At the tree line, he'd let go of her hand. Her smile would tighten and her posture would straighten. Everything that had grown between them would fade into a haunting memory.

Since when had he become so melodramatic?

He opened his eyes to find Fang Weiyong and Ma Jun staring at him curiously.

Forget duty.

Had he just thought that?

Tian bolted up and ducked out of the lodge. He sprinted across the village as fast as he could through the snow, arriving at the princess' lodge within a dozen heartbeats. Standing at the doorway, he yelled in, "*Dianxia.* Please. Come out and talk!"

Muffled sounds and indecipherable conversation came from within. The fur blanket covering the doorway opened.

Lahi appeared. "Kaiya does not want to talk to a stupid piglike you." Before he could reply, she turned around and the blanket closed behind her.

Undaunted, he called again. "Kaiya, I'm going to wait here. You have to come out sometime."

More muted sounds. The blanket opened and Kaiya was pushed through.

Without saying a word, Tian took her hand. She let out a gasp and pulled back, but then finally relented. He pulled her to the stream, their path lit only by the plump White Moon.

Arriving in the quiet fields on the southern end of the village, he turned around and took both of her hands.

He repeated the words over and over in his head before finally speaking. "These last two days I have sunk into sadness. Unlike any other since we were first separated ten years ago. I had no desire to eat—"

Her brow furrowed. "Maybe because you cooked yourself?"

"—and could not sleep—"

She harrumphed. "Ma Jun's snoring?"

"—every day has been colorless and dull—"

"It *is* winter, after all." She rolled her eyes. She wasn't making it easy.

He sank to his knees. "Kaiya, my princess, my beloved. I realize now that I can't live without you. You are more precious than the air I breathe. Each morning I wake, my first thoughts are of you. I wonder when in the day I will be able to see you for the first time. I want to... wake up, and see you at my side every morning, forever... "

Her gaze bore into him. "What about duty?"

"My first duty is to you." Did he just say that?

The princess' eyes glazed over, hopefully with tears of joy. "Oh Tian, I'd decided never to talk to you again, to hate you forever. It was the only way that I could return to Cathay. To hate you. I wasn't going to come out tonight. I was going to leave you freezing at my door. But then... you called me by name for the first time. I couldn't control myself."

She threw herself into his arms and wept. He brought his cheek to hers, relishing her hot, salty tears.

After a moment, she pulled back and pressed something hard and round into his palm. He looked down. It was a smooth river pebble, black with grey striations. He sucked in a breath. "Is this—?"

She nodded. "You gave it to me when we were children. When we promised to marry each other. It's always been a reminder to me, of when life was simple."

She'd kept it all this time. Bowing his head, he presented it to her, just like he had when he was nine.

Three weeks later, on the ninth day of the eleventh month, Kaiya's entire body quivered as Lana and Lahi helped prepare her for the ceremony. A princess of Cathay would've worn the finest silks and jewelry to her wedding. Here, she was just another girl.

Her hair, now nearly five months removed from its unceremonious shaving at the hands of her groom-to-be, hung over two handlengths long. Although she had kept it in a child's style while living among the Maki, the women now straightened it out and decorated it with shell ornaments.

She wore a doeskin dress with tassels at the hem and sleeves, topped by a shawl of peacock and wild turkey feathers. A necklace of colorful river stones adorned her neck. Two horizontal red stripes were painted on her cheeks.

If only she had a mirror!

With Lahi and Lana serving as her maids, Yuha's parents guided Kaiya through the cheering villagers gathered around the drum platform. An imperial wedding would have been quiet and solemn, her face a carefully crafted mask of grace. Today, unfettered with joy, she smiled ear to ear. She looked up, and her heart rattled.

He was so handsome. Tian stood on the platform, wearing a buckskin tunic with tassels along the neckline and hem. A line of long shells hung from his neck. Two bright turkey feathers, held in place by a headband, adorned his hair, which was now about a handlength long.

Chief Nuwa and his wife stood beside him, in place of his own parents. Ma Jun, Hati, and Fang Weiyong smiled there as his seconds.

Though the event was straightforward compared to elaborate Cathayi weddings, Kaiya appreciated the simplicity. She clasped the hands of Chief Nuwa and his wife, his steady gaze calming her. At her side, Tian did the same with Yuha's parents.

Then, Kaiya turned to face her groom. Hands trembling, she used her finger to paint two horizontal red stripes on his cheeks, then placed a bead bracelet she had made around his wrist.

He braided her hair back into a single queue, denoting her status as a married woman, and fastened it with a shell ornament he'd made and painted himself. His touch sent her stomach fluttering like a hummingbird's wings.

Yuha, as the village's spiritual leader, spoke: "Tonight, the waxing moons represent your growing love. Your energies have entered this circle separately, but will leave it joined. That which the spirits bring together cannot easily be undone."

A shiver ran up Kaiya's spine.

At Yuha's command, she clasped hands with Tian. Their adopted family members placed their hands on their shoulders, and then everyone in the village followed, radiating outward until all were connected.

One with each other. One with the village. One with the spirits.

They held a grand feast in typical Maki fashion, with each household bringing a favorite dish to share. All enjoyed a wine fermented from the red berries.

Drumming and dancing lasted late into night, when the couple was led to their lodge.

Their lodge.

Many of the young adult Maki gathered outside. Following their custom, they'd raise a racket until they heard the marriage being consummated.

However, as the two had arranged, Fang Weiyong, dressed in his monk's robes, awaited them inside.

Despite not having all of the official trappings, Weiyong had scripted a highly-simplified Cathayi ritual which fused the legends of plain weddings—from the time when humans were slaves to the orcs—with current, more intricate symbolic marriages.

In the days prior, she'd painted a simple picture of Guanyin, Goddess of Healing and Fertility; while he drew a similar one of Yang-Di, Supreme God of the Sun. Both hung side-by-side on the far wall, above a makeshift altar—a long flat rock taken from the river bed—to their family ancestors.

Two round berries sat in a plain wooden dish in the middle of the altar, replacing the two oranges that would be placed in an elaborate porcelain bowl for a typical Cathayi wedding.

Weiyong motioned them to the altar. "Kneel."

Tian at her side, Kaiya dropped to her knees.

He gestured to the sketches. "Bow to the Heavens."

She and Tian faced the effigies of the gods and pressed their heads to the floor.

When they straightened, he nodded at the altar representing their ancestors. "Now bow to your families."

They bowed again. Kaiya prepared a cup of sweet evergreen tea, which they both shared. Finally, they bowed to each other.

"You may commit yourselves to each other."

Tian's gaze met hers, again sending her heart racing. "I take you as my wife, forever."

"I am yours forever, my husband," she answered.

Weiyong bowed low, and then held up their names, carved into wooden plaques. "I will invest these together in your new ancestral shrine, which I shall dedicate in this village. Having followed the rituals prescribed by the Emperor and Empress in Heaven, you now belong to each other."

He raised his head and grinned. "By the law of Cathay, an official witness is required to confirm that a member of the Imperial Family's marriage is consummated."

Heat rose in Kaiya's face. She stared at the floor.

Tian stood up and unceremoniously ejected the chuckling Weiyong from the lodge. Outside, the gathered crowd gasped and laughed at his sudden appearance.

Returning to his knees, Tian stared at the floor, too shy to make eye contact with his bride. An awkward silence ensued. He knew that *she* knew what should happen next.

Unlike their spontaneous kissing and touching before, the next part of the wedding was too scripted, too awkward.

Neither spoke, the silence exacerbating the playful taunts of the villagers outside.

He looked up.

Blushing in the flickering firelight, she looked down at her knees and started to unbraid her hair.

Kaiya was beautiful, even more so than in the finest silk gowns and bedecked in priceless jewels.

His *wife*.

To think that *she* loved *him*, the unworthy boy who'd once locked her in an armoire. He never thought he'd find love, let alone marry. She was more than he deserved.

She looked up at him through her lashes and offered a shy smile.

He'd wanted her for weeks now. All his passion, pent up by discipline.

It exploded now, like a spring river torrent bursting through a dam. He stood and pulled her to her feet. A surprised gasp escaped her.

He brought her to him, fiercely kissing her neck, moving up towards her lips. Her sweet fragrance filled him as her soft body pressed against his.

Kaiya groped at his shoulders and back. He reached behind her and unfastened the ties of her dress. It fell to her ankles, revealing silken undergarments from Cathay—her last vestige of vanity from a past life.

His hands had brushed across them before, and even ventured below, but never had he actually seen them. He paused momentarily to take it in, that which no man had ever laid eyes on before.

A trapezoidal-shaped red silk bust binder, embroidered with green, blue, and golden flowers, accentuated her perfect curves and was held in place by thin laces tied behind her bare back at the neck and waist. Red silken arabesque underpants hid her most guarded place, hinting at what lay beneath.

Heart pounding, Tian pulled her back and drew her into a deep kiss. His dexterous fingers unraveled the ties of her top, and she undid the knot holding up his breeches. Finally, he loosened the strings that held her underwear. It slid down to her knees.

He stepped back to pull off his tunic, and then took in her nakedness in the dimming firelight.

She crossed her shapely legs and covered herself with her arms. She looked down demurely, causing her hair to fall over her face. But presently, she lifted her gaze and brushed the tresses out of her eyes. The coy smile was an invitation.

He took her hands in his, which revealed the treasures she'd been hiding, and brought her down onto the fur bedding.

Kaiya savored the ache after their first lovemaking. The darkness of the lodge mingled with the warmth of Tian's body, enveloping her in a calm sense of security. Naked under the thick fur blankets, she lay on her side with her head on Tian's chest, his arm wrapped over her.

He breathed lightly in shallow sleep, while she lay there wide awake. She brushed her free hand over his firm chest and abdominal muscles. A cold wind blew outside, rustling the door to the lodge, allowing the merged lights from the blue and White Moons to peek in. Beyond that, a wolf howled in the far distance.

Her sisters-in-law had always told her to set her expectations low for the first time, but Tian's tongue and fingers had sent surges up and down her spine, made her lose all coherent thought, left her yearning to feel the length of him inside her.

That had been nervously awkward and over quickly.

It didn't matter. She now belonged to him, him to her. Two souls, two bodies joined as one.

She'd happily remain here forever, in this rustic village, away from Father's court and the associated burdens of duty, as long as she could share this life with him.

His embrace tightened. Was he thinking the same in his sleep? Allowing the darkness to hide her smile, she turned her head and kissed him on the chin, her hair brushing across his smooth chest.

The light touch must have woken him, because he slid his arm out from under her. He rolled her onto her back and buried his face into her neck, his breath hot and urgent.

Kaiya woke in Tian's embrace. High in the Heavens, the sun peeked in through the lodge's smoke hole. Languid, exhausted, and pleasantly sore, she rolled onto her side to look at her *husband*.

Sleep draped him in childhood innocence, exposing the gentle soul he hid underneath layers of discipline and duty.

She kissed him on the forehead and unwrapped herself from his arms. Dragging herself out of the blankets, she walked past her wedding dress, which laid in an unceremonious heap, to her plain doeskin clothes.

He yawned, and she turned around. His eyes creaked open and met her gaze.

And she was naked, hair tousled like a nest made by a drunken bird. With one hand, she covered her nether regions; the other arm, she crossed over her chest and brushed out her unruly tresses.

She fiddled with a strand of her hair. Silly girl. Not like she had anything to hide from her *husband*. Not anymore, not to the man she'd given herself to. Still.

Grinning, he covered his eyes. "I'll... uh, get dressed under here."

She turned back to her clothes and was about to bend down to pick them up, when she looked over her shoulder.

Tian still watched her, his expression yearning.

Should she be embarrassed? She cast him a mischievous grin as she shimmied into her underpants and slid into the dress.

With a pout, he disappeared beneath the blanket, emerging seconds later fully clothed.

He pushed open the flap and gestured her out.

Cheers and grins greeted them as they made their way through the village.

Heat flared in her cheeks, hot enough to melt the snow. She'd spent too many years in Cathay to acculturate to the Maki's open attitudes towards relations between men and women. Nonetheless, having abdicated her responsibilities, she looked forward to a life of simplicity here. Maybe one day, her children would assimilate fully into the tribe.

Children.

An old couple, hand-in-hand, grinned at them.

In thirty years, would they be like that, too?

Ma Jun ran up to them, dropping to one knee, first to the ground. "*Dian-xia*, the chief asks that you come to his lodge. A neighboring village reported seeing Bovyans."

CHAPTER 46:
Rude Awakening

Tian was relieved that the neighboring village's sighting of Teleri scouts was an isolated incident. At least for now. It wouldn't be long before winter loosened its grip on the plateau, and their patrols could move freely through the woods.

In the meantime, the idyllic lifestyle seemed like a dream, full of the joys and trials of new marriage. Living together exposed quirks he would've never imagined in her, and no doubt she found some of his habits no less strange. Passionate arguments, invariably leading to his capitulation, quickly gave way to passionate lovemaking.

Ma Jun married Lana late in the eleventh month. If Yuha was concerned about his sister wedding a foreigner, it was probably tempered by the relief that she had found someone who could tolerate her strong will and personality. They moved into a newly-constructed lodge right beside Tian and Kaiya's.

The snows petered out as quickly as they'd come that season. The red berries of the river shrubs reached their sweetest at the end of the eleventh month, and now, fewer and fewer clung to the branches. Tian's anxiety grew as the paths through the woods opened up with an early spring thaw.

Soon enough, the Omiki men who came to learn from Tian brought disturbing news. Ancient roads that had been long-lost to outsiders now teamed with activity. The Metal Men passed along the trails from east to west in ever-increasing numbers. Larger contingents carried supplies and tools. Horse-riders became more frequent.

Then, the slaves.

Hundreds of people from the eastern Kanin tribes, chained together with collars around their necks. They cut swaths of greywoods along the main path, while others worked to restore the ancient stonework beneath.

Stories out of the east suggested that several large fortresses now controlled strategic points along the road. The Omiki observed from a distance, avoiding confrontation. They feared it would not be long before more and more of these Metal Men would become frequent visitors to their lands.

One day, as Tian taught spearwork to a group of Maki and Omiki tribesmen in the fallow cornfield, a squad of ten Teleri light infantry stumbled upon their practice. Chainmail peeked out from beneath their black tunics. Swords and daggers hung at their waists, and they all carried Teleri spears. A Kanin man from an unfamiliar tribe guided them.

Keeping an eye on the newcomers, Tian continued with his lesson. They huddled together near the stream, just outside of earshot to be clearly heard. After some discussion among themselves, the scout approached. He extended his right open hand, held in his left, in typical tribal greetings.

Hati motioned for a break and stepped forward.

"Hello, brothers," the scout said in a dialect Tian could barely follow. "These men are exploring the forest, and I'm their guide. Would you mind if we rested here?"

Tian would've rather they move along. Nonetheless, the chief's son glared at the scout and pointed towards the edge of the field. "Unseeded ground belongs to no one. You may sit."

The scout walked back to the Teleri soldiers, and the tribesmen around began muttering among themselves.

Hati leaned in. "He belongs to the Shaki tribe, you can tell by his marks. They are from the east, very aggressive. Nobody likes them."

Tian draped an arm over Hati and edged toward the Teleri, straining to hear their conversation.

The Teleri leader poked the scout in the chest. "Demand some food."

The scout returned, head hung low. "The visitors are hungry and want food."

Face flushing, Hati shook his head. "Tell your master it's winter's end, and food is scarce. We have none to spare."

The Shaki skulked back to the Teleri. "He say no food in winter."

The captain squared his shoulders and glared in their direction. "They're not scared, but that's because they've never tasted Teleri steel. Tell them we would like a challenge. Let's see what these barbarians are made of."

The Shaki came back with the Teleri captain. "It is not often that we see our Maki and Omiki kinsmen practicing together. The visitors would like a friendly lesson with your leader."

Tian had been around the tribe long enough to know the invitation was a thinly veiled challenge. He also knew that Hati was not one to back down from a fight.

Predictably enough, Hati thumped his chest. "I'd be happy to teach it." Scowling, the young man wrapped cloth around the spearhead. Tribesmen demarcated an area on the field, a square the length and width of three men.

Tian pulled him aside. "Brother, these men are trying to gauge our strengths and weaknesses. You can't reveal all your techniques and strategies, but you must still win so they don't think we are weak."

Hati nodded, but the words didn't seem to be getting through.

With a sigh, Tian pointed to the Teleri spearhead. It was a new configuration, with multiple uses. "Look at the shape. The blade can be used to stab or slash. At the base of the blade is a hook, used to catch weapons or legs. On the other side, the hammerhead can break a bone."

The chieftain's son brushed Tian away and sauntered into the ring. He spun in a circle, pumping his fists. Amid the tribespeople's cheers, he thumbed his right fist over his heart.

The Bovyan returned the gesture, and then pointed his wrapped spear at Hati. The two circled each other. While the Maki yelled advice, the Teleri soldiers watched in silence.

The captain lunged with a skillful thrust.

Hati intercepted the spear with his own, guiding it harmlessly to the right, then swept down along the shaft and struck the Bovyan in the hand with the pole. Tian suppressed a grin. It was one of the early techniques he taught.

The Teleri wrung his hand, even though his gauntlet had probably absorbed a lot of the force. With the man's guard down, Hati landed a quick strike to his armored torso.

Grimacing, the Bovyan avoided Hati's follow-up, then came down with the hammerhead.

Hati lifted his spear up to block the blow, but the Teleri twisted his weapon on contact. With a quick pull back, the hook caught Hati's spear and yanked it from his hands.

The Teleri soldiers all roared taunts while the tribespeople fell silent.

Tian sighed. The next lesson would cover counters to the hook.

The leader waved a condescending hand. "Not bad, for an untrained savage." He picked up Hati's spear, unwrapped the tip, and grinned. He threw it back into Hati's hands. "Unfortunately, I doubt this stone head could penetrate our armor."

Tian hung in the background. It was true, one of his greatest concerns. When the Shaki translated, Hati bristled with rage.

The captain twirled his own spear. "Perhaps we can civilize your people, and teach you how to make metal weapons. All you need to do is become our vassals, as your Shaki kinsmen have."

He was goading them. Tian kept silent. Yet on translation, Hati's face flushed an ugly red. Shaking, and despite Tian's silent pleading, he drew close to the captain, glaring him in the eye, even if he barely came up to the man's chin. "I will fight again!"

The scout translated and the Bovyan laughed. "I've already defeated you. If any others are brave enough to try my spear, then let them step forth."

Upon hearing the translation, the tribesmen started chanting. "Warrior Beyond The Wall!"

Tian drifted toward the back. Up close, the Bovyans would likely be able to tell he wasn't Kanin.

Hati, oblivious to the danger, pushed through his people and pulled Tian forward. "Brother, you must fight for the honor of the tribe!"

Tian shook his head. "I can't. I'll explain later. If these men find out... that Kaiya and I are here. They'll come back."

Hati shook his head, his eyes dancing with excitement. "Don't worry about that. You're our family now, and we'll protect you. Your enemy is my enemy. If they come to our village with ill intentions, they will feel the points of our spears!"

Tian cringed. The boy was overconfident and inexperienced. Though their spearwork had improved, they were still no match for the organized ruthlessness of Bovyan shock troops, fighting in an armored phalanx. "These men are just the beginning. Many nations have fallen before them."

The captain's laugh made Tian look up. "It's too bad that only your leader is brave enough to fight. If the rest of you are such cowards, then you aren't worth civilizing."

Tian feigned ignorance.

The Shaki scout approached, head bowed. "If you do not fight, they will think you are weaklings and it will only be a matter of time before you become their slaves. Learn from our tribe's mistakes."

Just like the Nothori Northwest, which Tian had witnessed firsthand. With a sigh, he crouched and rubbed dirt on his face. Then, he stepped into the ring, spear in hand. In the Kanin dialect, he issued his challenge. "You've said our spears won't pierce your steel skin. Let's see if that's true." He turned to the scout. "Tell him!"

Paling, the Shaki translated. "He want fight, open blade!"

The captain laughed, unwrapping the cloth. "Very well, let's see how long you last!"

Tian gave the Kanin salute.

His opponent returned the formality, and then dropped into a fighting stance. Without waiting, Tian stabbed at him with a clumsy, slow thrust, which his opponent easily deflected with his own spear. He twisted it and locked up Tian's weapon with the hook. However, Tian had set the move up, and before it could be yanked out of his hands, he thrust his spear downwards so that the Teleri's blade drove into the soft ground. Letting go of his weapon, he jumped forward and stomped on the shaft of his enemy's spear.

It slipped from the Bovyan's fingers. With two quick steps, Tian closed the distance, drew the shocked Teleri's own dagger and pressed the blade at his throat. "Yield," he ordered in the Maki dialect.

The message needed no translation. The captain held up his hands. The tribespeople all cheered.

Tian looked over his shoulder. A crowd had gathered, Kaiya among them. She shrank back behind the others. Hopefully the Bovyans hadn't seen her. Since the Cathayi and Kanin people shared some physical similarities, perhaps they'd go unnoticed.

He turned back to his opponent and presented the dagger. "Well fought."

After hearing the translation, the Teleri captain sneered. He yanked his sword back. "I am only one man, but the strength of the Teleri Empire is in the coordination of our troops. Perhaps you would like to try five of your warriors against three of mine?"

Tian narrowed his eyes. The Maki had very little experience fighting in formation. Ma Jun would have to drill them. There had to be another way. "I'll fight all three by myself."

Kaiya let out a startled cry, and the captain looked at her. She quieted and disappeared back into the crowd. As his counter-offer was being translated, the Maki began to chant, "Warrior Beyond The Wall."

The captain laughed, with no hint of mirth. "You're a confident bastard, aren't you? Very well then, this should be interesting." He motioned for three of his men to enter the ring.

Tian yanked his spear from the dirt. He feigned worry, letting his eyes widen and his hands tremble. Yet to himself, he smiled. The Teleri's confident grins told him they'd fallen for his act. With the versatility of Cathayi spear techniques and the element of surprise, there was little doubt who'd win.

After saluting his opponents, who returned the gesture, Tian held his spear one-handed and let the point drop to the ground. He waited as the three soldiers encircled him.

One let out a war cry, and three attacks thrust in at three different levels. With his spearhead still touching the ground, he lifted the shaft so that it stood straight up, and spun to the side, out of range of two of the spears while the third brushed harmlessly against his weapon.

With an open hand, he slapped down on the hammer part of the head, sending a vibration down the weapon. The wielder dropped it, staring at his shaking hands.

Tian kicked his spear up. The blunt end struck the unfortunate soldier in the face, knocking him to the ground. At the same time, he caught the Teleri's spear with one hand and swept it in a wide arc. The butt of the weapon deflected an incoming stab, and hit the second soldier in the head, crumpling him over. Three seconds, two down.

The Maki cheered loudly in the background. Even Kaiya applauded at the sudden shift in momentum.

The last Teleri disengaged and reset. Sweat gathered on his brow. Tian kicked his own spear up into his hands and advanced with multiple stabs and sweeps. The Teleri scuttled back to the edge of the ring.

"Attack, coward!" The captain stomped.

The soldier shouted and surged forward with the full arsenal of Teleri spear techniques: thrusts, slashes, and hammers.

Tian nonchalantly evaded them all, backing up until he stood over one of the fallen men's discarded spears. He twisted his legs with the haft between his feet, and the spearhead slashed into his opponent's unarmored shins.

With a yelp, the Teleri limped backward, holding his spear up defensively. Tian lifted a foot so that the spear rose into his hands, and he advanced purposefully towards his wounded foe. He avoided one last thrust, and used the hook of the weapon to catch the Teleri's good ankle. A jerk sent the man tumbling to the ground, and Tian placed the point at his throat.

The villagers erupted in louder cheers. Silent, the Teleri soldiers went to help their fallen comrades.

The captain strode up to Tian and studied him. "You're good. I look forward to the opportunity to meet you again, when it really counts."

Which might be soon, after today's events. Tian stared at his feet. Hopefully, the officer wouldn't spot the features that separated a Kanin from Cathayi. He spun and walked back to the celebrating tribespeople.

Kaiya threw her arms around him, burying her face in his chest. "What were you thinking? Fighting against three?"

So little faith in his abilities. That was the least of Tian's concerns. He turned to Hati. "We can't let them leave the village yet. The chief needs to know the entire story. Let's invite them to rest and offer them some food."

Hati's lips tightened. Nonetheless, he went to talk with the Shaki, and the guide translated to the captain. From where he was standing, Tian could tell the prideful Teleri had refused.

Had the Bovyans recognized them? There was too great a risk to the village. As distasteful as it was, the Teleri and their Shaki guide would have to die, and their secret with them. The only question was how to wipe out the patrol and minimize casualties to the Maki.

Tian tightened his grip on the spear and pushed through his cheering compatriots.

CHAPTER 47:
Dilemmas

Kaiya's heart pounded in her ears, drowning out the excited villagers. What had Tian been thinking, taking on three men at once?

And now... oh, no. His hard stare and clenched jaw was like the unfeeling automaton from their escape.

He planned to kill the Teleri.

She placed a hand on his forearm. "No, Tian. Maybe they didn't recognize us."

He looked through her at first, and then his expression softened. He was her husband again. "All right." He turned to one of the young scouts, Noki, and pointed at the patrol hobbling out of the village. "Track them, find out where they are going."

Noki nodded and slunk off.

When Tian returned her gaze, he looked defeated. Had she made the wrong decision for them? The village?

"Come," he said. He waved Hati down. "We must tell Chief Nuwa."

In the confines of the chief's lodge, the Cathayi gathered with Hati, Lana, and Yuha around the fire pit. She told their story: she was a princess of Cathay, betrayed while on a mission of diplomacy. They never expected the Teleri to be in the Wilds, never intended to bring harm to the village or tribe. At the end of her story, she pressed her forehead to the floor in apology. The Cathayi all followed suit.

"Rise," Chief Nuwa said after a moment of silence. "My children, you have nothing to apologize for. If the Metal Men are as ruthless as you say, and if the stories out of the east are true, then we would have faced this threat eventually. On the contrary, you have enriched our lives, and taught us a means of defending ourselves. I am grateful that the spirits brought you here."

Kaiya shook head. If only it were so simple. "If they recognized us, then I'm afraid that we will have brought this threat sooner. The Teleri are efficient and vengeful. Their armored infantry have met little resistance in two centuries of conquest."

The wise chief stood and walked over to the wall. From the floor, he picked up a long object, shrouded in a fur blanket. He unwrapped it, revealing a spear, much longer than the typical Maki spear, with a steel head.

"When I was young," he said, "our horse-riding brethren in the plains tried to incorporate our lands into their kingdom. But the tribes joined together to fight. We knew these forests, we knew not to engage them head-to-head. I was just a boy, and I felled one of their generals with my bow, and took his lance as a prize."

So much dignity and pride! Kaiya smiled in spite of herself.

"If the tribes were willing to unite against our distant kinsmen, I have no doubt that they will put aside their differences to fight outsiders. I will send word to the Maki tribal council, and they in turn will reach out to the other tribes. Now return to your home and rest."

Kaiya looked at Tian. If the lines of worry etched into his forehead were any indication, the chief's inspiring words had done little to assuage him.

It was late afternoon as they headed back to their lodge in silence. Villagers all smiled and patted Tian on the shoulder, congratulating him for his performance. His own smile looked like that of a condemned prisoner resigned to his fate.

Kaiya leaned into him. It didn't make her feel any better. What made her think it would comfort him?

Five young warriors waited at their door. As was Maki custom, Tian invited them in, offering them a seat around the fire pit. Kaiya started a fire and began heating water to make some sweet evergreen bark tea for their guests.

"Your fight was amazing!" Kona, a wide-eyed sixteen-year-old, had developed good spear skills under Tian's tutelage. "Your techniques were so unpredictable. How did you think to use your opponent's weapons?"

Tian's expression brightened. Leave it to a martial discussion to make him feel better! "Beyond skill with your weapon," he said, "you also need to develop an awareness. Of your surroundings. You can use them to your advantage."

The youths nodded excitedly, soaking up his words. Kaiya hoped they would never have to make use of the lessons.

Tian grinned. "Know your enemy's weapon. Then you know his strengths and weaknesses. Kaiya's ancestor banned all bladed weapons in our homeland. Except in the armies. When his widow, the Queen Regent, had to put down a rebellion. She found the peasants had developed unpredictable fighting techniques with their farming tools."

Kaiya looked up from the boiling pot. Was it true? She'd never heard of a rebellion. Perhaps the Black Fist knew more about these things.

Tian outlined the shape of the Teleri spear. "Their new weapon has four modes of attack. But at long range, the thrust is most common. It is the fastest way of covering distance. That makes the threat one-dimensional. Your response can be three-dimensional."

"So we can beat them!" Kosa, Kona's twin, clapped his hands.

Tian shrugged. "Each Teleri is formidable. However, their true threat is in formations. Ma Jun can tell you more."

Kona jumped to his feet and dashed out of the lodge. A moment later, he came back, dragging Ma Jun along with him. Lana followed close behind, smiling at Kaiya as she entered.

Thank the Heavens. Any more talk of fighting and weapons would be even more depressing. While she and Lana prepared dinner for four, the men continued with their discussion. On occasion, she would glance up to see Ma Jun and Tian working together to show how individual techniques worked in formation.

The teens all stared wide-eyed, so excited about combat.

Kaiya shuddered. All the sacrifices made for her: Xu Zhan. Li Wei. Zhao Yue. Chen Xin. Perhaps more she didn't know of since their escape. Had Jie survived? War was ugly business. Hopefully, these youths would never experience it.

After an hour, darkness fell and the youngsters were called back to their homes for dinner, leaving the four adults to eat in peace.

Around her, Ma Jun and Tian wore somber expressions, habitually talking in the Cathay language. Since Lana had picked up only a little, Kaiya tried several times to bring it back into the Maki dialect, to no avail.

Ma Jun poked at the food with his chopsticks. "If the Teleri recognized you, they'll be back with a larger force."

Tian sucked on his lower lip, almost like Jie. "We need to find where their base camp is. We can find out how many there are. And how soon they will return."

What was he thinking? Kaiya shivered. "Our presence here endangers the village."

Lana shook her head. "The chief is right, whether or not you are here makes little difference. Sooner or later, we will have to face this threat."

Ma Jun peeled back part of the rug and drew a map on the floor. "Strategically speaking, for them to come here would divert their attention from closer objectives. The only reason for them to come here in the short term is *us*."

And if the Teleri knew who they were... Kaiya shuddered. "Perhaps we should leave the village."

Lana frowned. "My brother never told you, did he? Last year, the spirits came to him in a vision, informing him that our people would soon face a great danger we could not overcome ourselves. He would find answers if he made a pilgrimage to the Land of the Spirit Messengers, on a night when the White Moon hid and the Blue Moon was half-lidded."

Kaiya calculated when that would have happened. Maybe several months ago, which meant—

"That is how you came to meet him on the trails west of the river."

Goosebumps rose on Kaiya's arms. "What did he learn?"

Lana locked her gaze on her. "He looked into the sacred pool and saw the reflection of the Blue Moon as straight swords. After Nadi and Waka told him how you defeated the ogre, he was certain the spirits brought you to us. You would save us from the danger. That's why Chief Nuwa accepted you into the tribe."

Save the tribe from danger? How was she supposed to do that? Kaiya looked at the floor. "I am no warrior. My encounter with the ogre was luck. I had to be saved from them the night before."

She leaned in to Tian, savoring his warmth, and he draped an arm over her. Why so hesitant?

Lana shook her head. "You do not need to be a warrior to protect others. The spirits do not speak directly, only in metaphors. Yuha's pilgrimage could be interpreted in many ways. Our people believe it is you."

Kaiya fell silent, lost in contemplation. They couldn't stay here, couldn't risk the village.

That night, after they'd gone to bed, she lay awake, unable to vanquish the thoughts clashing in her head. It was useless. She sighed and looked up through the hole in the roof at the stars.

Beside her, Tian whispered, "You can't sleep either?"

"I'm sorry, I didn't mean to disturb you."

"I was not asleep, *Dian-xia*." He shifted on his side, his gaze heavy on her in the darkness. His speech was so... *formal*.

And had he just used her title? She rolled over to face him. "I can't help but to think, if we returned to Cathay, then the village would be safe. But if we go back, what will happen to *us*? I know that my father would never approve of our marriage. And I never told you this, but I was courting Zheng Ming before I departed for Iksuvius."

Tian's tone carried unusual shock. "My brother would not take kindly to our marriage."

"Even *if* they recognized our marriage. I couldn't continue living if we were forced to be apart." She nestled her head into his bare chest.

Tian rubbed his hand against her back. "Fang Weiyong would vouch for it. He administered our vows. He made sure it was all done correctly. We should return. If we stay here... it's only a matter of time. Before Teleri subjugates the Maki. The tribesmen know the forest. But the empire's armies would win. With overwhelming numbers. And superior weapons."

She looked up from his chest, into his eyes. They were pools of blackness in the night. "What if we just ran away? We do not stay here, nor do we return to Cathay."

"Where would we go? We can't live on love alone."

Kaiya's chest tightened. How could he feel that way, after how far they'd come? She turned her head.

He reached for her, but she rolled onto her side, away from him.

"I'm sorry," he whispered.

She barely heard him over her own soft sobs.

Tian didn't sleep well that night. With her back to him, the princess' breathing suggested she barely slept either. All these people, his new family, faced danger because of them. The road back to Cathay would mean their separation. His sense of duty nagged at him. The only way to ensure everyone's safety, the princess' included, was sacrificing his own feelings.

At dawn, when the pink and purple clouds drifted past the smoke hole, she rustled beneath the thick fur covers. Was the dream almost over?

Only if he let it. He sat up and leaned over. "I'm so sorry. I didn't mean what I said. Last night. Let's leave here. We can go anywhere in the world. I'll find work as a bodyguard. You can perform."

Kaiya turned and gazed at him. "We can't run from our responsibilities, and right now, our duty is to the Maki. I am sorry, I was not thinking well last night, but I see things very clearly now."

Tian studied her, amazed at how she could still look so beautiful, even first thing in the morning. He bent down to kiss her, and she pulled him down.

Her hands worked his pants off while he tugged the shirt over her head. He brushed his lips over her closed eyes and worked his way down to her mouth.

Emerging from under the blankets, no more reassured from their lovemaking, Kaiya looked up through the hole in the roof. Dust motes shone in the beam of mid-morning sun that streamed in. She tightened the covers over her shoulders, as if their embrace would strengthen her resolve.

Outside, Hati's voice rang out, frantic. "Hurry! Everyone to the village center!"

CHAPTER 48:
Clear and Present Danger

The village buzzed with rumor, the noise drawing Tian out of Kaiya's embrace. Hopping one-footed into his pants, he poked his head out of the lodge.

Hati ran up, grabbed his arm, and pulled him down the path. "Hurry, everyone is gathering!"

Kaiya emerged, sweat matting her hair to her forehead, and Tian beckoned her to follow. Not that she needed his prompting.

At the village center, most of the tribespeople crowded around the drum platform, their chatter drowning out all other sounds. Near the drums, the Teleri's Shaki guide, left arm in a sling, conferred with Chief Nuwa. The remaining villagers trickled in, including Kaiya, who sidled up and clasped Tian's hand.

The chief raised a weathered staff with wild turkey feathers tied to the end. The villagers fell silent.

"My people!" The chief's voice boomed, carrying through the assembled tribe. He always spoke softly, and it was startling to hear his tone of command. "We have ill tidings. Shoma, a Shaki tribesman enslaved by the Metal Men, stumbled into the village this morning, with an arrow wound in his shoulder. Yuha has treated him. However, he brought ominous news, which he will share with all of you now."

Shoma staggered forward. "My Maki kindred, I know that our peoples have not always gotten along—"

Low muttering erupted, but the chief raised his staff again, quieting the crowd.

"—we do not serve the Metal Men by choice, but only because they hold our women hostage. Seeing your warrior fight yesterday, I was given a glimmer of hope that we may one day be able to win our freedom." He paused, his eyes sweeping over the assembled Maki.

That seemed too easy. Tian tapped his chin.

Shoma tapped both hands on his chest. "When I heard of their plans, I came back here as quickly as I could, even though they tried to stop me. They are looking for her." He pointed at Kaiya, who sucked in a breath.

Tian stepped in front of her. So the Teleri had recognized her. Hopefully, young Noki, who he'd sent after the patrol, would return soon with more news.

"A runner headed back to their base camp, which is a two-day march for them in their metal armor. At the camp, there are three hundred warriors, much like the ones you saw yesterday. Their sole purpose is to find the girl. They'll be returning in force. You must be prepared to either turn her over, or fight."

The crowd murmured again.

"Fight," one said.

"Fight." More took up the chorus.

Tian's pulse quickened. Though heartwarming, none of them had ever faced Bovyan infantry.

Shoma shook his head. "I forewarn you, three days beyond that, they've built a great fortress, which houses nearly two thousand of them. There, our women are forced to serve their soldiers while our men work like animals. If you resist and lose, you will share our fate."

Tian tapped his chin. It sounded like the Teleri way, but... "How can we trust you?"

Shoma placed his right hand over his heart. "I swear by the spirits that I speak the truth."

His oath was greeted by chatter. Yuha had told Tian in no uncertain terms that breaking a promise to the spirits had dire consequences: the oath breaker's life energy would never reunite with the universe when he died, cursing him to forever wander the netherworld between life and death.

The chief raised his staff again, silencing the crowd. "My people. I wanted you to understand this threat before telling you that my decision has been made. Kaiya, Tian, Weiyong, and Jun may not be of the Kanin race, but they are members of our village, our tribe."

Heads nodded in approval, even as dread grew in Tian's heart.

"We will never sell out one of our own. It will be war."

Cheers erupted.

Tian looked among the villagers. Only the middle-aged and elderly, who'd fought in the Kanin wars, remained subdued.

"We have three days to prepare. Heads of households, come meet with me. Everyone else prepare for our warriors' departure."

War chants resounded through the morning forest. Tian's heart sank. The village of almost three hundred only had about eighty men of fighting age. Even with the advantage of terrain, it would be almost impossible to defend against superior numbers and weapons. He exchanged glances with Ma Jun, who shook his head.

Tian looked to Kaiya. Maybe he had been right to begin with. It would be better to leave.

Hati pushed through the crowd to meet him, and hustled him towards the platform.

As soon as the war council convened, Tian stepped forward. "Chief Nuwa. We can't possibly defend this village. Not from their invasion force. Please do not throw your lives away for us. Kaiya and I will flee."

The chief smiled, his wise countenance the calm at the eye of a maelstrom. "Tian, who said we will defend the *village*?"

Tian fell silent. If not the village...

Chief Nuwa's expression returned to its usual gravity. "A wise warrior chooses the place where he does battle. A day east of here, along the river trail, is Omiwa Gorge. The north bank between the cliffs and river is such that only two men can pass at a time."

The chief held up two fingers, then brought his hands a finger-length apart. "At its narrowest point, only one man can fight at a time. The river flows so rapidly that not even the great horses of our plains kindred can negotiate the current."

A bottleneck. The strategy could work, though it would only be a matter of time before the Teleri would send more men. It might prove to be a temporary reprieve.

The chief drew lines in the air with his fingers while the warriors nodded. "It is one of only three paths that lead to this village from that direction; one of the other trails is treacherous, winding up the cliff; the last is out of the way. We will also do our best to draw them away from those other paths with ambushes."

Tian frowned. What if the Teleri took one of the other paths? It wouldn't have been the first time an enemy did not stick to script.

The chief continued. "Our men will engage their troops in the gorge, at the narrowest spot. I will send word to our Maki kinsmen to the north to bear down on them from the cliffs above; and I will further request to the Omiki tribes in the south to rain arrows from the south bank of the river. Does anyone have any suggestions?"

Ma Jun, a household head like Tian, stepped forward. "What happens if we don't hold the gorge?"

Chief Nuwa smiled grimly. "Then we will fall back, with half the men returning to the village for defense while the rest of us harass them with arrows along the path."

And dozens would die for nothing. Rehearsing his words in his head, Tian stepped forward and dropped to his knee, fist to the ground as if he were addressing Cathayi royalty. "Chief Nuwa. I humbly request the honor to enter the gorge first."

The chief favored him through pursed lips. "Normally, that would be Hati's right. But if he is willing to relinquish that, then you may be the point of our spear."

Tian turned to Hati with pleading eyes. "Brother, please. It is Kaiya they want, and I will take the responsibility of being the first to fall."

Hati nodded. "It's been a generation since we went to war, and I had very much hoped to prove myself as my father did before me. I relinquish this honor, for you, my brother."

Fighting a tear, Tian extended his right hand in his left in the Maki motion for thanks. "I can't possibly face three hundred men, one right after the other. You will have your chance."

The chief clapped his hands once. "Depart after lunch. Let all the warriors prepare for this generation's struggle."

The men erupted in cheers. Still, Tian's stomach flipped. How many would die because of them?

As the group dispersed, Chief Nuwa motioned Ma Jun over. "Jun, you will stay behind and formulate a strategy for the defense of the village. Keep in mind that our most robust warriors will go with the war party."

Ma Jun opened his mouth, but no words came out. He simply nodded.

He must have wanted to join the war party, even if he was still not in fighting condition after these several months. Had the roles been reversed, Tian would have felt the same way, to be first to defend his family.

He placed his right fist in his left hand, saluting Ma Jun in Cathayi fashion for the first time since they arrived in the village. "Lieutenant, I temporarily relinquish my duty to protect the princess, and return it to the capable hands of the imperial guard."

Ma Jun straightened and returned the salute, bowing his head.

Tian placed his hand on his shoulder, in Maki fashion. "My brother, please protect my wife."

The next several hours blurred by as the frenetic activity around Kaiya bewildered her. Many small drums were set up in the village square around the two large drums.

Mothers and wives painted the faces of their children and husbands. Grandmothers prepared food for the march, while grandfathers told stories of the last time an aggressor tried to invade. Middle-aged men beyond their fighting years sharpened spearheads and arrowheads, and children made good-luck charms of shiny river stones.

At last, the hour of departure arrived. Husbands and wives, mothers and sons all bid tearful farewells. Kaiya held Tian for a long time, memorizing the feel of his body against hers. He would surely sacrifice himself if the need arose. Was this the last time she would feel his warm embrace? Even after the call to march had been given, she pressed against him, unwilling to let go.

The chief presented Tian—as head of the column—a relic from the past war: a Kanin horse saber. Kaiya hid her smile. He already had one from their first disguise escaping Iksuvius. How long ago that seemed!

Tian hefted the weapon and smiled. With his free hand, he rubbed her on the back. "Don't worry, my love. These sabers will serve me well in a close-quarters engagement against Teleri spears."

He shouldered his pack and turned to leave. She held on to his strong hand as long as she could before he pulled away. His fingers brushed over her palm.

As the seventy-five warriors filed out down the path to the river, women played the drums to send them off. Wiping tears from her eyes and summoning up all the bravery she could muster, Kaiya joined them. The beating of her drum echoed from her heart, and the sound carried deep into the forest. The warriors answered the drums with a hearty cheer.

After several hours, the last rays of sun disappeared into the west, leaving a foreboding red glow on the horizon. The village grew eerily quiet, with even the littlest children seeming to comprehend the gravity of the situation.

To distract herself, Kaiya sought out Lana. She found her at the village center with Ma Jun, who'd already laid out plans for the village's defense. He was explaining the evacuation plan when a young scout rushed up.

Noki, a refugee from another Maki village, was one of Tian's original lodge mates. The one Tian sent to follow the Teleri patrol. Panting, he collapsed. "The Metal Men are coming! After they left the village yesterday, they split up at the river. One group headed east with the Shaki guide, and I followed the captain and two others west."

The villagers muttered among themselves. Kaiya's heart pattered.

"Where did they go?" Chief Nuwa's shoulders slumped.

"They stripped off their armor and ran to Wild Turkey Island, arriving around midnight. It was horrible. What was once our Uloki kinsmen's village, guarding the Shrine of Kahala, is now overrun with the Metal Men and ogres. Many tribespeople from all over the plateau were held in chains."

Where was that? Kaiya searched faces as a wave of upset murmurs rippled through the crowd.

Young Noki sighed. "As soon as the captain entered, their camp went wild with cheers, and it looked like even at that late hour, they were making preparations for war. I hurried back as fast as I could."

Ma Jun's face flushed. "A trap. The Shaki lied to us to draw our fighting-aged men in the opposite direction.

He is with our warriors now, maybe ready to betray them as well."

Kaiya shuddered. They were undefended. "The men must be warned."

The old chief seemed to age even more. "All the able-bodied men are gone, and we're all tired from today's preparations. No one will catch up with them."

"Lana, then," Kaiya said. "She's a shaman, like Yuha. Can they communicate?"

Lana shook her head. "I've expended myself, coaxing thorn brambles to grow around the village."

Chief Nuwa shoulders slumped. "Spend the rest of the evening collecting what is dear to you, and rest well tonight. We evacuate the village at dawn."

CHAPTER 49:
War on Two Fronts, Part 2

After a forced march to ensure they would reach the gorge before the Teleri, Tian rested among fifty of the Maki men. With no word back from the vanguard, all seemed relaxed for the time being.

He looked at each of the inexperienced warriors' faces, looking for signs of frayed nerves. Perhaps it was the ritual Yuha led to help ward off harm, though Tian didn't feel the calm relief flood over him like the others claimed.

On the southern side of the path, the waters of the North Kanin River roared, fed by the melting snows. Cliffs rose twenty feet above them on the left, their white rock faces creating a glare off of the afternoon sun. At the top, Maki kinsmen from other villages, fifty in all, also waited. In the unlikely event that the Teleri took the higher, narrower path, they might very well have to fight for their lives. The more probable route would result in Chief Nuwa's villagers bearing the brunt of the attack.

On the cliffs along the south bank, a hundred feet away, fifty Omiki archers—many of whom had learned spear techniques from Tian—also waited. This was the first major conflict the region had seen in a generation, and none of the warriors here had fought in those wars. Indeed, many had not yet been born. A nervous excitement trickled through the ranks. All hoped to win glory.

Tian tapped his chin. Perhaps the Teleri weren't even coming. Something was off. A trap, maybe? This location was almost too easy to defend. Unless the Teleri came by a different route. Yet the path above them along the cliff would be too treacherous in armor. The path on the south bank was wider, but there was no place to ford further downstream.

No, this would be the route they would have to take. It was just a matter of waiting. He sat down with Hati and shared some cured elk meat.

He'd hardly eaten three bites when shouts rang out from the eastern reaches of the gorge. The yells came closer. It was their own advance scouts. They ran through the gorge, none looking wounded. Tian sprung to his feet, making way for the vanguard.

The last man through stopped and caught his breath. "One hundred Metal Men, with spears and shields, supported by fifty Shaki archers. Our arrows couldn't penetrate their shields. They're close behind."

The men cheered. Hati grinned. "Less Metal Men than we thought. A third of what Shoma predicted."

"I am happy to have been wrong." Shoma's smile spread ear to ear.

Tian bit the inside of his lip. Certainly the Teleri were not so arrogant as to think they could take a village in unfamiliar terrain with so few swords.

Hati motioned everyone to quiet down. "Signal our Omiki kinsmen to target the Shaki archers when they are in range. They're our most dangerous threat."

The sound of heavy boots echoed down the gorge, just above the roar of the river. Then the first Teleri troops came in sight. Heavy infantry, wearing dress uniforms and steel helms with T-slots. Their shields were made of heavy ironwood, reinforced with steel. They carried short Teleri spears, meant to be used one-handed.

Behind Tian, all bravado melted away, overcome by worried chatter. Tribesmen pointed and muttered.

Swords and daggers hanging at the Bovyans' sides clanked as they marched single file, in perfect unison. Black banners with the gold sun fluttered in the gentle breeze.

Tian looked back and took stock of the men. None seemed to have panicked, though many clutched their spears with white knuckles. "Steady, my brothers," he said. "They can still only fight us one at a time. Their peripheral vision is poor because of their helmets."

Yuha flashed him a smile and chanted an invocation to the spirits. The men behind him settled down. Tian felt no different, though perhaps it was because he had fought for his life before.

At about twenty paces, the Teleri leader raised his hand to stop his troops. He walked forward, the insignia on his uniform and taller height marking him as a commissioned officer. A Shaki man skittered along the narrow gap between the soldiers and the cliff face, trying to reach the front. Tian and Hati went to meet with them.

The officer spoke first. "Brave and noble savages, you are hopelessly outnumbered by a better-armed force. Withdraw now, and you and your villages will be spared."

The Shaki started to translate, but Tian interrupted him. "Teleri captain, your numbers are meaningless in this gorge, and your armor is not impenetrable. Return to where you came from, or meet the point of our spears this afternoon." He raised and shook his spear with a falsetto shout, and even if the tribesmen didn't understand what he had just said, they joined in.

The officer laughed. "You must be the Cathayi who defeated our men. *You* may have faced us before, but *they* will cower in fear as they taste Teleri steel for the first time."

"You speak in big words for someone who hides behind the rest of your men. Or are you brave enough to try my spear first?"

The officer laughed again, though now with a hint of anger. "That stone spearhead will break on my armor. It is hardly a challenge. But perhaps if I dispense with you now, the savages will surrender." Turning back to his own men, "I will fight the Cathayi first. If I fall, Lieutenant, you take charge and begin the assault."

He turned to face Tian and dropped into a fighting stance, left foot forward and spear cocked back in his right hand. Both sides cheered.

Tian motioned Hati back and assumed a relaxed side stance with his right foot forward. He held his spear at the ready, left hand at the butt and the right about two feet up the shaft in the power-thrusting position. Standing ten feet away, the Teleri officer saluted.

Tian returned the greeting.

The officer hurled his spear and charged as he whipped out his sword.

Tian swatted the spear out of the way with a subtle motion. He stepped forward with his left foot, and stabbed with only his left hand to reach maximum spear range.

The Teleri ran right into the unconventional attack. The surgical thrust slipped through the opening of his helm, and he collapsed to the ground in a loud clatter.

Both sides fell silent, the only sound the gushing river at their side.

"Archers, shoot!" the lieutenant shouted. "A virgin to the man who fells the Cathayi!"

Tian rolled forward and worked the fallen officer's shield off his arm. He hazarded a glance up. Arrows arced from behind the Teleri line and descended. He held the shield above his head like a parasol and slunk back towards his comrades. Several stone arrow tips ricocheted off the wood.

"Omiki archers, shoot!" Hati yelled. "Maki men, attack!"

The Omiki on the south cliff and the Maki above them emerged from where they lay under the Teleri line of sight. Arrows filled the air.

The barrage at Tian ceased and he dropped the shield to the side. Retrieving his spear from the head of the fallen officer, he strode towards the Teleri troops.

They adjusted their shields to cover themselves from the enemy volleys coming from the south. Though the Omiki arrows just bounced off the shields, some hit the soldiers in the legs, slowing them down. Large rocks and arrows rained down on them from above.

Tian knocked the helm off the next Bovyan before he could even lower his shield. The back swing slashed across his eyes. Screaming, he covered his face. Tian stomped through his knee.

A spear thrust past the collapsing man, at Tian's face. Tian dropped his own weapon, caught the incoming attack, and yanked the attacker into the first. The two collapsed into a heap. Tian punched the steel-tipped spear through the second's knees. Yet, more Teleri came, picking their way among their fallen comrades. Injuries from arrows and stones didn't deter them.

Tian was precise and efficient, oftentimes killing or incapacitating an enemy with a single thrust. He gritted his teeth. It was easy. Too easy. The Bovyans' attacks, though skilled, left openings they meant for him to exploit. Why? He shot a glance back, seeing if he could pick out Shoma from the tribesmen gathered behind him.

Each Teleri he faced seemed more tired than the last, having faced a constant barrage of arrows and stones in the bottleneck. His own limbs tiring, Tian yielded his position at the head and allowed Hati to take over.

With his improved spear technique, Hati dispatched several while suffering only a few cuts. When he tired, he gave way to the next warrior. The Bovyans barely tried to defend themselves. And within an hour, they had fallen to a man. The surviving Shaki archers fled.

With the Maki's respect for life, they treated the Teleri survivors. Yuha led a prayer that would help guide the spirits of the fallen to rejoin the energy of the universe.

The Teleri lieutenant had suffered an arrow wound through the leg and sat up against the cliff wall. Tian picked his way toward him through the carnage. Like the others with exposed heads, the lieutenant looked older. Perhaps older than First Consul Geros. With the ancestral curse over their head, perhaps they had volunteered to be part of a suicide squad. But why?

The lieutenant nodded at him. "You are truly a hero of the ages. I would be honored if you helped me end my life, for I cannot bear the shame of leading my men to defeat."

Hold the butterfly with care, Kaiya had said, *for even their fleeting lives have value*. Tian bound the man's wound. "You lost on purpose. Why?"

The lieutenant choked on his laughter. "This is but one battle, and we have served our purpose in fighting it. There are not enough bottlenecks in this godforsaken forest to dam up the flood of Teleri soldiers. Once we control this region, the story of your valor tonight will be nothing but a footnote in history. If it is remembered at all."

A Bovyan would not break under torture, nor would the Maki condone it. With no other means of coaxing an answer out of him, Tian shrugged. "Maybe we will meet again on the field. Until then, farewell."

He turned to rejoin the warriors, who finished collecting valuable steel weapons. He searched for Shoma and was met with blank stares and shrugs when he asked about the Shaki guide. Had he been injured? Tian would've noticed. Suspicion gnawed at his gut. Perhaps the Bovyans were just gauging the natives' strength.

Or perhaps it was a diversion? But from what? If what Chief Nuwa said was true, there was no other practical approach from the east; and there were no reports of Bovyans to the west.

A few of the warriors went east to scout, but the majority headed west out of the gorge, looking forward to returning home with the story of their victory. Tian couldn't blame them, though worry fluttered in his stomach.

It was nearly nightfall when the tribesmen left the gorge. Coming to a pool in the river, Yuha made them strip down and bathe. He held a ritual to cleanse their spirits of their deeds, which Tian found surprisingly refreshing. Afterwards, they set up camp and ate dinner before settling down for the night. They sent the young twins Kona and Kosa ahead to send word to the village.

Most fell into a well-deserved sleep, though some sat around the fire, recounting the fight.

Hati grinned ear to ear. "It will be remembered like the battles of my father's time."

"It will only be remembered," Yuha said with a frown, "if our people maintain their freedom."

Just like the Teleri lieutenant had said. Tian nodded. "This is just a single battle. It won't stop their soldiers forever. They are ruthless and relentless. They will come again, maybe within a matter of days after they learn of their defeat."

Hati pumped his fist. "When word gets out that we can win, the other tribes will join hand to expel the Metal Men."

"We need to prepare for the next wave." Tian sighed. "Their fortress is four days from here. It will take their Shaki archers two days to take news there. If they run without rest. Then another four days for them to reach the gorge. We must set up our defense there again. Within at least six days."

"I prayed for the spirits to bring rain," Yuha said. "Combined with the melting snows, the gorge will be inundated in five days and remained closed for two to three weeks. By that time, we will have held a tribal council so that we can set up a collaborative defense of the gorge."

Tian pictured the terrain in his head. "Are there any other means of them reaching us?"

"Yes." Yuha nodded. "But in order to move so many troops, they would have to follow the old road going northwest, then turn back south along the path which we took when you first came to us. It would take them nearly three weeks, and our kinsmen would harass them the entire way."

Hati's tone sobered. "If they had enough boats, they could go along the south bank of the river and then cross at Wild Turkey Island. But they would have to carry the boats to that point, at least until the melting season ended."

Tian blew out a breath. "Then it seems that for the time being, we are safe."

Doubts and worry kept Tian from sleep. The others woke by dawn, ready to return home to a hero's welcome. The trip at regular pace would take fourteen hours, but the weather was pleasant, allowing them to forge ahead.

Tian's mind raced the entire time. Something still felt wrong. There must have been a reason for the Teleri to lose on purpose. Had they sent soldiers on the longer path?

At least the others' spirits were high as they reached the path off the river trail that would take them home. They arrived at the village not long before midnight, fully expecting late-night revelry.

All were taken aback by the sobering quiet, as Chief Nuwa greeted them with tears in his eyes.

CHAPTER 50:
War on Two Fronts, Part 1

Tian's gut churned. The mood among the villagers was too somber as they waited to greet a father, son, or husband. More concerning was Chief Nuwa seeking him out, even before talking to Hati.

He placed a firm hand on Tian's shoulder. "My son, I have awful news. Kaiya fulfilled Yuha's vision. She saved the village by sacrificing herself."

Tian staggered back. In the past, he had lost comrades on missions without flinching, but this... He choked back tears. "Where is she? What happened?"

His friends all gathered around, putting their collective arms around him. The chief let out a heavy sigh, and began recounting the cascade of events from the previous day.

On the morning of the evacuation, dog barks jerked Kaiya out of sleep. She panicked when she did not feel Tian by her side, forgetting in her foggy waking moments that he had left the day before. She shook her head clear. Outside, the village drums beat wildly. Erratically.

Danger.

Knowing that they would leave at first light, she'd slept in her clothes. Her hair was unbraided, certainly not proper for a married woman in public. She reached for her double swords and peeked out the lodge.

Shadows in the dim light ran by. The drums beat urgently, and one of the older tribesmen appeared, running through the village yelling, "We're surrounded by the enemy! Go to the center and prepare to fight!"

Fight? The warriors were all gone.

She hurried to the middle of the village.

Ma Jun stood at Chief Nuwa's side, giving instructions. Spears, bows, and arrows rested next to the drum platform. Middle-aged men, many who hadn't fought in thirty years, took up weapons and formed a perimeter around the village center.

Behind them, women also armed themselves with bows. Other villagers streamed in from all directions, many helping young children and the elderly. Arriving at the platform, Kaiya slung her swords over her shoulder and picked up a bow and a quiver full of arrows.

She waited for instructions, ignoring the drums, the murmurs of worried villagers, the crying of young children, and the barking of dogs.

Through the chaos, from the edge of the village, rang a loud voice with a distinct Shaki accent. "Surrender unconditionally, or face the wrath of the Metal Men."

Chief Nuwa raised his own voice. "We will not purchase our lives with our freedom, and you will not take either easily."

Mocking laughter echoed back. "Then prepare to die!"

A horn blared from outside the village, and the war cries and stomping boots approached from all directions.

Children wailed as mothers tried to comfort them. Men on the perimeter faced outwards with deathly resolve. Women nocked arrows, waiting for the first enemy wave to appear among the lodges.

Kaiya's heart raced. How useless she was. The bow in her hand would do little to save the people upon whom she brought doom.

No, there was a way. She placed her bow and quiver on the ground and climbed up to the drumming platform. The higher vantage point afforded a view of imminent disaster. Hundreds of Teleri light infantry marched in orderly ranks, supported by Shaki archers. Their bootsteps stomped in steadfast rhythm.

Taking up a pair of drum sticks, she set herself between the two drums, *Nimewa* and *Himewa*. Taking a deep breath, she channeled the valor of King Evydas of Iksuvi when he faced the First Consul; Sameer the Paladin; her loyal guards Xu Zhan, Li Wei, Zhao Yue, and Chen Xin; and of course, her beloved Tian. She struck the Soul of the Village. The drum's bellow resonated through the village, its steadfast rhythm meant to encourage the villagers.

Kaiya spun to face the larger drum, and used a single beat to send an ominous tone into the enemy ranks.

The Bovyans jolted to a stop.

She turned, rapped three beats on the smaller drum, and then leaned back and struck the larger. The rhythm filled her heart. Her limbs moved of their own volition, much like they had when she danced for Prince Dhannanad in Vyara City and First Consul Geros in Iksuvius.

The tribespeople chanted war cries in unison with the smaller drum. The fearless Bovyans backed off a step. Then they faltered back a few more. Heavens, it was working! All discipline collapsed. Teleri soldiers fell into full retreat.

Victory was in hand.

A single man stepped forward into the square. His feather and bead ornaments marked him as Shaki tribal shaman, and one of such power that her drumming dispersed around him. He raised his staff, whose crystal head captured the red rays of the now rising sun, and yelled, "Spirits, hear me!"

The villagers shot, but their arrows caught up in a whirlwind around him. He slammed the end of the staff on the ground. A thunder clap blasted forth. The Maki tribesmen collapsed to the ground, covering their heads in fright.

The rumble met the drum beats and dissipated. Fatigue rippled into Kaiya's limbs.

The shaman's face contorted. He raised his staff again, and shouted in a deep voice, "Spirits, shake the earth!" He pounded the staff.

The ground trembled. The pitch of the drums softened. The larger clattered to the platform. Kaiya twisted out of the way, barely avoiding it. Quickly regaining her footing, she continued to beat on the smaller drum to restore the Maki's confidence.

Beyond the first ring of lodges, Teleri horns blew again.

Her heart sank. They were regrouping, ready to resume their attack.

A dignified-looking Teleri general stepped forward and spoke in Arkothi: "Princess Kaiya Wang of Cathay, surrender yourself to the Teleri Empire, and the village will be spared. Not just for now, but for as long as the Empire endures. It will pay no tribute, nor take part in the Mating. It will for all intents and purposes be independent."

Kaiya ceased her drumming and met his gaze. "If you will extend the protection to the entire Maki tribe, then I will surrender."

The general's brows furrowed. "You have no room to negotiate. You are outnumbered by the best-trained, best-equipped fighters Tivara has ever known. Your men, elderly, and children will die; the women will be taken to serve our soldiers. And in the end, we will still have you."

Kaiya's stomach clenched. Like at the Battle of Wailian, there was only one bargaining chip left. Taking a deep breath, filling her heart with resolve, she unsheathed a sword and held it to her neck. "Then I will take my own life."

The general studied her, smirking. "You wouldn't."

She closed her eyes. She'd never feel the sunshine on her face, or feel the joy of a Dragon Song coursing through her again. Never see Tian again. Never have his children. Never hold those children in her arms. She took a blade and started—

"Stop!" The general let out a sigh. "Very well, we accept your offer."

Kaiya pulled up. Hands trembling, she staggered back a step. She'd almost killed herself.

He turned to a Shaki warrior and shouted in Arkothi. "Let it be known that immediately following the surrender of Princess Kaiya Wang, the Teleri will cease hostilities with the Maki tribe, and its peoples shall remain outside of our control in perpetuity. We will only fight them in self-defense."

Kaiya took in several breaths, trying to calmed herself as the Shaki translated the words.

The Maki murmured and wept among themselves. They made a path for Kaiya to walk through, many reaching out to touch her shoulder or thank her as she passed.

A figure stepped forward to block her way.

Ma Jun dropped to his knee, fist to the ground. "*Dian-Xia*, I will accompany you."

Kaiya found her tone of authority, long unused. "No, Ma Jun. This is my order. You must take care of Lana, your unborn children, and these people who have so generously accepted us."

She dropped her voice into a whisper and leaned in. Her voice hitched, forcing her to clear her throat. "Pass my message to Tian, these words that I could never say myself, even though we are no longer bound by the conventions of Cathay."

Ma Jun nodded.

Her brush with suicide had opened her eyes to truths she never told herself. "Please, tell him that I... love him. I love him so much, and want nothing more than to spend the rest of my life with him in this land and raise our children together. But I willingly make this sacrifice for something greater than me or him."

Ma Jun slid to the side, his head remaining bowed. Tears dripped down his cheeks.

A second person stepped in her way. "My daughter," Chief Nuwa said in his ageless voice. "We cannot trust that the outsiders will keep their word. We are willing to fight."

Kaiya shook her head. "Despite their evil ways, the Teleri are always true to their word. If they make this agreement, then they will abide by it. If you fight, you will surely perish."

He placed a heavy hand on her shoulder. "We will gladly die at their hands to spare you the indignities. You are one of us, and we never abandon our own."

Tears came unbidden, and she threw her arms around the chief. "As one of you, how could I allow my family to die at their hands? I gladly trade my freedom for yours."

Tearing herself away from his embrace, she strode towards the general. She then bowed, and extended her sheathed swords in two hands.

As the Teleri troops cheered, the general received the swords in one hand. He motioned for a captain. "The collar."

Collar? Were they already reducing her to a slave? Kaiya edged back.

The general locked eyes with her. "We will not consider you to have surrendered until you wear it."

Kaiya swept her gaze back at the villagers. Men too old to fight. Women, children. They'd all be slaughtered. She took a step forward and lifted her chin.

The captain bowed his head, and then affixed a hinged ring of grey metal around her neck. When he bolted it shut with a lock, the ubiquitous whisper of the world's energy was muffled in her ears.

"Now, General." Singing the next words, she said, "Withdraw your soldiers." The power surged in her chest, only to gutter at her throat. Energy trickled from her limbs.

It didn't work!

"In due time, Princess," the general replied. "First, there is the matter of the Teleri imperial seal. Where is it?"

The seal? Kaiya stared at him in genuine confusion. In the escape from Iksuvius, she'd forgotten about it. It must have been months. "I do not have it. It must be lost."

The general's eyes narrowed. "Lost? I find it hard to believe you would misplace such a valuable relic. Lieutenant Espios, search her."

An unarmored Teleri man, whose features and ruddy skin tone suggested his mother was likely a Kanin human, stepped towards her. He was slightly smaller than the average Teleri, which made him a likely candidate for a spy. Kaiya shrank back a step. How humiliating, to be touched by a stranger, an enemy.

"I swear by the spirits that it is not on my person," she said, invoking the oath of the Kanin tribespeople.

"I am afraid that means nothing to me," the General said. "However, if you swear on your honor, then we will delay the search until the doctor at our base camp examines you."

A doctor examining her. Kaiya shuddered. "I swear."

The general smiled, not unkindly. "Very well. Lieutenant, take a detail to search the princess' home. Remember, she belongs to the Consuls. I will ready the troops for our return to camp."

Belonged... of course, this was what surrender meant. Kaiya's heart tittered. She forced a serene composure. At least her dignity was safe for the time being, since the Consuls must be far away in the Teleri homeland.

"As you command." The lieutenant pounded a fist on his chest. He turned to her. "Take us to your dwelling."

She led them to her lodge. They upturned everything, even the cinders of the fire pit. Although their family altar was a simple flat river stone, it symbolized her tie to her ancestors, and she couldn't bear to watch the soldiers casually defile it. They went through her clothes, exchanging comments about her undergarments and looking sidelong at her with leers. The shell hair ring, which represented her marriage, was thoughtlessly crushed underfoot. By the time they were finished, tears clouded her vision.

The lieutenant motioned for the soldiers to leave. "We will give you two minutes to prepare what you want to take with you."

Left to herself, she cried. Was surrender worth it? Through tear-filled eyes, she gathered items of sentimental value and put them in her pack: among them, the remnants of her hair ring, her drawing of Guanyin, a head ornament of wild-turkey feathers, and the wooden bowl from the altar.

With a stick, she scribbled a message for Tian into the ground and covered it with a blanket.

After two minutes, the lieutenant pushed aside the door. "It is time."

Kaiya wiped away the tears. With one last look, she bid her home among the Maki goodbye.

It was still early morning as the Teleri troops departed the village. The Maki lined the path back to the river, bidding her sorrowful farewells. Despite the foreboding that sent shivers through her spine, she carried herself with a long-forgotten pride and poise. The villagers greeted her with looks of awe and inspiration. Her life as a Maki tribeswoman was coming to an end, and she was once again, a princess of Cathay.

Inside she shuddered. The dream was over, and a nightmare about to begin.

Tian hung his head, avoiding the gaze of the villagers. His wife, so courageous! Pride welled in his chest, even as his stomach twisted at the stark reality. Kaiya was a prisoner of the Teleri, enduring hell.

He squeezed his hands into bone-crunching fists. He would kill every last Bovyan, inflicting injuries that guaranteed a slow, painful death.

Chief Nuwa's voice radiated with a sad, fatherly pride. "Kaiya was so calm, so dignified. It brought inspiration to us all. Then, more than ever, we were so proud to consider her one of our own."

Tian shrugged the pack from his shoulders. It would only slow him down. "Where did they take her?"

"A scout followed them west to Wild Turkey Island. There used to be a holy shrine and a village of our Uloki kindred. It has since been taken over by the Metal Men."

"That is a twelve-hour march along the river." Yuha pointed west.

Tian straightened. He'd storm the camp alone if need be. "Then my brothers, I bid you farewell."

The chief placed firm hands on Tian's shoulders. "My son, you must rest. You will only be going to your death if you go alone and exhausted."

There was general murmur of agreement, but what else could he do?

He shrugged out of the chief's grip and took two purposeful steps before Hati crushed him in a bear hug. Tian twisted his hips, sending the chieftain's son to the ground. Three more warriors wrapped him up. Tian strained to break free, pulling them along. If they didn't give up, he might have to really hurt them.

Yuha placed a hand on him and chanted.

The energy of the spirits surged through Tian. A cool wave settled over him, the frenetic sensation of his rapidly beating heart and trembling limbs giving way to clear thought. The aches and fatigue weighed him down.

Yuha smiled at him. "There now, my brother, think with your head and not with your heart. Let us rest tonight. My prayer will calm your mind so that you will sleep well, and the spirits will show you a path if you allow them."

Every fiber of his body protested, but the spirits hushed their voice and lulled him into calm. Tian acquiesced and allowed Ma Jun to guide him to his lodge. Hati picked up the pack and followed.

Inside, it looked as though a storm had swept through. He ignored the clutter—even his compulsiveness to take stock of things was muted—and threw himself into his bedding, the one he would sleep alone in for the first time. Despite all the worries and concerns that should have nagged him, he fell into a deep slumber.

He woke up at dawn, feeling completely refreshed, as if the battle from two days prior and the hard march the day before had never happened. Yet, an unsettled feeling nagged at him. Had he dreamed? If so, he couldn't remember.

The morning light flooded in through the smoke hole, illuminating the mess made by the Teleri solders. Kitchenware was strewn haphazardly around the fire pit, bringing a bitter smile to Tian's face—although Kaiya now loved to cook, she was never good at cleaning up afterwards. It always fell to him to tidy up. Their clothes lay scattered about, each article bearing signs of a thorough search. What had they been looking for?

He turned to the long flat stone set up as their family altar. The wooden bowl they used for leaving a small daily sacrifice to their ancestors was gone. The altar's position seemed odd. He looked up. His crude sketch of Yang-Di, God of the Sun, looked at the empty spot on the wall where the drawing of his consort Guanyin once hung.

The blank spot on the wall! In his dream, Yang-Di had been looking down, pointing an open hand at the ground.

Tian turned toward the spot, covered by his bedding. He lifted it. Words were scrawled in the dirt, in beautiful Cathayi script: "I love you forever."

She must have written it, possibly in her last moments in the village. He choked on his tears. He should have told her the same, much like the young Maki lovers whispered in each other's ears.

The dream! In the dream, the words were not, *I love you forever*. What was written there? Try as he might, he couldn't remember.

He emerged from his lodge to find Ma Jun, Fang Weiyong, Lana, and the twins Kona and Kosa there waiting for him. They were packed.

Ma Jun bowed his head. "We will go with you, to Wild Turkey Island. Under the terms of their agreement with the Teleri, the Maki cannot engage the enemy, but they will be able to give us guidance."

Tian nodded, handing Ma Jun a steel Teleri longsword and dagger. "The Teleri troops have a two-day lead on us. However, it is light out. We can take a boat to the island. We'll arrive by mid-afternoon. I will free her tonight. Then we'll go by boat back to Cathay. We can't return to the village. Not until the Teleri threat has ended."

Buckling on a longsword and dagger of his own, Tian went to visit Chief Nuwa and Yuha. Even if he succeeded in rescuing Kaiya, he might not see the Maki for a long time. If he failed...

The chief, along with several others, waited for him in the middle of the village. Despite Tian's urge to get underway, he took long moments to warmly embrace all of these people whom he had become so close to, and bid each a farewell.

To Yuha, he said, "It was fate that brought us together on that cold autumn day. Among your people, I learned so much about what was missing in my life before."

Yuha placed a hand over his heart. "May the spirits guide you, my brother."

He turned to the chief. "I've had many fathers. The one who gave me life. The master who taught how to take life. I consider you my third father. The one who showed me how to live."

The chief looked at him with grave eyes. "May the spirits guide you to your love, and find her unharmed. Regardless of where you float on the tides of war and peace, you may always return here."

Tian then embraced Hati. "My brother. You will become a great leader. Like your father. With spear in hand. Bravely and proudly defend our people."

Hati crushed Tian in his hug. "Thank you, Brother, for all that you have taught me. You are a hero of our people, and the Warrior Beyond The Wall will live on in our songs as long as we have mouths to sing them. I had hoped you would honor me by serving as second in my wedding to Lahi next month, but I know that's not possible. So go now, with the spirits as your guide."

With a final look at the people he had come to love like family, Tian left the village, greeted on both sides by the tearful farewells of the tribespeople.

CHAPTER 51:
Hope and Fear

As the enormous Tree of Light came into sight, the symphony of natural sounds sang in Kaiya's ears. The chuckling river danced with the rustling wind, waltzing in harmony to the myriad chirps of a dozen different bird species. Like Ayudra Island, where she'd met the Paladin Oracle; like Shakti's Hill in Palimur where she'd faced Avarax, magic permeated the area.

She tried to remember a Cathayi chronicle of the ancient Kanin Empire:

The land around Wild Turkey Island is one of the last forested areas on the Kanin Plateau. It is now the private hunting preserve of the Emperor of Kanin, an oasis of trees among farmland stretching as far as the eye can see. A giant Tree of Light grows there, planted by the Elf Angel Aralas himself, just before the War of Ancient Gods. Yet even before that, legend has it that beneath the island is one of the glittering caves, where the elves unearthed a Starburst to aid them in their struggle against the orcs during the Twilight of Istriya.

She sighed in frustration. The resonance of the world called to her, should have made her body tingle with power, but the grey metal collar walled the energy off, keeping it just out of reach.

The Teleri troops had left the village some twelve hours earlier, marching along the path with tireless efficiency. They rested for only short amounts of time, affording her a pack horse so that she would not slow the fast-moving, well-conditioned troops.

General Altos di Bovyan strode beside her and had proven to be a gentleman. He allowed her hands to remain unbound and treated her with the utmost respect. He certainly didn't paint the picture of a brutal rapist.

A member of the elite Teleri Prospecti—the military officers and administrators—he stood even taller than most of his men. He called for halt and extended a hand to help her off the horse. "Your Highness, this is our last break before we reach our destination. Please rest well."

With a last glance at the Tree of Light in the distance, Kaiya took his hand and slid down. She curtseyed in the manner of the Arkothi. "General, I thank you for your courtesy. I imagine you might have made a fine Bovyan Knight, bringing order to the chaos following the Hellstorm and Long Winter."

The corners of his lips tugged slightly upwards as he bowed his head. "I appreciate your compliment, though I do not deserve it."

Maybe she could appeal to his sense of honor. If only she could convince him to take the collar off. "From what I have read, the Bovyan Knights were a noble order, and you certainly honor their legacy."

"They were. Their code of honor was derived from the Last Testament of Geros, our esteemed progenitor Geros Bovyan, mortal son of Solaris. Nowadays, we are taught we are successors of the Bovyan Knights, but sometimes I wonder if the code hasn't been corrupted to fit state ideology."

She studied his earnest expression. Apparently, Cathay's historians took an oversimplified view of the Teleri. "How did that happen?"

He returned her gaze. "In the time of our first ancestor, it was acceptable to take multiple wives. After the Hundred Years of War, the Hellstorm, and the Long Winter, there were so few men compared to women."

So it had been in Cathay, until the Queen Regent banned polygamy—not even the *Tianzi* could take a concubine. Kaiya nodded, prompting him to continue.

"Within a century, the ratio balanced and monogamous relationships became the norm. But since we can only have one child, always male, our population declined with each succeeding generation. It would have led to our extinction."

"I would think the Bovyan Knights would have rather gone extinct than resort to institutionalized gang rape." Which would probably be her fate, at the hands of the Consuls. Kaiya shuddered.

General Altos sighed. "The North was in a perpetual state of chaos. Had the Bovyans died out, how many more people would have suffered? Solaris meant for his son's descendants to bring peace. It was the only way. "

Was it? Apparently, even good men could rationalize evil deeds. "It's a peace bought with the dignity of all the girls you violate." And they were just girls, just starting their monthly cycles.

Brow furrowed, General Altos pressed his lips together. "It is hard for the conquered, but within a generation of Teleri rule, participation in the Mating is considered an honor." The retort came out rote, forced.

"You don't sound convinced."

He sighed and lowered his voice. "It *is* the case for women living in our heartland. Those who've given birth to a Bovyan enjoy a greater social station than non-Bovyan men. Their position is better than women in your country."

Kaiya favored him with a dubious eye, but prodded him to continue.

"But then, I became close to a woman. She confided in me the horrors we committed in lands we absorbed. It forced me to critically look at whether the peace and order we bring justifies the cruel means we use to achieve it. I began to question the Testament of Geros. It is written in a language that only the Keepers of the Shrine of Geros understand, so they control how it is interpreted."

"Surely there are others who share your sentiments?" If there were a rebellious faction, perhaps the Teleri could be changed from within.

He shrugged. "My views are in the minority, but there are those who idealize what the Bovyan Knights once were. Many of us were deployed to the Wilds instead of on a major front."

"It saddens me to think that even those who realize that the Teleri system is wrong do nothing to change it."

He gazed at her. "There is only one way to change us."

There had to be one. She raised an eyebrow.

He looked up to the sky. "An end to the Curse of Tivar, that cuts our life short at thirty-three, that bears us only sons, that keeps women from having but one Bovyan son."

If she could help end the curse... "How?"

"Fulfill our bargain with the Altivorc King. Or... " Altos regarded her with a curious eye. He leaned in and whispered, "There are some among us who believe an old story. When the Bovyan Edict was passed a hundred and twenty years ago, one young Keeper dissented, saying the methods were too brutal and that the Testament did not justify it."

Kaiya stared at him. At least some Bovyans took a moral stand. "What happened to him?"

"He was expelled from the Shrine of Geros. However, he used his newfound freedom to go on a pilgrimage to the pyramid in Arkos. The seer there prophesized that a Bovyan who knew his father and mother would take the Teleri imperial crest to the Tower of Light on the Eldaeri's Forbidden Isle. The knowledge he gained there would bring about the end of the curse."

Hope sprung in her. Jie had saved Aelward, an Eldaeri Prince and ship captain. He owed them a favor, and the Eldaeri would love nothing more than for the Teleri to leave them in peace. How hard could it be to find any number of Bovyans who knew their mother and father?

Altos shook his head, quashing her optimism. "Unfortunately, there are two sides to every story. The majority of the Prospecti dismiss the prophecy as a fairy tale; or worse, believe it prophesizes the world plunging back into a darkness rivaling the Long Winter. This is why magic is banned as the work of demons, why those with the gift of foresight are murdered. Bovyan boys who are born outside the Mating are quickly brought in, or hunted down and killed."

Kaiya's chest tightened. The murder of children, even Bovyan boys, was horrifying. Cathay might've been immoral in its weapon sales, but it didn't compare to the evil of the Teleri Empire.

He held his hand out to her. "We must be going. I will do my best to protect you, but know that once we reach Wild Turkey Island, I will not be the highest ranking officer."

After three hours, they reached a fork in the river. A bridge crossed over a narrow strait onto an island stretching about a *li* from end to end. The gigantic Tree of Light blocked the view of the Iridescent Moon, but from the height of the sun, it was clearly getting late. Her heart raced, the foreboding looming over her even more than the tree.

Besides the dozens of wooden structures, the island had a familiar feel. A few shrubs peeked out from the flat, rocky ground. A single hill rose at the southern end, jutting out into the larger river. Its hum, perceptible from where they had taken a break, buzzed in her ears now, the frequency so similar to... Palimur, where she'd confronted Avarax. Even the shape resembled the island where the Temple of Shakti stood.

Holding her chin high as if it would hide her fear, she strode across the bridge. What had the elf wizardess Ayana said about Palimur? That it was a glittering cave site, a place where the energy of the world welled? Her hand strayed to the collar. If only she could tear the damned thing from her neck, maybe she could repeat the improbable feat that had earned her the title of Dragon Charmer.

On the other side of the bridge, a waiting Bovyan yanked her wrist from the collar. Another clamped a hand on her shoulder. Her chest seized. Together, they pushed and pulled her towards a squat wooden building. No! What was happening? Where was General Altos? Struggling futilely against their powerful arms, she looked back.

He stood there, head hanging as the rest of the column dispersed around him. He'd said he'd protect her.

But now... Were these men going to violate her now? Pulse throbbing in her ears, she jerked against the men's grip, to no avail.

With her shoulders and head slumped, the Kanin woman standing by the entrance looked even more defeated than the general. She pulled back the animal fur door, the blue outline of a nine-pointed sun tattoo marring her wrist.

The two Bovyans shoved her in.

It was warm and humid compared to the brisk air outside, and dimly lit. Kaiya's heart skittered and her limbs froze up. Was this where she was to suffer a gang rape? She blinked away tears, and the room came into focus.

Steam drifted above a large wooden tub filled with water. The girl from outside—was it the same one, or was this a different girl? In her own panic, Kaiya hadn't noticed, but the body language was the same, screaming of hopelessness.

"They want you to take a bath," the girl said. "Please undress."

Kaiya looked back. The door had closed, the men out of sight. She blew out a long breath. The panic had been for nothing. As General Altos said, her rape would be at the hands of the Consuls themselves.

Perhaps even the First Consul.

She shuddered. Not that reassuring. Still, they would march her back to Tilésité, which might give her up to two months to preserve her dignity.

And perhaps escape.

At least a tiny bit assuaged, she shrugged out of the dress, which the woman took before leaving. Once alone, Kaiya sank into the comforting embrace of the water. It'd been months since her last hot bath, going back to the hot spring inn in Iksuvi. Probably one of the happier times. The warm waters soothed her now.

Maybe it was no different than calming a farm animal before taking it to slaughter. While she soaked, a maid entered, bringing towels and a clean white robe that smelled of honeysuckle. On top of it lay the undergarment she'd worn for Tian.

Kaiya rose from the bath, dried herself off and the clothes.

As she tied the open-faced robe in front, a young woman entered. Her broad features, fair complexion, and dark hair spoke of the Arkothi North. Her right wrist bore a sun tattoo, though unlike the girl's from before, it was brown. She bowed her head. "Greetings, Your Highness. I need to ask you several questions."

Kaiya's insides quivered, but she nodded. There was little point in fighting.

"When was your last menstrual cycle?"

It shouldn't have been a surprising question, given the Bovyans' abhorrent customs. Still, heat flared in her cheeks. She counted back. "Thirteen days ago, on the new White Moon."

Taking notes, the doctor maintained a professional expression. "Are you having any discharge, like raw egg whites?"

Heaven's Dew. "For two days now."

The doctor's brows furrowed. "Is that normal for you?"

"Always for a few days, before the full White Moon."

"So you are very regular. Please forgive my forwardness. Have you lain with a man recently?"

She nodded. "Two days ago."

Eyebrows clashing together, the doctor searched Kaiya's eyes. Then her expression relaxed. "Thank you. Be strong." With a bow of her head, she turned and left.

What could the doctor's expression mean? It would be months before they'd reach Tilésité, where the Consuls would do the unspeakable to her. If it turned out she was pregnant beforehand, would they force her to drink a poison which would kill Tian's baby? Her belly churned. All sense of relaxation from the bath drained out of her.

Two soldiers came in. Anxiety gripped her heart. Kaiya took deep breaths to calm herself as they bound her hands behind her back.

Flanking either side, they took her to the largest building. Inside, it was octagonal, with knotted wood floors and animal skins covering the windows. The roof slanted upwards on eight sides into a tip. What was this place?

Her focus fell on a throne, perched on a wood dais across from the entrance. A sconce in each of the eight corners held a light bauble. Maybe two dozen Bovyans lined the walls, all eyes undressing her.

Ice crawled up her spine. She pushed her shoulders forward as much as her bound hands would allow, as if it would cover her any better than the robe.

"Kneel." One of the escorts prodded her toward the center of the black octagonal carpet, which covered almost the entire floor.

They would get no satisfaction out of her, at least not without a little resistance. She straightened and lifted her chin.

The other guard shoved her down like a peasant, the plush wool softening the blow to her knees. His heavy hand pressed down on her shoulder as she fought to rise.

He was too strong.

Exhausted, she gave up the futile struggle and choked up a breath. She stared at the carpet's gold lattice designs so as to focus on something else besides the men's leers.

"Salute!" a soldier by the throne barked.

All the Bovyans thumped a fist against their chest.

She refused to bow, not from a kneeling position. Only the *Tianzi* himself deserved that respect.

The soldier at her side rewarded her defiance by pressing between her shoulder blades, pushing her prostate.

She gasped. She tried to straighten herself, but the man was unbelievably strong. Her nervousness and fear quickly gave way to anger.

From the entrance, heavy footsteps approached, stopping right in front of her. Kaiya tried to look up, but whoever it was placed a heavy hand on the top of her head.

Every muscle locked up. All she could see were large, bare feet, right by her face. He seized a handful of hair and jerked her head up. Fire flared in her scalp. Then every nerve went ice cold.

Geros Bovyan, First Consul of the Teleri Directori, glared at her.

Her heart leaped into her throat and she squirmed to back away. Her limbs wouldn't move. There weren't supposed to be any Consuls here.

Least of all *him*.

The one who'd sworn vengeance. Blood rushed from her head, and her vision dimmed. No, she wouldn't give him the pleasure of seeing her faint.

"Feisty as ever. I cannot help but admire your spirit." He patted her on the cheek before turning and strolling to the dais. Geros was dressed simply in a black, open-faced robe, which rustled as he walked. He lounged back on the throne, exposing a hairy chest.

On his right stood General Altos, still in uniform, his eyes downcast.

Kaiya winced. Geros wasn't supposed to be here. How? She forced herself to take a few deep breaths. Her heart slowed and her thoughts came into focus. Now upright, kneeling with a straight carriage, she returned his glare.

A long-term planner, Geros never expected his moment of vengeance to come so soon. He had left Iksuvius to personally oversee the restoration of the old Kanin roads, thinking the princess was trapped in the south of Iksuvi. Revenge had to be delayed in favor of starting the flow of shipbuilding lumber to his new deep-water port.

Or so he thought.

Geros now looked at the princess, proud but helpless as she knelt before him. No swords, no poison tea, the power of her voice bottled up by the Altivorc King's collar. Despite the image she tried to project, she reeked of fear.

He savored the scent.

Her eyes shifted to a spot behind him. Geros had seen it often, when someone hid their intimidation by trying to look through him.

It was easy to shatter that façade.

"It was a surprise to hear you were here in the Wilds. Quite the gamble you took, braving the dangers here." He leaned forward, and her gaze met his. He grinned. "Welcome to our new capital in Kanin."

Her expression remained unchanged. How could she stay so poised?

"But I digress," he continued in a pleasant, contrived voice. "We really do need to catch up. What has it been, six months already since we last met? I love what you've done with your hair."

Still no reaction, save for a shift in her eyes. Was it at General Altos? A childhood friend, a capable man in his inner circle, but weak.

It was time to make the princess squirm, to let her know who controlled the situation. He made his tone threatening, enough to intimidate a Bovyan officer. "You took something of mine. Something valuable. Where is it?"

Her irises darted back and forth, her expression one of genuine confusion.

"The imperial crest. This is the last time I will ask nicely." He tapped the spot where the pin once graced his chest.

The princess remained silent, her face serene, but her hands trembled. Just a girl. A scared girl.

Geros sprung to his feet. He yanked a dagger from the officer at his left and bounded towards her.

Mouth open in a silent scream, she shrank back, her bound hands not finding purchase as she tumbled to the floor.

He was quickly upon her, straddling her stomach. He let his weight sink onto her slight frame, leaving her gasping for air. He grabbed at the lapel of her robe and raised a fist.

She flinched, and he reveled in her terror. Now she knew how *he* had felt, when she left him on the Heights, helpless.

She turned her head to the side, and her voice came out as a hoarse whisper. "I don't know. I swear, it was lost."

He scowled. "Truly? When do you remember last seeing it?" Shifting his weight off of her, he wrapped a hand around her delicate neck and pulled her into a seated position. Her pulse fluttered beneath his grasp.

"It was here," she stammered. "In the Wilds, about five months ago. We were pursued by ogres."

Geros growled and tightened his grip. "Unbelievable. How could you lose the heirloom of our people? It has been passed down for three hundred years."

Her voice choked. "In the chaos of our escape, I forgot it was even in my possession."

He released his hold on her throat and shoved her onto her back as he rose to his feet. She gulped like a fish out of water.

"We will pursue this later." Stupid ogres. He turned to Altos. "At first light, send word to the ogres, find out when and where they captured this bitch. Our men will burn the forest down to find it, if need be."

The girl struggled to sit up, freezing in place as he turned back to her.

He sat on the edge of the dais, leaning forward with elbows on his knees. "Next order of business. Since you have been gallivanting through the Wilds, I will forgive you for not knowing about my recent promotion."

He waited, taking in her bewildered expression.

"I am now emperor."

Her brows furrowed.

"Which means I'm in need of an empress. And while the Keepers of the Shrine tell me I must keep three dozen concubines pleased, I really only have one woman in mind." He winked at her.

She shuddered.

So satisfying! He grinned. "So quiet. Are you going to make me ask? Very well. I want you to be my consort."

The soldiers shuffled, their discipline lost. Many exchanged glances.

General Altos stepped forward. "Your Eminence, what about your agreement with the Directori and the Keepers? What about the prophecy?"

Geros did not bother to look at the general, quieting him with an open hand. "Silence! I want to hear her answer."

Altos withdrew, and the men straightened. She looked at the floor, her lips quivering.

"If you do not tell me the answer I want to hear by the count of three, I will send orders to Iksuvius to torture and execute all seven hundred and forty-two of your countrymen, women, and children in our custody there. If you agree, they will all be released."

A tear trickled down her cheek.

"One."

Her voice came out, barely louder than a whisper. "Coercing consent and wrapping violation in formality is no less a rape."

Pretty words, deserving a clever response. But not now; this was too much fun. "Two."

The princess slumped, her voice choking. "I have no choice, then."

"Is that a yes?" He leaned forward.

A tear trickled down her cheek. At last, she nodded.

Geros looked around the room, triumphant, pointing an open hand at her. "She accepts!"

She let out a stuttered breath.

He strode over, squatted and lifted her chin with his hand. "I am overjoyed. Arrangements will be made tomorrow."

Tears trickled down her cheeks.

He leaned in and whispered in her ear. "In Iksuvius, you left me helpless and vulnerable, just as you feel right now."

She pulled against his grip, but it was easy to hold her fast.

He loosened the lapels of her robe, pulling them down to bare her shoulders as she tried to twist away. "Remember how I told you it was a mistake to leave me alive? What you would expect once I caught you?"

He dug his hands into her soft arms, relishing the fear and despair etched in her beautiful features.

"I don't care about your consent. Whether you are my consort or my bed slave, you will suffer the life of fear and humiliation I promised."

CHAPTER 52:
Wild Turkey Island

The dugout journey downriver passed in a haze for Tian. The focus and observational skills he relied on were useless. His stare locked on the muddy waters kicked up by spring melt. On occasion, food would be put in his hands, or some tribesman along the shore would draw his attention with a wave. Otherwise, it was all a blur.

A gigantic cherry tree appeared on the horizon, its trunk as thick as a castle, its canopy vaulting far above even the towering greywoods. A similar tree supposedly grew near the Cathay pyramid by Teardrop Lake, but Tian had never seen it himself. The sheer immensity jolted him out of his grief-induced stupor.

How much time had passed? He looked towards the Heavens. The afternoon sun nearly drowned out the Iridescent Moon, which waxed to its second crescent.

He turned to Lana. "How far are we from the island now?"

"Maybe two hours?"

And another four hours until nightfall. Tian tapped his chin. "Let's stop. Before we come within sight of the island. To scout the area out. The White Moon is full tonight. I'll only have a narrow window of opportunity. To penetrate the camp while it's dark."

Lana shook her head, pointing at the enormous tree. "No, when the sun goes down, the tree glows."

Tian favored her with a dubious eye, though he vaguely remembered hearing something about the tree in Cathay glowing at night. He would soon find out, either way.

About three *li* away, they came ashore on the north bank of the river and stowed the boat among pink-budded shrubs. Avoiding Teleri patrols, they crept along the bank until they were close enough to observe activity on the island.

Tian pointed them in different directions to get multiple vantage points, and gestured for them to regroup at dusk.

Working his way through the brush, Tian came to a large tree. Its knotted trunk provided handholds and crevices. He slunk up, coming to a high perch with a view of the entire island.

Never before had he seen such an almost perfectly oval, one-third a *li* wide and one *li* long. The western side bordered a swift-flowing tributary—the same one they'd had followed months ago just before the ogres captured them. Despite the name, there were no signs of turkeys.

The southern end of the island jutted into the North Kanin River, right where the riverbed made a hard turn south. Horns blared from a guard tower that stood atop an almost perfectly circular hill there. It probably provided a commanding view over the entire area, making a daytime insertion difficult.

Ogres led a train of bound Kanin tribespeople over a bridge at the northern tip of the island, which spanned over the tributary to the opposite bank. They wove through the dozens of tribal lodges and newer wooden barracks, and delivered the slaves to the stockade.

Black smoke billowed from two stone buildings, along with hammering that suggested armorers hard at work. Shaki tribesmen fished from the shores, while others rendered large game. Kanin women slaved at roasting the meat over large fire pits. And of course, Bovyans drilled in an open field in the middle of the island. They were holding Kaiya somewhere.

Fists balled tight, Tian shifted his gaze to the eastern bridge near the field, not far from his hiding place on the opposite shore. Narrower than the first, it spanned a strait of slow-moving water. With two guards at the bridge, rotating watches precisely on the phases of the Iridescent Moon, he'd likely have to swim.

When he regrouped with the others, they formulated a plan; one which had little probability of both him and Kaiya surviving. If he found her at all.

Late at night, after activity on the island died down, Tian stripped down to his underwear. Carrying only a dagger and his pouch of tools, he swam through the cold, dark waters of the strait. Though not a religious man, he could not believe it was just luck that storm clouds gathered above, blotting out the full White Moon.

Just as Lana said, tendrils of pale blue light trickled out from the tips of the gigantic tree's buds. Hopefully, it was not enough to expose him during his approach. He paused as he drew closer to the shore, waiting for a patrol to pass. When he gained the bank, he dashed towards a fire pit and covered himself in ash and soot.

Keeping to the shadows, Tian crept over to the cabin where he'd seen female prisoners held. A Teleri soldier paced the length of the building's front wall. Tian set himself up around one of the corners.

The Bovyan approached.

Hold the dragonfly with care. No, not tonight. Tian tightened his grip and—

Another solider stumbled out the door.

Relaxing, Tian waited and watched. The two soldiers exchanged greetings and the second ambled off into the camp.

The sentry reached the corner and turned on his heel. Tian stepped behind him, covered his mouth, and slashed his throat. After a quick glance to ensure no other Bovyans were around, he dragged the body inside.

Gasps greeted him. With their faces dimly lit by shuttered light baubles, a few Kanin tribeswomen covered their mouths. Their right wrists were tattooed in a blue outline of the nine-pointed Teleri sun. Their expressions spoke of fear and humiliation. Several others lay asleep on crude beds. To the far right of the entrance, crude animal skins covered four doorways. Behind one came the grunts and whimpering of forced intercourse.

His blood boiled. In all likelihood, it wasn't Kaiya serving the rank and file; it certainly didn't sound like her. Nonetheless, her rapist deserved nothing less than a painful death.

Tian motioned for the women to stay silent. He pointed to the side rooms and then the dead soldier. Hopefully the women understood him.

The closest put up one finger and pointed at the occupied room.

He made a quick appraisal of each. Glimmers of hope peeked out from expressions of defeat and despair.

In the occupied side room, the sounds stopped. Tian bounded over and waited at the side with dagger in hand. When the Bovyan stepped out, Tian severed his carotid artery while muffling his yelp with his free hand.

A couple of the women sucked in sharp breaths. Luckily, none screamed.

He dragged the body into one of the empty rooms, which reeked. When he emerged, most of the women were awake.

"Have you seen a Cathayi woman?" he asked.

One of the women nodded. "She was brought to the doctor two nights ago."

"Where's the doctor?"

The woman pointed east. "Two lodges over."

"Wake the rest of your sisters. Tell them to prepare to flee. I'll be back soon for you."

Tian ducked out of the cabin and slunk over to the doctor's lodge. Shadows cast by the flickering firelight in the pit indicated one person was awake. Waiting for the silhouette to move closer to the door, he burst inside. In the split second it took him to reach the person's back, he noted nobody else was there. He put a hand over the man's mouth and the dagger at his neck.

"Not a word," he whispered.

His now-rigid hostage nodded. The size and build... it was a woman. Likely another slave.

He spun her around, keeping the blade at her neck. She was... Arkothi, late-twenties, with dark hair and broad but attractive features. "Where is the doctor?"

"I *am* the doctor." Her voice was low and she showed no fear. "Who are you, and what do you want from me?"

Such bravery. And a doctor? Tian stared at her. "Where's the Cathayi woman?"

Her expression deflated. "Kaiya. She is gone. Such a nice girl, poor thing."

"What?"

"She was very fertile when I met her. You know what Emperor Geros did to her."

Emperor Geros? Emperor? Here? Tian's heart squeezed. It was all he could do to draw a breath. "I'm her husband."

The doctor's eyes narrowed at first, then softened. "I'm so sorry. They left yesterday morning by boat, en route to the next fortress downstream. After the threat of snow ends, they plan on taking her along the restored roads eastward, back to Tilésité."

Tian's stomach roiled. He was too late. He jabbed a finger at her. "How can you willingly be part of this?"

She looked down at the ground. "I'm from the city of Mirkos, conquered by the Teleri nearly fifty years ago. My grandmother was a noble there, subjected to the Mating by members of the Teleri Prospecti. After she gave birth and went home, she married someone of her station and my mother was born and suffered the same fate. Later, I was born. When I was fourteen, I happily went to the Teleri." She held up her hand, exposing the nine-pointed sun tattooed in brown to her wrist.

She didn't look sad or traumatized. Still, there was something she wasn't telling him. Tian stared at her feet.

"Though I never knew them, I have both a Bovyan brother and son somewhere. Maybe my unknown son is still alive after all these years of constant war. I have to hope the Bovyans are not all evil."

No telling who her brother or son had harmed. Tian snorted.

She glared at him. "The circumstances of my Bovyan brother's conception, according to my mother, gives me faith. He will end Tivar's Curse."

Fairy tales. Or rationalization. Tian leveled his gaze at her. "You act a lot on your faith in a story. To me, you are deceiving yourself. You're aiding an evil empire."

Her angry look melted. "My faith was rewarded by a kind Teleri general. As much as I abhor their practices, I came here to serve under that general, to see to the well-being of not just the soldiers, but also the prisoners."

Perhaps she was sincere. He pointed out the door. "I'm going to free those prisoners. Will you help me?"

Her eyes searching his. "Yes. If you can disable the guards at the stockade and women's quarters."

"Those at the women's quarters are taken care of."

She jabbed him in the chest with a finger. "No killing. Meet me by the eastern bridge in ten minutes. Take me hostage, and that will buy the prisoners some time to escape."

She seemed sincere enough. Could he trust her? If she could take a leap of faith about Bovyans, he could do the same for her. Not like there was any other choice, except to kill her now. *Hold the dragonfly with care.* Tian nodded.

Making sure nobody was outside, he snuck back to the women's cabin. All twelve women were prepared to leave.

He handed a woman the dagger from the slain Teleri soldier. "I'm going to free the men. In three minutes, head to the eastern bridge. As quickly and quietly as you can."

After another quick look into the camp, Tian moved on to the stockades and signaled the men inside to keep quiet. He rendered the guard unconscious with an artery block and took his dagger. Finding the key, he unlocked the chain securing the prison door. "Follow me to the eastern bridge. Quickly and quietly."

They didn't meet Tian's standard of quiet. It was such a large group. In the two-minute run to the bridge, horns blared throughout the island.

Near the bridge, two guards were talking with the doctor.

"Guards!" Tian yelled. It was the signal for Ma Jun to neutralize the sentries on his side of the bridge, and would hopefully attract the two guards with the doctor.

It worked. They rushed him, weapons drawn.

Tian flung two daggers, which hit each in the throat. The doctor screamed and ran over to the fallen men.

A voice roared to his left. "Spirits, hear me!"

Tian turned. A Kanin shaman strode towards him from thirty feet away. He held a crystal-headed staff in hand.

Only one dagger left, and no other choice but to use it on what could be a major threat. Taking the doctor hostage would have to wait. He charged, dagger ready to throw.

The shaman pounded the butt end of his staff into the ground. "Open the clouds!"

The storm clouds above flashed, and a bolt of lightning shot down towards Tian. Even a Paladin's superhuman reflexes wouldn't save him against the speed of nature. Yet the electricity sizzled and dissipated around him.

Tian stopped in his tracks, stunned but unharmed.

If he was surprised, the shaman looked even more so. His mouth stood agape, his eyes wide. Tian resumed his charge, coming within fifteen feet. He hurled his weapon, just as the shaman raised his staff.

Instead of a chant, nothing but a muffled groan came out as the shaman staggered back, clawing at the dagger lodged in his ribs.

Tian scanned the area to reassess the situation. Prisoners flooded over the bridge, pursued by several Teleri soldiers. Horns shrieked, rousing the camp out of sleep. He picked the doctor out of the crowd—she still crouched over the fallen men, pressing on their wounds.

He bolted over to her, and she stood up with a bloody dagger in hand. Tears glassed over her eyes. "Why did you do this? We had a deal."

Tian shook his head. "No time to think. No other way to free the prisoners." Would she still play along with being taken hostage? He'd soon find out.

Her eyes darted behind him, and she clumsily stabbed at him.

Tian caught her arm, twisted it behind her back and swiped the blade away. He then turned to face the approaching Teleri, backing his way towards the bridge with the point of the weapon to her throat. Waiting until the last prisoner passed, he retreated to the middle of the bridge and stopped. The Teleri soldiers followed, keeping their distance. They stopped about ten feet from him.

Tian pointed the tip at them. "Bring your leader."

The Bovyans discussed his demand among themselves, but before they said anything, a handsome man, taller than the other soldiers, approached. His unbuttoned white shirt exposed firm muscles and his pants hung unbelted at his hips.

"I am General Altos, and I command this camp. Release the doctor."

Tian smiled tightly. "Only if you agree to let the prisoners go and to never take any more."

The general's lips pursed. "You know I cannot agree to such terms. However, release her and I will give the prisoners a one-hour start."

Tian shook his head. "Wait until first light."

"Very well." The officer nodded. "We are agreed. We would have a hard time tracking them in this dark night anyway."

"Back off to the island, and I will send the doctor across. If you show any signs of trickery, I will throw this dagger into her back."

"You have my word. We will not pursue the prisoners until daybreak."

"Nonetheless, back off the bridge." Tian repeated.

The general retreated, motioning his men with him.

"Thank you," he whispered into her ear. He pushed the doctor forward and let her get about thirty feet in front of him—about the maximum accurate range of his dagger—then followed her to stay in range. Once she reached the island, he turned and broke into a run towards the other side.

"Now, now!" he yelled.

On the opposite bank, Lana chanted. A deafening roar rumbled from upstream, and the bridge shook as the waters swelled beneath it. Tian teetered over the planks, his balance just barely keeping him from being pitched into the rushing waters in the strait below. The less agile Teleri soldiers, running behind him, lost their balance.

On the other end, Ma Jun and the twins waited in the dugout, and Lana was just climbing in. Tian leaped aboard, right as the deluge picked it up and carried it downstream.

Ma Jun stared in awe at his wife. "I didn't realize that your tie to the spirits was so strong."

"It was the island itself," she answered. "This is where our ancestor relearned the way of the spirits, when the lights of the Tree guided him here during the Long Winter. His invoking of the spirits began the transformation of the barren farmland around. The forest reseeded and grew at an accelerated pace. All shamans used to make a pilgrimage here, because the spirits speak louder here than anywhere else on the plateau."

Tian looked back towards the island, the sparkling tree above it disappearing in the distance. "I wonder why their shaman's lightning strike did not affect me."

Lana cocked her head, her eyebrows furrowed. When she spoke, she didn't seem convinced, herself. "At night, when the Tree lights up, the spirits cannot go under its canopy."

Tian nodded. However, he hadn't been under the canopy when the lightning struck.

Back on the island, General Altos looked over his assembled staff, his heart beating with excitement. "Get the Shaki to track the Cathayi. I need him captured alive."

The Doctor Myra turned to him, her hand over her mouth. "General, you have never gone back on your word! Were you not going to give him until daybreak?"

Altos was surprised that she would question him in front of his men, but grinned, nonetheless. "I gave the *prisoners* until daybreak."

Her lips pressed into a tight frown.

He turned to one of his officers. "Send word to all of our outposts, base camps and fortresses: the Cathayi man has the Teleri Imperial Crest."

Myra leaned in. "He is the one who slept with the princess before Emperor Geros."

Altos jerked his head back. "If she's pregnant, and Geros raises a non-Bovyan as his own... "

CHAPTER 53:
Impossible Mission

Tian looked up as the storm clouds parted, allowing columns of sunlight to shine through after days of continual rain. Though Lana's invocation of the spirits had transformed the downpour into a drizzle, the boat ride was far from pleasant. Each night, they camped on the eastern side of the river, to avoid the Teleri soldiers marching up and down the west bank.

Late on the fourth day after their escape from Wild Turkey Island, they turned a bend in the river. A massive tower rose high above the sweet evergreens, looming larger and larger as dugout approached. The bridge arching across the river was so big, Tian could see it from many *li* upstream. As they drifted closer, it became apparent the tower and bridge were all part of one massive fortress.

The one where the Bovyans held Kaiya, at least according to the doctor. Tian's every nerve stood on end. If they could see the tower, then anyone there with a dwarf scope could see them. Clearly.

They brought the dugout ashore on the east bank, far from the fort. Finding a dirt trail with no signs of human use, they hiked the rest of the way under the cover of the canopy. The path rose along a gradual slope, eventually opening up onto a thirty-foot-wide corridor through the forest. A broad road paved in stone ran through it.

Tian peeked around a tree. The road connected to the bridge, which in turn led into the fortress. Along the sides, slaves cut down trees, hauled lumber, and worked on the roads. Shaki hunters carried game back. Bovyans marched in formation to and from the fort. If the wilderness had claimed the stone roads after the Hellstorm, it looked like the Teleri were taking them back.

Across the river, the fortress looked like a feat of engineering. It sat atop an embankment the height of three men, on a peninsula formed by the bend of the river. A log palisade, twelve feet tall, encircled the mound. The single entrance, connected to the bridge and flanked by two guard towers, sat at a height of fifteen feet above the river.

Tian looked up. Though it was hard to tell from the lower vantage point, the central keep rose about three stories high, with a towering greywood growing out of the center. Wooden steps circled up and around the trunk, leading to a lookout post near the top, under its canopy.

The forest beyond the palisade had been cut down in a one-*li* radius, and the few small buildings in the clearing would provide little cover if someone tried to approach from that side of the river. It didn't look promising.

Tian looked among the men, evaluating. Ma Jun and the twins, Kosa and Kona, could fight, and Fang Weiyong could help tend their wounds. None would be helpful for scouting out the fortress interior, and it would be suicide to storm it.

He turned to Lana. "I need to find out about the inside of the fort. Most importantly, if Kaiya is there. Can the spirits do anything to help?"

Lana withdrew her talisman, a bright blue river rock, polished by time. "Spirits, hear me," she whispered. "Summon the eyes and ears of the forest to do my bidding."

Eyes and ears of the forest? Tian looked around, blanking his expression to hide his doubt.

Birds, squirrels, and other small animals trickled in by foot and wing, their chattering growing to crescendo.

Lana squatted down and smiled. "My little friends, tell me about the house over the river." She gestured toward the Cathayi. "Please find out if there is a female like these men inside."

Tian suppressed a snort. Most humans had a hard time differentiating between Cathayi and Kanin. How would a stupid animal tell?

Lana narrowed a critical eye at him. Were his thoughts that obvious? "A bird of prey can pick out a squirrel in a tree branch from high in the sky. The squirrel can sense the bird. Do not underestimate my friends."

The animals all glared at him. Tian placed his right hand over his heart in apology.

With more chattering, they scattered off towards the fortress.

After sending Ma Jun and Lana to survey the road, and assigning Fang Weiyong to watch the river, Tian and the twins climbed sweet evergreen trees to get a better view of what lay beyond the palisade. What he saw made the prospect of attack all the more daunting.

Besides the guarded entrance from the bridge on the east, there was another entrance on the western side, from which the stone road continued. The main keep appeared to be made partially of living trees, with horizontal log walls covered by dried mud. Soldiers milled around barracks, while slaves came and went from another large building. Kitchens, warehouses, a smithy, and a lumber mill all stood within the palisade walls.

Tian pictured the map in his mind. Right now, they were about one thousand, eight hundred *li* from the Teleri border, less than six hundred *li* from Cathay. If at least some of what the Shaki guide said had been true, another outpost stood west of here, even closer to the motherland. These old roads, which the Teleri worked hard to restore, must connect several fortresses so that the empire could project their power into the Wilds.

How long had the Bovyans been here? How had they built up the infrastructure so quickly, especially with so much of their attention focused on the Eldaeri kingdoms and Arkothi states in the Northeast? With Cathay's distance from Teleri, their threat had never seemed imminent. Perhaps First Consul Geros truly was the genius the stories portrayed him to be.

Tian swallowed his sigh. Cathay could no longer be content in its neutrality, resting secure behind its walls while promoting trade to fatten its own coffers. Beyond the practical need to maintain its own security, there was also a moral obligation to take a stand and choose a side. Being a member of the Maki, even for this brief time, had taught him that.

Yet to convince the *Tianzi* and the *Tai-Ming* nobles would be an entirely different matter. Perhaps Heaven had willed for the Teleri to capture their beloved princess, to wake them out of their complacency.

The vision from his last night in the village flared in his memory. The words on the ground in his dream were *accept fate*. Was he meant to accept this, the kidnapping and rape of the only woman he'd ever loved? Were they to make this sacrifice so that others would learn?

He tightened his hand around a tree branch. No. Forget Heaven, forget fate. He'd make his own destiny.

Night fell, and activity died down in and around the fortress. The group reassembled back at the dugout and used the cover of darkness to pass beneath the great bridge. Reaching the other side, and following the river as it bent west beside the fortress, they set up camp in the woods.

"I estimate their fortress can hold three thousand soldiers," Tian said.

"There are hundreds of our own people as well," Kona added.

Lana shook her head. "I can't imagine how horrible they must feel, forced to cut down the trees."

"Even if the tribes united, they couldn't take this fort," Kosa said.

Kona nodded. "And the rumors say there are other fortresses like this one throughout the plateau."

Tian tried to keep the agitation out of his voice. "Its defenses are daunting. Even if I had a layout of the main keep. Even if I knew where Kaiya was being held. I'm not sure I could get her out. Let's sleep on it, find out what Lana's forest friends learn."

Tian didn't sleep well. His thoughts were on Kaiya.

The next morning, Lana related what the forest animals had told her: a Cathayi woman was staying in a third-floor room on the northern side of the main fortress.

At least Kaiya was close. Still, she was beyond his reach, at least with the resources at hand.

Tian withdrew Chen Xin's ring, bowed his head to it, and pressed it into Fang Weiyong's hand. "Take the boat down the river to the East Gate of Cathay. Show the ring to the imperial garrison. Inform them of our situation. Have a message delivered to the capital. Asking for twelve Black Fist."

"Black Fist?" Fang Weiyong raised an eyebrow.

Tian frowned. "Just do it. Take Lana with you so that she can guide you back to us. It will take a week for you to get there by boat. Two weeks to return by foot, at best. If there's any change in the situation, I will leave a message on this tree that my brothers-in-arms will understand." He patted a greywoood trunk.

Fang Weiyong nodded, though his pursed lips made clear what he thought of the plan.

As long as he did what he was told. Tian turned to the others. "In the meantime. We'll learn as much as we can. About the fortress and surroundings."

After the doctor and Lana pushed off, Tian sent Kona and Kosa east down the river to investigate the progress of the road, while Ma Jun watched the entrance. He, himself, scouted out the strengths and weaknesses of the fortress.

Over the next few days, he noted that several tribes besides the Shaki had allied themselves with the Teleri. All wore unfamiliar clothing styles and face paint, but they clearly served in support roles: as trackers, hunters, and archers. The slave overseers among them were lazy, and on the third day, Tian isolated a pair of Maki slaves sent to fell a tree.

He greeted them with a right hand in his open left, and spoke in their dialect. "I am Tian. From Swiftrun Village. Who are you?"

They gawked at him. "The Warrior From Beyond The Wall," one said. "I am Nala, from Blackhawk Village."

The other furrowed his brows.

Tian pointed toward the fort. "Is it true that a Cathayi woman was brought here?"

Nala bobbed his head. "Yes, the Willow Beauty. She arrived several days ago with the Metal Man chief."

"The chief?" Likely First Consul Geros himself. Tian clenched his fists.

"Yes, but different from other chiefs. He never leaves the main fort. The maids say he's always with the Cathayi girl."

Tian's face flushed hot. Damn Geros. He would die horribly. "Which tribes help the Metal Men?"

Nala clenched his fists. "The Pomaki from the west. The Lahoki and Shaki from the east, and the Komaki from the south. All made deals with the Metal Men."

Someone speaking a Kanin dialect yelled from the distance. "Hey! You lazy Maki get back to work!"

Tian backed into the trees. "Thank you. I will try my best to free you. In the meantime, please find a way to tell the Cathayi woman I am here."

Tian wasn't sure if the Maki passed his message on. He continued with his surveillance, nonetheless. It was hard to fight the urge to go find Kaiya, but information could improve his chances of success. Thousands of Bovyans arrived from the east and departed west along the road. Undoubtedly they were building strength closer to Cathay. Delegations of many of the Teleri-allied tribes arrived on the twenty-first day of the month, and left two days later.

By then, he'd learned the patterns for the changing of the guards, sending out patrols, mess times, and slave routines. The eastern wall, facing the river, was the least guarded... probably because the slope up to the palisade and river provided formidable defense against an attack.

Confident in this knowledge, Tian tried a few dry runs during the night, to see if he could get in unnoticed. The most daunting obstacle was trying to swim across the river, whose current flowed strong with snow melt.

Instead, he climbed under the bridge inverted, then landed on the narrow bank on the eastern side of the fortress. He crept to the south and found the earthen ramparts easy to negotiate. At the top, his cat-claws made scaling the palisade manageable. After two nights of experimenting, he was finally in. Still, as dexterous as she was, Kaiya would never be able to do the same.

It had been five days since the others had departed. If all went well, a team of Black Fist would be there to assist him in two weeks.

Two weeks!

The next day the twins returned, reporting that the restored roads stretched west for at least another three-day march, if not more. They witnessed plenty of activity, with slaves cutting down trees and dumping them into the river, and heavy infantry marching down the road.

For each of the next three nights, Tian infiltrated the fortress, identifying hiding places and locating potential access points to the main keep itself. There was just one entrance, facing south, flanked at all times by guards. The windows were all too small for him to fit through— if only Jie were around, she could squeeze in some of the upper windows.

On the second-to-last night of the twelfth month, the small sliver of the White Moon threw the fortress into darkness. Tian took advantage of the dark and scaled the western outer walls of the central keep to investigate the roof. With sixteen guards circling along the perimeter, he didn't climb all the way up, but instead peeked over the edge. Open space surrounded the single greywood tree tower protruding from the center of the building. Stairs spiraled down the tree to... another entrance. A way in, if only he could get by the sentries... Impossible without a diversion, given their patrol pattern.

If Lana's forest friends were right, Kaiya was close. On Tian's descent, he edged across the third floor, listening at each fur-covered window he passed. The sonorous sounds suggested large, sleeping men.

Arms aching and listless, he somehow rounded the corner to the fort's north face. Fifteen window slots were spaced ten feet apart. If she wasn't in one of those rooms, his energy wouldn't last long enough to find her.

Heavy wooden slats blocked the twelfth window. The thick fur cover muffled the sounds inside, but... yes! Kaiya's familiar breathing. He reached between the slats—

Wood furniture creaked in rhythmic screeches. Geros Bovyan's voice, husky in a loud whisper, professed his love for Kaiya. Her heavy breaths sounded wrong in his ears.

Rage boiled in Tian's head. His foot slipped from one of the crevices, with only the cat-claws on his hands keeping him from falling.

Kaiya was suffering.

The man who caused it needed to die. Slowly, painfully. Tian's vision dimmed at the edges.

Years of training brought his immediate impulses under control. His foot found purchase. Logically, what could he do? He had no leverage to break the heavy wooden bars, no way to slip in even if he could get past the slats. Anything he did now would just get him killed and leave Kaiya helpless at the rapist's hands.

No. His only recourse was to climb down and move far enough away that other noises would drown out the terrible sounds crushing his heart. Only then could he think clearly.

He fled the fortress as quickly as he could, trying to banish the memories of Kaiya's ordeal still echoing in his head. Muttering a terse greeting to Kosa and Kona, he climbed a tree to be alone with his thoughts.

After this foray into the fortress, two things were clear: even if he could break in, he wasn't sure how he could escape with her; and if Fang Weiyong had reached Cathay in eight days, he would still have to wait another two weeks for reinforcements. Too long. And maybe still not enough resources to free Kaiya.

Though his strategic intelligence told him there was zero chance of success on his own, his impulse said otherwise. Tomorrow night, he would go in alone.

CHAPTER 54:
Realizations and Confessions

Kaiya was late.

She was never late. Always as accurate as a dwarf-made clock, her monthly cycle reliably started when she woke the day of the new White Moon.

She'd looked forward to the debilitating cramps this morning, hoping it would provide her a temporary reprieve from the daily violations at Geros' hands. Now its failure to appear raised new fears.

What had Doctor Wu told her? *From when the flood waters receded, until about two weeks after it began, Heaven's dew would allow a seed to find fertile ground?*

If only she'd listened more carefully instead of drowning out the graphic details. She counted off the days. Nineteen days since last making love to Tian. Eighteen since she surrendered to the Teleri. Sixteen since the emperor had taken her for the first time.

She choked back bile at the thought of Geros' calloused hands. Sitting on a soft bed in a narrow room, Kaiya brought her knees to her chest and wrapped herself tightly in her arms. A tear trickled unheeded down her cheek.

When her nightmare had begun, she'd forced herself into a state of denial, tried to emotionally numb herself to the humiliation of his assault.

It didn't work.

His insatiable lust dragged her down into depression. She considered throwing herself from the top of the fortress; but a bird came back day after day and sang to her. Its song perked her spirits up and gave her some resolve.

On several occasions, Teleri generals prodded Geros to go oversee construction of the next fortress downstream—one which would put them uncomfortably close to Cathay, if her poor map skills were even a little accurate.

She had to keep him here.

Without the power of her voice, all she had were her body and wiles. Like the tale of Lady Lanyu, concubine of a warlord during Cathay's Warring States Period. He'd sent her to a rival king, ostensibly to seal an alliance. Really, it had been to break his enemy's focus as he became besotted with the girl. Still, a little part of Kaiya died each time she pretended to have fallen in love with the vile monster.

Then, word from a Kanin slave girl that the Warrior From Beyond the Wall was outside the fortress gave her a glimmer of optimism.

That was nine days ago. With each passing day, her hope guttered. Perhaps she'd have to keep up the act for the rest of her life.

The all-too-familiar sound of Geros' booted steps approached from down the hall. He only came to the third level to visit her.

A stifling sensation in her chest seized her breath. She rose from the bed and stumbled to the window for air. Outside, the first colorful buds began peeking out from the branches of trees and shrubs. In the past, these heralds of spring had made her happy. Now they were a reminder of this prison.

A lighter set of footsteps caught up to Geros.

"Your Eminence, Captain Miris in Fortress Ten expects you tomorrow. It is a one-week march."

She glanced back at the door. A week's journey from here must be at the Cathayi border. If only she was better with maps.

Geros' voice sounded bored. "Then I will take swifthorses after lunch and be there tonight."

"Your Eminence... certainly you know the road restoration and horse relays only reach Fortress Eight so far."

Kaiya frowned. From what she'd gathered, they were now at Fortress Nine.

"The captain is a smart man. I am sure he can build a fortress without me looking over his shoulder." His footsteps resumed, stopping right outside the door.

Shuddering, she turned back to the window.

The door swooshed open behind her.

He came up behind her and wrapped her in an embrace. With supreme effort, she kept every muscle in her body from locking up. He kissed the back of her head and turned her around, almost gently.

Kaiya composed her most adoring expression, and hated herself for doing so. "Your Eminence."

His voice was tender. "My love... "

Her stomach lurched into her throat, leaving a sour taste. Did he believe his words? To think, this might've been her fate had she gone through with marriage to Lord Tong in Wailian, three years ago.

He continued, "I was told your lunch was coming up soon, but I figured you might want an appetizer."

Kaiya suppressed a wince. His idea of an appetizer was the reason she had no interest in food. Today, though... "Your Eminence, as much as I hunger for you, I cannot. Not today."

His eyebrows smashed together and his faced flushed red. He pressed himself against her. "What do you mean? Why not?"

She pushed herself back against the wall. She swallowed the fear choking her words. "I have good news, Your Eminence. I... .my... . I am with child... " Was she? Hopefully, it wasn't... "Your child."

He staggered back, as if struck by a physical blow—one that didn't hurt, but caused confusion. His angered expression relaxed and his tone softened. "Are you sure?"

"You know there was no one else." She acted demure, casting her gaze at the floor. He'd either ignored or forgotten what the doctor on Wild Turkey Island had told him. "He will be third in line for the Dragon Throne of Cathay."

Geros turned toward the door. He paused and looked back. "A doctor will be visiting you shortly. You had better be telling the truth."

Kaiya shuddered again. She went to the washbasin to scrub where he had touched her, as if doing so would wash away his odor, which lingered in her imagination.

Before long, a middle-aged Arkothi man came and asked several questions. When was her last cycle, when her next one was due, when had she lain with the emperor, was she experiencing certain symptoms.

Though leaving out any mention of Tian, she answered honestly, wanting to know the result as much as Geros. After he finished taking notes, she asked, "Am I with child?"

The doctor's mouth shut like a trap and he rushed out the door.

Ill at ease, she turned back to the window, hand over her belly. Please let it be Tian's seed that had taken root in her. How devastating it would be to carry the spawn of a depraved rapist.

Presently, Geros' heavy steps approached, more rapidly than usual. He burst into the room, bounded across the floor and wrapped his huge arms around her.

Again, she fought to keep from shrinking in his embrace.

He then released her and leaned back. "Kaiya, I am so overwhelmed by the news. Despite the many sons that I must have sired, I never expected to know any of them, lost as they must be among the hundreds of Prospecti. I can describe the feeling as nothing short of joy, a joy that we will have a son together. I will see to it that he will rule Cathay and Teleri. Sharing our blood, he will be a strong emperor, ensuring the peace and order I have worked so hard to establish."

The man was delusional. Kaiya forced back a tear. How ironic. Her brothers' wives had both gone years of trying without success to conceive an heir to Cathay. She'd spent a week out of every month consoling them as their disappointment dragged on.

Now, she might carry the product of rape, who might very well become a pawn in the occupation and subjugation of her nation. Her countrywomen would share her fate, forced to endure violation, only to bear more tools of Teleri conquest.

Heavens, let it be Tian's.

Tian spent the day alone in a tree, mentally walking through his rescue plan. It wasn't really much of a plan, with too many uncertainties and variables. Had the memories of the previous night not haunted him, he'd never even consider it. Some Architect he was.

Late in the afternoon, he came down from the tree to discuss his strategy with Ma Jun and the twins. They all hovered around as he sketched a layout of the fortress grounds.

Tian pointed at the bridge. "I'm going to attempt the rescue tonight. Through here. Before the Blue Moon rises. With the new White Moon, it will be dark."

Kosa clapped his hands in excitement. "Did you scout out the interior of the main keep last night?"

Tian shook his head. "No, but I know exactly where she's held. There's an access point on the roof."

Ma Jun's jaw dropped. "How do you plan on getting the princess down from the rooftop, assuming you can actually get her out of her room?"

"Not from the roof. I'll take her out through the entrance."

Ma Jun's eyes and mouth widened. "You haven't even been inside the fort. Even if you get her out unseen, she can't climb under the bridge like you."

So much for the man's infectious optimism. Tian leveled his gaze at him. "That's where I'll need your help. You and the twins will create a diversion here at the eastern gate. It'll hopefully draw the garrison's attention to you. I'll take her out the back."

Ma Jun glared at him. "Hopefully? There are too many uncertainties. When the *Tianzi* ordered us to accept the Black Fist as adjunct protection for his family, he assured us you were meticulous. This doesn't give me confidence." He had slipped into the Cathayi tongue, but even Kosa and Kona looked at Tian with creased foreheads.

Tian jabbed a finger at Ma Jun. "We can't wait for word from Cathay. They're two weeks away. Every day Kaiya is imprisoned, a part of her is dying."

Ma Jun shook his head. "I don't want you to risk yourself, but it *is* your life to throw away. However, I can't let you risk the princess."

Had their roles been reversed, Tian would've agreed. Nonetheless, he couldn't let Kaiya suffer another day at the emperor's hands. He turned to Kona and Kosa. They idolized him and would accede to his requests regardless of what they thought of the plan. "I want you to—"

"Ma Jun is right," a female voice said. A familiar voice.

Tian spun around, looking left and right to find the source, one which could not possibly be there.

Jie.

Jie launched herself into Tian's chest, wrapping her arms around him as they tumbled to the ground.

She'd followed the Kanin tribeswoman, her heart racing at the imminent reunion with Tian. She admired how Lana could speak some of the Cathayi language.

Even more impressive was the shaman's ability to pick her way through the forest, barely making a sound.

Meanwhile, Jie had constantly stepped on a hidden twig or dry leaf. Maybe the enemy would think it was a rabbit.

A very large rabbit.

Who was she fooling?

Lana had dropped into a crouch, and Jie froze. When the shaman beckoned, Jie crept up to her side. There, in a small clearing, squatted Tian, Ma Jun, and two Kanin boys.

Her heart had nearly leaped out of her chest. She started toward the clearing—

Tian and Ma Jun were bickering. And with just cause. Tian's plan was idiotic, something she would've expected of... well, nobody was *that* careless.

Now, she lifted her head and looked into his eyes, trying to read his blank expression. Feeling the weight of the stares around her, she picked herself up and helped Tian to his feet. When she spoke, her voice sounded too husky in her ears. "Zheng Tian, I thought you'd died."

He flashed a grin, but it seemed forced. "I'm glad to see you are alive and well, too. My plan can't fail with the two of us."

What? Someone deserved a painful reminder—

Tian opened his mouth to continue, but knowing what he'd ask and wanting him to *see* the answer, Jie cut him off. "Were you hit on your head so hard that you can't see the holes in that ridiculous plan? I never thought an imperial guard would have more sense than a Black Fist."

Tian shrugged. "It'll have twice as much a chance of succeeding now that you are here."

Something was wrong about his demeanor. Her stomach hollowed. This was not how their reunion was supposed to be, even with a princess to rescue.

Ma Jun disentangled himself from Lana's embrace and pulled Tian aside. He leaned in and whispered, though Jie's elf ears heard it all.

"Neither Weiyong nor Lana told anyone in Cathay the whole story. That is between the two of you. But you can't let your emotions get in the way of objectivity. It's one thing to risk your own life, it is something entirely different to risk all ours. And hers."

What was that all about? Jie sucked on her lower lip.

Tian looked up. His distraught, almost guilty expression settled into a Black Fist blankness as his eyes met Jie's. "I think the two of us can do it."

"We have more assets a few *li* away, and I have a better plan. Follow me." She nodded towards Lana. "Or rather, follow her."

Tian trailed behind Jie in silence for a half-phase, remembering all the things that were left unsaid in the haste of the escape from Iksuvius half a year before. Had their mutual feelings been clarified, perhaps things would have turned out differently.

But now, Jie's magnetism no longer pulled on him. That attraction, no matter how brief, now transformed into guilt.

He started to confess, but other words spilled out instead. "How did you escape Iksuvius?"

Jie glanced over her shoulder, her expression speaking of a silent hurt. "The Teleri destroyed the embassy, killed most of the staff and imperial guard." She cast Ma Jun a sympathetic eye. "They rounded up all the Cathayi residents and imprisoned them."

All those comrades, killed. And Tian had left Jie there.

"Then," she continued, "the *Tianzi* sent a dozen ships to blockade the coast. I took the fastest ship back to Cathay with word of the princess' escape into the Wilds. Search parties embarked on futile forays into the plateau, but heavy snow forced the *Tianzi* to call the search off for the winter."

Tian nodded. "They would've stumbled on Teleri fortresses before they found us."

Jie shrugged. "They would've resumed their search tomorrow, but the embassy doctor and his guide delivered the news of the princess' capture two days ago. In the meantime, your brother Zheng Ming mobilized three thousand soldiers. They're heading this way."

Of course. Dashing Eldest Brother would volunteer to swoop in and save the princess. From the East Gate of Cathay, they were two weeks away. Still too far, given Tian's urgency. But if they were two weeks away, "How did you—"

They stepped out into a meadow. Tian's unasked question was answered as he gaped at the five enormous birds resting there. The Cathayi called them *Difeng*, with some foreign cultures erroneously naming them phoenixes. With a wingspan of thirty feet, they were a fourth the size of the even rarer true phoenixes, known as *Tianfeng*.

They had heads that resembled pheasants, but a peacock tail. Their legs were long and taloned like cranes, while their wings were much like swallows. Their brightly colored gold-and-silver feathers sparkled in the sunlight.

Tian sucked in a breath. Eight lived in the imperial aviary, and came out for the New Year's processions. Besides female members of the royal family, only a handful of female imperial guards were trained to ride them. They hadn't been used in times of war since the *Tianzi*'s ancestor reunified Cathay nearly three hundred years before.

Five women in the regalia of the imperial guard tended to the birds, pausing to greet Ma Jun with a right first in their left palm.

Two other women wearing Black Fist stealth suits took stock of weapons and equipment. One, the thirteen-year-old girl Feng Mi, had helped him storm Wailian Castle one thousand, four hundred and forty-six days ago; while he'd trained alongside nineteen-year-old Yina at the temple. He'd met the boy among them, ten-year old Zan, on trips back..

Jie went over to a saddle on the ground. "I brought you presents." She withdrew his curved *dao* sword, a black utility suit, and a bandolier of small throwing weapons. "You left these in Iksuvius, and I couldn't bear to imagine Bovyan paws on them."

Hefting the sword, Tian gazed at the phoenixes with a curious eye.

As always, Jie seemed to read his thoughts. "The *Tianzi* wanted his sister rescued as soon as possible. We knew you wanted a team of twelve brothers, but only five of the eight phoenixes were deemed fit to fly under the conditions. Weight also affects their range, so I picked three of the lightest Black Fist to join in. We can send the imperial riders back and have another five of us within four days. Zheng Ming's troops are two weeks away, but there is also a fortress under construction halfway between here and Dongmen which may slow them down."

Tian shook his head. "We can't wait that long."

Jie narrowed her eyes at him. "Can five of us do it?"

Ma Jun also glared at him, his expression answering, *no*.

"We have to try." Tian sighed. Ma Jun's silent objection was right. Tian lacked objectivity and needed someone with fresh eyes.

He motioned for Jie to follow him back into the woods, dreading what he had to tell her. Ma Jun and Lana both offered him sympathetic smiles.

Out of sight and earshot of the others, he turned around to face his long-time friend and almost-lover, afraid she'd throw herself into his arms before he could open his mouth.

He didn't have to worry.

She stood at an angle, her eyes at the ground. "I concede our chess match. Your queen was in too strong a position. It's written in the expressions of your friends, and even your expression speaks louder than words."

The hurt in her voice yanked at Tian's heart. He'd betrayed his duty, betrayed his best friend. He hung his head, contrite. "Then you know why I need you now. The First Consul is doing horrible things to her. I heard it myself. All I can do is think about how much I need to free her." And kill him.

Jie didn't answer, and he looked up to meet her scathing glance. It hurt worse than any sword cut. He wouldn't blame her if she refused to help.

The half-elf let out a sigh. "I would like to believe the princess is my friend, and it's my duty to protect her where you couldn't. Come back and share what you know about their defenses with the rest of the team. Know that I will not risk the lives or virtue of the women in my charge unless there is a good chance of success."

Among the others, Tian was meticulous in his details: the position of buildings, the timing of the guard changing, their posts, when Kanin tribesmen were coming and going. The Black Fist and imperial guards asked questions and provided input; Lana volunteered her tie to the spirits.

Jie's solution was simple.

CHAPTER 55:
Confrontations

With no indication of any weather besides clear skies, Jie gawked at Lana's invocation of the spirits. Clouds rolled in and blotted out the stars, and even the soft light of the Iridescent Moon. Thick fog billowed at ground level, to a height of a dozen feet. None of that affected her elf vision's ability to see either the sixteen soldiers circling the fortress roof, or the two guards in the crow's nest.

She looked behind her. Tian's phoenix lagged behind, burdened by his weight. Yet one more reason he was worthless.

Jie shook the bitterness out of her head. There were more important things to take care of. Like capturing the crow's nest.

The large guards there leaned against the tree, neither taking their duties seriously. Her superior hearing allowed her to discern the two men's conversation over the rushing wind.

"The emperor has been here a long time," the first said in a low whisper.

"Yes, he's too preoccupied with the Cathayi princess."

"Amazing to think the distinguished Emperor Geros, the greatest leader in our history, has lost his focus because of a woman."

"He spends so much time with her. What if the prophecy comes to pass?"

Jie signaled her rider with a tap on her shoulder, and the woman withdrew a bow from the saddle and nocked an arrow.

"Bah! Prophecies are fairy tales, meant to keep us in line."

"But—"

Jie opened the shutter of a light bauble lamp for a split second, spotlighting the guards. The man never had a chance to finish his sentence, as an arrow lodged in his throat. Several other arrows followed from different angles, felling the second before he could react.

Jie patted the rider's back, admiring her ability to shoot from a flying mount. Even more amazing was how she guided the phoenix into a smooth landing on the rail of the crow's nest. In short order, the others joined them, with Tian coming last.

The five Black Fists dropped soundlessly to the platform, followed by the five lithe riders. As planned, Jie motioned for the latter to stay, while the rest darted down the stairs wrapping around the tree trunk.

She gauged the distance from the rooftop entrance to the sixteen soldiers circling the perimeter—too many to take out before they could raise an alarm. She passed the message with a series of pats on the sister behind her.

Quiet as death, they bypassed those guards altogether, instead continuing downwards into the fortress and onto the landing of the third floor.

The landing opened into a hallway, and Jie peered out. The interior light globes were shuttered at this late hour, leaving the corridor barely lit by a window at the end of the hall.

Her elf sight barely made out a blurry shape about sixty feet away to her right. His breathing capacity implied a large man, almost certainly Bovyan given the circumstances.

She extended a leg into the hall and placed her foot gingerly on the floor. Hardwood. She gradually shifted her weight onto it to test the sound. Firm, no squeaks.

She reached back and tapped Tian. The series of signals would let him know about the guard. If his brain wasn't too addled by love, he'd pass the order for the others to continue with their plan: the two women were to continue down to guard the stairwell on the second-floor landing, while the boy Zan would hold his position on the third floor.

Jie crept towards her victim. He showed no signs of noticing her presence, and when she was close enough, she covered his mouth and slashed his throat with a curved dagger. The man crumpled to the floor.

She waited until the body went limp before removing her hand.

On her tactile signal, Tian moved to the door and ran skilled hands over it. He reached back and tapped her arm. *Locked. Can't see.*

She produced her magical light, cupping it carefully in her hands so that only a small sliver shone on the door handle's plate. They worked so well together, like the gears of a dwarf clock.

Tian removed his lockpick pouch and withdrew a tool. His hands trembled, causing the pick to scrape with a light sound.

Jie rolled her eyes. Taking the deceptively heavy pouch from him, she felt for the correct tool. With an expert twist, the lock yielded in her hands, and she gently pressed the door to test the hinges. The tremor on the door suggested they were well-oiled. She silently pushed the door open.

Tian slid in without a sound, while Jie stood guard at the doorway, wondering what to do with the body.

The room was almost pitch black, but Tian heard someone breathing. He knew the pattern. Kaiya. Heart racing with excitement and joy, he glided over and knelt by her bed. He put one hand over her mouth and another over her wrist.

Kaiya gasped in surprise and started to struggle.

"Shh. It's me," he whispered.

She sucked in a breath and sobbed. Sitting up, she wrapped her arms around him, her slim shoulders shaking against his body, her hot tears warm on his chest. Her hand rose to his face, which was covered by his mask.

He pulled down the mask and pressed his cheek into her forehead. Her suffering, the result of his decisions. He leaned in and whispered in her ear, "I'm so sorry. I'm so sorry to have put you through this."

She only shuddered. He stroked her hair, trying to calm and reassure her.

When she quieted, she whispered, "Tian, I'd given up hope."

Jie quietly dragged the dead guard into the room. "Tian, we must get out soon." From her tone, she must've been wearing the most sarcastic expression.

Tian stood and helped Kaiya to her feet. "We need to escape before anyone knows we're here."

He took her hand and guided her back through the dark hall towards the stairwell. Tian winced. Kaiya, though light on her feet, still made too much noise. If anyone heard...

The rest of the team waited at the stairwell. One grasped Tian's hand and tapped.

Emperor. Asleep. Second floor.

Tian's free hand clenched into a fist tight enough to crush rocks. The bastard! The night before... he would pay. For that, and what he must have done for the last two weeks.

Tian placed Kaiya's hand in Jie's and started toward the steps.

Kaiya grasped his sleeve. She tugged, even as he drew away. "Tian."

She'd broken the silence! Tian tensed, listening for telltale signs of guards. The rustling sounds suggested she and Jie were engaged in a minor tussle of wills.

One which Kaiya won. "Tian, don't leave me... " Her pleading voice chipped at his resolve. She needed his protection. He thirsted for revenge.

He whispered, "The emperor will pursue you. As long he lives. I'm going to punish him. For what he did to you, my beloved."

Around him, the Black Fist drew sharp breaths, tensed up.

Jie hissed in a barely audible voice, "Tian, remember the mission. Remember objectivity. And if you cannot do that, remember your duty to your *beloved*."

"Tian, please." Kaiya drew him close, taking his hand and placed it over her belly. She leaned in and whispered in his ear. "I need you more than ever. To protect my unborn child."

Unborn child? Heavens. Tian's heart thudded in his chest. His child? With her?

All the keen-eared Black Fist must've heard her. The collective gasp confirmed his worry. He stood dumbstruck.

Jie poked him. "If you don't want Geros raising your child, you need to come *now*."

Yes. Protecting the child and Kaiya took first priority. He took her hand and guided her up the steps. All they had to do now was gain the roof and slip quietly up to the tower without the perimeter guards seeing them.

The heavy thud of booted feet came from above. A glimmer of light danced near the exit to the roof.

"Hide," Jie whispered.

The Black Fist women slipped inaudibly down the stairs, while the boy vaulted upwards into a ceiling corner and suspended himself there. Jie glided into the hallway. Tian and Kaiya, however... they were already halfway up the stairs.

Two Bovyans froze there with light bauble lamps in hand, eyes wide, mouths agape.

In the blink of an eye, Tian reached into his bandolier and threw three spikes. With the narrow stairwell, the lead Bovyan took the brunt of the attack and tumbled down with a pin in his throat.

The last spike grazed the other Teleri along the temple. He fell back. "Intruders!"

"Intruders!" The message relayed above them, shouts ringing out and horns blaring.

Tian groaned. Now they had to get past fifteen guards on the roof.

Bright lights flooded the top of the stairs. Heavy boots thudded and crossbows cocked. The fortress would soon be on full alert.

"To the tower. Eliminate all threats," Jie ordered.

Tian pulled Kaiya down to the third-floor landing. "They're gathering at the top. Armed with crossbows."

"They are mobilizing on the lower levels," announced Feng Mi from below.

Outnumbered above and below! Tian's stomach clenched.

A chorus of pained grunts came from above. A Teleri voice yelled, "Archers in the tower!"

Jie growled. "That's our escape. The imperial riders don't stand a chance against the Bovyans in hand-to-hand combat."

The Teleri footsteps below were nearly upon them.

Feng Mi's voice from below shook with disbelief. "They have... muskets."

Muskets. When and where had the Teleri acquired them? Their range threatened a phoenix, though their accuracy was suspect. Tian tapped his chin. They couldn't take a chance with Kaiya's safety.

"We are trapped between a hammer and an anvil." The boy's tone sounded like he'd already accepted his fate.

Accept fate.

The words from Tian's vision echoed back to him now. Ever since he'd locked Kaiya in an armor cabinet a decade ago, it'd been his fate to selflessly toil as a cog in Cathay's spy network. He found acceptance and belonging there. Work became his passion. In falling in love with Kaiya, and worse, acting on those emotions, he'd shirked fate, abandoned his duty.

It was time to correct that mistake now. *Accept fate.*

Tian gazed at Kaiya, memorizing every line of her angelic face. "I'll hold the stairwell. The rest of you make sure the princess escapes."

Kaiya's eyes widened in the dim, wavering light. "No, Tian, you must come with me. I beg it."

"I am sorry, my love. It's my fate to die here. So that you... and our child... might live."

Kaiya squeezed tight at his arms. "Come, Zheng Tian, I command it."

Tian ran his hand through her hair and down her cheek, brushing the tears away. "The penalty for disobeying your order is death. That is my fate."

She pressed herself against him, burying her face in his shoulder, clutching at him. His resolve faltered.

Accept fate.

He met Jie's eyes. The bitter expression she'd worn since their most recent reunion melted away, her face softening as she haltingly shook her head and blinked away tears. She could always read his mind. She understood the message, even if she denied its necessity. Her voice caught in her throat, but he made out the words, *I'm sorry.*

"Do it," he said. "The *Tiger's Eye.*"

Jie had grown tired of the lovers' quarrel almost before it had started. Tian had been more derelict in his duty than she imagined, had crossed lines that might very well lead to his execution if he returned to Cathay.

That didn't matter if he planned to die this night.

She felt petty for harboring a grudge at a betrayal of unspoken feelings, made possible by time and distance.

And history. She'd wanted him to feel as awful as she felt, though knowing that they'd eventually resolve their differences. As they always had. Now, this would be the last time she saw him.

Flustered, her words tangled on her tongue.

Yet, Tian's slight nod indicated he understood her unspoken apology.

The *Tiger's Eye*. It'd buy them time. She locked eyes on him and made a simple gesture with her hand. "Your mission is to ensure the princess escapes."

Tian's expression transformed, the sad uncertainty replaced by an inhuman resolve. He returned her secret gesture with the subconscious hand sign that indicated he was locked in the *Tiger's Eye*.

He held the princess in his cold gaze, likely calculating the impact of his actions. Tears streamed in rivulets along her cheek. With obviously contrived gentleness, he slipped out of her grasp and disappeared down the stairwell. Sounds of metal crashing against metal rang out.

The princess started to lurch after him, but Jie blocked the way with her body. Her words came out surprisingly smooth. "*Dian-xia*, Tian is buying your escape with his life. Do not waste his gift."

The princess wiped her tears and straightened. While not exactly regal, she put on a brave face.

Jie pointed at the others. "Feng Mi, you stay with the princess. Zan and Yina, come with me. Attack after they shoot their first volley." With that, she turned onto the landing, into the Teleri line of fire, and hurled several throwing stars and spikes in their direction.

In the split second before she ducked away, she counted ten defenders in a formation that maximized their volley. One tumbled down the steps, cut down by her weapons. A barrage of crossbow bolts lodged into the floor and walls where she had just stood a second ago.

No sooner had the bolts cracked against the walls than three Black Fists surged up the stairs, drawing their swords while the Teleri reloaded. Covering ten feet of height and fifteen feet of distance in the flash of an eye, they were now among the enemy.

The Bovyans dropped their crossbows and drew swords. Too late. Black Fist lacquered swords danced like shadows. Some of the men cried out in pain, while others simply fell silent.

There was still a chance.

Kaiya's pulse thumped in her ears, though not loud enough to drown out the sound of swishing blades and screams. Her stomach twisted in a knot. Tian...

Lights and shadows danced in the third-floor hall behind them, from where rasps of weapons being drawn rang out. The rapid pattering of booted feet coming up the steps grew louder, echoing the pounding in her chest.

They were trapped. She'd be recaptured. With Tian gone, it didn't matter. Nothing mattered. Better to die here and now than to go back to Geros' bed.

"*Dian-xia*, follow Jie up." The female Black Fist urged her forward with a push. "I'll hold the third-floor landing."

With a last wistful glance at the stairs where Tian had disappeared, Kaiya hurried up the steps towards the sound of fierce fighting. Reaching the roof, she skidded to a halt. The boy Black Fist had fallen, while the young woman drew off four Teleri with her sword. Jie dashed up the steps to the crow's nest, pursuing several more soldiers trying to retake the tower.

And above, four phoenixes! They circled the roof, their riders loosing arrows at enemy soldiers. Maybe there was a chance. At least for her. But Tian...

Kaiya bent over and picked up a dagger from a fallen Bovyan. Splinters bit at her bare feet as she climbed the winding stair.

A body dropped past her. From above, Jie's voice called out. "All clear."

Kaiya looked down. One of the Black Fist women hobbled towards the stairs as well. Back towards the opening to the rooftop, there was no sign of Tian or the younger female Black Fist. Nonetheless, no Teleri burst through the entrance to the rooftop.

The phoenixes were landing as Kaiya gained the crow's nest. Chest squeezing, she scanned the rooftop again. Still no sign of Tian. She looked askance at Jie.

The half-elf shook her head, her eyes sympathetic. "Please mount up, *Dian-xia*. I'll go back down to investigate."

Kaiya nodded and climbed up behind one of the riders. The last Black Fist also reached the top of the platform and eased her way over to the next phoenix.

Below, several Teleri soldiers surged out onto the roof. If they had made it that far... it must mean Tian... No.

A sob wracked Kaiya's shoulders. In years past, she might have put on a brave face for her people, but for all that had happened to her, all that had been taken from her, the tears trickled down her cheeks.

Jie reappeared on the platform and mounted up behind another rider. Her eyes, too, glistened. She met

Kaiya's stare, her expression quickly turning stoic. "*Dian-xia*, we must go. Please give the order."

"Wait... " Kaiya choked on her tears. "There might still be a chance." A slim chance. Maybe no chance.

The soldiers filed up the steps, their collective weight sending vibrations through the crow's nest.

"We must go now, *Dian-xia*." Jie motioned for the riders to take off.

One at a time, the phoenixes spread their great wings and lifted gracefully into the air. From the higher vantage point, Kaiya continued to look down at the rooftop, hoping beyond hope that Tian would somehow emerge.

"Look!" Jie pointed down towards the southern side of the fortress, now bathed in the light of raging fires.

Kaiya followed the half-elf's gesture. A single figure fought viciously through waves of enemies.

Tian.

She looked back at the path of carnage he had taken, and to her horror, even at this distance she could pick out Emperor Geros pursuing her beloved at a deliberate pace.

"Fly in closer," she ordered the rider.

"What?" Voice shocked, the rider turned her head.

"Do as I command!" Kaiya snarled, unslinging the woman's bow from the saddle and fitting an arrow from the side quiver.

Around her, the phoenixes veered with their leader. Riders shot into the Teleri ranks. Many fell. Others looked up.

Now closer, Kaiya could see Tian clearly. Her stomach twisted in knots. He'd suffered numerous cuts, and his shirt was ripped to shreds. Yet he still fought on.

With a Teleri longsword in one hand and a dagger in the other, he hacked and slashed through the sea of

Bovyans. Her heart surged with hope as he cleared the last enemy in front of him and broke into a run towards the palisade.

Geros had watched in admiration as the Cathayi man tore through his soldiers like Tivar's Archangel of Death. The Eye of Solaris painted it all as he littered the steps with dead and dying Bovyans, and now somehow gained the yard.

In the bright firelight, Geros remembered having seen the man at the banquet in Iksuvius. At the time, he was just another weakling.

He was now proving Geros wrong. He worked his way towards the palisade, and if he managed to get away, Geros would not begrudge him a temporary victory.

One of his officers pointed up. "Cathayi phoenixes!"

Geros followed the gesture. Five huge birds circling downward. The fools! They were descending into crossbow range.

Several ranks raised their crossbows, and Geros lifted a hand, ready to give the signal.

"First Consul!" A male voice called from near the edge of the fortress.

Who dared address him by his former title? Geros looked. It was the Cathayi man, now ignored by his men after their attention turned to the phoenixes. Their eyes met.

Geros feared no one, let alone a lesser human. Nonetheless, a chill flared up his spine at the sight of the man's singularly focused glare.

Geros took a crossbow from a soldier by his side and leveled it at the Cathayi, who now limped back towards him.

He squeezed the trigger.

The bolt tore across the Cathayi's arm and ricocheted off the fence.

Unbidden, his own soldiers lowered their weapons and leveled them at the man.

Geros snatched a loaded crossbow and took aim again. The Eye of Solaris painted a yellow rune on the man's chest.

Just as Geros shot, yellow flashed high in his visual field, the Eye warning of an incoming attack from that direction. An arrow grazed his own thigh, throwing his aim off. The bolt would have sped past the man's head had he not plucked it out of the air with a quick swipe of his hand.

Ignoring the pain in his leg, Geros took another loaded crossbow, while looking up to see one of the phoenixes veering. The princess rode astride, a bow leveled at him. Her shot would be ludicrous from that range, launched from a moving platform. He turned his focus back to the man, who now broke into a hobbled run towards him.

A few men took shots at him, but he sidestepped the bolts with remarkable agility.

Yellow flashed in Geros' vision again. An arrow from above grazed his arm, just as he pulled the crossbow trigger. Gritting his teeth at the pain, he watched as his own bolt flew.

It slammed into the man's right upper shoulder with a dull thud, knocking him onto his back. He tried to crawl to his feet before collapsing into a sitting position.

Above, the princess screamed.

Flashing a taunting grin at her, Geros limped over with another loaded crossbow. Maybe the princess would be stupid enough to come closer. He turned and locked gazes with the man, who stared back with deadly resolve.

Geros almost faltered.

Then, the man's look faded into a peaceful tranquility, revealing neither fear nor defeat. His eyes rolled back into his head and he went limp, sagging forward.

Geros drove his heel into the man's chest. When he simply flopped to the ground, Geros knelt down to take the pulse at his neck. Nothing. His own shot should not have been a killing blow, but perhaps all of the other wounds had taken their toll.

Looking up at the princess, his mouth curled into a smile. They now hovered on the outer limits of crossbow range. "Bring those birds down! Take aim!"

His soldiers raised their crossbows in unison.

The phoenixes flapped their wings, gaining height.

"Shoot!"

Clicks of triggers and the twang of bows sounded in unison, sending a deadly barrage into the air.

Fighting through her tears, desperately wanting to recover Tian's body, Kaiya loosed arrow after arrow in reckless abandon until the quiver was spent.

"Down, down!" she ordered, pounding on the rider's back with her fists. Even still, the phoenix continued gaining altitude.

The rider would continue their escape regardless of what she said or threatened. It was useless. She looked down.

Oh, Heavens, no. Tian's body lay unmoving. Geros stood above him, shrinking as the phoenix flew.

Oh, Heavens, no.

Her chest squeezed so tight, it was impossible to take a breath. Jump. She could reunite with Tian in death. It would take all the pain away.

But no.

She carried his child. It had to be his. For his child, for his sacrifice, she had to live. Kaiya closed her eyes and sank into the saddle. The rush of cool night air was comforting, but how could she enjoy her freedom? Too much had been taken away from her.

CHAPTER 56:
Farewell

Jie's logical Black Fist mind clashed with her emotions, the conflict between duty and friendship, love and betrayal, tearing her apart more than her elf and human halves ever had. She wiped the tears from her eyes as the phoenixes settled down in the meadow.

Beside her, the princess tumbled from her phoenix and collapsed onto her knees. She wrung her hands, shamelessly crying.

Hollowness seized Jie's chest. She'd treated Tian so curtly. He'd always survived.

He wasn't supposed to die.

She stumbled over and placed a shaking hand on the princess' shoulder. Wracking sobs reverberated into Jie's body, and her own tears flowed freely.

The imperial riders and the surviving Black Fist sister, Feing Mi, slid off their saddles. Ma Jun joined them, and all dropped to one knee, fist to the ground.

The princess looked up at her. "We must recover his... their remains. Before the Teleri desecrate them."

Jie shivered, imagining the Bovyans hacking up Tian's body. As much as she agreed with the princess, it was an impossible task. And of course, protecting the princess was top priority. She shook her head. "*Dian-xia,* I am sorry."

The princess ripped at the collar around her neck, jerking her head from side to side as if it would loosen it. When the collar didn't so much as budge, she collapsed again, sobbing.

Lana sidled up to the princess, wrapping her up in an embrace. She held the princess' head to her chest, brushing her hair and whispering words in her own language. Such an open display of sympathy!

The princess nodded a few times before breaking away. She rose to her feet and raked a red-rimmed gaze over all assembled. She then bowed her head. "Thank you all for... for your hard work."

All of the Cathayi bowed their heads at the ceremonial words.

The leader of the imperial riders looked up. "*Dian-xia*, the phoenixes will be too tired after their long flight from Cathay. If it is your order, we will rest for night and leave before dawn tomorrow."

The princess nodded.

Without any bedding, the riders all offered their cloaks for the princess to sleep on. After they settled the birds down, everyone found a place on the ground. Jie stood first watch, but was barely able to take her eyes from the trembling mass of cloaks that was Princess Kaiya.

Kaiya lay awake, curled on herself like a newborn, trying to will away the memories of all the awful things that had been done to her. With Tian gone, she was alone and abandoned, not unlike the feelings that she had suffered as a slave to a depraved man's sick fantasies.

Her thoughts strayed to her unborn child. Would Cathay recognize her marriage to Tian, legitimizing the baby as the scion of the *Tianzi* and a *Tai-Ming* family? What if it was the first Bovyan member of the Imperial Family? She balled herself tighter.

It was in this position that Kaiya found herself when she awoke with a start before dawn. It had been the most restful sleep since her capture, the brutal emperor unable to haunt her dreams at least for that night. Warm arms cradled her.

Tian's? Her heart leaped. Maybe the last month had been nothing more than a horrible nightmare. But no. The arms were too small, the body pressed against hers slight compared to Tian's. She turned her head to find Lana asleep by her side.

Around her, the camp already stirred, with the imperial riders saddling the phoenixes.

Kaiya lay still, unwilling to rise. She'd once been confident and strong, beloved by her people. Cathay's allies and enemies alike admired her for her poise and ability to manipulate affairs of state. Now, with her dignity stolen from her, she was a dried-out husk of her former self. To make matters worse, the man who'd sworn to love her forever, and with whom she'd shared her most intimate soul, was gone.

She untangled herself from Lana's embrace and pushed herself into a seated position.

Jie sat cross-legged nearby, watching her, and then transitioned to one knee, fist to the ground. "*Dian-xia*. I have something for you." Her voice was hoarse, her eyes red. Walking over, she withdrew a small pouch from her own and placed it in Kaiya's hands. "These belonged to Zheng Tian. His lockpicks. You should have them."

Kaiya turned the pouch over in her hands, feeling the weight of it. She opened it to find the rings of the imperial guards. The pouch flap itself was deceptively heavy, with Tian's haphazard stitching near the edges.

Her shoulders shuddered as sobs threatened to wrack her body again. She so wanted to be strong in front of her people. How had Tian been so focused in their escape?

Her gaze locked on the half-elf. "Jie, what did you do to Tian in the stairwell? How did he bring his anger under control so quickly?"

Jie frowned. "Our clan uses a technique called the *Tiger's Eye*. We use it on suicide missions, or on those who have been grievously injured and would not be able to otherwise complete their assignments. It helps him achieve a singular focus and objectivity, feeling no pain or emotion."

How convenient; a tool to keep someone from crumbling under the weight of their grief. "Can you perform it to someone else? Someone not from your clan?"

Jie's eyes narrowed. "I am not sure. Someone who has not undergone our mental training might not be affected at all. Or, the effect could be permanent."

"Then do it to me. I do not want to feel anymore. It is the only way I can survive right now."

Jie sucked on her lower lip. "*Dian-xia...* If I do that, then you will cease to be everything that the people love in you... that *he* loved in you."

"I am no longer that person anyway. I don't care. It takes all of my strength and willpower just to draw a breath. I don't want to feel anymore."

Jie sighed. "I have told you the risk. Is that your command, my liege?"

"It is."

Jie dropped to a knee, fist to the ground. "Then I obey." She took a deep breath and locked her gaze on Kaiya's eyes. She made a gesture with her hand.

A cool wave washed over Kaiya, all of her racing thoughts and emotions coalescing into a singular focus. The tightness in her neck and shoulders relaxed, and the vice-grip on her chest eased.

For maybe the first time in her life, she achieved absolute mental clarity. Perhaps if she were a *Black Fist* warrior, who served the realm unquestioningly, she might have lost herself to obedience to serve her country's interests—even if those interests conflicted with her own values. Instead, those values of life and dignity became her compass—an unambiguous beacon that would serve as a guide through this difficult time.

She straightened her carriage. "People of Cathay, to me."

The riders, the *Black Fist,* and Ma Jun all dropped to one knee, fist to the ground.

"As the princess commands," they shouted in unison.

"My first command is silence. Even if the *Tianzi* himself asks you about my relationship with Young Lord Zheng, or the product of our union, you will beg for death before betraying my secret."

"As the princess commands."

She turned to Ma Jun. "Imperial guard Ma Jun. You are released from active service to the realm." Ignoring his shocked look, she held out the rings of the imperial guards who had sacrificed themselves for her. "For now, your duty is to pray for the repose of your fallen comrades in arms: Xu Zhan, Li Wei, Zhao Yue, and Chen Xin. Know that in the future, you may be called upon again. When you have settled in your final destination, send word to Cathay of your whereabouts."

Head bowed, Ma Jun received the rings. "*Dian-xia.* Your humble servant accepts your command."

She took his hands in her own. "Jun, although you have always been my loyal guard, you are also my Maki brother. Please take care of Lana and the village."

She then turned to Lana and clasped her hands. "Sister, thank you for making me a part of your family, and then coming for me in my most desperate hour. Please take care of Jun for us."

Lana simply smiled. "Go with the spirits, Sister. Remember that you always have a home here, with us, among the trees."

After bidding the twins farewell, Kaiya mounted up behind the lead imperial rider. The phoenixes spread their great wings, taking flight. A spring headwind whipped through her hair as the meadow disappeared into the distance, along with the carefree life she'd always wanted.

Late in the day, Kaiya spotted the Great Wall, snaking its way above the forests through Cathay's mountainous border. Stone watchtowers placed every dozen *li* along the wall sent smoke signals, relaying word of her return.

They landed near the Great East Gate of Cathay. Here, the Kanin Plateau ended, and the North Kanin River spilled into the Cathay basin as a six-hundred-foot-wide, fifty-foot-high waterfall not far from Tian's hometown of Dongmen.

Swollen by spring melt, the falls roared above all other sounds. The mist formed a rainbow that danced in the sunlight, providing a spectacular backdrop for the delicate pink plum blossoms that now reached peak bloom. Over the centuries, hundreds of poets had written thousands of verses about the stunning scene.

Kaiya's reaction was completely different. In years past, she would visit the falls in spring, allowing the breathtaking vista to fill her spirit with inspiration. Today, she did not feel her heart stirring; her mind simply analyzed the composition and mechanics of the scene.

On her command, the imperial riders set the phoenixes down in the central square of a town bordering the waterfall lake.

Dismounting, she turned to Jie. "I am going to Dongmen Castle. Spread rumors that I have sequestered myself there to recover from my trek through the Wilds. Send word to Doctor Wu in the capital to meet me there. I do not wish to see the *Tianzi* until after I have had time to consult with my doctor."

Jie's eyes wavered. "*Dian-xia*, your father is dead. Your second brother Kai-Wu is now *Tianzi*."

Had her emotions not been locked away by the *Tiger's Eye*, Kaiya imagined she would be reeling in shock. Not only was Father gone, but her second brother, the less capable of the two, now ruled. "Why did Kai-Guo not inherit?"

"He, too, is dead." Jie bowed her head.

Kaiya considered the implications with complete impartiality. It could not be coincidence that both her father and healthy brother had died in such a short time.

After Kai-Wu, the next in line to the Jade Throne was... her cousin, the traitor Kai-Long. Or perhaps her unborn son?

Epilogue

In his fury at Princess Kaiya's escape, Geros executed many of the slaves who rose up that night. Their severed heads adorned the palisade walls as a warning to any others who dared defy him. Their mutilated bodies were left out for carrion birds to feast on.

However, Bovyan culture glorified valiant death, with enemy soldiers afforded the same respect as their own. The bodies of the three Cathayi, a boy and woman among them, were cleaned and set on a crude raft with the Teleri dead. Their cold hands clasped weapons. Geros himself set the broken *dao* in the dead man's hands.

With a light bauble at the head of the raft to guide their souls into the netherworld, they were sent downstream in a solemn ceremony.

Geros watched the raft as it disappeared downriver in the direction of Cathay, where his operative worked to weaken the country from within. Civil war would tear the nation apart within two years—coinciding with Teleri pacification of the Wilds, and making it ripe for the picking. The Directori would again hail his genius.

With the Curse of Tivar, he would not be alive to witness it.

Or would he?

The words of Princess Kaiya's ancestor came unbidden to his mind: *The best-laid plans rarely survive the first encounter.*

Geros had not expected to battle the Cathayi this early. Even though he had ostensibly won the first engagement, he left himself with an unenviable decision. He would not stand for his unborn son to be raised by a nation of artists and merchants.

He turned to a general. "Send word to Captain Miris in Fortress Ten. We will begin amassing soldiers for the invasion of Cathay immediately."

Soon, Cathay would be his, two years ahead of schedule... along with Princess Kaiya and their son.

For four days, Kaiya sat by a window in the private wing of Dongmen Castle, waiting for her doctor to arrive. If anyone could tell her something about her unborn child, it would be the ancient and mysterious Doctor Wu, who could look at a tongue and discern how long her patient slept on a specific night three years prior.

Kaiya's next move hinged on her baby. If it were Tian's, she would wed his brother Zheng Ming immediately. If it was Geros'... well, there was a Bovyan prophecy to consider.

"*Dian-xia.*" One of the castle servants came to the open door and dropped to a knee. "Doctor Wu has arrived from the capital."

By habit, Kaiya's hand lifted to the collar that marked her as Geros' slave—since removed by Jie's lockpicking skills. Her heart beat in her ears, slow and steady. "Show her in."

With Fang Weiyong in her shadow, Doctor Wu entered and dropped down to her knees with the grace of a woman a quarter of her age. How old that really was, no one was really sure; though some speculated that as Master of the *Dao*, she had achieved immortality.

Pulled up into an austere coil, her long silver hair had a faint bluish sheen. Her eyes were unique among the Cathayi: a luminous pale blue, reminiscent of the moon Guanyin's Eye. Hair-thin lines of wisdom fanned out from the edges of those startling eyes, yet left her cheeks unmarred.

"*Dian-xia*, I have come at your summons. What is your bidding?"

"Thank you, Doctor. Please, take my pulse and tell me what you feel."

Doctor Wu motioned towards Fang Weiyong and smiled. "A master is as only good as her student."

"*Dian-xia*, forgive me for my impertinence." Weiyong bowed and placed three fingers on both of her wrists. After a minute, he looked up, his eyes sparkling as if a secret were passed between them. "You are pregnant. I would guess it is a boy."

Kaiya shrugged, and turned to Doctor Wu. The old woman brushed Fang aside as if he were a cherry blossom in a spring wind, and took up Kaiya's wrists in the same manner as Weiyong had.

She held Kaiya in her gaze. "Not *a* boy. Two."

Coming out of a coma on a funeral barge next to a dozen cold bodies was not as unsettling as knowing he had somehow intentionally put himself into that coma... the *Viper's Rest*? Though he didn't remember how he'd gotten on the log raft, or even who he was, he knew he'd awoken too early, before his injuries had stabilized.

His raft had come ashore, lodging in the rich-smelling earth. The river, swollen by spring melt, tumbled past, while the wind rustled in budding tree branches. A cool breeze brushed across his bare chest, causing his skin to erupt in goosebumps.

He groaned and pushed himself up into a sitting position. A warm sensation trickled down his back, emanating from the spot where pain seared in his shoulder. That stab wound, unlike the numerous cuts all over his body, would bleed him out. Each heartbeat brought him closer to death.

Two lithe figures dressed in doeskin clothing stared at him with wide, almond-shaped eyes. With the streaks of red and white paint across their face and feathers in their hair, they looked as rustic as the untamed forest around them. They were... elves. Though how he knew it, he couldn't tell.

The silence lasted only a few seconds. One—a brown-haired male with sharp features and a sharper dagger—put his hands on his hips and pointed at his feet. When he spoke, the threat in his voice belied the flowery language. *"Amane esaya na!"*

The Dragon Songs Saga concludes with <u>Symphony of Fates</u>, available April 2021.

Acknowledgements

First, I would like to thank my wife and family for the patience they have afforded me as I pursued my childhood dream of fiction writing.

A shout-out goes out to my old Dungeons and Dragons crew: Jon, Chris, Chris, Paul, Conrad, and Julian, for helping to shape the first iteration of Tivara twenty-five years ago. Huge thanks to Brent who contributed so much backstory to the new literary version.

A gigantic thanks to my sister Laura for her spectacular job with the maps.

Thanks to the readers and writers on Wattpad for their encouragement and feedback.

Infinite gratitude to writers over at critiquecircle.com who motivated and helped me along the way. Jason, for patiently providing countless ideas. Kelly, for amazing input, character development and all the other advice. Victoria, for showing me how to layer scenes. Andy, for unparalleled wordsmithing. Ernie, for teaching me the fundamentals of fiction writing. Lindy for her sharp eye. Taylor for the numerous suggestions. Laurel, Joyce, Tracy, Traci, Larissa, Alicia, Kathyrn, and Ardyth for beta reading; and all the others who critiqued.

Finally, a huge thanks to all my readers for the encouragement you've given me. The Sisterhood of Tivara knows who they are.

Special Thanks

This special edition of Songs of Insurrection was only made possible by many generous pledges and donations.

From Patreon, I would like to especially acknowledge Elena Daymon and Samantha Mikals. I'm humbled by your support; as well as Dianeme Weidner, Spring Yang, Nicholas Klotz, Scott Engel, Mary Luu, Dexter Bradley, and Lindsay Shurtliff.

From Kickstarter, many thanks to Dyrk Ashton, Wraithmarked Creative, Zach Sallese, Dian, Ben Nichols, Rich Chang, Henrik Sörensen, Dan & Robert Zangari, Philip Tucker, Steven Hall, Jan Drake, Michał Kabza, Cody Allen, John Idlor, Kathy Jones, Nic Guinasso, Doug Williamson, Susan Voss, J. Zachary Pike, KE Sizemore, yesterspectre, Bobby McDonald, Andrew Barton, Michael Tabacchi, Emmanuel MAHE, Nicholas Liffert, A.Y. Chao, Artgor, Michael Mattson, Alexander Darwin, Krystal Xu, Caroline Atkins, Angela Engelbert, Shawna Dees, Nicolas Lobotsky, Justin Gross, Joey Hendrickson, Sarah Polk, Lawrence Wight, Eddie, Graham Dauncey, Jennifer, Virginia McClain, Christian Holt, Christopher Kranz, Leanne Yong, Kanyon Marie Kiernan, Scott Engel, Ivor Lee, Dan K, Mike Filliter, Ryan Kirk, James Yu, JC Cannon, Michelle Rapoza. Craig A. Price Jr., John Jutoy, Derek Freeman, Gerald P. McDaniel, Mat Meillier, A. Hakes, Helena Jones, Ashley, Charlie Gipson, Lapiswolf, PurpleSteamDragon, Laura E Custodio, Megan Mackie, Ashli Tingle, Stacy Shuda, Anna Lee, Don Quaintance, Anne Kinney, Jessica Stone, Stanley, Derek Alan Siddoway, Ting Bentley, Ernesto, Gary Phillips, Dianeme Weidner,

Timandra Whitecastle, Paul Cassimus, Paul, Walt Mussell, JohnYu, Chris, and Andre.

About the Author

JC Kang's unhealthy obsession with fantasy and sci-fi began at an early age when his brother introduced him to the *Chronicles of Narnia, The Hobbit, Star Trek* and *Star Wars*. As an adult, he combines his geek roots with his professional experiences as a Chinese Medicine doctor, martial arts instructor, and technical writer to pen multicultural epic fantasy stories.